If you hate Armenians,
don't read Book One.

If you hate Jews,
don't read Book Two.

If you hate Arabs and Palestinians,
don't read Book Three.

If you hate all or any of them,
boy, you have a problem. Read the Coda, it may
help you and it may open your heart."

The Mother of Jerusalem is Crying is a sweeping historical novel that begins in 19th Century Armenia, then under Turkish control, and tells the interwoven stories of three families - Christian, Jewish and Muslim over three generations and three continents. The story describes their lives in terms of their tradilions, triumphs and tragedies, and how they contended with the violence of the Armenian Genocide, World War Two, the Holocaust, and the founding of Israel. Many of the characters do not survive the enveloping violence. Despite these tragedies, the message of this book is hopeful. The story illustrates that people of different faiths can live togelher, marry, and raise happy children. Ordinary people, perhaps more than their political leaders, have the capacity to bring an end to the Suffering and death that mark our time.

Advanced reviews

Le livre de Rosemary Cohen donne au roman historique —
et au roman tout court— ses plus belles lettres de noblesse. Il
stimule constamment l'intelligence tout en s'adressant à ce que
notre âme recèle de meilleur : la générosité et l'amour vrai de
l'Autre. En le lisant, je songeais à ce bel aphorisme de Bernanos :
« l'espérance est un risque à courir ».

On l'aura compris : l'ouvrage de Rosemary Cohen est une
sorte de « bombe douce » (« bombe » par la force du message, «
douce » par la délicatesse du style et des sentiments) qui nous
réconcilie définitivement avec le genre humain. A mots feutrés, il
démontre, en effet, que les préjugés les plus solides et les haines
les plus tenaces ne sont que des obstacles provisoires quand les
peuples —ou les individus— décident de prendre courageusement
leur destin en main.

A tous ceux qui, comme l'auteur de ces lignes, ont toujours
cru —avec quelque raison, il est vrai !— que l'Histoire est
tragique, Madame Cohen rappelle qu'il n'est pas de limites à ce
que la volonté peut accomplir ; que l'impossible prend juste un peu
plus de temps ; et que c'est au plus noir de la nuit qu'il faut croire à
la lumière.

Dr. Patrick Wajsman
Fondateur et Directeur de la
Revue *Politique Internationale*
Professeur de Relations Internationales
Conseiller auprès du Président du Groupe *Figaro*

A Reflection

One can read in Rosemary Hartounian Cohen's moving and inspirational book, *The Mother of Jerusalem Is Crying*, accounts of great exultation and deep sorrow, of human achievement and inhuman cruelty, of immense strength and devastating weakness and of unbounded hope and crippling hopelessness. It fills our minds with images of the suffering of the innocents in the maelstroms of two genocides and ongoing violence that have shaped the human experience over the course of the past century. The ultimate message of book, however, is very clear: Affirm faith in God, affirm faith in one's own capacity to find light where there appears to be only darkness and dedicate oneself to a life in which such faith is realized in sacred acts of loving kindness.

Human suffering can evoke a wide range of responses. Some people who have been stricken by a great personal tragedy retreat from the world because they lose hope and find little purpose in life. Their continued existence seems to be simply a function of the natural instinct in living beings to stay alive. One can hear the echoes of Ecclesiastes 1:2-3 reverberating in the emptiness of their souls: "'Utter futility!' – said *Kohelet* – 'utter futility! All is futile! What real value is there for a man in all the gains he makes beneath the sun?'" In her book, Rosemary Cohen rejects this message.

Other folks confront tragedy by making a vow that as long as the breath of life fills their lungs they will not allow death to overwhelm them. They commit themselves to finding profound meaning in life, to living a life informed by the noblest of values and to devoting themselves to serving causes that promote the sanctity of life. Knowingly or otherwise, they accept the Biblical mandate in Deuteronomy 30:19-20: "I call heaven and earth to witness against you this day: I have put before you life and death, blessing and curse. Choose life – if you and your offspring would live – by loving the Lord your God, heeding His commands, and holding fast to Him." These are the principles for which Dr. Cohen advocates in *The Mother of Jerusalem.*

Rosemary Cohen does not dwell on the magnitude of the Armenian genocide or of the Holocaust or on the number of victims of Middle East terror. Those who recount these events today, while not denying the significance of such figures, tend to focus more on the stories of individual people, be they victims or survivors. These stories touch the souls of those who read or hear them much more powerfully than do the mega-numbers. Statistics are cold and distant; a reader or listener can relate more personally to those who suffered when they are drawn into the experiences of real people like themselves. If we are called upon never to forget these black holes of human history, then retelling the stories of the individual lives that were lost or broken will ensure that we and the rest of humankind will remember. Though the characters in *The Mother of Jerusalem* are fictionalized, their stories are based on the events of real people who experienced the history presented in the book, and that is why the book is so impactful.

Those of us who know Rosemary Cohen understand that the passion, emotion, struggling and commitments expressed by the characters in this book, in the final analysis, are those of the author. Rosemary has experienced her own personal "holocaust," losing a brother-in-law to terror and witnessing the death of a beloved daughter in an accident that defies comprehension. And yet, her outlook on life is so much healthier than that of most of us, and she has become a source of healing to her family and to anyone who has turned to her in need. She has emerged as a relentless advocate for what is the foundational message of *The Mother of Jerusalem is Crying* – "Choose Life," and for this we are all in her debt.

Joel Rembaum

Rabbi Rembaum is Rabbi Emeritus of Temple Beth Am in Los Angeles, where he served as Senior Rabbi for 25 years. He was ordained a Rabbi in 1970 by the Jewish Theological Seminary of America. That was preceded by his having been awarded a BA by UCLA in 1964 and was followed by his receiving an MA and a PhD in History from UCLA in 1973 and 1975, respectively. Rabbi Rembaum served on the faculty and administration of the, then, University of Judaism from 1970-1985, following which he assumed the mantle of Spiritual Leader at Temple Beth Am. A published scholar, Rabbi Rembaum also served the American and Southern California Jewish communities in a variety of leadership capacities and has been deeply involved in the activities and support of the Conservative/Masorti Movement in America and in Israel, as well as in support of and advocacy for the State of Israel in general. He is married to Fredi Rembaum, herself a respected Jewish communal leader; and they have four married children and seven grandchildren.

تراژدی های تاریخ و ایده آل های انسانی

کتاب های داستانی رزمری کهن Rosemary Cohen از بسیاری جهات در میان کتاب هایی که با موضوع های مشابه نوشته شده اند، بی نظیر و یکتاست. شاید کمتر نویسنده، و داستان سرایی مطالعات این نویسنده و تجربیات ویژه شخصی و اجتماعی او را برای نوشتن این داستان ها که دارای منابع تاریخی است حائز باشد.

رزمری کهن تحصیل کرده رشته دکترای جامعه شناسی از یکی از معتبرترین دانشگاه های جهان، سوربن Sorbonne پاریس است. وقتی یک جامعه شناسی به نویسندگی و داستان سرائی روی می آورد، مسلما نگاه متفاوتی با یک نویسنده و داستان نویس معمولی نسبت به زندگی و حوادث و شخصیت های آن و حتی تخیلات ادبی دارد.

زمان تحصیل رزمری در پاریس دهه ۱۹۷۰، اوج قدرت دوران پهلوی ها بوده است و رزمری سپس مانند بسیاری از هزاران روشنفکر ایرانی مقیم خارج از وطن خود وهمراه ده ها و بلکه صدها هزار نفر مهاجران انقلاب مذهبی ایران که شاید یکی از خونین ترین انقلاب های تاریخ بوده و یکی از حیرت انگیزترین تحولات بعدی جهان که در ارتباط با این رویداد بوجود آمده، تحت تاثیر کامل ابتلائات آن قرار داشته است. بر این اساس جامعه شناسی او ، از مرحله آکادمیک و جر و بحث های مجالس دانشگاهی به صحنه بزرگ زندگی که از جمله بحرانی ترین دوران معاصر بوده کشیده شده است.

سفر رزمری کهن با خانواده اواز فرانسه به امریکا خود رویداد دیگر اثرگذار زندگی اوست و سپس وقتی یکی از فرزندان او دختر ۱۸ ساله اش لیانا Liana درست زمانی که برای ادامه تحصیل عازم شهر دیگری درامریکاست در یک حادثه اتومبیل در برابر چشمان او و دیگر اعضای خانواده جان می سپارد، جهش دیگر و بزرگتری در زندگی او بوجود می آید. رزمری کهن شرح بسیار حساس و نکته به نکته این رویداد را در کتاب خود به نام قربانی Korban- The Sacrice of Liana آورده است. کمتر مادری است که گریه و شیون از دست رفتن یکی از محبوب ترین فرزندان خود را صرفا دردرون خود نگاه دارد و آنرا به دنیای عمیق انسانیت خود رهنمون شود و متقابلا و درست در همان زمان حادثه به تسلی شوهر و فرزندان زنده خود از این ماجرای خونین بپردازد.

کمتر مادری است وقتی که درجلسه دادگاه با خنده راننده مستی که از دست رفتن دختر نازنین اورا موجب شده است روبرو میشود، با این تجزیه و تحلیل درونی که قضاوت

زندگی و رویدادهای آن تنها با خداست، این جوان گناهکار را ببخشد. و این دکتر رزمری کهن، یک خصیصه منحصر به فرد دیگر هم دارد و آن این استکه وقتی در پاریس و در زمان آشفته ترین حوادث روز با مردی عمیقا مهربان، ساکت و ضمناً محقق ، یک استاد لبنانی مقیم پاریس آشنا میشود، با او عهد زناشویی می‌بندد و به دین او میگراید بدون آنکه هیچگاه و هرگز احترام خود را و اعتقادات روحانی خود را نسبت به مسیحیت قبلی خود از دست داده باشد.

همین دکتر رزمری کهن است که بعدها در جامه یک زن یهودی و با خانواده ای یهودی یکی از هولناک ترین حوادث تاریخی ارامنه ایرانی در شهر خوی ویران شده را به هنگام هجوم و حملات بیرحمانه و خونین نظامیان ترکیه عثمانی در اثر بخش ترین یک اثر داستان نویس تاریخی عرضه می‌کند.

من قبلاً ۲ بار درباره این کتاب بنام Survivor به زبان انگلیسی ، و زمانی که ترجمه فارسی آن با عنوان «بازمانده» منتشر شد، نقد و مطالبی نوشته ام.

رزمری کهن، نه فقط فصل مهمی از تاریخ ارامنه ایران را بصورت جامعتر تاریخ خود ایران که برای بسیاری از پژوهشگران نیز تاریک بوده است آشکار کرده بلکه با زبانی بسیار شیوا و راز ورمزی داستان گونه ، خواننده را از آغاز تا پایان کتاب به دنبال خود میکشاند تا رنج ها و شادی ها، مرگ و زندگی وعصاره بخشی از حیات موجود ما را دریابد و آنرا در احساس و تفکر خویش همراه سازد. رزمری کهن باز وباین بار در عرصه بزرگتر و کلی تری همان نگاه عمیقا و احترام آمیز خود را به نفس انسان ازهر قوم و مسلک ومذهب ابراز میدارد و خونباری مهاجمان ترک را نتیجه ترک بودن و یا مذهب خاص آنها نمیداند بلکه بخشی از شرارت هایی میداند که سیستم های خودکامه جهان در مردمان از هر قوم و گروه ممکن است ببار آورند. انسانیت دکتر رزمری کهن و صرف نظر از شیوه بسیار سحرانگیز نویسندگی او، در یکی از جدیدترین کتاب های داستانی او «مادر اورشلیم می‌گرید» The Mother Of Jerusalem is Crying همچنان مشخص است.

۳ خانواده یهودی، مسیحی و مسلمان در این داستان در یکی از حساس ترین وبحرانی ترین زمان های تاریخ معاصر و در تحولات خاورمیانه درگیر هستند. قصه پر غصه سه خانواده در ۳ اقلیم جهانی وطی ۲ سده ، واینکه چگونه بعضی از آنها در قتل عام ارامنه در ترکیه عثمانی و در خطه ای از ایران از بین میروند، در بازداشتگاه مرگ آلمان نازی سوخته میشوند و جان می‌بازند و چگونه در بحران های ناشی از بازگشت یهودیان به فلسطین و تشکیل کشور اسرائیل نفوس دیگری کشته میشوند، و ضمناً آنهائی که از همه این بحران ها و مصائب و بهرحال جان سالم بدر می‌برند و در جستجوی یافتن روح سالمی نیز هستند.

رزمری کهن دراین داستان ترکیب یافته بر بخش هایی از تاریخ معاصر جهانی، نگاه حتی عمیق تری به این نکته دارد که ما همه انسانیم، همه زاده یک پروردگار، و باید که برای رفع

انبوه مشکلاتی که زمانه به ما تحمیل کرده است، راهی مسالمت آمیز وانسانی پیش گیریم.
رزمری کهن در این جدیدترین داستان خود یادآور این شعر سعدی، شاعر بزرگ و ارزشمند
ایرانی است که گفته بود:

تو کز محنت دیگران بی غمی   نشاید که نامت نهند آدمی

تاریخ، تراژدی های بزرگی را به همراه داشته است ولی تراژدی یک امر محتوم نیست. و این
رزمری کهن است که ضمن نمایش بخش های دیگری از تراژدی های انسانی که گاه خونین
ترین آن نیز هست، روزنه ها ی امید را نشان میدهد. شادی های مردمانی را منعکس میکند
که ازجمله لذت بخش ترین نکات داستان های اوست. در آثار داستانی رزمری کهن، چه
این داستان اخیر او و چه نوشته های سابق او، حوادث و اتفاقات زمانه چه آنها که مبتنی بر
واقعیت است و چه آنها که با چاشنی تخیل اورقم خورده است، جزء به جزء تصویر میشود.
نوشته های رزمری کهن ما را به یاد نویسندگان بزرگی در شرق وغرب جهان چون
داستایوسکی و بالزاک میاندازد بسیاری از آثار ایندو نویسنده قبل از آنکه در دوربین های
جادوئی سینمایی بصورت تصویری در آیند، در ذهن وفکر خواننده حتی تصاویر جامع تر
ودرخشنده تری داشته اند رزمری کهن نیز با داستان های خود ما را به همین جهان سرشار از
واقعیت خیال انگیز و خیالی استوار بر واقعیت رهنمون میشود.

پرویز ناظریان ژورنالیست، نویسنده، تهیه کننده و کارگردان تئاتر وسینما در ۳۰ سال اخیر که مقیم لوس آنجلس
بوده و دو نمایش درباره دوشاعره بزرگ ایرانی، فروغ فرخزاد و طاهره بر روی صحنه برده است. بیش از ۲۰۰ مقاله
درباره فرهنگ و ادب و هنر ایران و جهان نگاشته و در اغلب رادیو و تلویزیون های فارسی زبان، سردبیر خبر و یا
برنامه ساز بوده است. فیلمی که وی در دهه ۱۹۷۰ با عنوان «یک اصفهانی در نیویورک» کارگردانی کرد، نخستین
فیلم ایرانی بودکه در امریکا تهیه شد. از پرویز ناظریان به زودی کتابی با عنوان «ضد خاطرات» حاوی دیدگاه
های شخصی و اجتماعی او از ۴ دهه فرهنگ و هنر ایران و جهان منتشر میشود.

Parviz Nazerian
Author, movie and arts critique

The Mother of Jersualem is Crying novel humanizes Middle East conflict

Dr. Rosemary Hartounian Cohen is perhaps one of the rare authors and academics you'll ever come across today because of her identity as an Iranian, Armenian and a Jew. Her unique background, her life experiences and those of her own family have enabled her to see the world— especially the conflict in the Middle East in a totally different light. So when she asked me to read and review her latest book, *The Mother of Jerusalem is Crying* I gladly accepted. To my delight Dr. Cohen does indeed manage to convey the heart wrenching personal pain that the three families in the novel who are Jewish, Christian and Muslim encounter because of the blind hatred and lack of human decency in their world.

I particularly enjoyed learning about the tremendous hardships Armenians living in what is now Turkey encountered at the hands of the Turkish military during the early part of the 20th century. It was not easy reading the story of the Armenian family in her novel that was decimated and devastated in the genocide, but it is an example of just one of the thousands of true life stories many Armenians today carry with them about their own families. The Armenian genocide is among one of humanity's worse episodes and its occurrence must be recognized. My hope is that this novel and others will continue to raise awareness in the world about the Armenian genocide and encourage human beings to stand up against future genocides! Dr. Cohen's ability to humanize the suffering endured during the Armenian genocide, the Holocaust as well as Arab and Israeli conflict in this novel is remarkable. The emotional, historical, religious and cultural complexity of the Middle East and its people are often very difficult for authors, journalists and even politicians to explain to individuals not from that part of the world. The Middle East is just not easy…but Dr. Cohen's message in this novel lays out the overriding solution to the suffering endured in that part of the world— that with love and tolerance, those who truly cherish life can overcome all difficulties. Readers of *The Mother of Jerusalem is Crying* will not be disappointed because the novel tells three compelling stories and conveys a powerful message for humanity's need for co-existence in the world.

Karmel Melamed
Attorney and an award-winning internationally published journalist covering Middle East affairs for various publications. He is a contributing writer and blogger for the *Jewish Journal of Greater Los Angeles*.

I had the opportunity to interview Rosemary Cohen and was astounded at her innate ability to graphically express the sides of life that most people never have to deal with. After reading this amazing work, I am convinced that Rosemary is a voice that must be listened to.

Stephen F. Kaufman
Founder of Self-Revealization Acceptance
Host, Hanshi's World TV and www.hanshi.com

The Mother of Jerusalem is Crying offers readers a wonderfully rich, powerful and heartfelt story that truly captures the pathos of the Jewish legacy from the early 20th century to modern times, with some brilliant reflections on the mysteries of life and human nature. Author Rosemary Cohen is a masterful storyteller who artfully presents the poignant human drama often lost behind factual history. She chronicles the full spectrum of historic events as the backdrop for showcasing the emotional legacy of generations of Jewish people who have faced so much oppression in such a short span of time. She tells their tales with grace, courage and a memorable style that will touch the hearts of every reader who will never forget her fascinating characters.

Catherine Rourke
Editor/Publisher/Journalist, *The Sedona Observer*,
Editor911 Literary Service

Explosive and emotive – captivating and gripping!

In her *The Mother of Jerusalem*, Dr. Rosemary Hartounian Cohen tells the incredible story of human love and survival, through adversity and ultimately sheer resilience. With her artistic talent and palette of descriptive words, Dr. Cohen has painted a panorama of scenes and characters that evoke pure emotions about the frailties and strengths of the human heart.

With her heightened ability to sense life, and equipped with a pair of perceptive eyes, Dr. Cohen sees and describes events with artistic and stylistic strokes. In her book, a doctor's tear falls on the face of a fallen soldier, mixes with the blood on his face, and rolls down the face like a ruby; a weeping woman adds her salty tears to the seawater; the breathing of a sleeping child becomes a sweet melody accompanied by the beat of night music; the smoke of cigarettes in a bar climbs lazily to the ceiling and is blown into intricate patterns each time the door is opened.

With her fearless and free style of writing, Dr. Cohen takes on taboo - head on - and daringly describes the love affair between a Christian Armenian wife-and-mother and her Moslem lover of Turkish descent, in the post-Genocide era. She then unites the child of that union with a Jewish man, whose own story is every bit as fascinating and touching as the novel's other characters. She painstakingly describes the common bond that unites humans of all races and religions: pain and love.

Whether you're a Christian, Moslem or Jew, in Dr. Cohen's story, you will find the comfort of our oneness. You will revel in the knowledge that we are all leaves and branches from the same tree, united and woven together in the intricate web of destiny.

Naris Khalatian
Attorney at law, a writing enthusiast, and former chairperson and active member of the Parish Council of St. Gregory the Illuminator Armenian Catholic Parish in Glendale, California.

The Mother of Jerusalem

Is Crying

Rosemary H. Cohen

Lico Publishing
1541 South Robertson Boulevard
Los Angeles, California 90035

The Mother of Jerusalem Is Crying
By Rosemary H. Cohen, Ph.D.
Copyright 2011 by Rosemary H. Cohen, Ph.D.

LIBRARY OF CONGRESS CATALOGING – IN- PUBLICATION DATA

Cohen, Rosemary H.
The Mother of Jerusalem is Crying/ by Rosemary H. Cohen
1- Historical Novel. 2- Middle East. 3- Armenian Genocide.
4- Holocaust. 5- Family Relations. 6- Grief - Physiological aspects.
7- Women Studies. 8- Widowhood. 9-Single Parent.

pp: 434

ISBN 978 – 0 – 9667361 – 4 - 4
UPC # 794808-41888
FIRST EDITION 2012

Contact the author at: rosemary@atelierdeparis.com
Published in the United States of America
*12 13 14 15 16 17 * 7 6 5 4 3 2 1*

Cover Design by Chad Carpenter & Rosemary H. Cohen
Book Design by Elia B. Cohen

Dedication

I dedicate this book to my daughter, Liana, who taught me the taste of real pain and who made me a member of a very precious group in this world: the compassionate humans.

She helped me to learn the meaning of suffering, to cherish happiness and, most importantly, to understand the true value of life, death and beyond.

Acknowledgments

I thank my husband, Ishac, and my children – Mabelle, Ruben and Elia – who have always believed and supported me in anything that I do.

I would like to thank the following persons for their valuable time that they have given so generously. I really appreciate it very much.

My heartfelt thanks to Rabbi Jacob Pressman, who always read my manuscripts and returned them to me with some words of praise and valuable suggestions that I cherish and keep among my life's treasures.

To Rabbi Albert Axelrad for believing in me, for always providing encouragement, and for having "Godly" words in his mouth.

To Ari Noonan, for publishing so many of my articles in *The Front Page*.

And, finally – but not least – to the many friends who have encouraged me in whatever I do.

Preface

THE CLOCK was approaching nine at night in California. It was August 28, 1992, and my family and I were returning from Friday night prayers. The air was deliciously filled with the breeze coming from the Pacific Ocean. The sky was clear and we could see bright stars twinkling above us. It was one of the most peaceful and beautiful summer nights in Los Angeles. The perfume of the night flowers filled our lungs and we could hear the songs of some night birds.

We had decided that, once we arrived home and had dinner, I would help my two daughters pack their luggage, since they were going to leave on Saturday night for Boston. Mabelle was in her second year of college and Liana, who had just finished high school, was going to start her first year of college. Five minutes before arriving home and exactly twenty-five hours before the scheduled departure of our daughters, a drunken driver hit us head-on.

When I found myself, I heard Mabelle and our younger son, Elia, calling me. When I looked for the rest of my family, I discovered that my husband, my older son, Ruben, and Liana were apparently dead. But immediately I somehow knew that it was only Liana who had left us and that, despite of all the blood around them, Ishac and Ruben were going to be okay. Liana was just eighteen years old.

From the very first moment, regardless of my injuries and the tragedy present around me, I felt that God had come to my rescue. It was as if I had been injected with a magical potion, one containing an unusual mix of logical reasoning, peace and courage. I told myself that Liana was with God and thus did not need my help anymore, but there were my husband and three surviving children who needed me. The next morning one of our friends who visited us at the hospital told me, "Look at them. You are the main pillar of your family. If you fall, they will all fall."

I still believe that God helped me in dealing with the enormous tragedy of losing a child and the uncertainty of not knowing the fate of the rest of my family. Even now, looking back to that moment, I am surprised that I had amazing calm and courage to find my strength in order to stay on my feet, forget my own wounds and pain, and take care of my family.

Everyone was surprised to see me – a mother who had just lost a beautiful daughter – able to remain so calm. I wanted to cry and complain, but then I remembered my grandmother and felt ashamed of myself, for I realized that I had the best example in my life to follow.

Within minutes of the accident, Liana and the rest of us were transported to the best hospitals in the city. Later, Liana was buried with prayers and all honors, and we had the luxury of a week of mourning and prayers with our friends and relatives.

That was in stark contrast to the experience of my grandmother, who had lost her entire family and belongings in a very short time. Her husband was killed in front of her and her daughter. She was only eighteen years old and her daughter was three years old. Ottoman Turkish soldiers had killed my grandfather, tied his legs to the tail of a horse, and drawn his body through the streets of Khoy. He was an honorable and innocent man who was guilty only of being born to a Christian family in a Muslim country during the wrong period of time.

The lives of my grandmother and mother changed in hardly more than an instant. They were the wife and daughter of a well-respected, kind and wealthy man. Suddenly they had lost everything. The wife became a widow and her daughter was without her loving father. My grandmother lived the life of a survivor and struggled to secure a roof over the head of her daughter and put enough food on the table.

Both my grandmother and mother survived the evil with courage, their heads held high, and smiles on their faces.

ॐ

Many years later my sister, Seda, died at the age of sixteen. My mother and grandmother, who had struggled bravely for so many years, had to face tragedy one more time.

So didn't I have good examples in my family to follow?

ॐ

Just hours before the accident, I met with one of my customers, whom I had known for a long time. I do not know why he chose that fateful day to share his life story with me.

"I lost my entire family in Auschwitz," he told me. "While I was all alone on the deck of the ship that was bringing me to the United States, I met a young girl who, like me, had also lost her entire family at Auschwitz. With no special aim and hope, we were both coming to the United States. Regardless of the tragedies and sad experiences, I do not know how and why we opened our hearts to love each other. I later asked her to marry me. We had not yet made peace with this world when we had our children!"

ॐ

Some years later my blameless and innocent brother-in-law, Haim Cohen, was kidnapped by Muslim fanatics. They held him hostage for nine months and then, on the eve of Christmas, his body was thrown in the yard of a church with three bullets.

My mother-in-law, who was crying for nine months, died of grief over her son's death.

His fault was being born into a Jewish family.

Haim just wanted to live a simple life with his wife and children, but he had chosen a wrong time and a wrong place to be born.

ॐ

After going through all these experiences, it is normal that any conflict in any part of the world would break my heart, especially the Israeli-Arab conflict that has existed for decades. Knowing the pain of the loss of a child gives me the automatic right to cry for victims on both sides. I have learned firsthand what a mother goes through when she loses a child. But it is not only the mother who grieves, of course; the father, sisters and brothers suffer from the loss all their lives. It changes and affects everyone. When I hear or see some of the parents who are obliged to face the media and put a smile on their faces or affirm that they are proud of their son or daughter's martyrdom or receive some money from certain groups, I am able to see the traces of tragedy and sadness deep in the wrinkles of their faces. What about the next day when they do not hear and see their child anymore?

Nothing in the world can replace the child who is absent, even if there are twelve other children present at home. That lost one has his or her own unique place. No money can replace a word that can never again be heard from the child who is no longer present. No money or glory can replace that one child!

ॐ

In honor of Liana, we organize music competitions and festivals every year. In the second year, I wanted to do something more than a concert. We invited an Israeli and an Arab musician for the festival – a young Jewish girl violinist and an Arab pianist. Both were very talented and they played some solo and duo pieces. If they were able to play such beautiful duos in harmony, the question was: "Why couldn't the politicians play the same rhythm and tune together during all these years?"

It was while seeing these two young people together that the idea of *The Mother of Jerusalem is Crying* found shape in my mind. I thought, perhaps, I was the best delegate to write about this subject.

I had seen the suffering of my parents all my childhood. I was not present during the genocide, but I had nightmares about it all through my childhood. And, although my parents never talked about it in front of me, I knew all as if I had been present there. I also knew how much different our lives would have been if my grandfather had not been killed.

I can understand the depth of the tragedy just as if I had experienced it firsthand. In addition, I understand the meaning of religious conflicts, since I have experienced them all myself. I have lived in many countries and speak many languages; sometimes people forget what I am and express themselves as freely as if I were one of them. So I can understand the reasons for the conflicts and the pain of suffering. But I still believe we are all part of one family. We are tied together like the pearls of a necklace, hanging from the same thread for a given time. We can stay there only as long as we can hold onto and watch out for each other.

Although the story I am about to tell begins in the late 1800's in Asia Minor, it really is without time or place. It has happened before and since.

TABLE OF CONTENTS

BOOK ONE: The Armenian Family

TIMELINE: The Armenian massacre of the first several chapters occurs in Turkey in 1890. Ani and Ara marry in 1910. Vartan is born in 1912, and Sara is born in 1914. Sara marries Raffi in Beirut in 1930; Sako is born in 1931 and then Sarina in 1933. Sara meets Wahab in 1935 and their relationship continues through 1947 in Lebanon and Iran. Ruth is born in 1941 in Iran and marries Daniel in Paris in 1969; Joseph is born in Paris in 1970. Ruth, Daniel and Joseph leave for Los Angeles in 1984. Daniel dies in Beirut in 1985.

BOOK TWO - THE JEWISH FAMILY

TIMELINE: Avraham is born to Yaakov and Musya in Russia in 1882 and is sent to Belgium in 1900 to live with his Uncle David. Avraham marries Miriam in 1904; Jacob is born 1905. He marries Rivka in 1928; Esther is born in 1930. Jacob, Rivka and Esther move to France in 1939. Jacob and Rivka are seized by the Gestapo in 1940. Esther gives birth to Leah in late 1941. In 1951, mother and daughter emigrate to Israel. Leah marries Solomon in 1973; Rachel is born in 1974.

BOOK THREE - THE PALESTINIAN FAMILY

TIMELINE: Wahab is born in 1914 in present-day Lebanon. Abdulah and Aisha Khaled have five children: Habib, 1926;

Ameerah, 1931; Faisal, 1934; Naseem, 1936; and Layla, 1942. Wahab and Layla marry in Beirut in 1970; Rana is born in 1974; Ahmed in 1976. The Six-Day War occurs in 1967 and the Yom Kippur War in 1973.

CODA

INTRODUCTION

Jerusalem
August 30, 2002

SARA, THE MATRIARCH OF THE FAMILY, was walking with her daughter Ruth, her grandson Joseph, his fiancée, Rachel, and Rachel's mother Leah. They headed toward the jewelry store in East Jerusalem to buy the final and most important emblems of Joseph and Rachel's union – two golden wedding bands. The ceremony was only forty-eight hours away. They talked and walked happily in the narrow streets of the Old City. Their joy and happiness shone in their eyes and on their faces. It seemed that an aura glowed around them because even strangers stepped aside, letting their happy chain remain connected.

Joseph was in his early thirties. He was a handsome young man with dark curly hair and large deep blue eyes. His fiancée, Rachel, was in her late twenties. Her curly golden hair framed her face and her beautiful clear blue eyes shone with happiness. Holding their hands and looking very much in love, they were delighted to know that in two days they were going to be pronounced husband and wife.

Joseph's grandmother, Sara, who was in her late eighties, still looked very energetic and pleasant. She had devoted her life to her daughter, Ruth, and her grandson, Joseph, and was very thankful to be alive to see her grandson's wedding. Aware of her great joy, the young couple asked her to be present at all decisions and, thus, also to be present when they bought their rings.

An attractive woman in her sixties, Ruth's facial expression clearly evinced her kindness and intelligence. She and her family lived in the United States but, since the couple had decided to get married in Jerusalem where most of Rachel's family lived, they had come to Jerusalem and rented an apartment for a month in order to spend time with the family and visit the city where the wedding was going to take place. Ruth was known for her delicious meals and had invited the two families for dinner. Earlier she had prepared everyone's favorite dish for *Shabbat* – the Sabbath – dinner before the wedding. She had set the table before leaving their temporarily rented home. In her mind, Ruth was still planning where to seat everyone and how to arrange the food on the table.

They walked into the jewelry store so that the couple could pick up their wedding bands. Carved inside each were Hebrew letters that read *Ani le dodi, Ve dodi li* – "I am my beloved's, and my beloved is mine." Joseph had also asked that their names be carved in Arabic next to the Hebrew letters. When the jeweler put the bands in the boxes, he wished everyone good luck in both languages –*Mabrouk* and *Mazel Tov*.

Since they still had time, Sara invited them for coffee at Café al Ahmar on the way back. Ruth looked at her mother tenderly and smiled. She remembered this café from her mother's stories about the time when Sara lived in Lebanon and traveled to Jerusalem. She always told these stories about the little café there with fond nostalgia. As a young woman, Sara was lively and beautiful. Now, with her snowy soft hair, she still remained attractive. Years earlier, at the time of Sara's stories, the café was in Jordanian territory but, after the Six-Day War, it fell under Israeli jurisdiction.

Omar, the owner of the café, stood near the entrance as usual. Time had marked him with lines on his face and an emerging hump on his back. His dark hair had turned snow white and his strong body, which reminded Sara of a cedar of Lebanon, now seemed more like an old olive tree, bending down from all sides. He recognized Sara immediately and was pleased to see her and greeted all of them with a wide smile. After all these years, Sara thought that everything looked the same, as if time had stopped inside the café.

She chose her usual table. The waiter brought them glasses of cold water and they ordered Turkish coffee. Sara introduced her grandson and Rachel to Omar. "Can you imagine?" she asked him. "My grandson, Joseph, is getting married in two days."

Omar looked happily at Sara, his eyes twinkling as usual, and said, "I am sure that you and your family are the luckiest persons on Earth. *Mabrouk* – congratulations." He then ordered the waiter to bring a tray of sweet Middle Eastern pastry and baklavas.

Omar and Sara had known each other for a long time. As a young woman in love, she often used to meet her lover in this very Arabic café, far from the sight of others. Years had passed and all those memories had turned to dusty dreams. Later, Sara came to this place alone since she liked to drink her favorite Turkish coffee in her usual place. Whenever she sat at her favorite table, she immediately turned into a young woman in love – crazily in love – with Wahab, her forbidden love! She was a married Armenian young woman and Wahab was a handsome bachelor from a mixed Arab and Turkish parentage.

Now her world was limited to her daughter and grandson, and their happiness was hers as well. She kept her memories to herself in her inner private garden. She had never told anyone – not even her daughter, to whom she was so close – about her secret from so long ago.

The giggling of the young couple brought her back from her thoughts and she joined the moment with her loved ones. They drank coffee and ate the fresh sweet pastries made with honey and rose water. Omar came over to them with a smile and wished the couple a sweet, happy and long life.

When they were ready to leave, Joseph asked for the bill. Omar waved him away. "You are my guests, and you know that I am always delighted to see your grandmother. You are like my own family. This was also a happy occasion for me to see you and your bride. *Inshallah* ("God willing"), you will grow old together and fill your grandmother's arms with healthy babies." Joseph knew Oriental hospitality and traditions very well and, therefore, he did not insist. He thanked the old man and left a generous tip for the young waiter.

As they walked out, Rachel's mother, Leah, proposed that they stop at the famous "Khaled & Sons Gift Store of Jerusalem." "The owner, Layla, is a beautiful Palestinian young woman," she explained. "This store has been here for a very long time. They have the best handicrafts and I would like to offer each of you a souvenir of Jerusalem to remember this day."

They entered the store and looked at all the unusual gift items. Leah asked the clerk if Layla had returned to Jerusalem. He answered sadly: "Unfortunately, no. I think it is not easy for her to come back here. As you may be aware, beautiful Layla faced many tragedies in her life. She lost almost all of her family members and finally went to visit her sister in Beirut. She met her *kismet* ("destiny") there, got married, and now lives with her family in Paris. She has a son who is actually with his father visiting Jerusalem. He wanted to see his ancestral house and store for the first time."

They each chose hand-crafted objects, wall hangings, paintings with different images of Jerusalem, and jewelry designed by talented artists and left the store.

Since they still had time, they stopped at the *Kotel* – the Wailing Wall, situated in the midst of the Old City in Jerusalem. As the Western wall supporting the Temple Mount, it has remained intact since the year 70 A.D., when the destruction of the Second Jerusalem Temple took place. They all prayed and thanked God for their accomplished wishes.

ॐ

It was not very long ago that Rachel had started her new job as a resident in surgery at Hadassah Hospital. All was going well for her but she had not yet met her *beshert* – her destiny. One day she went to the Wailing Wall and, after prayers and meditation, pulled a small piece of paper from her pocket on which she had written her wish of meeting her real soul mate. She chose an open space in the joint between two old stones where a little grass had grown, pushing out from the small crack in search of the bright sun. She told herself that the growing grass showed the force of nature and was blessing and took it as a good luck sign. She timidly inserted the well-folded paper inside the wall and finished her prayers.

At the end of her medical training, she was accepted for a year-long fellowship for an exchange program in the United States. It was not long before she met Joseph in the operating room at Cedars Sinai Hospital in Los Angeles. She admired his ability and knowledge. They fell in love and, after some months, Joseph proposed. Rachel happily accepted the engagement ring.

Now, at the Wailing Wall, everyone in her little party prayed and meditated in silence. Each thanked God for His blessings and for the upcoming wedding. Rachel wanted to pray and thank the Holy One for sending her the wonderful young man who was praying in the men's section. Ruth had learned not to ask anything specific from God, since she believed that He knew better what to do; therefore, who was she to order or interfere in His future plans? She always thanked God for what she had and, like everyone else, she finished her prayers, wishing for peace and good health.

After prayers, they took the short walk back home. Soon *Shabbat* would start and Ruth wanted to warm the food ahead of time. The sun was setting. The sky's palette had already mixed hues of purple, red, orange and blue together and was waiting to receive the last magical brush strokes before darkness would cover all. People who took the time to look at the wonders of creation were able to see a masterpiece of nature painted freshly just above their heads each evening. Others were hurrying to reach home in order to get ready to welcome the "*Shabbat* Bride." Some men had bought *Shabbat* flowers for their wives. Others had *challahs* – braided bread – under their arms. Some children were still playing on the sidewalk. Teenage boys and girls stood in small groups, talking and enjoying themselves. The tourists were looking around with admiration, taking pictures; others sat in cafés, lazily enjoying the beautiful weather.

Physically, Sara was following everyone in the present but her thoughts were flying back to the past. She had a mysterious face with a kind smile that was well-known to her daughter. Suddenly, at that precious moment, Sara saw Wahab in the distance walking directly toward them with a young man. She was surprised at all these coincidences on that special Friday. She had just returned from Omar's café and, deep in her heart, remembered the old days and wondered what Wahab was doing at that moment. And just then, by some amazing coincidence, there he was walking toward her.

She had not seen him for a long time. She admitted to herself that, even from a distance, Wahab was still the handsome man she knew years ago, with his deep blue eyes and black wavy hair. Now his wavy hair was snowy white and he looked older, as did Sara herself. But still he was very attractive. She felt guilty as even now, decades later, her heart started beating hard and she felt the warmth of love filling her whole being. She was a young girl again; her dried veins flashed hot blood to her cheeks.

Sara understood how much she had missed him. They loved each other truly and deeply even though she had stopped her forbidden love and their relationship years ago. Obligated by the difference of their religions and cultures, they were separated from each other but neither forgot the love that they were carrying in their hearts for the other. Through all these years, she pretended and locked her emotions in her chest and sealed them with her tears. She thought she had buried her love but now, at that exact moment, she realized that she had cheated herself. She was aware of how much she had missed him and suffered in silence, surprised to realize how much his love was still present in her being and that time was not able to diminish the depth of her feelings.

She asked herself how was it possible that she could still feel love and emotions the same way in her old age. And, at that moment, she felt like a very young woman! She wondered and, meanwhile, understood that love was not the monopoly of youth. The human body takes the curves of time and age, but in reality, the human spirit always stays young, even inside the body's fragile frame.

She, again, felt the old guilt but immediately comforted herself by repeating, "For all these years, I never did anything wrong that I should be ashamed of. On the contrary, I became a role model to my daughter and a devoted grandmother to Joseph."

She was surprised at how quickly she had recognized Wahab with all the details of his face – from a distance and in a short glance, even without her eye glasses – after so many years. She understood that she had carved his image so deeply in her heart that a sudden short glance was enough to awaken his clear image in her mind again.

Wahab was also looking intently at her. She trembled and was uncomfortable as she experienced the magnet of his eyes pulling her heart and mind toward him. She moved her eyes from Wahab to the young man walking next to him. Wahab, who was the same age as Sara, had married very late in life, so from their resemblance and age difference it seemed that the young man was his son. As she looked at the youth, suddenly all her excitement disappeared and she felt a chill along her spine.

The young man looked to be in his late twenties. He was handsome like his father but had darker skin and hair and did not have his father's friendly blue eyes and sweet look. He was walking almost like a ghost, with a flat expression. He was pale, as if he had just been discharged from a hospital after a long illness. She trembled and felt his negative energy hitting her and its darkness spreading all around him.

There were many Israelis and Arabs around them – children, as well as young and old people. Some were sitting in the hot weather of Jerusalem on terraces of the coffee shops, sipping their orange juice, eating ice cream and drinking sodas in order to cool off. Others were reading newspapers or talking and arguing loudly with their friends. Some were hurrying into shops for their last-minute purchases. Lovers were just enjoying a walk in this beautiful city. Foreign tourists were admiring the historical buildings and were snapping photos, while groups of visitors were pointing to the sky of Jerusalem, which always seems to be so close to the earth.

Suddenly, Sara heard a little voice inside her. She collected her strength and, as her sixth sense called upon her louder and louder, she started trembling. It was Wahab's son who was inflicting all these negative feelings within her. She asked herself why he was dressed in such a long coat during the hot weather. Suddenly she cried loudly out of control. Joseph and Rachel looked at her, surprised, and held her hands, not knowing what was happening to her.

Ruth remained at a distance. She had seen all and knew what her mother was going through. Although Sara had never shared any word about her past love to her daughter, Ruth knew all about her mother's secret. From a very young age, Ruth had been an intelligent and curious person and, therefore, she had discovered her mother's illicit love. But she had kept this secret to herself out of respect for her mother's silence and for her honor.

Sara was able to cry loudly, but she did not have the time to utter the words that were blocked between her throat and lips. Wahab and his son were only a few feet away. Wahab was also confused by her cry. He took a step toward her without thinking, in order to see if he could help her. He thought his presence probably disturbed her as much as hers had disturbed him but, right at that moment, everyone heard a loud call of *Allaho Akbar!* – "God is great!"

And then the sound of an explosion deafened the ears of everyone. Very strong and loud, it emanated from the young man, whose body was girdled with a powerful bomb and who seemingly disintegrated in the blast. The sound came from where the bride- and groom-to-be stood, offering them an evil wedding gift of fireworks. Then blood and body parts started flying in all directions through the air, like fountains of the devil in hell.

People screamed and cried uncontrollably. Others were shocked, and it seemed as if they were pinned to the ground like stone statues. Some started running crazily toward where the sound had been, while others fled from the explosion's center.

An army officer, who was a military doctor, immediately pulled out his cellular phone and called for help. He ran toward the explosion's center. It looked worse than any war zone he had seen during the Six-Day or Yom Kippur wars.

Innocent men, women, children and elderly people were cut into pieces. Many were present only in tiny pieces of flesh and burnt fibers and others lay in rivers of blood. The smell of human sacrifice filled the noses and lungs of those still breathing. Some who were able to speak asked for help; others, holding the wounded parts of their body with their hands, were frozen – wordless. Some were crying quietly, and others were yelling hysterically. Death, blood and tears descended throughout the world's Holiest City.

The army officer had taken care of many patients during his long years in army hospitals and on battlefields but, at that moment, he did not know what to do or where to start. Nearly in shock himself, as well as sad and angry at the same time, he asked himself how people could commit such horrific actions against innocent civilians, in this Holy City, where all prophets and religions dwelled side-by-side.

He approached a victim who was a young soldier. His body was massively injured but his last breath was still present in him. He was bleeding hard but his bloody face looked calm and angelic. The doctor kneeled and tried to put pressure on a large artery to stop the bleeding until the arrival of the ambulances. He thought that, perhaps, the vigor of the soldier's youth would have pity on his life. The soldier was mumbling: *"Shema Israel Adonai Eloheinou Adonai Ehad"* – *Hear, O Israel, the Lord our God, the Lord is one.* He looked at the doctor calmly, his eyes reflecting enormous pain. But, at the same time, that special light was shining in his eyes – that last bright light in the eyes of departing patients with which the doctor was so familiar. The soldier's lips moved slowly and in a weak voice he told the doctor, "I am finished. Please go help others who have a chance. Don't waste your time on me."

The doctor was amazed at this young man's selfless courage. He was still pressing on his artery and had pity on his youth. He then heard a sharp breath and understood that the young body had given up its life at that very moment. As his tears dropped on the young man's face, they mixed with the dark blood that had dried on the soldier's cheek. A red ruby rolled down the lifeless face.

The doctor was still pressing the artery with one hand and holding the soldier's head in his other hand. He carefully placed the young man's head on the ground, as if he were afraid to hurt him more than he had already suffered. His head touched the earth – the earth that was soon going to swallow the brave young man's body. The soldier's two beautiful blue eyes stared motionlessly at the sky of Jerusalem, now covered with dark, dirty smoke. The doctor gently closed the eyelids and pulled down the curtains of his life forever.

The doctor moved to the other victims who were calling for help, but he knew that, for the remainder of his life, the young soldier's bloody face and the clear blue eyes reflecting his kind spirit would always stay with him. During all his years of practice, he had never heard any patient – even the terminal ones – ask him to leave them alone in order to help others.

The loud voices of the ambulance sirens and the police cars gave him courage and woke him to the reality present around him. Without protective gloves, he started helping other injured victims. It was not the time to worry about AIDS and other viruses that could be present. His lips repeated the prayer *Shema* in order not to see and think about all the horror surrounding him. He was feeling the pain of the victims – Europeans, American, Japanese and other tourists as well as local Israelis, Palestinians and Arabs. He was repeating to himself that all these people were *korbanot* – sacrifices – but asked himself, "*Korbanot*, yes, but for whom and for what reason?"

In moments the police, medical technicians and other emergency personnel were busy helping the wounded. Officials from the coroner's office collected the dead and the body parts and put them in white sheets and bags. The religious men – the fringes hanging on the side of their shirts – cleaned the blood from the street in respect for the lost lives.

Ruth was able to see and hear everyone. Large tears poured out from deep within her spirit. She was not sure if she was dead or alive. She tried to move her legs but discovered she had none. She saw them moving without control and in different directions at a distance, and then she saw a man collect them with respect and place them in a white bag.

She tried to move her arms but she did not feel them either. She saw only her hands and realized that they were still holding the bloody fingers of her mother, Sara, and her son, Joseph. Joseph's other hand was holding Rachel's hand. Their engagement rings were shining on their fingers and a bright light was spreading around them. Somehow all the hands were gathered together in a corner far away from the busy crowd.

In all that chaos and confusion, Ruth felt no physical pain and was not frightened. She realized that she was not dragging a heavy body anymore. She felt very light, almost like a feather. Then she felt that she was rising from the ground where she had been walking minutes ago, happy and proud at the thought of seeing the wedding of her only son in forty-five hours. She looked down and saw Rachel's torn body shattered on the ground, the same beautiful body that was supposed to be dressed up in the white lace wedding gown.

Ruth knew that the wedding gown was still waiting for Rachel in her bedroom. More tears rolled down from her inner eyes, and she felt the heat of each drop burning inside her being. She did not dare to look at her son. She looked farther left and saw her mother, Sara, and Rachel's mother, Leah, in pieces scattered all over, lying in the bloodbath. There were no signs of life in either of them. Then she saw the handsome future bridegroom, in pain and in blood, cut in pieces but still holding to life and pronouncing his last words weakly. He was calling for Rachel, his beloved bride.

She saw some people like herself, without bodies, joining her on the top of the carnage and watching all the movement down below. Peaceful but sad, they were all quiet, able to understand each other without words.

Down on the ground, everyone worked very hard to collect whatever they could. They gathered the body parts that once formed human beings. The cry and pain of the people penetrated the spirit of everyone on Earth and above it. All the pain formed a huge cloud of darkness over Jerusalem.

Suddenly, at that very dark moment, a beautiful bright column of light shone on them from inside the deep blue sky. It was so bright and warm that everyone forgot the pain, horror, carnage and blood. They all heard the choir of angels singing the glory of God – the same song that had come in the vision of Isaiah, which is read in everyday prayers. Then everyone started repeating the same words: *"Kadosh, kadosh Adonai Tzeva'ot, mlo khol ha-aretz k'vo'do"* – *Holy, holy, holy Lord of the armies of Heaven, the whole world is filled with His glory* – and followed the light to reach the final path.

Ruth stayed behind. She was still concerned about her son, who was covered in blood and in pain down on the ground, and she was still thinking of the wedding. Then she looked up and saw that everyone was rushing upward toward the sky, as if they knew exactly what they were doing and where they were going. She was surprised that the victims – Buddhists, Jews, Christians and Muslims – were all singing the same song and rushing in the same direction. She asked herself how and when they had all learned to sing the same song in such harmony.

Suddenly she felt someone pushing her forward. A familiar voice told her that finally they were all going to be united together forever and that no one could ever separate them anymore. She looked back and saw her mother and Wahab, both young and vibrant like old times, following all the others. For a second, she took a little step forward, happy for their reunion – something that she had wished for over many years. But she stopped and told them not to wait for her. She had some unfinished business left behind.

They smiled sadly, did not insist, and continued on their way. Then Ruth saw Rachel bending over Joseph and, in a second, the two of them were flying up, side-by-side. They seemed very happy, as if it was the day of their wedding and they were walking toward their *Chuppa* – or canopy. Suddenly they saw Ruth and asked why she was waiting. They asked her to hurry and join them. She answered, "Later, my loved ones; later."

After a while, she heard a much stronger voice ordering her to follow the others. She ignored the order and descended lower and lower instead of flying up with the others. She looked around and saw the *Migdal David*, the Tower of David, on the top of one of the gates of Jerusalem. She descended farther and sat on its highest point, where she could watch and see almost all of Jerusalem and beyond. She told herself that *Migdal David* was the most appropriate place for her to stay. David was a wise king who did many good things but who had also committed adultery with the beautiful Bathsheba and lost their son for his sins. And now it was her time to finally pay for her mother's adultery. But her case was much more complicated and justified than David's. She felt that she was going to carry the cross of the entire region on her shoulders from that moment on. Now she was going to pay for the sins of others but also ask God for justice.

She again heard the firm order to fly up. She turned to the voice that was so impatient. Ruth recognized him but was not afraid. She answered calmly and with strong conviction.

"Angel of death, you have followed your orders and have taken the lives of many innocent people. Tell me, for what reason? I am not afraid of you, since you have taken me out of my body, too. But I have decided to stay in this place with the free will that I was born with. Isn't it written in the *Torah* that we are born with free will? I am going to use my right and sit here as long as it takes to finally receive my answers and wishes. No one can push me away from this place. I have eternity in front of me. I will ask and pray for justice, since the people are not able to give or to obtain it anymore.

"My tears are abundant like the waters of the ocean. I will sit here and cry day and night. I will cry for the unmarried brides and grooms; for the Jewish, Muslim and Christian children who are falling on your holy grounds; for these brothers and sisters who are fighting against each other without knowing why they hate and kill each other. I will cry so much that finally everyone will see and feel the deep pain that they have afflicted upon a mother and upon each other, in the name of the Holy One, who has turned away from His beloved City of Jerusalem. I will cry so loudly that I am sure He will finally hear my voice wherever He is, and then maybe the long lost expected peace will be sent to all humanity."

The entity who was the collector of souls was not able to persuade Ruth to obey his order. He told her in a sad voice that he did not have enough time to wait for her, for he had much to do. Ruth looked at him and saw two large crystal teardrops falling from his eyes. Surprised, she declared to him, "So, the angels also have tears!" She added, "While I was living on the Earth, I had suffered a lot but nothing comparable to the last moments of my life. This was the most horrific experience! I would wait and cry for as long as it would take me to finally see the arrival of peace on the Earth. Then, on that day, I will join my loved ones forever."

He looked at her with compassion and sadness and told her that she had chosen a very hard, long road filled with pain and tears. He left her behind and entered the column of light that was still shining down from the sky. While flying up and joining others, he turned back, looked at Ruth for the last time, and announced loudly, "The mother of Jerusalem is crying."

❧

To judge a person's acts and establish justice, one should learn the entire story and the whole existing truth, so as to understand all of one's actions.

I am going to tell you the complete story of my family, starting from my great grandparents and the events that led us to this moment and this place. I will do this so that you will understand where I am coming from and why I have become so passionate to stay on the top of this gate and cry for everyone. I see that, regardless of our differences, finally we are all simply a big family. We are all heading to the same place at the end.

Ruth

BOOK ONE

THE ARMENIAN FAMILY

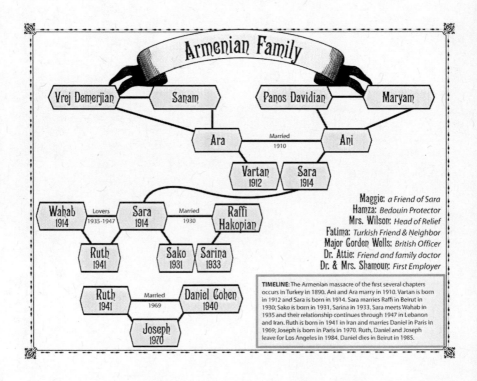

Armenian Family

Vrej Demerjian — Sanam   Panos Davidian — Maryam

Ara — Married 1910 — Ani

Vartan 1912   Sara 1914

Wahab 1914 — Lovers 1935-1947 — Sara 1914 — Married 1930 — Raffi Hakopian

Ruth 1941   Sako 1931   Sarina 1933

Ruth 1941 — Married 1969 — Daniel Cohen 1940

Joseph 1970

Maggie: *a Friend of Sara*
Hamza: *Bedouin Protector*
Mrs. Wilson: *Head of Relief*
Fatima: *Turkish Friend & Neighbor*
Major Gorden Wells: *British Officer*
Dr. Attie: *Friend and family doctor*
Dr. & Mrs. Shamoun: *First Employer*

TIMELINE: The Armenian massacre of the first several chapters occurs in Turkey in 1890. Ani and Ara marry in 1910. Vartan is born in 1912 and Sara is born in 1914. Sara marries Raffi in Beirut in 1930; Sako is born in 1931, Sarina in 1933. Sara meets Wahab in 1935 and their relationship continues through 1947 in Lebanon and Iran. Ruth is born in 1941 in Iran and marries Daniel in Paris in 1969; Joseph is born in Paris in 1970. Ruth, Daniel and Joseph leave for Los Angeles in 1984. Daniel dies in Beirut in 1985.

CHAPTER 1

Ara

ARA DEMERJIAN was born to a long established and well-respected Armenian family in Zeitun, Turkey, in 1880. As long as anyone could remember, the family lived in this same house, generation after generation. Ara's father, Vrej, was a highly regarded carpenter, as was his father. As the tradition was in those days, fathers passed the family business to their sons. With each coming generation, new techniques were added to their skills and over time their craftsmanship turned to fine art.

Ara followed the family tradition without question. As a child he went to his father's workshop, watched his father and grandfather create beautiful objects from wood, and learned the art of carpentry. He had seen and smelled wood from early childhood. Even at a young age he was known for his ability to recognize all types of wood while blindfolded; he could name each just by touching and smelling it. His grandfather was proud of his grandson's talent and liked to show him off to his friends; he was also happy to see that the family tradition would continue long after he left this world. Ara's fingers learned to dance around a piece of ordinary wood and transform it into a piece of beauty. They became known as "the golden hands of Zeitun."

During the Armenian massacre of 1894-1897, many Armenians, including Ara's grandfather, were killed by the Turks. Ara, his father, Vrej, and his mother, Sanam, were spared because they were hidden by a kind Turkish friend, a Muslim whom Vrej knew well.

Armenians had lived in Turkey for as long as anyone could remember. (By 600 B.C., Armenia sprang into being as a nation and, in the tenth century, Armenians established a new capital at Ani, affectionately called the "city of a thousand and one churches." In the eleventh century, the first Turkish invasion of the Armenian homeland occurred. Thus began several hundred years of rule by Muslim Turks. By the sixteenth century, Armenia had been absorbed into the vast and mighty Ottoman Empire – the Turkish Empire at its peak.).

Some said that this part of the country had once belonged to Armenians and became a Turkish territory only after many wars. In any Muslim country, anyone who is not Muslim is considered a second-class citizen and a minority. Such discrimination was true in those days and remains true even in the twenty-first century. Regardless, Armenians felt that Turkey was their country, since this was the only one they had ever known. They were born there and grew up speaking Turkish like all their neighbors. It was true that Armenian parents sang sad lullabies to their children and spoke to them in Armenian. Yet Turkey was their homeland. They all knew that.

The Muslim Turks themselves had their own regional dialects and traditions. Sometimes they teased each other and made jokes. So did the Armenians. Although they had their own traditions and religion, they still considered themselves real citizens of the Ottoman Empire, just like their neighbors. They had strong friendships with most of their Muslim neighbors, some of whom respected them even more than they respected other Muslim Turks. After all, Armenians were known to be skilled craftsmen and sometimes better educated than the rest of the population. Virtually all Armenians spoke at least two languages and sometimes more. Once in a while, due to new government policies, massacres and killings took place in different villages of the country. The minorities suffered dearly, but they thought that atrocities like these happened everywhere in the world.

Later the Armenians would admit that sometimes bad things happen. The world is a complicated and dangerous place, and men in power can act foolishly. But, they concluded, every country has its own advantages and disadvantages. So they had good reason to believe that these horrible events would not happen unless the person responsible had a change of heart or was dismissed from the position he occupied. Each time there was a massacre, a few Armenians left the country. But most returned to their destroyed houses, rebuilt them, and resumed living their lives.

After the Armenian massacre of 1894-1897, Vrej, the father of Ara, found his own father's simple tools and resumed the family business. He crafted beautiful wooden pieces to reestablish his life. When the smell from the cut wood enveloped him, he remembered his murdered father and tears fell on the log. Now he was carrying the responsibilities of his family, and his happiness centered around his wife and son. Vrej had lost almost all other members of his family and learned not to ask any questions. He prayed that God would keep his wife and son in good health and far from such awful experiences. He put so much energy into his work that everyone gave him compliments and remarked that his craftsmanship even rose above his father's.

Ara grew into a handsome young man and learned the secrets of the trade from his father. He was so skillful and talented that later his father passed the business with all its responsibilities to Ara and enjoyed a type of oriental retirement. Vrej came to the shop late in the mornings just to give his son some advice and help him when needed.

Vrej was happy to see that his son had mastered their family craft and that he already was a well-respected craftsman while still in his late teens. While staying with his son, he drank tea and Turkish coffee, smoked the *nargileh* with his friends, proudly watched his son, and admired how well he worked and communicated with customers. In the afternoons, his wife, Sanam, always brought them a tray of freshly baked cookies with dried fruits and sweets. The smell of the rose water and honey that she used in her syrup mixed with the smell of the wood in the shop created a new and exotic perfume in the workplace. She always poured a cup of hot tea for her son and asked him with motherly love and concern to take a break.

Sanam had lost all her family during the massacre. Ara and her husband were all she had left in this world. She loved her son dearly. He was such an honest young man, with a soft voice and kind heart, that everyone from Armenians to Turks and Greeks adored him. People from all over the country commissioned Ara to make different kinds of interesting pieces. He carved a wooden door for the entrance to a mosque. Then he restored the old doors of the beautiful, local Armenian church. He made tables and chairs for government offices and beautiful chests and cases for brides to store their dowries. He even made utensils for kitchens and toys for children. He never charged enough money for his time and work, and sometimes he gave pieces to needy families.

He did not own any sophisticated tools, but he was able to create intricate pieces to show that he was using his God-given talent. Superstitious people would say that at night there were angels in his studio helping him work. If not, how could he create such beautiful pieces all by himself? Sometimes children asked him about the angels and fairies. He always smiled and answered, "If you work hard with your hands and keep a clean heart with God, you too, will also discover the existing talent inside and achieve all your dreams."

CHAPTER 2

Ani

ANI DAVIDIAN was born to an educated family in Adana, Turkey. Her father, Panos, was a well-known Armenian businessman who traveled all over Turkey and Europe. He exported Turkish dried fruits and other local products and, with the money he earned, imported goods that were in demand by the Turkish population. Panos and his wife, Maryam, were blessed by a beautiful daughter. They had given her a very comfortable life and good education. During one of his trips inside Turkey, he heard about Ara's talent. When they met, Ara's expertise, honesty and goodness fascinated him. Panos ordered some wooden pieces for his house and later for export. They became good friends. Ara became the son that he had wished for and, little by little, Panos started dreaming of having him as his son-in-law. The only obstacle was the distance. Panos loved his daughter and did not want her to live so far away. But he knew that his daughter would live a happy life with Ara. Her happiness was very important to him.

One day he told Ara about his beautiful daughter, Ani. Finally, when Ara was delivering a piece of furniture to the Davidian family, Ani's mother, Maryam, introduced her to Ara. The two young people were attracted to each other at first sight. Since Ara had the blessing of his parents and especially the love of Ani's father, Ara asked her father, Panos, to spread their friendship wider and become relatives. They agreed and chose a date.

Ara and his family traveled to Adana. As soon as Ara's parents saw Ani, they fell in love with her. Ara had already carved a beautiful wooden ring, which he gave to Ani, and then all the family went to the bazaar the next day to buy a real ring and other jewelry. They invited the priest, relatives, friends and neighbors to the engagement party, which included music, national dances and a big feast. They decided that the wedding should take place in two months. Ara wanted to marry her immediately but Panos wanted to organize a large wedding party, which would take time. He said, "We have always been invited to many weddings and parties and now it is time for us to pay back and invite everyone in return."

Ara and his parents returned home with bittersweet feelings. Ara wanted to have his future wife by his side but everyone told him that he should be patient since the two months would pass quickly.

In reality, Ara experienced the longest two months of his life. During this time, he and his parents remodeled their house. They added a large bedroom for the bride and groom. The best tailor in the town measured Ara for his wedding suit. All the family's friends helped his mother prepare the house for the happy occasion. Because of the long distance, many of their friends were not able to travel with them to Adana, so they decided to have two weddings – one in Adana and another in Zeitun.

Ani's father organized the largest wedding in the town's history. It lasted a week, as was the tradition. They invited all their family, friends and business associates – Armenians, Greeks, Turks, Jews and even some Europeans. All gathered together to celebrate the wedding. As the musicians played Armenian, Turkish and Greek songs, the bride and groom and then their families and guests danced the entire night. They ate and drank to the health of the bride and groom and their families and prayed for long lives and happiness for the couple. There were abundant Armenian, Turkish and Greek foods and pastries. The smell of lamb kebab filled the lungs even at a distance, and a special place was set to feed the needy all week long, since the family wanted everyone in the town to share their happiness.

After the week of wedding ceremonies, the bride, groom and their families and relatives rested a couple of days and then returned to Zeitun, where a second and equally lavish wedding was celebrated. A week after that wedding, Ani's parents had to return to their hometown. They kissed their daughter and son-in-law goodbye and wished them a happy and healthy life. The separation was difficult for both sides, but they promised to visit each other soon.

CHAPTER 3

A New Family

ARA AND ANI established a loving family and lived happily together with Ara's parents in their house. Ara's mother, Sanam, showered Ani with all her love; Ani became the daughter she never had. In addition, Sanam was aware of how difficult it was to leave one's home and live in a strange city with new people. She herself had been born and raised in a neighboring city but, since her marriage, she had lived in Zeitun. Her entire family was massacred in 1890 and the memories of that horrible period haunted her. Later the love of her husband and son had lightened her burden and she appreciated every moment that she was able to see and feel her family near her.

Sanam was like a real mother to Ani. During the day, they visited relatives and neighbors together. She taught Ani her cooking secrets and how to handloom lace. Twice a year they went to Adana to visit Ani's family. Ani's parents came to Zeitun to visit them as often as they could.

Life was very pleasant for the newlyweds. Ani loved her husband very much. She and her mother-in-law visited their husbands in the shop where father and son worked together. Ani loved the smell of the wood and enjoyed watching her husband create beautiful wooden pieces every day. She admired Ara and his talent. Life was beautiful – as if they had created a little paradise under their roof.

Yet it seems that life is never complete without a sorrow.

For the new couple, the sorrow was over the absence of hearing the sound of a baby in their house. All were eager to become parents and grandparents. But it seemed that God had sealed the womb of Ani, since she was not able to become pregnant. She listened to the advice of many elderly women. She drank all kinds of herbal teas and ate all kinds of fruits and herbs. She and Ara prayed in different churches, mosques and other holy places. They burned candles in all the sanctuaries. But nothing helped. She remained barren, regardless of all efforts, and was unable to conceive a child.

When they finally gave up hope, Ara made a beautiful wooden baby out of an old log from a tree that they had cut down in their garden. The little wooden baby was so real that everyone suggested he should offer it to the church. But both of them loved the wooden baby so much that they were not able to separate themselves from it. Ara promised himself that, if by any miracle God gave them a child, then he would offer the wooden child to the church.

On the very day that they had completely given up hope of becoming parents, Ani woke up sick. She and Ara thought that she had caught one of the diseases going around. At first they kept this horrible secret to themselves and prayed to God for help. But, as the extended family was living under the same roof, it was only a few days before Sanam noticed the changes in her daughter-in-law. After she questioned Ani, she cried loudly and started praying and giving thanks to God. When her husband and son ran to her to find out what the problem was, they were surprised to find Sanam standing motionless, with a large smile on her face, next to Ani, who was throwing up. She told everyone that they should thank God for the miracle that had taken place. Vrej and Ara looked at her puzzled and, when they asked the reason, Sanam announced that soon the two men were going to become a father and grandfather.

On that same day, Ara bought a new Singer sewing machine for his wife and mother. This was an expensive and exotic gift. It had taken him all day to search the city, tipping several merchants before he was finally able to buy one. Ara took the sewing machine home that night and presented it to his mother and wife, telling them that they were going to be able to sew all the necessary clothes for the baby.

After nine months, the miracle baby boy was born. They named him after his grandfather, Vartan, who had died during the Armenian massacre of 1890 and was himself named after Saint Vartan, a beloved and revered saint who died to protect his Christian faith. This was the tradition. By naming the baby after a deceased relative, they were keeping alive the name and the memory of their dearly departed.

After a week they organized a big party and invited many relatives, friends and neighbors to the baptism and baby-naming. The priest placed the baby in the pure water that the family had pulled out of a deep well. He poured some of the holy water – *Meron* – in the basin and washed the baby. The baby was smiling at the beginning but started crying when he felt the cold water. As the priest pulled him out of the holy water and drew a cross with it on his forehead, everyone saw the beautiful smile on baby Vartan's face. The *kavor*, the godfather, offered a golden chain with a cross and hung it around the neck of the baby. When the priest pronounced the child's name, Vartan, aloud in a strong clear voice that carried throughout the church, the infant officially became a new member of the Armenian community and of the Apostolic Gregorian Christian faith of Zeitun. (Armenia was the first nation to adopt Christianity as its state religion).

The Christian Armenians had lived in Turkey side-by-side with the Muslim Turks. Neighbors loved and helped each other, accepting their differences and respecting one another. Ara knew many Turks, since he worked directly with them; they all liked and respected him. On this big festive day, many Muslim neighbors and customers were present to welcome the baby to their wider community.

Late that night, as the priest prepared to leave the party, the couple offered him the wooden baby, which was in a wooden bed filled with golden straw. With her new machine, Ani had sewn a blanket and decorated it with her mother-in-law's beautiful hand-loomed laces. Ara told the priest that the wooden baby was a sign of hope and strength for his family. He hoped that it would have the same meaning for the entire community and said its proper place was in the church. Everyone looked at the artwork with admiration; no one could believe that the baby was made out of a simple log. Later, whenever people looked at the wooden baby, their eyes shone with hope and their hearts felt the warmth from the color of the golden straw.

Vartan was two years old when another baby was added to the family. This time it was a girl, just as Ara and Ani had hoped. She had beautiful black eyes and gleaming black hair. She resembled her father. Her older brother, Vartan, looked more like their mother. Ara and Ani's joy was complete. They named her Sara, after Ani's grandmother. Very soon there was a big celebration for the baby's baptism. Tradition required that the ceremony be done early in a baby's life. Should the baby die, he or she was already baptized. Everyone enjoyed the party and prayed that the baby would grow under the shadow of her parents in peace and with good health.

In the early 1900's, Turkey was going through political changes. The Young Turks – Talaat, Enver and Djemal – had deposed Abdul Hamid, the bloody Sultan of Turkey and had established a constitutional system. The Parliament guaranteed freedom of the press, free speech and equality to all its citizens. Everyone in Turkey was hopeful. The minorities and especially the Armenians were pleased and looking forward to a better life when they heard the speeches that declared, "We are all brothers under the same blue sky. We are all proud to be Ottomans."

Ara was not politically active, but he was optimistic about the future of his children. He hoped that they would grow up in a country where they would no longer be considered second-class citizens. Unfortunately, after four years, these hopes faded and the birth of democracy ended bitterly. The world was going through chaos, and the Turkish nation became more impoverished during these changing years. The masses in Turkey were altogether too ignorant to understand and practice the true meaning of democracy. Soon the Young Turks reclaimed total power, with the help of assassinations. Men were arrested and deported.

In the beginning, everyone believed that the brother of the Sultan, Mohammed V, who had ascended to the throne with a democratic program, was going to carry the people's hope for the future. But Sultan Mohammed did not use his power and played only the role that protocol asked of him. Fear spread through the country as political opponents were hanged. Soon the Young Turks completely controlled the sultan, the Parliament and the entire country.

The Armenians were well-integrated into Turkish society. Many were lawyers, soldiers, doctors, craftsmen and merchants. Some were very rich and had all the comforts and beautiful houses that came with wealth. Others were poor and uneducated. Some lived in large cities and others in smaller towns and villages. Some of the Armenians even worked in government offices or were dedicated career soldiers or high-ranking officers. The Minister of

Posts and Telegraphs was an Armenian. Whatever situation the Armenians had, they loved their country and were loyal citizens. They paid their taxes and, since they were hard-working people, helped to advance the country's economy. Soon most of the young Armenian men were called into the army, serving side-by-side with their Muslim countrymen. For the first time, they carried guns legally and later they were sent to war to fight the enemies of Turkey.

Unfortunately, a large-scale storm was already forming in Europe. Germans were preparing their supporters inside Turkey to fight against their European enemies. The political mood changed rapidly in Turkey. Slogans such as, "We are all proud to be Ottomans" changed to completely opposite ones like "Turkey for the Turks." Every day such nationalistic slogans were heard louder and louder. Turkey needed more youths in the army. From all different classes of people, both single and married men were obliged to leave their families and join the army. But this did not help the country's economy or the life of its citizens. The government confiscated cattle and whatever else was needed from its own citizens for the army.

A state of fear prevented people from opposing these actions or even protesting openly. The newspapers ran stories about the future war in Europe but, at the same time, Turkey had decided not to get involved in the conflict. Yet, there were occasional troubles along the Russian and Persian borders.

All of this was not comforting news for the Armenians. They knew from their old experiences that, whenever the country became embroiled in a conflict, they were one step closer toward an organized Armenian massacre. Even so, most Armenians held fast to the beautiful words of the democracy that they had heard. No one wanted to believe or admit that those words were already history. People who had proclaimed them loudly not so long ago had already forgotten all their meaning and now were headed in a completely different direction.

By then the Germans were everywhere in Turkey. They acted as if the country belonged to them. They helped build the army and train the inexperienced and mostly uneducated men in military skills. Turkey was falling more and more under the influence of the Germans. The Young Turks had cast their lot with the Germans because they were sure that, in the case of war, the Germans were going to be the winners. Therefore, they were already counting on the future advantages from their new partners.

Little by little the British, French and other foreign diplomats and residents – even the ones who were born in Turkey – worried about their future and their safety. They were all afraid of possible harm and a massacre against them and their families. This concern was well-founded, for soon the Turkish government officially sided with Germany against the Allies. The world war that started on August 1, 1914, would last four years.

On October 29, 1914, when the Allies' ships fired on the Turkish ports in the Dardanelles, Turkey officially entered the war. Foreigners in Turkey were trapped. The Turkish government tried to use them as hostages. After difficult negotiations and diplomatic intervention, the Turkish government finally permitted only foreign diplomats to leave the country. Foreign-born residents were not allowed to depart. The situation became more confused and dangerous.

Because Ani's father often traveled abroad, he was able to meet and talk with many people from different backgrounds. Panos was aware of the explosive situation in Turkey and in Europe.

Therefore, he and his wife decided to visit their daughter and her family and talk to their son-in-law while they had the opportunity.

Everyone was happy at their visit, especially the children, who were in heaven and spoiled by the gifts and love that their grandparents showered upon them. Ani showed her mother the new pieces that she had sewn and they passed their time talking, cooking and offering guests and neighbors Turkish coffee. The women told the future by looking at the designs that were formed by the settling of the coffee grounds in the bottom of the cups. In the past, the grounds revealed only happy tomorrows, but this time all the coffee cups predicted problems on the horizon.

The men stayed up nights talking together in a somber mood. Ani could see a shadow of sorrow and worry on their faces. Whenever she served them tea or coffee, she tried to catch a word, but they pretended that they were talking about regular business matters. This time her parents stayed with them longer than usual.

One night Panos asked that all the members of the family, the women as well, gather in the room since he wished to share something. Ani saw some large and small leather belts on the table. Her father started speaking in a low voice.

"On my last trip to Europe, all my business friends asked me to pray for the world peace as everyone expects that a war is inevitable," he began. "They believed that, if a war started, it was going to be a long and a bloody one. This is the main reason that we came to visit and discuss the situation with you – to see what we can do as a family to protect one another."

Panos first suggested that they should all leave Turkey, but he was met with a blizzard of objections. "Where would we go?" "How do we know it would be better somewhere else?" "We would lose everything we have." "This is our home. We can't leave it." Finally, they all agreed that, at least in Turkey, they knew their neighbors and had their houses and their jobs. Anyway, if the war was going to start, it was going to spread to all the countries. So, they thought that, since they were Turkish citizens, they would be better off in Turkey than anywhere else, where they would be considered foreigners.

After many hours of discussion, they agreed that they were going to continue their lives in Turkey as their ancestors had for centuries. Still, they would take some protective measures.

"I ordered some custom-made belts," Panos said. "You see them on the table." He offered one to each member of the family and even to the youngest child, who was only three years old. "These are intended only for peace of mind and no one should worry or be fearful for the future."

He took one of the belts, which looked like an ordinary belt, and opened a hidden pocket along the inside. Everyone was amazed to see that so many gold coins, small and large, could be hidden nicely inside the pocket. Then he showed them how to close and wear the belts. He summoned each person by name and showed each how to fasten the belt around the waist so that it would not attract attention. He was trying to smile but there was concern, even fear, in his eyes. When his beautiful daughter approached him, he looked at her glowing face with love and, when he kissed her forehead as usual, she felt a hot teardrop on her skin.

Ani's heart ached. She wanted to hug her father and cry loudly for the uncertainty of the future. Then she saw her two children looking at her with their innocent smiles. She controlled her emotions. She showed a brave face and a big smile. All the adults were aware of the danger, but they played happy roles as best as they could. When the belts were being fitted on the children, their joy at receiving another gift from their father and grandfather broke the hearts of the grownups.

At the end, when everyone had a belt fastened around the waist, Ani's father told them, "Our country and the world are going through a crazy time. I am praying that God will protect all the population of Turkey and the world, and especially our community, the Armenians."

He paused, as if greatly tired, and then added, "Everyone in this room should remember that, until now, you were blessed to have such a loving family and a comfortable life. Everyone should remember that, regardless of whatever will happen in the future, the thought of our deep love for each other will become our strength. Our belief and hope in Almighty God will become our best instrument of struggle and survival. Even you children, although you're very young, must remember that you belong to this ancient nation of the great and brave Armenian race, which has survived through all kinds of difficulties during thousands of years. Everyone should continue working toward your future just as your ancestors had done before, regardless of what might happen. I know and believe that despite all the difficulties and troubles we now face, the Armenian nation will survive and grow strong in future."

He then asked all his loved ones to wear their belts a few hours every day in order to become accustomed to the weight.

That night Ani and Ara were unable to separate themselves from their children. They all slept in the large bed, smelling and hugging each other. Vartan had golden hair with light honey eyes, but Sara had dark thick hair and black eyes. They were so beautiful that Ani admired them for a long time as if she were seeing them for the first time. The children fell asleep almost immediately, like beautiful angels, and she put them back in their beds. Ani kissed them gently and prayed to God for the protection of their children, that they be kept away from evil and that they should be safe in the future.

When she returned to bed under her thick, warm blanket – made of camel hair and sewn especially for them as a wedding gift – her husband pretended to be asleep. She knew that he was playing a sad game and that his eyes were shut in order not to discuss the unthinkable subject. She did not want to disturb the artificial peace present in the room. She knew well that, if she said a word, she would break down in tears. So she respected the silence and slipped into her place quietly.

She stared at the ceiling in the dark, remembering everyone's face in the room moments ago, and her warm tears ran slowly down on her cheeks. She knew her father well and was aware that something bad was lurking in the near future. She asked herself what could she do and knew that she could only be a good mother and wife for as much as time and life allowed her. The rest was in the hands of God; she had no other power. Slowly her eyes dried from its tears and closed in the darkness. The sweet music coming from the breathing of her children on the other side of the room lulled her to sleep.

In her dream, Ani saw all the family walking hand-in-hand in a large and peaceful garden, filled with the aroma of all kinds of exotic flowers that she had never seen. Huge, colorful butterflies fluttered all around and the children joyfully ran after them. Her parents and in-laws were walking next to them and everyone looked very happy. Suddenly, at that wonderful moment, three ugly, monstrous animals appeared before them. The animals stomped savagely on the beautiful flower beds and ate the colorful butterflies. The children started crying. Ani tried to calm them, but she was unable to utter a word. The animals threw dirt on them.

Her parents and in-laws pleaded for help, and then she saw one of the monsters savagely drag Ara away from them. She tried to cry for help but no sound came out of her mouth. It was as if her mouth was shut and her lips were glued together.

Suddenly she saw herself dirty and empty-handed in the middle of a bare desert, with the sun blinding her eyes. She was lonely and tired. She heard the cry of her children and her husband at a distance. They were calling for help but she was unable to move, since her legs had turned to stone columns. Her hands were bleeding and her blood was soaking into the sand. She tried to call to them as loudly as she could. She heard only her painful voice echoing back to her, and her tears fell like heavy rain on her face.

She felt two warm hands shaking her, and she was happy to realize that her body could still feel the warmth of these dear hands, which then wiped away her tears. She made a painful effort to open her eyes. When she did, she saw her husband's worried face close to hers, begging her to wake up and stop crying.

The sun was already warming their room. Sara and Vartan looked at her with wide, beautiful confused eyes. They had never seen their mother in tears and had never heard her yelling so loudly. She shook her hands and legs and saw that she was completely healthy. She looked and touched everyone and understood that she had had a nightmare and was relieved that she was in her bed, safe and surrounded by her loved ones. She hugged and kissed all of them and said, "You can't imagine how lucky we are to be able to hug and feel the warmth of each other."

CHAPTER 4

Day to Day

THAT MORNING AFTER BREAKFAST, when Ara and the men had left for the shop, Ani told her mother and mother-in-law about her dream. They both made crosses on their faces and pleaded loudly to God for help. *"Meghaim kez Der, Meghaim kez Der Astvatz."* The mothers said that they all should immediately go to church, pray and give donations so that the effect of the dream would disappear. They dressed nicely and took food and money to donate to needy families. On their way, they also gave coins to the beggars who were all over the city.

When they entered the church, they crossed their faces with holy water and lit candles. The children were happy to light candles. The smell of the incense and the soft, shaky glow of the candles pulled Ani toward the bright light in the middle of the sanctuary, flowing from the windows surrounded with beautiful carvings. She looked at baby Jesus in Mary's arms and felt her inner peace. Then her eyes stayed fixed on the little miracle wooden baby that they had given to the church. She remembered that God had always been kind to them. She knew that miracles happened all the time, even in the darkest moments of life, especially when no one was expecting them. She smiled at the wooden baby, and they all left the church with lighter hearts.

That night, after dinner when all the family was relaxing, Panos asked everyone to bring their belts and fasten them around their waist and keep them on for a while. After that, it almost became a ritual for all of them to wear the belts while doing their everyday work. Time heals all hurts, and soon everyone started making jokes about the belts. Slowly, the uneasiness hidden behind these exercises faded.

After two weeks the guests decided to return home. At the moment of their departure, there was a lot of noise and confusion. The children and adults were crying, hugging, kissing and holding each other as much as they could. They were smelling and touching each other's face, as if they were thinking of the worst and were trying to keep as many memories as they could in their minds. Ani's father promised to visit them again soon, but no one was certain of that. They were just repeating, "Please be careful; watch each other; love you; God will protect you."

Once alone, Ara and Ani were sad and silent. But soon the children broke their somber mood by asking questions and, with their innocent laughter and cries, they pulled their parents out of their dark thoughts.

The days passed one after the other as usual. Everything was back to normal. Ara was busy filling orders at his workshop; Ani was taking care of the children. She had become a skilled seamstress and now was sewing new dresses for the children and Sanam and sewing whatever else was needed around their house. She was even making pieces for her Turkish neighbor and friend, Fatima. While sewing, her mind was free to travel back and forth, to beautiful and loving scenes from the past and to dark and unknown places in the future. She read newspapers and was aware of the explosive situation in the country. She hated to hear the slogan, "Turkey for Turks." She always viewed herself as an Armenian and had a deep love of the country and a strong attachment to the soil because she knew that her ancestors once governed on these lands and were powerful people. She considered herself a Turkish citizen who loved her country ever since she could remember. Now she was not sure what others would consider her.

She often looked at her innocent children and asked herself what they had done in their short lives to face such an uncertain future. She and Ara had so many plans for them. Ara had always talked about giving them the highest possible education. They imagined both of them as doctors in white uniforms, healing the poor in their city; now she was not even sure of their immediate future. She was living day-to-day. The war with the British and French was continuing in the Dardanelles. Nearly everyone in Turkey hoped that the Allies would win this war soon and, as a result, the oppressive government of Ottoman would be replaced by a better one. This wish never came to be. The Allies' ships were sunk, and people waited nervously for new attacks.

One day, while Fatima was visiting as usual, she gave Ani a flyer and asked her to read it. "My brother had this piece of paper for some days and was talking about it to my husband and his friends," she told Ani. "He seemed very excited so I want to know what is written on the paper." She was afraid that it was an invitation for her husband to join the army. In tears, she revealed her anguish to Ani. "What would I do if my husband left for war? Who would support me and our children?" She told Ani that one of her husband's friends was very excited but, when her husband read the flyer, he was sad for his friend's excitement.

Ani took the flyer and started reading aloud but then her voice died in her throat and tears flowed to wet the flyer. Fatima asked her to read louder since she was not able to understand her mumbling. Ani repeated the words slowly like a ghost: "Let every Muslim, wherever they are in the world, kill at least three infidels who rule over him. Get organized and slay Christians."

Her Turkish friend's eyes opened wide and she also started crying. "I swear to Allah, my God, that Prophet Mohammed never said such a thing, that Judaism and Christianity were accepted in the Koran that I pray with every day, and that Abraham is the father of all the nations." Fatima then added, "You know that I and my family love all our Armenian neighbors and especially you and your family, who are like our own family. I assure you that the words written on the paper are not coming from the heart of a real Muslim but probably from a thief, an assassin and an enemy of Turks, a non-Muslim but not a Turk." The young and confused women hugged each other and cried bitterly.

That night, when Ara came home, Ani told him that her father was right – that they should leave the country, at least for the safety of their children. Ara looked at his beautiful wife sadly and desperately. "And just where would we go?" he asked.

Europe was in the throes of war. Russia was in early revolution and war. Turkey's other neighboring countries were predominately Muslim and probably had similar feelings toward foreigners. At least, in Turkey, they knew their neighbors and had many friends among them. How could they travel to an unknown country with little children and old parents? Both felt like a mice caught in a trap. They felt like the first Christians thrown to the lions in the Coliseum of Rome. The gates were closed; Romans were cheering; and hungry lions were surrounding them. Ani saw and felt all the horrors but she had no choice. Her legs were rooted deeply in Turkish ground, where her ancestors had lived all their lives. She remembered her nightmare and hot tears rolled down her cheeks and a cold shiver rolled down her spine. They hugged each other, kissed their children, and after a quick dinner they continued practicing the belt exercises.

The world was getting crazy and the Ottoman Empire was getting even crazier. Every day something new and bad happened. Mobs attacked Armenian shopkeepers and restaurants. The government was going after the "foreigners." Christians, who were born and had grown up in the Ottoman Empire, were considered strangers. High officials talked about deporting descendants of foreigners to their "home" countries. The government arrested some and then freed them as if to show its superiority to European countries. Some children and women who were born in Turkey were sent to the countries of their fathers and husbands, while their fathers, brothers and husbands were kept in jails.

The Armenians thought that as long as the government was busy with foreign residents, they would be ignored. The Armenian community was aware that it was going to have its fair share of horrors one day – of being blamed, because Armenians were Christians. Armenians knew that dark clouds surrounded them but they did not know when and how they would explode into a storm.

Ara had received an important commission from one of the government leaders. He finished the order early in April, 1915. He took the pieces and delivered them personally to the official's residence. Among the pieces was a beautiful wooden cabinet carved with unusual motifs. When he finished assembling the cabinet on April 23, everyone admired his work. But he was not paid the agreed-upon price; instead, a lowly bureaucrat gave him a fraction of the original price and dismissed him with a wave of the hand.

Ara knew he had no recourse. Who could stand against a government official? Ara decided to return home as soon as he was able to get transportation, which was becoming increasingly unreliable. The overall situation was getting worse every day, and he wanted to be near his wife, children and parents in order to protect them. The government had arrested several hundred Armenian intellectuals, leaders, writers and professionals – the most important Armenian citizens in the city of Constantinople – and they were now in jails like criminals. Everyone was shocked. No one was able to understand the real reason or meaning behind these actions.

The next day Ara learned that the government had executed all these Armenian intellectuals. The Armenian community was shocked to learn that their most educated fathers, brothers, sons and husbands were killed by these butchers for no reason. All the victims had studied for many years in Turkey and abroad and had worked hard to become doctors, attorneys and teachers in order to help their community and country and make a difference for humanity. Now a bunch of uneducated criminals took their precious lives for no reason. Ara was sick to his stomach. He thought of running all the kilometers back to his city to be with his family. He understood that the end had arrived for the Armenians and told himself that at least he should try to stay near his loved ones for as long as his destiny was going to allow.

After some days he finally found a way to return home. But, during his entire trip, he kept seeing the faces of the martyrs, especially the ones that he had known as customers. These images would roll in his mind, one after the other. He was able to see their anguish and heard their unuttered cries for justice. In his mind, they were asking the reason for their arrest and assassination. He knew one of the slain attorneys, who was a very talented and honest man. He was a famous attorney who spoke Turkish, German, Russian and French perfectly. He defended many innocent people in his career and now he was killed, without being able to defend himself or his fellow prisoners in a court of law. No one gave them a chance to defend themselves because they had committed no crime. They fell victim to a group of ambitious killers with a thirst to drink innocent Armenian blood.

When Ara arrived in Zeitun, his wife was surprised to see a sad and tired face. She asked if he wanted something to eat. Instead of answering, he took his wife and children in his arms and smelled, kissed and held them so close that the children asked to be freed, saying they had no air to breathe. Once alone with his father, Ara told him all that he had learned. He was surprised to see that his father was already aware of the situation. Both admitted that they had no hope and no solution but could only wait for a miracle. They just promised each other to protect and keep the women away from all these troubles and bad news as much as they could.

One morning soon after, they heard about the draft. All able-bodied men were called to join the Turkish army, since the country needed every one of them regardless of race or religion. The soldier who came to pick up Ara was one of his neighbors who knew him well. He was nice to Ara and said he would try to keep him in the city because he knew he was needed by his family.

Ara had no choice but to follow the orders. Ani prepared a little bag of food and supplies for him. She kissed him in tears and asked him to pay attention to his well-being. He marched away like a ghost with no complaint or fear. He looked back to see his beautiful wife, his young children and his tearful old parents standing at the gate of his ancestral house that he loved so much. They waved to him with their hands and handkerchiefs. He looked back for as long as he could see their images. He felt the pain in his neck as he twisted for a last look, but the view of his family was his only source of warmth and hope.

The shadows turned to little dark dots and then there was nothing. Dust covered the road and he remembered the faces of his mother and father before his departure and the last kisses that he received from both of them. He still felt their snow white hair touching his face like a soft feather, and he thought of all the years that they lived together while he witnessed their hair turn from a shiny intense black to snow white. Then he felt Ani's tears washing his face and his heart ached as he recalled the cries of his children.

Ara could not think anymore since the Turkish soldiers asked them first to walk faster, then to run, and finally to stop. They gave Ara and his fellow conscripts all kinds of illogical and even unreasonable orders. That night they stopped in a valley and everyone slept on cold beds, for the dusty ground was their mattress, the sky was their blanket, and their knapsacks were their pillows.

In the morning they had just a short moment to eat from their packed food. Ara took a very small bite since he understood that their situation was going to be worse in the future. He thought of saving his food for the coming days. All the officers had changed. His soldier friend was no longer present; probably he had left late at night when everyone else was sleeping. He looked at all the new faces. Some seemed kind and some appeared soulless. He knew well in his spirit that the end had come for him; he was not afraid of death but was worried for his family. His father had promised to take care of them, but he was an old and weak man.

Ara was sure that his father's remaining days were also numbered and little time was left for him too. The Turks were first going to kill the young men and then the elders. Ara thought about his poor children. They had not lived long enough in this world to see all the miracles of God. Everything seemed cruel, and the future looked very uncertain and dark. The sky was still blue and the sun still shining, sending its rays of light and warmth equally to everyone and every place on Earth, yet Ara felt a chill as if evil had overtaken all of the Ottoman Empire and was trying to cover entirely the world's beauty with human darkness.

❧

For days they walked without proper hygiene or any comfort. As time passed, their knapsacks emptied, so at night stones took their place as pillows. The soldiers asked them to build roads and do all kinds of odd work. Those men who were sick, tired or weak were beaten or were left behind alone. Ara could sometimes hear the single gunshot, signifying that a small piece of metal was ending a human's life and dreams.

One day they arrived at a bare valley between two mountains. It was a cold and gray day. Ara thought it looked like a sad day. This time the officers ordered the recruits to dig a large hole in the ground. No one was allowed to ask the reason. If someone worked too slowly, sergeants used their clubs to hit them with no pity. It seemed that even the soldiers were tired of their own games and were eager to return to their wives, children and homes. The soldiers had their orders, and they had to execute them. The Armenian "soldiers of the Turkish army" dug the designated pit.

Before sunset the Ottoman soldiers ordered the Armenians to stay together close at the edge of the large hole. The Turkish soldiers who wore khaki uniforms were ordered to line up behind the Armenians and when Ara heard the officers give the order, he immediately started praying loudly in Armenian – *"Hayr mer vor herkins es"* ("Our Father who art in Heaven…") – while at the same time making a sign of the cross on his face. He felt a sharp metal object strike him, then his warm blood ran over his face and body. He tasted a salty warm liquid in his mouth but was not sure if that was the taste of his own blood or the blood of fellow Armenians who were under or over him. What was the difference? It was all innocent Armenian blood. It was the source of life of every man, pouring on this bare land so far away from any witnesses.

As the Armenian recruits fell dead or half alive on each other in the pit, some of them asked "Why?" Others called the name of their loved ones, and a few asked God to be witness to the horrors. Ara was still able to see and think. He saw his parents' loving faces close to his, comforting him like the times when he was sick as a child by putting a cold damp cloth on his forehead to reduce his fever. They would smile and repeat that tomorrow the sun would rise all glorious and he would feel strong and well again. He felt the damp cold hand of a dead soldier on his forehead and smiled. He saw the beautiful face of his wife and the angelic faces of his children. They were holding his two hands and were asking him to stand up. Ani was calling his name and urging him to hurry. She was saying that they did not have much time left, and she was asking him to be strong and to stand up.

Ara was very weak; his blood had drained down onto other soldiers and onto the cold ground. Then he felt lighter. The voices of his children and wife were giving him the needed strength. He remembered that some Sunday mornings he would sleep longer than Ani, and his children would pull him from all sides and remind him that they were late for church services. Suddenly he saw his little carved wooden baby, with its curly blond hair and deep eyes. It was approaching and talking to him. He felt warmth and saw light. He wondered if he was alive or dead, and he was not sure what to do.

The little wooden baby angel told Ara that an innocent victim had nothing to worry about and asked Ara to follow him. He told Ara to look back at the pit for the last time in order to detach himself from the earthly world where he was a guest for such a short life. Ara did not want to look back as he knew what he was going to see, but he was unable to ignore the command of his guide. Ara looked down at the pit; there were no Armenian soldiers swimming in their blood. He was amazed to see a beautiful field covered with golden wheat, waving gently north and south with the mild wind. Then he saw many blood-red poppies mixed with the golden wheat, waving their heads east and west delicately, and he heard and joined the choir of the Armenian victims singing:

"Oh, stranger, crossing these beautiful fields, when you see these beautiful red poppies, remember us and don't forget that each red poppy represents the face and life of an innocent victim. Stop, look at them, and listen. You will hear their voices and the cries of hundreds of the innocent Armenian fathers, husbands, brothers and sons who lay under these fertile fields. Their crime was to be born and live in the darkest period of the human history, in the year 1915, in Turkey."

CHAPTER 5

Deportation

SOON AFTER ARA'S DEPARTURE, Turkish soldiers knocked on the doors of the Armenian houses and told the residents that the army had been ordered to take all of them to a new location for their safety and that they should be ready to leave the next day immediately after sunrise. Ani had not heard even a word from Ara and now she, her children and her in-laws had to get ready on such short notice and move out. Her mother-in-law helped her collect as much food as possible. They also gathered other necessary objects that they could carry. Everyone wore their money belts and one garment on top of another as much as they could. Vartan happily asked if they were going to see his father.

Ani's in-laws hid some valuables under bricks in the basement of their house that night, but the rest of their belongings remained behind. Ani gave the house keys to her best Turkish friend and neighbor, Fatima. While they were crying and hugging each other, Ani told her: "Fatima, if I or any of the members of my family do not return in the future, it is *hallal* for you to take our house and its belongings."

Her Muslim friend cried hard and said, "My countrymen have fallen into the hand of evil as we Turks never behaved like this before. I will pray to Allah for everyone to return home safely and soon."

But Ani knew in her heart that it was the last time that she would see her house and city. In reality, her life ended when the soldiers took away Ara for the army. She was alive and present only for her children's sake. She held Sara and Vartan's little hands in hers and they started their march toward the unknown destination.

The soldiers asked everyone to stay in line and ordered them to walk in a row. All the Armenians of the city were like ghosts, sandwiched between the soldiers. No one knew why they were leaving or where they were going. Nearly all were women, children and the elderly, for the young men and boys had been taken to serve in the Turkish army. It was still early in the morning and some children were sleeping in the arms of their mothers, while older ones were holding the hands of their relatives. The elderly walked slower and some who were not healthy wondered how they were going to walk for hours.

At first the soldiers were nice to them since there were many Turkish neighbors who were watching the march. Most Turks looked on quietly but in tears. However, soon some young boys started shouting, "Dirty Armenians, leave our cities. Your place is prepared in hell." Some even threw small stones at them. None of the Armenians responded. How could they? All this was happening so fast that everyone was in shock. Their held their heads down, and they did not know what was happening or why.

As the march continued, the Armenians found themselves in an increasingly difficult situation. Mothers, children and elders had different needs; some soldiers were gentle and helpful; others were savage and cruel. By the end of the day, Ani already saw some sick people left behind, unattended by soldiers. She heard the cries of the families and her heart ached. Fortunately, her children were calm and sweet; they were tired but at least they were not crying. She gave them just enough food to keep them going; already she had cut her own ration, not knowing what they were going to face in the future. Her in-laws said nothing but she could see the pain and fatigue on their old faces. Her heart was with her husband and her mind was flying far away, looking to find a way to protect her children from suffering.

At the end of the day, as the sun began giving its place to the moon, the soldiers ordered hundreds of people to stop and prepare to sleep. Everyone was happy to rest, and people started making a place to sleep. They ate a little portion of their food and went to sleep tired and scared, not knowing their future. Vartan asked when they were going to see their father. Ani held back her tears and answered, "Soon."

When night fell, Ani opened wide her beautiful eyes. She looked at the shining stars and suddenly felt a pain in her soul. She saw Ara's face, formed by the stars, looking at her. She began crying and tasted her salty tears. Then she looked around and remembered her dream. It was over; everything was coming true. She hoped that at least it would end soon. Death was honorable, but a life of humiliation was not worth living. Then she thought of her children and her tears came faster. She felt her mother-in-law's hand on her shoulder; Sanam whispered and begged her not to cry and stay strong. The exhaustion closed her eyes and she slept.

In her dream, Ara came to her. He brought her a big basket decorated with red poppy flowers and filled with sun-colored apricots on a bed of golden wheat. He said, "This comes from the fertile valley of Ararat. Eat them; you have to be strong. Do not worry for me. I am in peace and I will be with you forever." He kissed her gently and disappeared. Ani started crying and calling after him. Again she felt her mother-in-law's hand on her shoulder, calming her down. She was ashamed of her weakness and decided not to give up so easily.

The next morning they were all ordered to get ready for another day of walking. Ani attached Sara to her back and held Vartan's tiny hand. At noon they approached a village that Ani had visited with Ara in olden days. The soldiers gave them a little time to rest and eat. Ani watched an older soldier who looked more fatherly near her group. She took advantage of a quiet moment and asked him gently if she could buy some fresh bread and milk for her children, putting a gold coin in his hand. The soldier looked at the cold piece of bright yellow metal; his eyes shone and he said, "Hurry. I will make the group walk slower for a while."

Ani covered her head and face with her veil like a Muslim woman and ran toward the village. As soon as Ani approached the vendor, she saw him looking at her with indifference. She told him what she needed. The man gave her all she asked for but charged her double the usual price. It was not the moment to bargain; she was simply happy to find some food for her children. She paid him and, while leaving, she heard her name. She looked around and saw her dear Muslim neighbor Fatima. Ani was surprised to see her there. She asked what she was doing in that village.

"Once I learned the marchers' destination, I begged my father to accompany me here," she replied. "I knew that you were going to pass near the village." She had tears in her eyes as she continued. "I am not able to help all of you, but at least I can help one of you. My husband told us many awful stories about the Armenians and their march. Listen to me with your brain and not with your heart. You know that you can trust me. Give me Sara. It is easier since she is very young; I will take her to my home, and she will be safe with me. When you are settled, send me the message and I will give your child back to you, safe and well. Later you are going to enter the desert and it will be very hot during the day and cold at night. You will not be able to buy food. You have your hands full with your in-laws and two children. But, if you give me Sara, at least you will have one less to worry about."

Ani looked at Fatima all confused and asked if she had any news from Ara. Fatima hesitated a moment and then said, "No, we haven't heard anything." Ani felt the dagger in her heart as she could hear the unsaid words. Like a lost spirit she unknotted and pulled the fabric that was wrapped around her daughter. She took her in her arms, kissed her sleeping face in tears, and handed Sara to Fatima, saying, "Whatever you find in her little belt is also *hallal* to you." She asked her to promise not to convert Sara to Islam even if she was not going to contact her anymore. Sara should know her origins, Ani said. Fatima promised and took the child in her arms. At that moment Ani heard the soldier calling her to join them, so the two friends kissed and hugged goodbye in tears. Sara was half asleep and did not make much noise as she was taken away in Fatima's arms.

Ani walked like a ghost to join her group. Her back was aching, as if she had a large hole in it, and her heart was bleeding. She knew that she had made the right decision. But she felt guilty and sad knowing that she would probably never again hear or see beautiful Sara. She was sure that Fatima would take good care of her; perhaps she could even sleep in her own wooden bed that her father had built for her with all his love. Remembering the old times gave some warmth to her frozen heart. Then she remembered Fatima's face and her answer about Ara. This returned her to reality. She promised herself to keep the secret to herself and report the contrary to her in-laws.

When she rejoined her in-laws, she gave them all the food that she had bought and offered some to the soldier. At first Vrej and Sanam did not notice the absence of Sara but saw the red eyes of their beautiful daughter-in-law and tried to give her hope and kind words. Suddenly, they felt Sara's absence and asked her what had happened. Ani told them about her encounter with Fatima.

With tears in their eyes, Vrej and Sanam admired and praised Ani for her brave and right choice. They said that, if they did not survive, they knew that at least their family's blood was going to run in Sara's veins for the continuity of their ancestry and the Armenian nation.

Ani marched while holding hard her son's hand in hers. When he became tired, she held his little body close to her heart. The beating rhythm of his heart gave her the power to continue.

૨જ

After many days of misery climbing through the mountains, they reached the edge of the desert, far from all the cities and villages. Everything was getting more difficult to understand. There was no reason for all of them to struggle and continue to live; yet, everyone tried hard to survive the difficulties that they were facing – probably, this is the secret of human nature. Once Ani thought of holding Vartan tightly and jumping from the top of a cliff, ending their miserable lives. But she heard Sara's voice and saw her in-laws and felt ashamed of her selfish thoughts.

By then, dozens of people were dying every day. Hygiene was getting steadily worse; often there was no water to wash. Sickness spread among the marchers. The weaker persons were left behind in the wilderness to die alone. Everyone was aware that young girls were raped after dark because they heard their cries every night and in the mornings saw their naked dead bodies, which the Turks left behind for wild beasts and nature to clean up after their savage acts. Older boys and elderly men were asked to remain in certain places in order to work, and then the women could hear shots and cries. Whenever men were taken away, they never returned to their frightened families.

Ani tried to be inconspicuous. She put mud and dirt on her face to keep her from appearing desirable. She knew that as long as the old soldier was at their side, she would be safe. Vartan looked weak and it seemed that his normal growth had stopped since Ara's departure. Ani was dressing him with what was left of Sara's dresses since it was safer to have a "female child." At each stop, many of the soldiers were replaced, which Ani thought was an ominous sign.

One afternoon one of the new soldiers came and asked Ani's father-in-law to follow him. Ani and her mother-in-law begged him to spare the old man, who gave the soldier a piece of gold.

"Well, you have fortune," the soldier brightly said. "So come with me. We have to check and see what else you are hiding."

Vartan hung onto his grandfather's pants; his old wife wept hard; and Ani begged the soldier to leave him alone. But the soldier was without a soul; he did not change his mind. In the end, everyone hugged and kissed Vrej and cried, but the old man told them not to worry as he was closer to peace. He walked straight like a young boy, proud and ready to die, since he knew that there was hope in death and greater promise in this situation than in the life that he was living. Both women hugged each other in tears and despair. Vartan was pulling their skirts and calling after his grandfather. The soldiers walked with him far away and, after a short time, they heard gunshots. The two women crossed their faces as tears dropped down their cheeks and their lips said Armenian prayers.

From that moment on, Sanam lost her mind. It was as if her spirit had joined her dear son and husband. Her face was pale with open flat eyes. She talked to herself and soon no longer recognized her daughter-in-law. She stopped eating and drinking. Ani insisted and begged her to come back to herself, but she knew that Sanam had lost the battle. Ani envied her. She envied her father-in-law. She asked herself why no one was shooting her. She held the cold fingers of her mother-in-law in one hand and the warm fragile fingers of her son in the other.

When they were ordered to rest, Ani tried to put a little dry bread in Sanam's mouth but was not able to pry apart her teeth. She refused to open her mouth. She was repeating the names of her husband and son. When Ani helped her lay down to sleep, suddenly her eyes shone and she looked like she had before. She held Ani's hand and kissed her and said in her fragile voice, "Thank you for being such a wonderful daughter-in-law. I am done and soon I will join my beloved husband and parents. You are young and have two children. Please take good care of yourself and don't worry for us. Keep your strength for the day that you would be reunited with Sara." She kissed her and Vartan and then asked Ani to remove her belt and wear it herself as it was getting too heavy for her. Ani did as she was told. Then Sanam kissed Ani and Vartan for a third time with her dry wrinkled lips, closed her eyes, and fell asleep immediately.

When Ani lay down near her, Vartan was already sleeping quietly. She kissed him gently and looked up to the sky full of stars. It was a beautiful but sad night. She talked to the sky and asked how all could stay so calm with so many tragedies and horrors occurring on Earth. She thought, "The sky with its calmness misguides people! The sky should change its appearance in order to alert the world of all the injustices happening around us. The beauty of nature deceives people. In other places, right at this moment, people are enjoying life and holding festivities without thinking about others who are suffering."

Ani saw two large shining stars twinkling at her. The wounds of her heart ached more and tears covered her face, but this time she did not feel her mother-in-law's hand on her shoulder.

She talked to Ara and to her God and wondered what was happening to her parents. She was sure that, like all Ottoman Armenians, they were marching through the country toward the bare desert. She asked Ara to come and take her away from her miserable life. She asked God's help but felt ashamed because she knew that, if she were spared from rape, she was already luckier than many young women of her march. And at least she was lucky to have saved Sara from suffering. But the idea that if she was going to die and not be able to see her again gave Ani another ache. She was aware that, in that case, Sara would become a Muslim girl; she would marry at a very young age and would never go to school. With those thoughts her weakened body received a shock and she promised herself to fight against any despair and stay alive in order to save her daughter from a life of ignorance. Her eyelids became heavy and closed, covering her two beautiful eyes that had seen so many horrors in such a short time.

When she awoke in the morning, she saw that Vartan was asking her grandmother for some water. He was saying in his childish language, "Grandma, water please. I am thirsty." Ani looked for water and, when she approached the little wooden cup to his lips, her fingers touched his cheek and she felt the warmth announcing fever. She held him in her arms and gently called her mother-in-law to wake and get ready as the march was going to start soon.

The old woman was lying peacefully and did not respond. When Ani shook her gently, she felt her cold and motionless body under her fingers. Then she remembered Sanam's last words before falling asleep and felt her kisses and understood their meaning. "Lucky woman," thought Ani. "She is free of the burdens of this world. She is at peace. Such a nice person! Why did she suffer so much? She did not deserve such an ending in life."

Ani pulled the body away from the others. She dug a shallow grave in the ground with her bare hands. Some women and children came to her aid. They dug a grave deep enough to cover Sanam with some earth in order to protect her body from wild animals. Unable to find a piece of wood to make a cross to mark the grave, she drew a cross on the sand and wrote Sanam's name with her fingers. She said some prayers with her neighbors but, by then, the soldiers had lost their patience and yelled at them to join the rest of the marchers.

Ani, who was holding Vartan close to her heart, said loudly to herself, "What an irony. The mother of the golden hands of Zeitun is lying in the grave without a wooden coffin and cross. The father of the golden hands of Zeitun, who worked with wood all his life, is lying on the sands without a wooden coffin, cross or even a simple burial prayer. For generations the men of the family built crosses and beautiful wooden pieces for everyone, and now they are buried in unknown places without a grave, coffin, cross or any sign. Why? Where is the justice?"

They walked and walked the entire day. Ani was surprised at her new hope and strength. Like everyone on the march, she had lost a lot of weight. Women and children now fell like autumn leaves. Some were dead and some half alive. Some were buried in shallow graves and others were left for birds and animals. Even in those horrible moments and in such miserable conditions, in which everyone was dirty, tired and hungry, young women and girls were raped every night. Some girls became pregnant and later the soldiers played a game with them. They lined up the pregnant women, bet on the gender of their unborn babies, and then slit open their bellies to see if they had won or lost the bet. This was the most horrific scene. Ani covered her ears and said prayers loudly in order not to hear the screams of these poor women.

Some of the young girls who had survived the rapes without becoming pregnant lost their spirit and turned into complete ghosts. Some were quiet and cried softly to themselves. Others loudly yelled Armenian and Turkish words that were incomprehensible. They still had mothers who tried to calm them but who themselves were in a more pitiful condition than their surviving daughters.

All kinds of sicknesses spread among the marchers. Some of them had high fever and soon died. Some suffered from malnutrition. Vartan's fever had dropped and he looked better. Ani bribed the soldiers with her golden coins and was able to feed Vartan enough to sustain him.

૨૭

One day they approached a river. The water was flowing abundantly, which gave hope to marchers. All were happy, as they thought that after such a long time they could finally wash themselves and drink as much as they wanted. But, as they drew closer, Ani was horrified to see many dead bodies floating in the river. Some were fresh and others were decomposed. It was a horror to see men, women and children and even babies being carried downstream or washed ashore. The smell and the view were sickening. Everyone lost their momentary joy and felt sick. The ones who were not able to control themselves and drank from the water were soon ill. Others continued on their way without stopping. Some who walked with closed eyes in order not to see the horrors tripped and fell.

The next day, as they were walking, they saw a big cloud of dust in the distance. Ani saw Kurdish soldiers approach their group, and she started trembling with fear. She had heard about their attacks and had to make a choice. She picked up Vartan and swung him onto her back, fastened him with a cord, and told him to hold tight. Within minutes before the Kurdish soldiers reached their group, she threw herself into the river. The water took her and Vartan away from the soldiers. She tried to make little movement in order not to attract any attention. She played dead in the water but was obliged to push some bodies gently away. Ani had not swum for a long time but the force of life and the need of survival pushed her to swim. When she felt that she was a good distance away from all the cries and misery, she felt more comfortable being surrounded with the quiet dead bodies.

She was exhausted and let the water take her and Vartan to shore. They landed at a deserted spot. There she felt safer. Vartan was also happy; they were clean but, once on the shore, the smell of the cadavers gave them nausea. She wanted to bury the bodies that were washed ashore but did not have the strength. Even if she had, how could she bury so many bodies all by herself?

CHAPTER 6

The White Horse

IN HER DREAM Ani saw Ara holding her in his arms and comforting her. He was kissing her face and touching her hair and saying all the nice words he used to share in the private moments of their life. She was so tired that, even in her dream, she was not able to touch him. She gave herself completely to his arms. He lifted her tired body and put her on his white horse. She smiled and asked him not to leave them alone anymore.

Suddenly she felt a big jolt. She opened her eyes and realized that an old Bedouin man was looking at her with sadness. She tried to cover her face and body with rags that were left from her dress when she suddenly realized that the man had already covered her with his large shawl. He started talking to her in broken Turkish and made her understand that she should not worry, that he would protect her and her son.

He gave her and Vartan water and some fresh dates and asked them to eat and regain their strength. He reassured her that they were safe with him. He said, "Allah is crying in this desert to see what my fellow Muslims are doing to the Armenians." He added that he himself was unable to understand this, because Mohammad had recognized Jews and Christians in the Koran. "Please," he continued, "you should make an effort to stand up so we can leave this place immediately. The river, which was the source of life for all of us here, has turned to a source of destruction. Even the farmers are not able to irrigate their lands since body parts are present everywhere and the smell horrifies everyone." Then he repeated many times *"Astaferolah"*, and added sadly, "Why should I say all these words when you have gone through all and know it better?"

Later he introduced himself as Hamza and asked the men who were waiting in the distance to help Ani and her son mount one of the horses. Ani saw all the Bedouin men for the first time. She had heard about all the atrocities committed against Armenians by certain Arabs and Kurds in the desert. Yet she knew that there were good and evil people in all nations. She felt that she could trust these Bedouins. She realized that she had no choice but to follow their orders. She remembered her dream with Ara and understood the meaning of the white horse; maybe Ara had sent these men to help her and their son.

Despite Ara's absence, she felt that she had been protected by him. She knew that although the Ottomans were able to take away her husband and their house, her in-laws and her parents, they were not able to break her spirit. After all the horrors she had witnessed, she was looking forward to saving her daughter and son. But she did not know why that whenever she thought of Vartan's future, she had a weaker feeling for him than for Sara. Even her mother-in-law at the end had asked her to remain strong in order to save and help Sara. Why didn't she say Vartan as well? The thought scared her. It was as if Vartan were her guest, and that feeling filled her with anguish.

She did not know how long she had marched with the Turkish soldiers. Was it weeks or months? So many events and horrors had passed that she could not even think clearly. She blocked all the bad memories in order to stay strong for her children. Her physical body had weakened, but she forced herself to keep her spirit strong for them.

The horse moved gently and Ani still was chewing slowly on the date that Hamza gave her. She had forgotten the pleasure of having a sweet taste in her dry mouth after such a long time. Her teeth were not able to chew hard on the date. Even swallowing was difficult. It was as if her intestines had dried out after such a long period of privation.

Hamza seemed to be the oldest and the most respected person in the group. It appeared that he was their leader, since everyone bowed in front of him and respected his words. No one looked at Ani but they were very kind to Vartan. They rode quietly a long distance. Then they stopped to rest and eat and to also take care of the horses and camels. Vartan was weak and pale; Ani saw his real condition for the first time. He had not grown enough for his age and was thin and fragile. He never laughed or jumped like a child of his age. He was quiet, sad and pensive, as if he were an old man living in the body of a child. All this caused her heart to ache, but she had done all she could for him. He slowly ate the date in his hand.

At nightfall they saw black tents in the distance and everyone made happy sounds and moved faster. Before they reached the tents, some women came toward them with water, making happy and loud noises with their tongues. Ani felt tired but comforted. Hamza jumped from his horse like a young man, and an older woman came to him and kissed his hand, then looked surprised at Ani and Vartan. He talked to her in Arabic and the old woman called other women for help. It was amazing: Ani did not know a word of Arabic but somehow she was able to understand them.

They took Ani and Vartan to a large tent. It was decorated with colorful fabrics, *kilims* and beads. They brought water and helped Ani wash off all the dust and dirt of the desert. They all helped wash Vartan and gave both of them new garments to wear. Ani and Vartan still had their belts on but they were empty. Ani had spent all the coins to bribe soldiers or buy food, even the coins from her mother-in-law's belt. Ani was wearing her belt to honor the memory of her father. She had kept a tiny gold piece for Vartan in his belt for his future and as a memory of his grandfather.

The women sat around. Ani was still beautiful and young. But everyone could see painful lines on her face and recognized that something had died in her. She thanked them in all the languages that she knew. They smiled at her and they all went to another tent to eat their dinner. Ani had forgotten all about the existence of a hot meal. The smell of the food filled her lungs. Vartan looked much happier. He was glad to have hot food and see all the smiling and friendly faces around him. The women served them and taught them Arabic words for the various dishes. Neither Vartan nor Ani was able to eat more than a few bites. They had almost forgotten how to eat and how to swallow. As soon as the food was consumed, the women guided them to a smaller tent and showed them their beds and made them understand that it was time for them to sleep. Ani knew how to say thank you in Arabic and all the time she was repeating, "*Shokram, Shokram*".

When they were alone in the tent, Ani took off some of Vartan's and her garments in order to feel more comfortable. Vartan was tired. He pointed to his stomach with his little hands and said, "Mama," and then threw up the little food that he had eaten. Ani cleaned him gently, kissed and comforted him. He soon fell into a deep sleep; she also lay down to sleep and covered herself with the soft blanket. For the first time in such a long time, she was in a warm bed.

All through the night, she dreamed and saw herself, tired and dirty, marching with the Armenian women and children across the mountains and into the desert. The pain was all over her. She could feel it inside her, as if a dagger was tearing her heart apart.

The pain was so deep inside her being that she knew no one could ever comfort her. In her dream, she was still marching among the weak, hungry and brave Armenian women, still looking for Ara, her parents, her in-laws and her children. But everyone had abandoned her. She was all alone, wondering where the others were and calling out their names. She was able to hear the cries of the young Armenian girls who were being beaten and raped by the savage soldiers. She was able to see the dead bodies all around her. Some were fresh and others were decomposed and half-eaten by beasts. Bones and rotten body parts left from the previous groups who had marched the same desert were all around.

When Ani awakened in the morning, her pillow was completely wet. She felt sorry for herself but she knew that, by some miracle, at least she and Vartan were in safe hands. But she also knew that she would never have peace of mind anymore. She wanted to die and join her family, but then she thought that she must stay alive to avenge this evil. She had to live in order to become a witness and show the world that she was a survivor of the Armenian Genocide. She was going to stay alive to show the Turks and the world that no one could ever destroy a race. She had to remind everyone of the atrocities and sufferings of the victims. It was not her choice but her fate to stay alive and she knew she would be aware of its pain for as long as she would live.

Vartan was still sleeping. She gently touched his forehead and was frightened by the heat at her fingertips. He was the only gift left to her from Ara. She tried to wake up Vartan gently. He sighed and Ani called his name again. As soon as he opened his eyes he pointed to his tummy. Ani was scared at the thought of losing him. She dressed him and asked for help. One of the women who had taken care of them the night before approached her and showed Ani her mouth to invite her for breakfast. But Ani pulled her hand and asked her for help. When the woman learned about Vartan's condition, she left the tent and after a few minutes returned with Hamza's wife and another elderly woman, who seemed to be the tribe's healer. She took a look at Vartan, left the tent, and came back with some herbs and a bowl of liquid. She put some sort of herbal mixture on his body, gave him liquids to drink and, using pantomime, told Ani what to do. She then smiled sadly at Ani and said a phrase that included the word Allah. Ani was able to understand only one other word, *inshallah* – God willing.

Ani forced herself to drink the hot tea and coffee and eat the dates and freshly baked bread. Physically she was feeling better but was worried sick about Vartan. Deep in her being she did not have much hope. "Poor little child, he was born at such a bad time in history. In his short life he had seen more suffering than happiness. What was he guilty of to be punished so bitterly?" Looking at his tiny face, Ani could see peacefulness and comfort. Yet his fever did not drop for days; he was not able to swallow even a drop of water. Ani knelt in front of his tiny body, rolling his curly golden hair around her fingers and talking to him, to God, to Ara and to her parents at the same time.

Ani had blocked her brain from thinking of Sara, for it was too painful. She had to concentrate and give all her energy and attention to Vartan at that moment. She was asking for a miracle but, in a way, she knew that she was being told that she should not expect much. Although the old woman came every hour to give new cures and treatment, and even though Hamza came and brought another older man who was a known healer, no one was able to help Vartan. Ani watched her son all day and all night; her legs had muscle spasms due to lack of movement. She kissed and talked to Vartan. She sensed the presence of the Angel of Death in the tent. She begged God and the angel to spare her son.

But in her heart she knew the truth. Probably Vartan had caught something evil from the river water. And because she had taken him into the river, she knew this was her fault. She looked at Vartan every second and carved his beautiful face in her heart and mind. She told him that soon his father would come and he would be able to be with him and his grandparents again. At these words, Vartan opened his blue eyes; a little smile brightened his face. For a moment Ani thought that Vartan was feeling better and a smile came to her face. While she was kissing her only son, she heard him whisper. "Mama, look, Papa is here." Ani heard a little puff of air and understood that she had lost her son and the battle.

She looked at his peaceful face. There was a little smile present and he had a very peaceful face after such a long suffering. She closed his beautiful eyes with her trembling fingers and made a cross on his face, and then her warm tears dropped on his face. But even her burning tears were not able to revive the little cold body of Vartan. Ani wanted to die with him. "Why should I live? What was there in the world left for me to live for?"

Then she remembered the beautiful face of her daughter, Sara, and her father's words, and she told herself that she was going to stay alive to protect and educate her daughter. She had to find her Sara. If not, her daughter would be converted to Islam and marry a Muslim man. Then she would never know who she was and where she came from. So Ani decided to stay alive and join her daughter, the only other survivor of a large family.

She promised herself that she would work hard to give Sara the best education possible, just as she and her husband had wished. She would help Sara to continue her education through university. Who knows – maybe one day she could become a doctor and help all the little boys who were sick like her brother and stop them from dying at an early age. These thoughts gave her courage and strength, and inside her being she heard a word of admiration from Ara. She heard her mother and mother-in-law telling her not to worry about Vartan and that there were many loving family members surrounding him right at that moment.

All the Bedouins were sad and in tears at the little boy's death. Hamza tried to comfort Ani with kind words and even gave her two pieces of wood so that she could make a cross to mark his grave. They buried him with respect and observed a week of grieving for him. All prayed in their own language and faith for the little soul of Vartan, who passed such a short and sad time on this Earth.

CHAPTER 7

The Survivor in the Desert

MONTHS, PERHAPS YEARS, PASSED. Ani had lost the meaning of time and space. She was living like a ghost, living with old memories. Some nights she was with Ara and the children in their old house. Some nights she was in her parent's house as a young girl, playing and studying, loved by her parents and relatives. Then she was getting married to Ara; she could feel his strong, warm arms around her. Suddenly, she would wake up and find herself in an empty tent – all alone. She would leave the tent, sit on a stone, and watch the bright stars that decorated the beautiful clear sky. The stars were her only companions on these lonely nights.

Some nights she saw faceless pregnant women, over and over, being cut in pieces and heard the echo of their cries torturing her spirit. She heard the young girls calling for help while they were being raped. Some nights she woke up from her own cries and trembled with fear of being raped but found that no one was around and she was safe.

Hamza and his wife treated her as their own daughter. She learned to weave rugs with the women of the tribe. She learned to cook new foods. But she never talked much. She visited the grave of Vartan every day, decorating it with wildflowers and leaves. Sometimes she found little feathers and took them to his grave. Sitting graveside, she talked to Vartan, to her husband, and to all the relatives whom she had lost. She asked many questions but never received any answers. Yet she was aware that, while walking back to her tent after visiting the grave, she had a more peaceful spirit.

One day Hamza and his wife talked to Ani and proposed that she marry one of the young men of the tribe who had lost his wife and was alone. "You know that we love and treat you like our own daughter," Hamza said. "We think the time has come that you should think of your future. You should start a new life and put aside your old memories. Life goes on. You should go forth and not live with the past."

Ani smiled and understood that it was time for her to leave the tribe. Although she loved the old man and his wife, she was not ready to marry and start a new life. "How can I stay here forever?" she asked them. "I want to find my daughter and learn what has happened to my husband and parents. I am not even sure if my husband has died."

Hamza and his wife did not say a word but had sad faces. Ani then thought that she did not want to leave her son's grave, but she knew that the Bedouins would always take care of it.

The killing of the Armenians and the Great War were over, and the atrocities around the world had also ended. The blood of the innocent victims in the deserts and rivers still silently called out for justice, but the time had come to put the past aside, start new policies, governments and lives. It was time for the living people to heal from the pain of loss and start a new life for a better future, regardless of everything. This was true also for people who had not been victimized.

But for those who had lost their entire families and their houses with all their belongings, life was no longer like before and it was not going to be better if they even lived a hundred years. The survivors had witnessed so many atrocities, had accumulated so much pain, had so many bitter memories, and had suffered such horrendous losses that forgetting was out of the question. Courage and endurance were their choices in order to continue life. At night they heard voices deep in their minds, and all the survivors, old or young, suffered from the continuous pain that they knew was their fate in this world.

One afternoon, while Ani was visiting Vartan's grave, she noticed a column of dust rise in the distance. As the shadows came closer, she saw some foreign soldiers approaching her. At first she was scared, thinking that the Ottoman cavalry was coming to take her away. But, when they came closer, their calm and smiling faces gave her assurance that she was not in danger. Since most of them were Englishmen, Ani tried to use her long-forgotten English. The one who seemed to be in charge asked her who she was and what was she doing in the middle of the desert. She answered that she was an Armenian survivor under the protection of the chief of the Bedouin tribe. She guided him and his lieutenants to Hamza's tent and left them.

Hamza invited the soldiers to stay as his guests and rest before continuing their trip. The commanding officer, Major Gordon Welles, learned all about Ani. Later he told Ani that he was sorry for what she and her nation had gone through. He told her that, if she was looking for a different life, there were relief organizations in different countries and the one closest to her was near Beirut.

At this time Lebanon was part of Greater Syria, ruled by the Ottoman Turks. When the war started, Turkey occupied Lebanon and appointed a Turk to rule over the country. But the Lebanese resisted the occupation and were freed from Turkish rule in September 1918, when British General Edmund Allenby and Faysal I arrived. In 1920 the League of Nations gave France a mandate over Lebanon and Syria, which become the State of Great Lebanon.

Major Welles explained to Ani that the relief centers were established to take care of the Armenian orphans and survivors, many of whom were living in tent cities and needed help to reunite with their families, find permanent housing, and restart their lives as independent beings. "If you are ready for a change and desire to move on, I can take you to the one in Beirut," he said. "You will learn new skills for your future and, perhaps, will be able to find your lost relatives. We will try even to help you find your daughter and reunite you again."

The last sentence opened a window of hope for Ani; in all her desperation, she still had a little hope. If she could get back her daughter, at least she could protect a part of Ara and give Sara all that she and Ara had wished for together since her birth.

Ani discussed her thoughts with her adoptive parents. The old man's face was sad and his wife had tears in her eyes, but they understood that they could never marry her to one of the men of their tribe because she was not willing to forget her past or to give up her race, religion and hopes of finding her daughter and husband. Since they loved her truly, they understood that her future with her daughter would be a much richer life for her than staying in the desert and living with them in old memories and with Vartan's grave.

In a few days, everything was decided. Ani mounted a horse and waved goodbye to these hospitable people who had saved her life. They had loved, protected and given her the courage and strength to continue to live. All the women were crying and she could hear the last words that they pronounced: "Allah will protect you and your daughter wherever you go. We will always love and never forget you."

CHAPTER 8

Beginning a New Life

THEY STARTED TRAVELING WEST. The British soldiers said that they would reach the city in a few days. They had enough food and water. For Ani this trip was not a deportation but an organized journey with hope and promise. Major Welles tried not to talk about war or the bad news about the Armenians. Once Ani turned to him and said, "Don't worry; you do not need to protect me. I know much about the fate of the Armenians since I witnessed all the horrors. I lost everyone I knew, and nothing in this world could be crueler than all I have seen and gone through."

Then she added that she needed only to have answers to her questions. "How many Armenians died, and why did no one or no nation come to our aid? Why did all the people of the world let those atrocities happen to the Armenians? How could all the governments know about it and watch silently?"

She knew that all the survivors like her were going to live with their memories and hear all those cries and see all those nightmares every night. But she now understood that, because the other nations did not stop the evil, it was permitted and accepted by everyone. Their silence was consent. Therefore, another evil could reappear and repeat all the atrocities again, over and over, in the future, since no one condemned these acts against the Armenians. It was very difficult for Ani to express her feelings and thoughts in a foreign language that she had learned so many years ago, but she was sure that Major Welles understood her.

The British officer looked sadly at her and listened quietly as if he himself were guilty. He never answered her nor did he address her the rest of the day. Each of them was plunged deeply in their thoughts and in their own pains.

They traveled all the day and rested when needed. In the evening, when it became too cold and dark to continue riding, they found a safe place to rest. At night the sky was deep blue and the stars twinkled all around. Ani was very tired but, after such a long time camping with the Bedouins, she had found a new hope and freedom. She was free to dream of finding her daughter and planning for her future. At least a little hope was given to her and she was able to come back to life and dream again.

Yet deep in her heart she was afraid of the reunion with her daughter. What if Sara did not recognize her? She did not know how long it had been since they separated. For young children even days were a long time. How could Sara remember her real mother? Maybe by now Sara had accepted and loved Fatima as her own mother. Maybe she would have to let her daughter live where she was. Sara would become a Turkish Muslim girl. She would have a country and belong to the majority of the population. No one would persecute her anymore because she was a minority. Why should she bring her back to a nation that had such a sad history?

Ani asked herself all these questions and received answers from the silvery moon that was looking at her with its white sad face. The sparkling of the stars worked to change her mind from one moment to the next. She sat there looking and thinking, unafraid of the snakes, scorpions and insects of the desert. She told herself: "If the Turks did not kill me, why should the scorpions hurt me?" She stayed up late till her eyelids became heavy. She could not struggle to remain awake any longer, went inside her tent, and fell into a deep sleep. She was so tired that she was sure that at least this night she would not have any nightmares like all the other nights.

Very early the next morning they resumed their trip and she was told that in the evening they would approach a village. They traveled all day and did not talk much. She was thinking of a new future built over a sad and tragic past. That night they reached a small village where Major Welles knew the authorities. A man who seemed to be the chief of the village invited them to his house. The houses looked much better than the villages that Ani had seen in Turkey.

Villagers prepared water for them to wash and hot food for them to eat. Major Welles stayed hours talking with the chief, but Ani was guided to a room where a mattress with clean sheets was waiting for her. After two days this was the first time that she slept in a comfortable bed. They stayed in the village for a day. Major Welles told Ani that they were going to leave for Beirut where she was going to live with the relief organization.

It took two more days to reach Beirut. They passed through villages and green cities. On the third day in the early afternoon, Ani saw in the distance the clear blue sky join the deeper blue Mediterranean Sea. Little waves skipped on the surface of the water and, as they approached, Ani thought of the times when she used to travel with her parents to the Black Sea to spend their vacations.

Warm tears dropped from her eyes. She thought of all her loved ones – of her lost husband, son and daughter. She was not able to forget anything. All her past was mingled with the present, and some nights, after dreams, she was confused in the morning to know where and with whom she was. She asked herself if she was living with them on the other side or all alone here on this Earth. The view in front of them – the combination of the sea and mountains – was more than beautiful. What a pity, she thought, being alone in this beautiful city. If only her family were present, she would have believed that she was in paradise. But now family life had ended for her despite her youth. In reality, she was a deeply wounded and dead person.

She looked around and was surprised to see that people were working normally in this city. No signs of all the horrors Ani had experienced were present. People were walking and talking, and some were swimming in the sea. Children played in the sand and were laughing and were calling out to their parents. Ani's heart ached as she felt the emptiness. She had lost so much. She was thinking of all that she could have had. Now, lonely in this foreign country, she had to start a new life with empty hands. She had no hope of finding her husband. She had seen how the soldiers treated her father-in-law, the children and the elderly. Sometimes she would imagine all that the Ottoman soldiers could have done to her husband. But the thought of Sara gave her a little light in her dark thoughts. Still, she was afraid. Would Fatima give Sara back to her as promised? Would Sara remember her mother and accept her again?

She was surprised that she had never complained to her God about being subjected to all those horrors. But she was aware that she was not the only one. Even so, looking at the happy people on the beach, she asked herself why the Armenians had gone through so much. Why did others live happily in another part of the planet but not the Armenians?

Finally, they arrived at a large house. The soldiers stayed at the gate, and Major Welles told Ani that they were going to walk to her final destination. Ani carried her few belongings, which were some Bedouin dresses and a small rug that she had woven for Sara with her own hands. She was anxious. While walking toward a white gate, Major Welles told Ani that he was going to introduce her to the director of the house, who was a good friend of his. Then he promised that he would arrange for the safe return of her daughter and reunite them very soon.

She looked at his deep blue eyes. They reflected kindness and assurance. She thanked him for all that he had done for her. He wished her courage in return and said, "Unfortunately, no one has any answers – neither for life nor for death. No one has any answers for human cruelty and tragedies, and sometimes it is just random and happens to anyone. One should only try to become compassionate. Although sometimes it seems that life is very long, in reality it is very short."

As they entered the building, Ani saw some young girls walking like ghosts in the hallways. She smiled at them; they looked through her. It seemed that they did not even see her. Some were talking loudly to themselves and some had tears in their eyes. Major Welles opened a door with a sign that said "Director." A middle-aged, gray-haired woman was sitting behind a large desk. A nameplate on the desk identified her as "Mrs. Wilson." As soon as she saw Major Welles, she smiled and walked toward him. They shook hands, and he introduced Ani.

They sat around a small table. Margaret Wilson offered them cold water and said, "Nothing is better than a glass of cold water when traveling in warm weather." Major Welles told her briefly about Ani and added that he had proposed that she join the relief organization since he thought she would have a better future living under the organization's protection than staying in the desert. "Beginning tomorrow," he said, "I am going to contact people I know to see how I can find Ani's daughter, Sara, and hopefully reunite them soon."

Mrs. Wilson smiled at Ani kindly and welcomed her to the house. She said, "Although there are some refugees present here who have lost all their dignity and presence of mind, there are also many courageous young girls and women who are very hopeful and looking for a better future. We try to teach them that life is a journey. Although the present is built on a sad past, the future can be built for a happier life. We try to give the necessary tools to everyone in order to reach our aim. I am sure that you will join this group and will make a better choice for the future, for yourself and your daughter."

Mrs. Wilson spoke Armenian fluently. She called one of her assistants and introduced Ani to her and asked her to show Ani the facility and introduce Ani to the residents. The assistant was an Armenian woman from Lebanon named Vart. She told Ani that she lived all her life in Lebanon and that it was a beautiful country whose people were very nice. Many different peoples and religions were present in Lebanon, and people were used to living side-by-side peacefully.

Ani was assured that life would be more pleasant there than living in Turkey, that she was safe, and that no one was going to hurt her anymore. Mrs. Wilson was sorry for what happened to the Armenians of Turkey and explained to Ani that many soldiers from all over Europe were killed in the Great War and that many changes had occurred in the world, especially in Russia. Many Russians lost their lives, while many wealthy Russians lost all their belongings, had fled the country and were scattered in foreign nations, where they lived in poverty.

Ani told Mrs. Wilson, "It is true that many people suffered in the war, but their situation was different from us Armenians. They were soldiers who had guns. They went to the war with ammunition to protect themselves and their countries. We did not have any means to protect ourselves and our families. We were not allowed to ask any questions. We endured such horror and had no one to stand up for us or protect us. No one came to our aid; no one heard our voices. Not a single person cared that our children were being slaughtered." Tears dropped quietly from Ani's eyes and her voice died in her throat. There was a long silence.

Ani and Vart entered a large room where there were many beds with clean white sheets. Vart showed Ani an empty bed and said that it was Ani's. She told her that she could put her belongings under the bed and then she showed her around. She introduced Ani to women around her age – some younger, some older. They went to the dining room, a large room where the refugees learned all kinds of skills and crafts for their future jobs. Vart told Ani that she was happy to see that she was a strong-spirited woman and she was counting on her for future help.

She said to Ani, "The administration sometimes faces difficult situations. Some of the young girls were hurt so brutally, physically and mentally, that they were not able to talk or function. Others have been impregnated by Ottoman soldiers and had their babies but do not want to take care of them. Some become suicidal and do not want to live. Others talk and repeat the same stories over and over. The worst happens in the middle of the night, as some of the girls cry loudly and wake up others, and then the ones who are able to sleep wake up and remember their past and start crying themselves. It becomes very complicated to help everyone at the same time. So we advise all the new residents to put some cotton in their ears before going to bed, so that they would not be disturbed by loud voices and cries."

She added immediately that there were also many courageous women who were very helpful and looking forward to learning and living again. They were determined to tell the world what happened to the Armenians of Turkey and to reconstruct a new life, regardless of all the difficulties.

Soon it was dinnertime. Vart took Ani to the dining room and, when everyone was seated, she introduced Ani to the other residents. Then some of them, who had kitchen duty, served dinner.

Vart told Ani, "For two days you would be considered as a guest, free to go around everywhere and make yourself familiar with everyone. Then you would become an active resident and work like everyone else."

Vart asked her if she had special skills. Ani told her, "My husband was a skilled woodworker; I had watched him work for many hours and probably would be able to use my hands. Also, my husband had bought me a sewing machine and I sewed many different garments. I also learned from my mother-in-law how to sew and make laces." Then she added, timidly, "I learned from the Bedouins how to weave rugs, fabrics and make jewelry. I also know how to read and write since I had studied before my marriage."

Vart was happy to see that they had received such a highly skilled person who could become a true asset and help in the future. She left Ani with the other survivors. Ani was questioned by some young women. Some were quiet while others told her about their experiences with the Ottoman soldiers. After dinner Ani was guided to her bedroom by a young woman by the name of Anoush, who told her that Ani needed to sleep more after her long journey. She told Ani in a low voice that it was better for her to push the pieces of cotton deep into her ears. Ani thanked her, washed and slipped quietly in her bed. She put the cotton under her pillow and immediately fell into a deep sleep. She did not hear others when they came to the room to sleep. They also talked quietly as so not to bother her on her first night, for everyone knew how sad and tired she was.

She did not know what time it was when she heard someone announce loudly that they should all collect their belongings as the Turkish soldiers were coming to take them to a new location. Then another voice was crying for help, repeating, "I am a virgin. I am only ten years old, sir. Please leave me alone; I want my mother. Where is my father? What did you do with my brother?" Another voice was crying loudly over the death of her hungry and sick baby.

Ani jumped from her bed and looked for her belongings to collect and run away, but suddenly she felt a gentle hand on her head and a kind voice asked her, "So you did not put the cotton into your ears as I warned you?" In the middle of the night she was not able to see her face but she recognized from her voice that it was Anoush. She continued, "If you want to wake up the next day stronger and healthier, you had better use the cotton. If not, every night you will be doubly tortured. We all have our own pain but some of us have bigger pains. Some can go on and live with their pain, but some are not able to put their past in the secret drawer of their head. Therefore, they are tortured day and night. Damn the Ottoman soldiers! See what they did to all of us!"

Then Ani heard her voice break into tears and she said goodnight. Ani took the cotton balls and pushed them deeply into her ears while crying quietly. She thought of her father and remembered what he told her, and she promised to herself that she would try to make him proud of her daughter. Then she suddenly thought: What if tomorrow she found out that her parents and Ara were also in Beirut? Joy and hope filled her heart, and her eyes closed only slowly.

While sleeping she had her old dream; she was stuck in the sand and was not able to help anyone. She cried for help but no one answered her. She knew that she was the only one who could help herself out of her situation. When she woke up, the sun was shining on her bed. No one else was in the room. She understood that she had slept very long.

᠈᠍᠋᠍

Ani learned to live and work in her new surroundings. Everyone liked her. She was a sweet soul; she had many skills and was very kind to the women who were suffering mentally. She found strength and comfort in helping and taking care of them. On Sundays they all went to the Armenian church to pray. Soon she learned that there was another house where young boys and men were living just like them.

One Sunday during the prayer she saw a man who looked familiar to her. After the prayer she remembered that she had seen him many times while visiting Ara in his shop. She approached him timidly and asked if he knew Ara in Zeitun. He looked at her with sad eyes and, in a trembling voice, said that he could not believe his eyes. She did not dare ask him again about Ara, knowing in a way that not knowing the truth was better – at least that way she still had hope. But, at the same time, she wanted to learn the truth. So she asked him if he had any news from relatives, family or friends.

He answered in a very low voice. "Sister, it is better not to have hope. We all have gone through horrors and have lived in hell. I wish I had good news to give you but, unfortunately, everyone perished in our city. I may be the only man of Zeitun to be standing here to witness the truth. The story of serving in the army and becoming national soldiers was false. Their aim was to finish us."

He started crying uncontrollably. Ani had never seen a man crying and she also started crying. She cried for the young man;

she cried for Ara; she cried for her entire family, friends, for the Armenians of Zeitun, and for herself. What a fate! What a life!

Two months later Mrs. Wilson called Ani into her office. First, she thanked her for all the work that she was doing, and then she said, "I have heard good news from Major Welles. I knew that he was a very kind person who always kept his promises. Although he lost his only son in the war, he has turned into a very compassionate person who is working hard to help everyone in need."

It was the first time that Ani heard about Major Welles' loss. When she had cried and talked about Vartan and her past, Major Welles had never shared his own sorrow with her. In a way Ani felt guilty and, with a broken voice, she mentioned that he never told her about the loss of his son.

Mrs. Wilson replied that she was aware of that. "Major Welles never tells anyone about his son," she told Ani. "It is a fresh wound and so painful for him. He never talks about it. Instead, he tries to help others."

Mrs. Wilson then said that she had called Ani to the office on another subject. She had a word from Major Welles that he had located Fatima and Sara. "At the beginning," Mrs. Wilson said, "your friend wanted to keep Sara. But, since she had also lost her husband in the war, she has had a hard time herself taking care of her own children. Major Welles offered her some money to make her life more comfortable. He thanked her for all the care that she had given to Sara and promised that she could come to visit you and Sara anytime."

Fatima admitted to Major Welles that, although Sara was very young when she was given over to Fatima, somehow it seemed that Sara had never forgotten her mother. She always had temper tantrums about little things, and Fatima has had a hard time with her. Fatima explained that she had taken Sara to her old house, but nothing had helped to calm her down.

Ani could hear the sound of her heart beating hard. She was crying, trembling, and repeating her gratitude over and over. She was thankful to hear that soon she would reunite with her daughter.

"In two weeks Major Welles and Sara will arrive in Beirut," Mrs. Wilson told Ani. "I have made arrangements for you to have a private room in another section of the house – one designated for families."

A week later, when Vart guided her to her new quarters, Ani saw a small room where there were two beds – one for her and another, smaller one for Sara. Once she was alone, she tried to arrange her belongings nicely so that Sara would like the room. The news was already spreading among the residents. Anoush told her how lucky she was to see her daughter again. Some were happy and others were crying for their lost children since they had no hope of ever seeing them again. None of them even had a photograph to look at. It was all but a cloudy memory for them, and their good memories were erased by the atrocities that they had witnessed. They never remembered the baptisms of their children or the holidays or the happy times that they had passed with their families in the past. They remembered only how their children were tortured and how they cried for some drops of water or a piece of bread.

Ani asked permission to weave a small rug for Major Welles after finishing her responsibilities. Her fingers ran fast to finish it on time. At night she sewed little dolls for Sara from scraps of fabrics and dried garbanzo beans that were given to her to make garbanzo bean dolls, a skill she had learned years ago from her mother. When the dolls were ready, she dabbed on paint to mark the eyes and mouth. Everyone loved the dolls, so she made some for the younger girls just to bring a smile to their faces.

The girls and women in the house were doing many craft projects, as were the men at the next house. Some of the more energetic young men were given the opportunity to go to the market and find customers for all the handmade products. Through this way, money was coming back to both houses and to their residents. The aim was to teach the refugees new skills in order to become self-sufficient and independent so that they could start their lives all over again. Different governments were helping them, but governmental assistance was difficult to obtain since many countries needed help with their own refugees.

CHAPTER 9

Reunion with Sara

ON SUNDAY AFTER CHURCH, the Relief Center usually served a more elaborate lunch than usual. On one such Sunday, when Ani and Vart were responsible for washing the lunch dishes, one of the girls called Ani just as they were finishing their task and said that Mrs. Wilson wanted to see her. Ani started shaking and tears rolled down her face. She understood that Major Welles and Sara had arrived. Ani ran quickly to her room, arranged her appearance for her daughter, and grabbed the little rug and some dolls. She froze for a moment and asked herself, "What if Sara does not recognize me? What if Sara does not like me? What if Sara wants to return to Fatima?"

All these thoughts worried her and, when she reached the door of Mrs. Wilson's office, her legs were almost frozen to the floor. She could not advance another step. Suddenly she heard a child's voice talking in Turkish and she pushed open the door.

As soon as she saw Sara, her heart stopped. It was as if Ara had been transformed into a little girl. When Ani entered the room, Sara looked at her timidly. And then, as if she had been asked, Sara approached Ani with hesitation and called, "Mama." Then she pulled back to Major Welles and looked with confusion at her with her big beautiful black eyes – probably wondering who the lady that she called mama was!

Ani was calm and reassured. She controlled her nerves and emotions and tried not to overdo anything that would scare or repel her daughter. She asked Sara in Turkish if she was tired and pulled from her pocket a little piece of candy and a little doll that she had made. Sara hesitated but took it and then turned to Major Welles.

"When can I go home?" she asked. At that moment, Ani realized that she had not seen and greeted either Major Welles or Mrs. Wilson. She apologized and thanked both of them, especially Major Welles, for all their efforts. The subject was changed, and Sara did not again ask her questions.

Major Welles watched the reunion with tearful eyes and told Ani that he was happy to witness such a miracle and that Fatima sent all her love and hoped to see both of them soon again. Ani again thanked him for all his kindness and then offered him the little rug, which was already finished. Major Welles was very touched by this. He thanked her for her beautiful work and added that seeing the reunion was the biggest gift that one could offer him.

Mrs. Wilson then insisted that Ani take the week off from all her Relief Center responsibilities in order to have enough time for a mother-and-daughter reunion.

Major Welles kissed Sara's forehead and said, "I am sure you will like this new country and, as I told you, you are a lucky girl to have such a nice mother." As soon as his word left his mouth, Sara started crying and asked to be taken back home to her mother. "Sara, Sara," Major Welles gently said, "Your real mother is right here in this room. You are going to be very happy now that you're with your real mother and in a new country. You will be able to visit Fatima, who is a very good friend of your mother's, later. Right now, you must get to know again your real mother."

Sara stopped crying and looked down. Doubt filled her face. Then Mrs. Wilson said that she and the major had to discuss some matters in the office and suggested that Ani and Sara return to their room. "Or," she said in her brightest voice, "take a walk on the beach. It's a beautiful day for that."

Ani thanked them both for their kindness and for the unimaginable reunion. She took Sara's few belongings in one hand and held Sara's hand with her other. Sara did not say a word. Ani told her to say goodbye and thank everyone. Sara repeated the words in Turkish but then ran toward Major Welles. She hugged and kissed his cheeks and then reluctantly returned to Ani and held her hand loosely. As soon as they left the office, Sara pulled her hand away and walked quietly by Ani's side. Ani's heart was broken, since she knew she had a long and hard time before her. She had to prove to her daughter that she was indeed her mother and that she loved her very much.

As they walked through the hallway, Ani introduced her daughter to some of the women residing at the center. Some said nice words in Turkish, but others just repeated random words in Armenian. Sara was happy to hear her language; she asked when they would go back to her home. Ani answered gently that this was her home. Sara stopped, stomped her feet on the floor, and cried loudly that it was not true; this was not her home. She wanted her "Nana." Ani said that she was her real nana and pulled her gently to their room. She showed Sara her bed but Sara looked puzzled. Ani then remembered that most villagers in Turkey slept on mattresses directly on the floor. So she explained to her gently and then asked if Sara was hungry or thirsty. Sara rudely answered no. Ani looked at the beautiful face of her daughter. Her eyes and face resembled Ara. But the way she was acting was strange; in her family no child talked and acted like that.

This told Ani that she would have to be patient since mother and daughter had been apart for several years and both had experienced very hard times. Everything was new to Sara, even her mother. Ani realized that she was a new person to Sara and had to prove herself. There were moments that Sara looked at her and her eyes appeared as if she remembered something, and then they turned flat with anger.

Ani took Sara to the seashore and asked her to take off her little shoes and walk on the sand. She did the same and suddenly she remembered her mother many years ago, holding her hand and walking with love, hand-in-hand on the sand. She was warmed by pleasant memories and, without paying attention to Sara's presence, she told herself in Armenian, "Mama, those were the nice days of my life. Where are you now?"

Suddenly, she heard a little voice answering in Armenian. Ani was stunned to hear "I am here, Mama." Was it coincidence or had Sara remembered some of her native language? She turned to her happily and started asking questions in Armenian, but Sara answered back in Turkish.

This continued for some time. Soon the warm sand and sun, the breeze blowing in from the Mediterranean Sea and the view of the mountains in the distance melted the icy relations between the newly reunited mother and daughter. For a moment both forgot their differences and their past. They were transformed into two children and started laughing and running on the sand and into the water after each other until both were damp and exhausted. They returned home, ate their dinner, and went to bed early. Sara did not talk much. She was very tired but seemed happy. She immediately closed her eyes and fell into a deep sleep.

For the first time, Ani was not afraid to sleep. She looked at Sara as much as she could see her in the dark. She was able to recognize every line on her face and every movement that she was making in her dream. Ani had a vivid image close to her to remind herself of her lost family. Each part of Sara resembled someone she knew and loved dearly. Sara's eyes were exactly like Ara's. Her fingers resembled Vartan's. Her hair and smile resembled her mother's. Her eyebrows were like her father's. Her lips were like Ani's father's, and her nose was like her mother-in-law's. Ani marveled: "One little survivor, with so many presences and similarities in her tiny body!"

She listened to the sweet melody that her daughter produced while breathing. She adopted the rhythm of her daughter's breathing as if she was trying to accompany her on the right beat of night music. Ani's eyelids became heavier and heavier until her eyes closed and she was in a deep and sweet sleep. That was the only night after many years that Ani did not have any nightmares.

The next morning, when Ani woke up, she was surprised to see Sara at her bedside looking at her with confusion. Ani felt guilty that she had slept longer than her daughter. She said, "*Bari-luise*", or "Good morning" in Armenian, but Sara responded in Turkish. Ani asked her if she was hungry and then they got ready to have their breakfast in the room. Ani wanted to put her hands around Sara and smell her hair and squeeze her body against her heart and fill her empty and broken heart with her warmth. But Sara kept her distance. Ani had imagined Sara's face in the darkest moments of her life and that image had brought her back to life, given her hope and strength.

But, actually, she was aware that they both were strangers to each other now. Ani knew that Sara missed Fatima, whom she surely regarded as her own mother and Fatima's house as her home. Turkish was her language, and Ani realized that she had even been taught their religion since Sara was performing one of the religious rituals each morning by putting a piece of cloth on her head and bowing down to pray.

Ani told herself that she should be patient. After they left for a walk, Ani found the right moment. She asked Sara about

Fatima and her past life. Suddenly Sara stopped, looked at her with anger and replied: "If you were my mother, why did you leave me alone? And why do you ask me all these questions now?"

Ani responded kindly with tears that she could not explain all because she was too young to understand. One day she would tell her everything and Sara would understand the real reason. But Ani realized that, even with all the love present inside her being, she was going to be a stranger to Sara for a long time. The truth broke her heart, but that was not Sara's fault. Sara was also a victim, and it was entirely reasonable that she should feel the way she did. She had already been hurt too much at such a young age.

After some days, Ani resumed her duties, carrying out what she had to do and at the same time taking care of Sara. Sara started opening up and socializing more with the other residents. She was talking to all the women. Some were upset when she spoke in Turkish and others helped her to learn Armenian. And others spoiled her as much as they could. It seemed that Sara was adapting to her new life well enough.

જ

Sara was now almost six years old. She had passed a little of her short life in her own family, surrounded with love and respect, and another part as an orphan in a crowded family that was very different from what she was used to. She missed her parents. She probably did not remember the deportation and her grandparents. She had seen and probably heard from her Turkish family about the suffering of her nation and knew little of the Armenian Genocide. Although Sara was young, Ani soon realized and was amazed to learn how much she had repressed good and bad memories and images. She had the influence of two religions, cultures and customs present in her little being. She loved and hated everyone she knew. She loved her Turkish family but she also hated them for giving her up to Major Welles. She vaguely remembered Ani and, at the same time, hated Ani for leaving her with strangers and now taking her away from her family.

Ani was confused herself. She had tried to forget her past in order to deal with the future but, with Sara's presence, all was coming back to her again. After some months, Mrs. Wilson asked Ani how the relationship between her and her daughter was working out.

"Sara is nice and angry with me at the same time," Ani explained. "I have a hard time making Sara understand that I am her real mother."

Mrs. Wilson replied, "In these types of situations, time is the most important element. Ani, you should be patient since, in the end, maternal love always triumphs."

Ani answered that Sara had brought a lot of joy and hope to her. In a way, Sara covered over all the horrible memories but, at the same time, she was living proof of the past. Ani was aware that she had a long struggle ahead but was ready for anything that would give a good future to her daughter.

After long reflection and thought, Ani asked Mrs. Wilson if she would help her find a real job outside the Relief Center so that she could help Sara grow in a more normal atmosphere, where the shadow of war and genocide would not be a constant reminder. Ani added that while she was aware that the center was a protected place for them, she believed that, if she could work and live outside, she and Sara would have a better life and greater opportunities. Mrs. Wilson smiled kindly and approved her approach and said that she would put all her efforts to find a job suited for her and Sara.

After a week, Mrs. Wilson called Ani. "There is an opening with a well-known family that is looking for a reliable person to take care of their newborn baby. The husband is a famous Maronite physician and the wife is from a respected Lebanese family. I know the family very well. They live in a nice area of the city and their house faces the sea. I am sure that both you and they will like each other and that Sara will find a loving family and comfortable life. Doctor Shamoun and his wife, Rashida, are very sympathetic toward the Armenian cause and they have helped the relief organization often."

The Maronite Church was a Christian community that originated in Syria in the seventh century A.D. and persisted ever since, despite the spread of Islam. Ani had heard only good things about Maronites, and this reassured her.

The next day Ani and Sara went for the interview. Doctor and Rashida Shamoun liked Ani at first sight and told her how sorry they were for all her losses. "We are sure you and Sara would be comfortable living with our family," Doctor Shamoun said. His wife, who was a young and a beautiful woman with curly dark hair, walked with Ani to the baby's room. Ani felt her heart ache when she saw the baby boy in the crib. He reminded her of Vartan and her past life. Her eyes filled with tears but she immediately controlled her emotions and smiled at the baby, who was sleeping peacefully. Mrs. Shamoun then showed her a nice room next to the baby's room and said, "I am sure Sara and you would be comfortable living here." From the window Ani was able to see the Mediterranean and hear the music of its waves filling the air, which added to the charm of the house.

Mrs. Shamoun told Ani the financial arrangements. In addition to a small monthly salary, Ani and Sara would have the room and all their meals. "At the beginning of summer, our family moves to our vacation house in the mountains where many guests and relatives visit and stay with us," she said. "Your family and friends are also welcome to visit you." Ani stopped looking at the sea, her eyes filled with tears and answered in a low voice. "There is no one left for me in this world but Sara. My daughter and I are the only survivors of our entire family."

Mrs. Shamoun immediately regretted her offer and was confused about what to say next. Suddenly the baby started crying. Mrs. Shamoun was relieved at the interruption and said it was time for him to be fed and that Ani and Sara could move in immediately if Ani accepted the job.

Ani immediately agreed. She couldn't believe her good fortune and thought that it was the luck that Sara had brought with her. When they returned to the Relief Center, she went directly to see Mrs. Wilson and, in an excited voice, explained that she had accepted the position. She thanked Mrs. Wilson for giving her such a wonderful opportunity. Mrs. Wilson was gracious and thanked Ani for all the work she had done while at the center. "You were very important to us," she said. "But you and Sara should take advantage of this opportunity. It will allow you both to live more normal lives. And, of course, to obtain the best education possible for Sara."

In the evening the staff prepared a modest farewell party for the mother and daughter, who were well-liked by all the residents. Most of the women were happy for her but sad to lose Ani and especially Sara, since Sara's presence gave them joy and hope. Ani promised to visit them as often as she could. "I love you all very much," she said, holding back her tears. "You are my sole family left in this world." Mrs. Wilson gave her a little envelope and said it contained the savings that had been put away in her name. With that small amount of money, she would not go empty-handed into the world. Everyone was in tears, and the night ended with kisses, promises, hope and more tears.

Back in her room, Ani put Sara to bed and started gathering her few belongings. When she got into bed, Ani felt tears pouring down her cheeks. She remembered all the farewells and the past kisses and goodbyes in her life. She remembered the day she had to leave her father's house and move to Ara's hometown. Although it was sad to leave her parents, it was a beginning of love and hope for the future. Then it was the departure of Ara – sad and unforgettable. Soon the time came for her own evacuation from her own house and finally the march toward an unknown fate. Then the goodbyes with her in-laws, life in the desert with strangers, and her last farewells to her Bedouin family. Ani loved Hamza, his wife and his tribe. They were kind and loving people; she loved them as if they were her own parents.

All the departures were heartbreaking memories. But the birth and death of Vartan was the worst. In the dark she looked at Sara and tried to see Vartan's presence in her. There were certain lines of similarities on her face that reminded her of Vartan, but Sara had a different coloration and personality. Vartan was all kindness and sweetness. Sara was completely the opposite: she had a strong character and was hard to deal with. Ani comforted herself by thinking that time would change all, but she was aware that Sara had already built her character and was not going to change completely. Probably, in time, she would be able to modify her behavior slightly. Sara was a part of Ani's being but still a very different personality. She had to accept that. Just as children are very different by appearance, so too they also have different personalities, since each child represents an independent spirit.

In her time, traditions and strong family ties were very important; the grandparents influenced the children on behaving with respect and love. Sara was influenced by Fatima's education, and Ani's absence had opened a deep scar in her memory. It was as if Sara could not forgive her mother – neither for abandoning her nor for taking her back. Ani was able to feel a separation and distance between her and her daughter at such a young age.

But she comforted herself by thinking that at least she was lucky to have a daughter. Many other Armenian women were less fortunate. Her challenge was to work hard in order to pass her traditions to her daughter. Ani hoped that, with her new job, she would be able to give her daughter a good education and many opportunities for the future.

She was exhausted by all her thoughts, the back and forth in time and in tragedies. She finally told herself that tomorrow was the start of a new life for both of them, and she was determined to work as hard as she could toward building a good future for her daughter.

CHAPTER 10

Life at the Shamoun Household

ANI'S WORK in Doctor Shamoun's house was not difficult. And even if it were, the family would not know because Ani did it all with grace and no complaints. Soon Ani and Sara were accepted as the members of the family. The Shamouns felt lucky to have such a sweet and dedicated person as Ani for the nanny of their baby, a happy infant named Robert. Ani liked to take care of the baby and, although she always had Vartan in her heart, she learned to keep her sadness to herself and give all her love and attention with a smiling face to the infant.

Days passed peacefully for Ani and Sara, but nights remained the same: The atrocities that Ani had witnessed during her march, as well as the faces and voices of the innocent Armenian victims, never left her alone. She always had nightmares and suffered long nights in absolute silence.

On weekends Ani and Sara took some sweet fruits and pastries and visited the residents at the Relief Center. They attended church services and then walked around the city and on the beach. Like her, some of Ani's friends had left for a new life and jobs. And others found new hope and love within the center. Boys and girls got married and started a new life. But there were always those who never returned to their former selves and, instead, lived constantly with their past horrors. They yelled, cried, talked to themselves, and never healed. This was the group that Ani often visited. She gave them unconditional love.

Sara was growing tall and beautiful. The Shamouns treated her as theirs and were kind to her. She was both attractive and talented. She never forgot the Turkish language and sometimes unknowingly spoke Turkish to her mother. Ani replied also in Turkish since she believed there was a need for Sara to speak Turkish and travel back in her subconscious mind. Sara no longer talked or asked questions about Fatima; it was as if she were making an effort to accept Ani as her mother. Sara had learned Armenian and spoke it quite well. She also had picked up some Arabic and French, since these were the languages spoken in Beirut.

Occasionally, when Ani was busy with her work and the baby, she would sense that Sara was quiet and sad. Probably, Ani thought, she was jealous and wanted her mother's total attention. Sometimes it was hard for Ani to strike a balance, especially when little Robert was crying or hungry. But most of the time she tried to give Sara her attention and love.

When the Shamouns had guests or more work, Sara was left alone to take care of herself. She often sat near the window of her room and watched families walking and playing on the beach. It was then that she cried silently over her lonely life. She wished that she had a father and mother all for herself. She wished that she had sisters and brothers. She dreamed of a real family life, with cousins, aunts and uncles. Sometimes she wished she had stayed with Fatima. She had played in the street with Fatima's children and, although they did not have fancy clothes like the Shamouns, she had fun. She missed everyone and everything about having a real mother present. Although she had Ani, Ani was more like an absentee mother and, even when they were together, Sara was aware that a part of her was always absent. She never had real fun with her.

Whenever Sara saw the baby in the arms of Doctor Shamoun, she remembered how she missed having a father who loved her. She knew that whatever her mother did, it would never replace the emptiness of having no father. She needed a man in her life with strong arms to hold her and protect her. She was never able to ask Ani about her father, and Ani never mentioned him. It was as if Ara never existed and this bothered Sara greatly. Sara wanted to know more about her father, but she had learned to respect the silence of her mother.

Sara created an imaginary family for herself. She collected some postcards with the images of parents and children. She looked at pictures of families in magazines and wished that they were her family. Small things would upset her, and Sara would turn in anger against her mother, who had abandoned her first to Fatima and now to her job. As Sara's fantasies grew, the Shamouns gave Ani more and more responsibilities around the house. Grateful for the security and comfort that her employers provided her and Sara, Ani was never able to refuse. But many evenings, after a long and busy day, she was too tired to do anything with her daughter.

Soon Ani registered Sara in a private French school, one of the best in the city. With the help of the principal, Ani was able to get a partial scholarship for Sara. She paid the rest of the tuition from her small salary. Ani was in heaven to see her daughter at a French school. Before the term started, she sewed her uniform, bought a new pair of shoes, and made nice ribbons for Sara's long black hair. Ani did not want anyone to consider her daughter an orphan. She promised herself that she would not make Sara feel less than any of the other students, most of whom came from wealthy families.

The night before the first school day, Ani asked Sara to arrange her uniform on the back of the chair along with everything else that she was going to need. She kissed Sara goodnight and told her, "I am sure that you will be happy at the school." Sara was excited to start school, not so much for learning, since she did not know what it meant, but for meeting other girls her age and finding friends. Once in bed, Ani was able to pour out her thoughts in the dark as she listened to the music made by the waves. She always imagined that the wind and the waves were telling secrets to each other at night. Sometimes she listened carefully in hope of discovering the subject of their discussion, but she had her own story to go back and forth too.

The moon was sending his bright rays through the sky and looked like a powerful king dominating the Earth. Sara looked quietly at the little stars that twinkled at her. She remembered the night with Major Welles, while they were traveling to Beirut. He showed her a twinkling star and told Sara that it was sent by her father. "He is asking how you are doing, and every time it twinkles he is telling you how much he loves you." Since that night Sara always searched for that star in the sky and smiled and talked to her unknown father. She looked again at the star and said, "Father, I start my school tomorrow." And her eyes closed for a deep sleep.

The next morning Ani woke up very early. She was probably more excited than Sara. She knew the real meaning of school and learning and how the life of a child would change because of a good education. If Sara studied as Ani wished, her life would change completely to a better one in the future. Ani looked at the little uniform and passed her loving hands over it as if she were ironing it with her palms. She checked on the baby and prepared everything so that, while she took Sara to school, if Mrs. Shamoun wanted something it would be just where she could find it. Then she woke Sara. Ani washed and combed her daughter's beautiful long black hair and braided it, with one braid at each side. Finally, she tied the nice ribbons at the end of the last knot.

She prepared breakfast and, after Sara had eaten, helped her into her uniform. Ani had tears of joy in her eyes and a large smile on her face seeing her daughter in a French school uniform. They walked hand-in-hand to school. Sara was a little worried to be alone in a new environment, but she had already changed countries and families and had learned to look out for herself. She was happy to finally be free for some hours and see other children her age and thought that perhaps she could even find some good friends to fill the empty place of a sister.

All went well on Sara's first school day. Ani was happy to hear her daughter's experiences. Days, months and years passed. But although Sara was a bright child, she was not motivated to study hard. Ani tried to help her with her homework, but she herself was caught up in her own work and relied on Sara to be responsible. After all, Ani's mother was not educated and her father used to travel most of the time, so her parents had to depend on her to study well all by herself. She expected that Sara would do the same.

But Sara was another spirit. Her experiences and expectations of life were very different from her mother's. She was only a fair student; learning for its own sake held no magic for her. Instead, she wanted to have fun and have friends; studying was her last objective. In time, she learned to lie in order to protect herself. She had already learned this lesson while living with Fatima, when she was told to call Fatima her mother even though she knew that she was not her real mother. She learned to pretend and to become what everyone wanted from her in order to survive. When she had bad notes from school, she hid them from her mother. She sometimes lost a notebook or a test paper in order not to show the truth to Ani.

Whenever her mother asked the teachers about her daughter, they always replied that Sara was a talented girl but also a very lively one who talked too much in the classroom and did not pay enough attention to the teacher. On the way home, Ani recited all the reasons why Sara should study and how it was good to study. She often asked her, "Tell me, Sara, which future you would like to choose for yourself? Would you like to become like Doctor Shamoun or like me?" Sara always answered with respect that she loved her mother and it did not matter what she did to earn her living.

After some years, Doctor Shamoun and his family decided to leave for France. They loved Ani and Sara. Their little boy, who had now grown, also loved Ani as a second mother. They had added two other children to their family and they all loved and respected Ani and Sara as well. Doctor Shamoun and his wife proposed that Ani and her daughter move with them to France. Although Ani never heard anything from either Ara or her parents and never found a relative among the refugees, after all those years she still hoped for a miracle. She thanked the Shamouns but refused to move to France.

Such a change would have been a very big move for her. She had already learned to live in the city and she did not want another change in her life. By living in the Middle East, she felt she was still close to her past life; she was waiting for her loved ones to show up one day. But, deep in her heart, she knew that no one would ever come back to her alive. On the day of the Shamouns' departure, everyone hugged and cried. Ani was sad to lose such a kind family but was happy that at least Sara was at school and not there to witness the departure of the family in which she had grown up.

Ani had already found a new job. She worked hard all her life; she never complained since she knew that life was always composed of hard and easy days, and complaining would only make the hard days harder. She had learned that a bitter medication should be swallowed immediately; no one wanted to keep a bad taste in the mouth for a long time. Life was like that too. If one did what had to be done, the day would pass faster and the taste of the bitterness would not last long. She learned that life was kind to some people, like Mrs. Shamoun, and unkind to others.

Ani sometimes compared herself to Mrs. Shamoun. Ani was as young and as beautiful, but she could never understand why her life was so hard and filled with suffering while Mrs. Shamoun's life was one of prosperity and happiness. Both were born in relative comfort and had married and lived in nice houses surrounded with friends and relatives. When very young, both enjoyed a good life. But Rashida Shamoun had remained in her luxury and comfort whereas Ani had become a hardworking maid tormented by nightmares. Still, she was thankful because she had seen people who were in worse condition than herself. Ani was not jealous but always tried to understand the secret of life.

One day she read a prayer in the Old Testament that said everyone was created as a very special entity and that God had given everyone a special life and destiny and that He loved them all. From then on, she understood the meaning of life and was comforted. She told herself, "Everyone's life is like the lot of a farmer. Some have fertile land, and they plant and work on their land easily and are able to collect abundant produce. Another farmer in another part of the world owns barren land with not much water, but he still works hard and plants. Even though he works hard and does not collect as much produce as the first farmer, he still is able to feed his family somehow. The secret to life is not to compare one to another. God gives all people a parcel of earth and watches how they work on it. At the end of the account, it is the way that they have performed that gives them the points, not the quantity that they have obtained."

Ani knew that she had a special destiny to achieve in this world and she was humble to accept her life with all its difficulties, since it was written that everyone was special and unique in this world. After all, life was just a passage and it never lasted very long. She learned to live in peace with herself and her portion of life and, perhaps, this was the reason that everyone loved her, since she always had a smiling face.

Yet, deep inside her, she knew that this did not mean that she was without troubles. She just did not have a choice. But at night whenever she was miserable, she ended up sleeping on a wet pillow. Then Ara would come to her in a dream to hug her, give her all his love, and comfort her. The next day Ani always woke up released of all her anguishes and pain and would tell herself that she had responsibilities. She lived only for the sake of her daughter. As soon as Sara became independent and did not need her anymore, then she would ask Ara to take her with him to wherever he was, because she knew that her real happiness was by his side and close to her lost ones.

CHAPTER 11

Sara Falls in Love

AT SIXTEEN YEARS OLD, Sara was already a flower in full bloom. Despite her young age, she had experienced and seen many tragedies in her life. Although her mother worked hard and was completely devoted to her, Sara felt the empty place of her father terribly deep in her being. She never experienced the joy of living with a full family in which the father was present and grandparents, aunts, uncles and cousins surrounded her. This was the life of all her girlfriends at school, but it was not Sara's life. She never experienced loving, sharing and fighting with a brother or sister like everyone else.

Her friends talked about their lives with their immediate and extended families. They were invited into each other's houses, went on picnics to the seashore and mountains together and did different activities. Sara listened to them and sometimes ran to the bathroom to wipe off her tears out of sight from her friends. She was too proud to show them her pain. She thought of all the good things that she could have if she had a normal family, and at night she wept quietly in her bed. She never shared her feelings with her mother since she did not want to break her heart more than it was. Ani also did all that she could and she herself never shared her pain with her daughter either. Both of them knew how to keep their sorrows to themselves and were resigned to live an apparently normal life.

The result of all these feelings was that, from a very young age, Sara always looked for a man to fill the void in her heart and life. She was attractive, bright and full of life. Regardless of all the sad experiences, she had a strong *joie de vivre*. Most of the boys of her age were attracted to her, but they were still very young and behaved childishly. She talked to them indifferently and did not think of them as protectors; they were not even real men to her. She had many close girlfriends and, because her mother trusted them, she was allowed to go to their houses to play and study. She was invited to her friends' birthday parties and, because parents and relatives were always there, she pretended that she were part of their families.

The young boys and girls danced folk and modern dances together. Sara danced beautifully. Ani had paid for private lessons so that Sara would learn traditional Armenian dances, but Sara had also learned modern dances like the rumba, tango and waltz. Unconsciously she was attracted to older boys, since they were more mature, more fatherly, and offered an umbrella of protection to her.

In those years, the relationship between boys and girls was distant. If a girl looked in the eyes of a boy, that was enough to kill him. As for the girls, they fantasized relationships platonically in their minds and were like actresses from their favorite movies. Both boys and girls imagined and romanticized the relationship in their minds since most were not able to date openly and those who could just went to the beach or a movie. If, for a moment, their hands would clasp together in the darkness of a movie theater, that would create an electrical current burning their young bodies. As soon as the lights came back on, they would pull back their hands.

Almost every ethnic group lived in a specific quarter of the city. The Armenians had their own section and, like the other communities, they married almost exclusively among themselves. The few mixed marriages that took place brought shame to their families and communities. By refusing interfaith marriages, every community was protecting its nationality, religion, politics and traditions. The Christians were more liberal and modern than the rest of the population, probably because of their contact with Europeans and the influence of the their religion. Sara was more open-minded than most; she accepted everyone in her heart equally. By attending the French school, she learned another language and culture and was in contact with all segments of higher society.

Sara was happy everywhere; she was attracted to Muslims as well as other ethnic groups of her class. From a young age she never accepted the idea that people should stay only in their own community. She lived with Fatima and her Muslim family in the early years of her life and loved them. She lived with Shamouns and found that they were wonderful people, so how could she discriminate against anyone? By now she had earned a strong Armenian identity and belief in her religion but, at the same time, she was aware that all her family's misery was the result of religious and ethnic discrimination. Sometimes her friends or her mother would reproach her about having friends from other communities, but she argued that people looked the same to her. Sara believed that, if everyone accepted one another and worked together without discrimination, there would be fewer tragedies, like her own family's history. It was only by knowing, understanding and accepting each other that peace could spread on the earth.

At one of the birthday parties, Sara met a young man named Raffi Hakopian. He had recently graduated from college and was teaching at a school. He was an Armenian from Egypt who had just turned twenty-six years old. He had come to Beirut to obtain an advanced education degree. His parents lived in Cairo and hoped that he would go to medical school or engineering college. This was the wish of all parents in those years since everyone thought that their children would have a secure future as doctors or engineers.

But Raffi was attracted to Armenian literature; he loved poetry and in his high school years he started writing poems that later were published in the most prominent Armenian newspapers. He was a very sensitive, honest, quiet and handsome young man. At parties he was always asked to recite his poems, and when he did, it seemed that he was another person – strong and daring, pronouncing the words in his warm, deep voice. Many of the older girls dreamed of marrying him, while the younger ones admired his handsome face and talent and some wished to become like him.

When Sara saw Raffi for the first time, she was immediately attracted to him. She listened to his poems and his deep voice and went into her usual dreamland and thought that he had written them only for her because they were full of love and purity. She did not have a chance to talk to him then, but after that day she dreamed only of him, and her life and mind revolved around him only.

Sara was at the end of the ninth grade. She was a bright student but, for the first time, she failed her term exams. Ani was very upset to see the results. She told Sara that she did not mind working hard and that she never asked anything from her except that she worked hard at her sole profession, which was being a good student. Sara apologized and promised that she would try her best for the final exams. But, in reality, she ignored her mother's supplication and continued on enjoying her life by passing time with friends, going to movies and parties, and dreaming about Raffi day and night.

Sara had seen many romantic movies and so she knew that she loved Raffi at first sight. Nonetheless, their personalities and interests in life were completely opposite of each other. Sara was lively and socially ambitious; her nickname was Fireball. Raffi, on the contrary, was resigned, quiet and humble. Sara loved talking, dancing and walking and running on the beach. Raffi liked sitting on the beach quietly while watching the waves and composing his poems. Sara always loved to have many friends around her, to talk and laugh. But Raffi liked his solitude and his writings. He was ten years older. Sara was still in school, but Raffi had already started his professional life.

Yet none of the differences mattered to her. The birthday parties continued and, at one of them, it became evident to both Raffi and Sara that they were in love with each other. At the beginning it was a platonic secret love. They started dating and Sara asked her best friends to cover for her absences so she could meet Raffi alone. They spent as much as time together as they could. They stayed on the beach; she watched the waves while Raffi composed love poems for her. At night she dreamed and imagined herself in the strong arms of Raffi. In his presence Sara felt protected, comforted and secure – something that she had never felt before. She did not know what was happening to her. She was not able to concentrate on her school work; she was not even able to read a book or learn new lessons.

Meanwhile, Ani was sometimes obliged to work longer hours. But she did not worry about Sara, since she was growing into a responsible young adult; besides, they lived in a safe neighborhood where neighbors watched out for each other. One weekend, while Ani had to work the entire day and night, Sara had her usual secret but innocent date with Raffi at the beach. After they walked all morning, they went to sit on Lovers' Rock and suddenly Sara's feet slipped and she fell into the sea. She was not hurt but all her clothes got wet. She proposed that they walk to her house so she could change. As they approached her house, Raffi wanted to leave but Sara insisted that it was too early to be separated from each other and that it would take her just a short time to change; then, she said, they could go to a movie and stay together a little longer. She assured him that her mother and neighbors were absent at that hour of the day and there was no danger that anyone would reveal their secret.

While Sara went in her room to change her clothes, Raffi turned his eyes in all directions and admired the clean and nicely decorated little house. He looked at pictures of beautiful Sara on the walls. After a short time, Sara entered the room completely changed and nicely dressed, carrying two cups of hot tea and, in a small transparent bowl, shiny fig jam. She told him that the jam was one of her mother's specialties and appreciated by all their friends.

Raffi was not comfortable to remain in the house alone with Sara. He felt almost like a thief invading the privacy of an honest family; he was afraid to be caught by her mother or a neighbor, which would ruin their future chances to be together. He really loved Sara and was waiting for the right time to commit to their future. In Middle Eastern countries, men almost always married much younger women, but still Raffi worried deep in his heart that ten years was too much of a difference in age between them.

Raffi preferred to give himself more time to settle down in order to create a better future for Sara and their children. By that time, Sara would have finished school and then he would ask for her hand. But Sara's lively character brought Raffi out of his thoughts and changed his serious mood to a happy one. Raffi suddenly felt free from his guilt and enjoyed the company of such a vivacious host. Sara was mature beyond her years and looked much older than her age. Because her mother was always absent for work, she learned very soon in her life to become independent. She had learned to take care of herself and behave more maturely than other girls her age.

Sara took the tray of cups to the kitchen to wash them in order not to leave any signs of their visit. Raffi followed her to the kitchen to help by drying the cups. Suddenly Sara felt that, for the first time, there was life in the kitchen. It felt so pleasant and warm to have another person to share the work and the moment. While Sara placed all the dishes on the shelves, Raffi stood within a short distance and looked at her with love and admiration. Sara finished placing the dishes on the shelves. As she pulled the towel from Raffi's hand, their fingers touched and, suddenly, the electrical current was connected in their young bodies. They both trembled and felt the warmth. Their blood rushed to their faces, reddening their cheeks. Both hardly breathed. It was as if there was no air in the kitchen.

Raffi wanted to pull her close to him but did not dare; his logic and brain controlled his actions and emotions, and he tried to walk out of the kitchen immediately. Sara, on the contrary, was more emotional and brave; she did not follow logic and gave up herself completely to her emotions. She grabbed his large warm hands and they both were pulled to each other. Their faces came closer and, as their eyes closed, their lips sealed their love and emotions silently.

Sara had never been close to a man, nor had she ever kissed anyone on the lips. She tasted the sweet kiss of love for the first time in her life. They kissed for a long time and, little by little, their hands moved around each other's bodies. They forgot time and space. They were in the best place of this world, where there is no time and no worry – only the sweet taste of love. Slowly they became tired of standing, and Sara pulled him gently to her room where they sat on the bed and continued kissing. They kissed, smelled and then tasted each other. Love, passion and curiosity captured their minds and they forgot all that they were taught by their parents and traditions. Raffi was trembling and Sara was completely overwhelmed by heat and emotions. Their hands moved further, discovering each other's bodies; each movement brought them closer to each other and, at the same time, took them to a new and unknown direction. Everything happened so suddenly and so spontaneously that both lacked control of their actions and themselves. Passion and love were present and nothing else mattered anymore.

They tasted each other and their new joy and hunger became even more demanding. Sara forgot that she was only sixteen years old; she forgot that she was neither engaged nor married to Raffi. Her love and passion had taken her where there was no reason and no limit. Then the unknown and unexpected happened, and she suddenly was one with Raffi. They started turning and dancing around each other with the natural music of love. Finally, they both were so tired that they were not able to move anymore. They fell into a sweet and deep sleep.

When Sara opened her eyes, she was surprised to see Raffi by her side in her bed and in her house. She was first surprised and thought that she was dreaming, but then she remembered all and became scared. But, immediately, she felt as if her entire body was burning and she started kissing him passionately. He woke up from her kisses but understood what had happened and told her that he should leave at once before they were caught. Sara reassured him that her mother would not be home until late that night since she had to work. She also suggested that he should stay longer because the neighbors were still out and about at that time of the day.

Again, they forgot everyone; they kissed and stayed attached together as two spirits in one body.

When the time came to leave, they were so exhausted and lost in their sweet world that Raffi begged her to push him out of the house. He told her that he was no longer able to leave her anymore.

The sun had already set. They watched from the window the neighboring houses. Then, although Sara wanted never to be separated from him again, she gently pushed Raffi out of the door and into the darkness. He felt that he was walking on the clouds and his entire being was singing like birds in springtime. He also was confused, like a person who had drunk too much alcohol, but this was because love and passion had taken him to another dimension of this world. Soon the cool salty breeze of the sea woke him up completely and he trembled with fear – fear of his actions.

Sara lay down on her bed but, in reality, she was flying high and above all the clouds in the sky. She had never been so happy and fulfilled in her entire life. Her body was still burning and she could feel the hands of Raffi knotted around her. She could smell and feel him close to herself. She looked out of the window and saw the stars shining in the sky. A soft breeze moved the branches of the trees, composing soft music.

Suddenly she got scared as if she felt the cold air within her body. She saw the twinkling star and understood that her father knew what she had done. She felt ashamed and guilty. Then she told herself that her father would never become angry with her, that he should be the one able to understand the emptiness that he had left in her life.

She thought of her mother and decided to arrange things so that she would not have any suspicions of what had happened. Sara immediately put on her nightgown and, like a skilled detective, walked around the rooms and inspected everything. She arranged little objects and placed them in their right places. Then she got into bed and, for the first time, did not recite her prayers before going to sleep. It was as if she had come to her senses and realized what had happened. She was ashamed and afraid to say the name of God.

She suddenly remembered something and jumped out of bed, took off her nightgown and stood naked in front of the mirror. At first she was afraid to look at herself but then she found the courage. She looked carefully at her image to see if anything was changed on her face or body. Raffi had been very gentle to her all the time. She had no marks on her body or on her face. Her lips were a little puffier than usual and her cheeks were rosy, but that was acceptable. She put on her gown again and told herself that, when her mother came home and checked on her, she would be very tired from working the entire day and would not see anything unusual. Sara's mother always tried not to wake her up when she was asleep and never put the light directly on her face. By the next day, Sara assured herself, all would be normal and Ani would never imagine what her daughter had done the day before.

As Sara expected, her mother suspected nothing. That night, once Sara and Raffi were alone in their beds, they understood that they could no longer live apart. They dreamed about the unforgettable day that they had spent together. Both of them trembled as they felt each other's presence in their hearts and knew that they were deeply in love. Both of them had a sweet, deep and long sleep; they were in each other's arms in their entire dreams. The next morning Raffi woke up early and composed his masterpiece, a beautiful love poem for Sara.

Sara stayed longer in her bed and pretended that she was asleep until Ani left for work. Sara ran to the kitchen and ate the delicious breakfast that her mother had prepared for her with love, just like every morning. She felt guilty betraying such a pure soul as her mother. Ani was a very kind and dedicated person. Sara knew well that she worked hard to give her a good life.

But she wanted to enjoy life at the same time; she had suffered enough from all the atrocities and their long effects. It was not her fault that every friend of her mother had lost a father or a mother, a husband or a wife, a brother or a sister, a son or a daughter. She wanted to have a normal life like others and forget the past. She was looking forward to life. She believed that she had come into this world for a short time to live and enjoy. She knew all too well that her brother and father had not lived long, so she did not want to waste the time that was given to her.

Sara stayed home that day. She was afraid to go out, visit friends or neighbors. She was afraid she would betray herself. She was thinking that just by looking at her everyone would find out the truth about her and Raffi. She wanted so badly to see Raffi and kiss and hug him, but instead she decided to stay away and think. In the afternoon Sara rearranged her room and later she warmed the food that Ani had cooked and set the table for dinner. Sara was trying to work off some of her guilt by becoming more responsible. She was blocking her mind so that she would not ask herself the real question: "What if Mother learns about my relationship with Raffi?"

When Ani arrived from work, she was thankful to see that her daughter had been so thoughtful. She thanked her and said, "I would have set the table. You have all your life to work as an adult, now you should spend your time only to study and learn."

After dinner, Sara sat in a corner of the room with an open book in front of her pretending that she was reading. She intentionally held the book high to hide her face so that her mother could not see any changes in her appearance. She was still afraid to look directly in her mother's eyes. She knew that mothers find out the truth just by looking directly at their children's eyes. At least that was what Ani had told her, and Sara knew that it was true. Whenever she lied or did something wrong and denied the truth, Ani always asked her daughter to look at her eyes and repeat the statement. Sara always lost the battle with her mother, but since she started dating Raffi she had practiced and learned how to lie so that her mother could not find the truth. For the time being, she had come to the conclusion to stay away from her mother until she came up with a better solution. A couple of times Ani reminded Sara to keep her book at a distance. She told her that reading too close may hurt her eyesight. But Sara tried not to converse with her and, with just "yes's" and "no's," continued to keep her distance. Later Ani went to the kitchen to prepare food for the next day. Once alone in the room, Sara felt more at ease.

All the time, while holding the book against her face, she was not even able to scan a word; she dreamed of Raffi and wanted him to be close to her. She needed his warm and large hands around her entire being. She had never felt so secure and reassured in life. She felt so good and was surprised that she was neither afraid nor worried about what had happened between them the day before. She knew that he loved her very much. After so many years she had finally found her security, a man who was good and loving, intelligent and kind. He was like a father, a brother and, at the same time, a real friend to her. She was sure that he would be the best husband in the world. She had no special needs for the time being. She was happy in his arms. She did not need a house, furniture or any luxury objects. She was fully satisfied just being at his side.

When Sara was in his arms and could feel the beating of his heart and the warmth of his body, the world belonged to her. For the first time, she realized the reason of the real emptiness inside her soul; she understood that she had missed her father and brother so much all these years. Her mother had given her a comfortable house, nice clothes and a good education. She had tried hard to fill up the emptiness. But her mother could never give her the essential need of her life, which was having a normal family. She always missed and needed a father, a brother and a mother who had time to take care of the real Sara.

She constantly had all kinds of childhood memories but they were cloudy and mostly ugly. She could hear voices but did not know whose voices they were. She was afraid of carriages, horses and donkeys but did not know the reason. She hated the color red but did not know why. She was still afraid of any man in a uniform. She always felt thirsty and drank a lot of water, yet was always afraid that she would die of thirst one day. When she heard the prayer songs from the minarets, she remembered Fatima and her family; the sad music and call of God broke her heart.

Many sad memories bothered her constantly. Finally she had decided to protect herself and close all the dark closets of her past. It was only in the presence of Raffi that she felt complete and composed. In his arms she forgot the past and all her memories and, for the first time, she thought of the future and even dreamed of sweet images instead of her regular nightmares.

CHAPTER 12

A Life Changed

SARA WAS TOO YOUNG and inexperienced to think much further into her future. She had learned not to look ahead too far since the future did not mean anything to her and was not a secure place. She had learned that the future could change in a second. She knew that once she had been happy and safe in her childhood but that one day soldiers came and took her father; then her life changed forever. So why should she bother herself with planning for a distant future that might not exist? She trusted only the present and wanted only to enjoy the time that was given to her right at that moment. For her, the important part of her life was now. For Sara, time was limited only to the present.

Ani was so innocent and had so much confidence in her daughter, that she could not imagine all that Sara had gone through. As usual, in the mornings, she always walked quietly around the house while Sara was asleep. She prepared breakfast for her daughter and left for her work very early while it was still dark outside.

Days passed. Sara attended school as usual but always found the time to meet Raffi. Sara told two of her best friends about the love that she had for Raffi, but not the entire truth. Her friends also had their little love stories, but all was platonic. As good friends, the girls covered for each other to evade mothers' curfews, and each was able to meet her loved one for a short moment. Sara and Raffi could not attend movies together but, instead, each went with friends and then changed seats to sit side-by-side for a short time. Since that explosive day, they never talked about their affair and they did not even have the opportunity to kiss each other. They just held hands tightly during the movie and then, as the lights came on, pulled away.

One morning, not long after their rendezvous, Sara felt uncomfortable and started vomiting. She thought that she either had not digested her dinner or had caught cold or some kind of sickness. She was not even aware that her periods had stopped.

On the weekend, when Ani was at home, she realized that Sara was using the bathroom very often and looked pale. She asked her what had happened and Sara replied that she did not feel well and did not know why. Ani started worrying about her health. She gave her some herbal tea and rubbed her feet and stomach with Lebanese Arak, a folk remedy made of anise and used by many people as medicine for adults and children. Sara felt better for a while and went to sleep, but soon she was up and running to the bathroom since all her stomach was turning upside down. Ani worried more and went to her bedside and asked some questions, but Sara did not talk much and pretended to fall asleep. This continued for several days but she refused her mother's request to visit a doctor. The next day Sara was not able to go to school. Finally, Ani took her to Doctor Attie, whom they had known since their arrival in Beirut.

George Attie was a kind and gentle man who teased Sara and told her that when she grew older he would marry her. But Sara always answered that, by then, he would be a very old man. Doctor Attie asked Sara some questions and then glanced sideways toward the door, asking Ani by this gesture to leave the room as he wanted to examine Sara and question her alone. Doctor Attie had a lot of experience in his life, and so he soon became suspicious and asked Sara more questions about her period and finally he brought her to the real point. Sara understood immediately and fear traveled through her body. She froze, felt that she was lost, and was not able to hold the secret all to herself anymore. She had to confess the truth to the doctor. Suddenly Sara, who had felt completely grown up and independent just minutes earlier, became like a little lost child and started crying bitterly. The doctor comforted her, for Sara did not want to believe what she heard.

Sara was thinking that all she tried to do was to enjoy her life for a short time. She did not know anything about pregnancy and certainly never considered the possible consequences of her actions. Moreover, although she recently had not studied seriously, she was not thinking of quitting school either. She was a teenage school girl who went to movies with her friends and wanted to spend a few stolen hours with Raffi. Motherhood was the game of old people, not the responsibility of a girl like her.

Sitting in the doctor's office, Sara suddenly realized that she was still very young. She had not done much in her life. She had not traveled anywhere; she wanted to see places and know other people in the world. Now she was going to be pinned down like her mother and have to take care of a baby. It was not long ago that she had put aside her doll and toys. Now she was going to have a real human doll in her arms. Bitterly, in a loud voice, Sara told herself that she was not ready to have a child. The doctor heard and said that there was no other solution and that he was sorry for her and especially worried for her mother. He knew that Ani had sacrificed all her life for her daughter. He knew that she would be heartbroken to hear the news; it was dishonorable for Ani to have a pregnant unmarried daughter at home.

He asked Sara to give him the name of the man who had impregnated her and said, "For a day or two we will keep this secret between us until I talk to him and find a solution." Then he told Ani that Sara was not in danger but that she had to rest at home for two days, after which he would visit her to see if she was getting better.

Ani was reassured and thanked God that all was going well with her daughter. Outside she proposed that they go to the church to light candles for her health. When they entered the church, Sara felt guilty for the first time. She prayed silently and asked God for forgiveness and help. For the first time she felt that a future actually existed, and she was worried about her future and the reaction of her mother. She felt sad for her mother since she was aware that Ani had suffered a lot in her life and did not deserve to be afflicted with a new pain.

Ani was still a beautiful young woman but she had closed herself off completely from everyone. She behaved like an old woman whose life was coming to an end. Again, in her mind, Sara justified her actions and defended herself in the presence of God. She accused Him of neglecting her entire family in his blessings. She asked angrily, "Why didn't you protect my father and brother? Why did I suffer so much at such a young age?" She knew that many of her reactions and feelings came from her past. Now it was too late for her to correct her mistakes. She was given the choice to study and have a better life in the future, but the emptiness in her heart and life had been so strongly present that it had taken her where she was at that moment in her life. She asked if God couldn't rid the tiny baby from her being. She promised that, if He did so, she would study hard and make her mother proud of her. She begged for His help at least for her mother's sake.

Then she saw the painting showing Mary looking with tears at her son who was on the cross. She understood that if Jesus and Mary were not spared suffering, why should others think that they should not suffer also? If God did not help Mary or Jesus, why would He help Sara or Ani? Sara told herself that she was a sinner and she deserved her fate, but poor Ani – what had she done in her life to go through so much pain and loss? A hot tear rolled from her eyes as the loving arms of Ani wrapped around her. Then Sara knew that, regardless of events, she would be always loved by her mother and this thought gave her courage and warmth.

The entire Armenian community knew Raffi well so it was not hard for Doctor Attie to find him. He sent Raffi a message and asked him to come to his office regarding an urgent matter that same afternoon.

The doctor received Raffi kindly in his office with a fatherly smile. At first he talked about events of the day to put him at ease; then asked him about his life and job and if he had yet met his future wife, since at his age he was ready for a new life. Raffi blushed and did not answer. He was too honest to lie, so he preferred to stay quiet. Little by little, the doctor pulled him to the focus of their visit. He asked Raffi if he needed any help to talk to Ani, since he knew that his parents were away. He added that he knew and loved Ani and Sara as if they were his own family. Raffi blushed again, and his mouth dried so much that he was not able to utter a word. The doctor put his words differently so that Raffi felt comfortable, and he answered shyly that he loved Sara very much but he was afraid that Ani would refuse his request to marry her. He added that he was probably too old for Sara and did not earn enough to give her the comfortable life that she deserved.

Raffi was confused but in a way happy that finally he could talk to someone about Sara. At that moment the doctor said that he thought that neither Raffi nor Ani had any choice about marriage. Raffi's eyes widened and he asked what he meant. "Sara is pregnant," he told Raffi. In order to save Ani and Sara's honor, Raffi had to immediately ask her hand for marriage. He added that he was sure that Raffi wouldn't like to hear people gossiping about his loved one and calling out names to his child and its mother.

Raffi was completely confused and lost in his feelings and thoughts. He considered for a moment that Sara was so much different from him; she was so young and lively while he was ten years older and restrained. Then he reassured himself that probably that was the reason they were so in love with each other. He suddenly told the doctor that he had never loved a person so much all his life. He really did not want to take advantage of her youth and had a world of respect and love for Sara and would do anything to make her and her mother happy and honored. Then he asked the doctor if he would help him to prepare Ani for Raffi's request and if he would agree to be their *kavor* – best man – at their wedding.

The deal was done. Deep inside, the doctor was not so sure of the success of their future union. But he reassured himself by noting that no one could predict the outcome of any union. He congratulated Raffi on his decision and asked him to come to his office with a nice bouquet of flowers and a box of chocolates the following day as he was going to formally introduce him to Ani.

Ani was cleaning and cooking after work like she did every day and Sara was again lying in bed reading a book when they heard a knock at the door. Sara opened the door and was astonished to see Doctor Attie and Raffi before her. Raffi held a beautiful basket of flowers in one hand and a large box of chocolates in the other. Sara's black eyes and beautiful mouth were wide open and she did not know what to say. Her first impulse was to tell him to go away because her mother was home. But seeing Doctor Attie, she froze before them both. Finally, Doctor Attie smiled and said, "Aren't you going to invite us inside for a cup of tea, or you are going to serve us out here?" Sara smiled and invited them inside.

Ani called out to Sara and asked to whom she was talking. When she came into the front room, she was surprised to see her daughter's doctor accompanied by a handsome young man. Ani had been baking pastry and the sweet smell of the cookies filled the room. She excused herself and went to the kitchen to wash her hands. When she came back, she had already put the kettle on the fire to prepare the tea and asked them if they wanted to drink tea or Turkish coffee. The doctor replied that tea would be perfect.

The four of them sat around the dinner table. Sara was controlling herself not to look at Raffi although her heart and thoughts were pulled toward him. She knew that, in a moment, the truth was going to come out and was not sure how her mother was going to react. Raffi was sharing the same thoughts. He was uncomfortable and, as he looked at Ani's beautiful face, he could see and feel the suffering and sadness on her face. He felt guilty of his and Sara's betrayal of such a kind woman. The love fever had calmed down, and now he was thinking logically and was aware that they and especially he had made a major mistake. He loved Sara and was ready for marriage, but still he wished that he had controlled himself. In any event, there was no way to turn the clock back. Now, he had to think of the future with Sara and put all his efforts for a better future for the sake of everyone involved. He knew that, if Ani agreed to the union, his parents would be in heaven to hear that he was getting married.

At first Ani thought that George Attie had come to propose to her once again. George knew Ani from the early days of the Relief Center, since he visited the patients there. He had lost his wife many years earlier and, after a while, asked Ani to marry him and share his life. But she refused without hesitation. He asked Ani every year but each time she declined and told him that she could never marry anyone because of the love that she had for Ara. Although she had lost hope of seeing Ara again, every once in a while she would read about a soldier who had been a prisoner of war and returned from captivity, asking for his family. She dreamt of the day when she would see Ara's name in the paper – a freed prisoner of war seeking his family.

She had kept a tiny hope for herself that brightened her sad life and made it worthwhile. After all, no one had confirmed the death of her husband. She had not seen his body and had not buried him, so she had the right to have a tiny hope. She always had answered gently to Doctor Attie that, if one day she decided to remarry, she would choose him. But, for the time being, she was not ready and, since she was not officially a widow, she would keep her hopes for the return of her husband. The doctor knew the truth like everyone else but never tried to force it on her, because he understood that this slender reed of hope provided energy for Ani to continue her life. So he stopped asking for her hand but was always attentive and kind to Ani and Sara. He had always played the role of a protector for them when needed.

Ani thought that it was the doctor who had brought the flowers and the chocolates; she thanked him, but the doctor gently waved her away and introduced Raffi and said that this time it was not he who had brought gifts. Ani immediately understood that he was there to ask for her daughter's hand and she bit her lower lip while thinking how to refuse him firmly. Although Ani immediately liked Raffi and found him a handsome and honest-looking man, she was not ready for her daughter to marry yet. After the introductions, the doctor smiled and said that the young man asked him to play the role of his parents, who lived far away, in asking the hand of Sara for marriage. Without breaking his cloak of sincerity, he said that he knew Raffi for a long time and guaranteed him as if he were his own son. He added that Raffi was a hardworking and honest man and he was sure that everyone in the family would like him.

Sara's eyes shone, yet she still kept her head down. Ani asked her to go and prepare the tea. It was a way for Ani to breathe, for she thought her heart was stopping; and it was a way to keep Sara from their conversation. It was always difficult for Ani to refuse people. She was so used to serving and helping everyone that she could never say no, even when saying yes was contrary to her own interests.

But the correct answer to Doctor Attie's request was so evident and clear to her that she immediately controlled her nerves and said firmly, "I find the young gentleman very attractive and well-behaved and that I have nothing against Raffi personally and am sure that he is a nice young man. But Sara is too young for such a commitment." She added that she and her husband always dreamed together that their daughter would complete her higher education and then marry. She repeated that Sara was just a child, that she was only sixteen. Her voice broke and for the first time in her life she complained that she had worked very hard and done everything all alone in order to keep her promise to her husband's dream.

The doctor knew the real meaning of her words. He knew exactly what she meant. She had always wished that her daughter would become a doctor or at least a nurse so that she would prove that even the Genocide could not stop the Armenians' old dreams. She worked very hard and for long hours to give the comfort and possibility to her daughter to achieve. She did not only dream in her mind but worked hard to realize her dream. The fatigue, loneliness and the hard work did not stop her. No one, not even Sara, knew how much Ani suffered because she never opened up to anyone and she never cried about her misfortunes in front of people. She kept her head up; she kept smiling and did not talk much. She was always thankful for what she had and did what she had to do in the best way that she knew how.

George Attie knew Ani well, and he felt sad about having to give her the bad news. He knew that he would break her heart by telling her the truth but there was no other solution. At that moment, Sara came in the room with the tray of tea and fresh baked cookies.

Ani turned politely toward Raffi. "I hope that you would not take my answer personally," she said, her voice a bit softened. "But the decision was made by my husband and me years ago. I really think highly of you but it is not the right time for Sara. She has to finish her school." Her large eyes were filled with tears and were almost begging without words to leave her and her daughter alone. Then Sara served the tea. Ani tried to change the subject in order to protect her daughter.

Everyone started drinking tea, although no one was comfortable in doing so. As soon as Sara swallowed some tea, she felt her stomach turn upside down. She ran to the bathroom without even excusing herself, and everyone heard her crying and vomiting. Immediately everyone, even Raffi, lost their self-control and ran to the bathroom. He suddenly felt fatherly since he knew by then that it was his seed that was growing inside Sara and causing all this discomfort to his loved one. Ani was surprised at his reaction and did not hear the words that Raffi was saying but suddenly she understood the truth. She put all the pieces of the puzzle together in her mind and, for the first time in her life, she cried loudly. "No, doctor, please don't tell me that it is true!"

Doctor Attie touched her back in a fatherly way and said that she made the right guess and he was sorry. He understood her pain but it was too late. He told Ani that they had no other choice but to cover the young couple's mistake in the best way that they could and help them for a brighter future. To be sure, all was not going in the direction that Ani had planned. But the doctor hoped that no one would regret the future resulting from the union of Raffi and Sara, and that the two would build a happy family together and a bright future for their baby.

Doctor Attie told Sara to lie on her bed. Everyone was crying but him. Raffi was confused and sad to see that he had hurt Ani, since he saw how pure and kind she was. Between sobs, Ani was repeating to herself, "What an unjust world. What a cruel world."

She had protected her daughter from the Turks and Kurds in war and now an Armenian – one of her own – had hurt her daughter in peace. She was sobbing and talking to herself and to her long-missing husband, Ara. She was talking to her God, to her parents and back to herself. George Attie had never seen her so desperate. She was never this way. Even on the twenty-fourth of April, an annual event when he accompanied Ani to the official Armenian Genocide Commemoration ceremonies, she always stayed calm and dignified. It seemed that the suffering of deportation, the disappearance of her husband, the death of her son and in-laws and parents and all her miseries were pouring out for the first time at that moment.

Ani had never been so desperate and lost in her life, even while in the desert resisting the Turks. But, now that her own daughter and a young Armenian man were going against all her principles and dreams, she did not know what to do. She felt that she had lost everything that she had worked for. It was like a farmer who had worked on his farm all year and, at the very moment he was going to harvest his crop, suddenly a bolt of lightning struck and all was burned to the ground. She felt betrayed by her own daughter, by Raffi and by her destiny. She had nothing to live for or look forward to.

Suddenly she heard the doctor's kind words. "Think of a little spirit who has decided to join your family. You can help the baby and Sara have a better life. She is too young and she is suffering, so be compassionate and forget what you had in mind for her. See how you can help her and the baby now. This is the real responsibility of a parent – to be there regardless of the outcome of your dreams and the situation."

At that moment, it seemed that Ani woke up suddenly from a deep dream. She became calm and quiet. She cleared her tears and sat near Sara, hugging her and asking how she was feeling, if she needed something, and how her mother could help her. Sara cried and hugged her mother and asked for her pardon. For the first time, Ani felt she was receiving true deep warmth from her daughter, and love enveloped their entire beings. Ani told Sara to rest in her bed while she discussed their future with the doctor and Raffi.

All three sat around the table with a better comprehension of the situation. The question was no longer "if" but "how." Ani turned to the doctor and asked what she had to do for the good of her daughter's future. The doctor opened the box of chocolates that Raffi had brought and said, "First, let us all eat a little sweet in order to start a new sweet future." They each put a chocolate in their mouths. Ani was hardly able to swallow the melted chocolate in her mouth but nonetheless tried to stay polite. The doctor suggested that they should arrange the wedding very soon so that no one would learn about Sara's condition. Ani timidly asked him how advanced she was, and the doctor answered that the pregnancy was probably at the end of the second month. He added that Raffi's parents would arrive by the end of the week and they could officially ask for Sara's hand on the wedding day.

When the visit was over and everyone was leaving, Raffi respectfully kissed Ani's delicate hand and said that he was sorry to have given her so much pain; he would try his best to give comfort and happiness to Sara in the future. Ani pulled back her hand gently and answered only with a sad smile and a cold goodbye. She closed the door immediately so that they could not see her large tears rolling down her face. Once alone in the room, she cleared the table and went to the kitchen. While she was washing the tea cups, she was crying and was talking to herself quietly. Sara was asleep.

Ani wanted to throw the flowers and the chocolates into the garbage but, instead, she put the basket of the flowers near Sara's bed and the chocolates remained on the table. She continued baking the pastry that she had started. While she was forming the dough into circles, they did not turn out exactly as she wanted, so she gathered again all the dough in her hands squeezed it in her palm, rolled it again, and there they were: nice circles just as she had planned.

While she was putting the tray in the oven, she suddenly asked herself why the doctor could not help them better. Wasn't an abortion the real answer to their situation? If George Attie performed an abortion on Sara, it would be sad but at least it was a better solution to a bad situation. That way Sara would become free of her unexpected lifelong responsibilities and she would be able to finish her schooling, graduate, and have a better future. She would be able to travel and have a real profession, and then find the man of her dreams and marry, even if that man would be Raffi.

She had nothing against Raffi; Sara was too young for marriage and motherhood.

Suddenly she realized that she was not even ashamed of her thoughts; she, who had seen so many pregnant women in the deportation being cut open by the soldiers. The unborn babies in all different terms did not even have a voice; they did not even utter a word in their defense. She heard only their mothers' cry of the horrible pain at what they were going through. She came to the conclusion that the little unformed and unborn embryos were not babies or humans for others yet. If not, how could the soldiers kill them with no outraged cries from others? The babies were real only for the parents who wanted them, who loved the unborn little bundles, who gave them names and built their images in their minds.

Then she remembered Raffi's kind attention toward Sara and her feelings toward the unknown baby and the love that she felt for the two-month-old fetus. She saw the tiny egg already being formed, looking like the mixture of Sara and Raffi. And, she wondered, who had any knowledge of the unknown? Would the baby resemble her son, or Ara, or even her father? The thought brought tears of joy to her eyes.

The moment that Ani was able to put a face on the unknown egg, she felt guilty at the thought of destroying it; yet, still, deep in her heart, she knew if she were courageous, abortion would have been the best solution for Sara. She recalled the proverb: "If you refuse and say no now, you should not carry a baby for nine months and take care of him for all your life."

CHAPTER 13

Raffi's Parents Bless the Union

ANI KNEW SARA VERY WELL, and she was aware that soon Sara would become a prisoner and slave of a moment of her passion. She would no longer be able to enjoy life like other young girls of her age. But Ani also knew that the hardheaded Sara would go through all her difficulties with her head up and would do her best. She remembered Sara's love for Raffi and her sufferings moments ago; then she remembered that Sara kissed and appreciated her mother truly for the first time. It was one of the sweetest moments of her life, and she did not want to destroy their relations anymore.

When Ani finished her work and made her resolutions about Sara's future, she found her daughter deeply asleep in her bed. She looked at her with love and affection and went to her own bed and stared at an indefinite point on the dark ceiling. Ani was not crying anymore. She was not even able to think. She was trying to look beyond the ceiling without blinking. She was completely exhausted and tired of her life, and she asked herself, "Why did I go through so much in life and why did I survive?" Survivor's guilt was not something people like Ani knew about, but she suffered from it greatly. Almost everyone she knew perished in the atrocities, but she was pulled by a strong hand out of all the dangers. What was the real reason for her staying alive?

The next morning Sara did not attend school since she was sick. She never went the following days either, because she had early morning discomforts and was also getting ready for her sudden wedding. Her friends came to visit her and she happily told them that she was going to marry Raffi. They envied her and wished that they could find someone to love and marry. They thought she was so lucky to quit school and marry and have a life of her own. Each one of them asked Sara to put her right hand on their heads so that the luck would come to them soon and they would find a husband. Of course she never revealed her situation to anyone; Doctor Attie had suggested that, after the baby's birth, Sara would tell everyone that her baby was born two months prematurely. She had to protect her mother's honor in the community – and her own as well.

The school's principal contacted Ani and asked if a financial problem was pushing Sara to get married. With tears in her eyes, Ani responded sadly that it was a youth fever and she was not happy that her daughter would not finish her studies.

Ani started gathering and making the dowry for her daughter. The following week Raffi's parents arrived from Egypt as planned. They were simple and kind people who were happy to see their son marrying, especially to such a beautiful, young and healthy girl. After meeting them, Sara felt much better. She was happy that she was finally going to leave her mother's house and obtain her freedom. She loved Raffi and he loved her very much, and so she was sure that they would have a wonderful life together.

Raffi's parents invited Ani and Sara to go with them to the jewelry store so that together they could choose the wedding bands. They already had brought a simple ring with them and, during their first visit to Ani's house, they placed it on Sara's finger as an official engagement promise. Ani had ached in her heart when she compared her daughter's situation to her own lavish wedding. She bought a nice but simple wedding dress since it was believed to be a sin for a pregnant girl to get married in the church like a virgin.

Doctor Attie had advised Ani and Raffi that everything was going to take place as a regular wedding and, as the *kavor*, he was going to accept their passionate sin on his shoulders. Raffi rented a small apartment, which Sara, Ani and his parents decorated as much as they could. It was only a short distance from Ani's home so that Sara could visit and receive her mother's help easily.

Ani and Sara invited friends, Raffi's family, and friends from the Relief Center to the wedding, which would be held in the evening, as was the tradition. Ani did her best to keep a happy face during the ceremony. But her heart was crying because of her daughter's early wedding.

On the night of the wedding, Sara was glowing and looked radiantly beautiful. After church, everyone was invited to the wedding dinner; the guests ate and drank. With each glass of wine, someone in the wedding party toasted to the health and honor of the bride and groom and their families. One of the guests, who had a nice voice, sang a song to seal the wish. Sara's friends danced popular, modern and traditional Armenian dances; they all told Sara that they admired her for marrying such a handsome, kind and talented man. Many told Sara how they envied her finding freedom.

Ani, regardless of her smiles and the apparent happiness on her face, was crying in sadness in her heart. Her daughter's wedding was not to be compared to her glorious one so long ago. But then she comforted herself with the thought that the end was more important than the ceremony itself. After all, she reminded herself, look what happened to her and her family after such big festivities! Yet, at the same time, she was sure that the union between her daughter and Raffi was rushed and she feared its eventual outcome.

Before the wedding ended, Raffi thanked his parents and Ani for all their kindness, and then Ani and some of the guests accompanied him and Sara to their new home. Ani still was not able to forgive herself for not having the big wedding that she had dreamed of for Sara. When she returned home, she found herself very lonely and, for a moment, she felt abandoned by her daughter. But soon she was comforted by the thought that a baby was on the way to this world. Although sad, she hoped in her heart that at least the baby would have a better future than Sara had. She prayed that he would grow strong and healthy under the protective and loving care of his parents.

The next day Sara and Raffi came to visit Ani and Raffi's parents, and then they all walked to their new apartment to open the wedding gifts. That night Raffi invited them to a restaurant on the beach. Everyone was happy, and Raffi's parents blessed them and prayed for them to grow old together and stay healthy and happy. Raffi's parents invited the new couple and Ani to Egypt so that family members who were unable to attend the wedding could meet Sara and her mother. Doctor Attie had advised Sara not to travel yet, so Raffi said that he was not able to take a vacation from his teaching job for the time being. But he promised to visit them with Ani and Sara later.

After a few days, Raffi's parents left for Egypt, and Sara and Raffi also left for their honeymoon in the mountains. But they did not enjoy it since Sara had nausea most of the time. Raffi often took his new wife into his arms to comfort her and he murmured into her ear how much he loved her. While this comforted Sara, she was telling herself that her actual married life was far from what she had dreamed it would be. She thought that, as Mrs. Hakopian instead of Miss Demerjian, she would have fun and freedom to do all that she was not able to do as a schoolgirl. But it seemed that the unborn baby was already stealing most of her newly obtained freedom. Their lovemaking was far less passionate than their initial encounter that fateful afternoon, which now seemed a lifetime ago. Sara felt that she was already paying for her mistakes. But a kiss or hug from Raffi pulled her out of her dark thoughts and, as soon as she was feeling better, they were walking hand-in-hand, enjoying the beautiful scenery.

After a week's honeymoon, they returned home. Ani had prepared her best recipes and pastry for the new couple. The next day Raffi returned to work and, for the first time, Sara stayed home all alone as a housewife. Her little apartment was clean, but still she cleaned and arranged everything. There was enough food left from the previous night so she did not need to cook, and thus she had nothing to do. She sat on the balcony and watched some young children play in the street, jumping rope, or running after each other with laughter.

Then for the first time she realized that she never had a real childhood. She immediately blocked these thoughts since she did not want to open a Pandora's Box to the world of what-if's. She looked farther and saw some youths walking home from school and felt better; she was happy not to be like them. She missed the fun and the talks she had with her friends, but she did not miss the homework, the teachers or the classrooms. Then she decided to take a walk.

She dressed up nicely and walked some blocks and found herself on the beach. She watched the waves, took off her shoes, and walked in the blue water. The little waves and the swirling sand massaged her delicate feet and the sun warmed her body and her thoughts. Soon after, she returned home and prepared the dinner table. Raffi arrived from work tired but happy to find his smiling wife at the door. They had dinner and held each other tight for a long time. Love and happiness pervaded their house. Raffi was very kind to her, and he was careful not to hurt the growing baby or Sara. Soon Sara felt more comfortable in her pregnancy, and they enjoyed walking on the beach, visiting friends, and passing passionate nights like new lovers.

જી

Days and months passed. Sara was getting bigger and heavier; by then, everyone could see that she was pregnant. They wrote Raffi's parents with the good news and, since Sara was able to travel, Raffi proposed that they visit his parents for the New Year and invited Ani to travel with them to Egypt.

Ani and Sara thought that Egypt was a beautiful and interesting country. Everyone was very nice to the expectant parents. They were invited to relatives' houses for lunch and dinner. Some of Raffi's relatives gave wedding presents and others offered baby gifts. Raffi's parents were in heaven at the thought of becoming grandparents. All the time they reminded Ani that she and they were going to become grandparents. They told Raffi and Sara that they were thinking of moving to Beirut so that they could help the new young parents and see the baby more often.

After returning from Egypt, Ani and Raffi resumed their work and Sara stayed busy at home as a housewife, cooking and cleaning. She made all the necessary clothing for the baby. She already knew how to sew and, under Ani's tutelage, learned how to knit beautiful sweaters for Raffi and the baby. She even knitted a jacket for Ani. She asked her mother or her neighbors for advice on her apparel-making. She made friends with neighbors, and her old classmates came to visit and give her the latest news. Life was nice but simple. Raffi earned a modest salary as a teacher, so Ani helped the new couple by buying whatever they needed but couldn't afford. Raffi was very kind and respectful toward Ani and Sara, but Ani was not able to forgive him for what he had done to her young daughter. She knew that it was their passionate love that had caused this unwanted event, but she thought that Raffi, as an older person, had not respected Sara. Ani believed that Raffi was the person at fault and, in her heart, she had not forgiven him.

From then on she tried hard to forgive both of them, but for all her life she was unable to. They had a modest life and Ani knew that they would stay always in the same condition since Raffi's profession was never going to be high-paying. She also knew that, however kind and honest he was, he was not an ambitious person; he would not be one to look for a better life. He was satisfied and happy with what he had.

Ani kept her feelings to herself. She felt betrayed by her own daughter and now her son-in-law. But she knew that, in reality, her dark destiny was created by the Genocide, which had turned her life completely in the opposite direction. If Sara had her father and grandparents beside her, her personality and her life would have been quite different.

Sara was getting bigger and heavier every day. She now was telling herself that, as soon as the baby was born, she would feel free and could become the young girl that she used to be. She could enjoy life with Raffi and they could have the same romantic life that they had tasted that unforgettable afternoon.

Finally, the expected day arrived and Sara was ready to bring her baby into the world. Ani and Raffi took Sara to the hospital. After almost twenty-four hours of hard labor, Sara gave birth to a handsome baby boy. Raffi and Ani received the good news from the nurse. Later they visited Sara, who looked tired and pale. Then they heard the baby's cry and saw the precious being. Sara and Raffi wanted to name the baby Ara, after Sara's father, but Ani refused to call the baby after her husband. She proposed that they give a new name with no old tragedies tied to him. So they called him Sako.

Everyone forgot the past and the early birth of the child. Raffi and Sara's love blossomed for Sako. He had a lot of dark hair on his head and was handsome. As Doctor Attie had suggested, they told everyone that Sako arrived two months early. Raffi immediately sent a telegram to his parents and announced that the baby was born prematurely but that mother and son were in good health.

Sara returned as a new mother with a baby to her house. She was happy to have had the baby and be rid of her large belly. Still a young girl, she was looking for a fun life in the near future. She loved her baby, but soon she found out that Sako demanded almost twenty-four-hour attention and was consuming all her time. She had lost the freedom that she had enjoyed during the short time that she carried her baby. Now that Sako had arrived, he needed to eat, to be changed, and to be washed, all of which was a full-time, day-and-night job for her.

Raffi was proud to have a beautiful wife and a handsome son who would continue his family name. To earn extra money, he started giving private lessons after the end of the school day. Meanwhile, the baby was changing and growing. Raffi's parents moved to Beirut and found a house not far from the couple so that they could visit their grandson and help the young mother.

The intimate life between Sara and Raffi never went back to that romantic afternoon that Sara dreamt of and looked forward to. Most of the time, Sara was tired after so much work at home. When Raffi returned home at night after a long day's work, he too was tired. Ani was doing her best to help them and Raffi's parents were also trying to be helpful so that the young couple could enjoy their life. Sara and Raffi walked on the beach from time to time, but they rarely went to restaurants or even to their friends' parties. The few times that they could enjoy their sex life, it turned into another bitter experience, for almost nine months after the birth of Sako, Sara felt the same nausea and discomfort and understood in horror that she was pregnant again.

Raffi and his parents were very happy to learn the news, but Sara felt trapped once more. Every day that passed, she found herself in a self-made prison. She often asked herself why she did not see the problems coming and why she did not listen to her mother's advice.

Since leaving Fatima to join her mother, Sara had everything that she desired; she was even able to buy whatever she wanted. She never worried about money or anything else. Her mother gave her all that she needed, yet Sara did not appreciate it at the time since she needed love and attention more than anything else. Now Sara had to stretch Raffi's monthly salary and spend every penny of it wisely in order to have enough money left at the end of the month. Raffi was kind, honest and hardworking and, although he worked all day and into the evening, he was not able to earn enough money to give Sara and his child a better life.

With every day that passed, Sara remembered the great life that Mrs. Shamoun and her children had. And then she remembered her mother's advice and understood that, if she or Raffi had finished their education, they could have had a better life. Now it was too late for her to turn back and run away from her problems, so she decided to stay strong and embrace her challenges with courage.

In order to have a more comfortable life, she decided to seek work and earn money. But, since she did not have any qualifications, she decided to use her hands and work from her home. First, she started knitting sweaters for customers who were ready to order and pay. Of course the amount that she earned for her beautiful creations and hard work was not much. But she was happy that at least her hands were earning some money in order to help the needs of her family. More customers came to her since her work was beautiful and word-of-mouth was her best advertisement. She worked mostly at night because, during the day, her hands were full with cleaning and cooking plus taking care of a young baby who needed her attention, it seemed, all the time.

When Raffi saw her working hard, he was disappointed in himself for not being able to earn enough money to give his young wife a comfortable life. He was aware that she had a lot of work to do around the apartment besides her knitting and, in his heart, he appreciated her greatly. Yet he never revealed his true feelings to her. On the contrary, when Sara was knitting at night, Raffi criticized her for having the lights on so late in the room because it made it hard for him to fall asleep. In reality, Raffi was thinking that if he could persuade Sara to turn off the lights then she too would be forced to go to bed earlier. He knew that the baby was going to wake her up very early in the morning. But she had orders to fill and, if Sara could not complete them on time, she would lose her customers.

Sara was hurt deeply by her husband's remarks since she expected him to appreciate her efforts instead of criticizing her. This lack of appreciation and communication became the source of unrecognized conflict between the two. Sara did not mind working hard, but she desperately expected to hear a word of appreciation or recognition from her husband. Yet the sweet words never came out of his mouth for he thought that, if he said a kind word about her work, he would be admitting openly that he was a failure and a weak person.

This was why Raffi had started looking for private students to tutor after his day at school. He taught long hours in the evening to both children and adults. Raffi was sometimes invited to eat the dinner with the family of his private students, since this was a way for the family to show respect to the teacher. Sara would wait hours for him and then, quite hungry, would eat alone. Later he told her that he was not able to refuse a family's invitation for dinner and asked her not to wait for him anymore. She felt betrayed when he innocently told her what they served for dinner, for it was a much better menu than she could afford. She envied him and felt bad that she was not able to buy and serve those same fancy foods at home.

Knitting was not the type of job that kept her mind busy. Sara's fingers ran fast on the yarn but her mind went back and forth across her actual life, her memories, and the lost dreams of the past. By this time she knew exactly what a big mistake she had made. She could see how her old classmates were happy and living a fun life. They had no responsibility but to study for their exams and worry about their grades. How lucky they were! They were going to parties and dreaming about boys and their bright futures. Some were already getting ready for higher education. A few girls from the wealthy families were planning to study abroad, in France or Switzerland.

For Sara all these dreams were dead and all those countries were far away and unimaginable. Now she could understand why her mother had been so opposed to her getting married. Now she was aware of her huge mistake, but she also knew there was no other choice left for her. She had a little child attached to her and a second one was already showing its presence in her belly. She decided to remain composed, to not admit to her failure openly, and to continue her present path with a smile. At least it gave her pleasure to see that many friends envied her life since she never complained to anyone, not even to her husband or mother. At least she was a winner in her failure.

Sara became larger and heavier every day. Her mother and in-laws told her that soon it all would be over and that the second child's birth was always easier and faster. They were right; when her labor started, it took her much less effort and time to see her second baby born. They were all very happy because this time she gave birth to a beautiful baby girl, whom they named Sarina. When Sara took her in her arms, she told herself that she had now added to her miseries another poor spirit. It was then that she felt as if another heavy chain had been added to her feet.

As soon as the baby started pulling the milk out of her breasts, Sara's heart opened to love her. Here was a precious being who depended on her for its very life. She knew that she had to give her daughter the best, just as Ani had done for her. After some weeks, when Sara felt better, she and Raffi decided to hold a real party and invite all their relatives and friends. Everyone helped her because the party was a celebration of holy baptism. Sako was not baptized yet so they asked the priest to baptize both children on the same day. They all went to the church and, after the prayers, the priest immersed Sako and then Sarina in the holy water and made a cross with the holy water – *muron* – on their foreheads. Each had a godfather, who fastened a golden cross on a chain around the child's neck.

Afterward, they all returned home and everyone ate delicious food and drank to the health of the children, their parents and grandparents. And, as tradition called for, they remembered and drank to the memory of their close relatives who were not present. Ani dropped little warm pearls from her eyes – a rare event – but soon she controlled her tears and enjoyed the babies and the guests. Sako and Sarina received some gifts. Sara and Raffi were proud and happy to have such a nice family. Sara's old classmates admired the babies and envied her life. Everyone danced and sang until late hours.

The next day life returned to its routine. Sara had her hands full with the two children. Raffi also was working very hard; sometimes, when he returned home, he was so tired that he was not able to do anything or even talk with Sara. He gently kissed his sleeping children and went to bed. Sara, who was home all day working, looked forward to seeing her husband at night and getting the attention and love that she had tasted during their first months of their relationship. She wanted to hear the sweet words and romantic poems that he had offered her so generously in the past.

Every night, when Raffi was asleep at her side motionless, her large beautiful eyes filled with tears and she asked herself what happened to their passionate love. In the morning she looked in the mirror and saw a beautiful young girl, still filled with dreams and passion, trapped in an adult life. Sara was not able to share her feelings with her mother because she was afraid to hear "I told you so." And she was too proud and hardheaded to admit that she had made a mistake. And, even if she had admitted that, what solution was there for her? She had two little children who needed her for years and years to come. Whenever Raffi's parents found Sara tired or in a bad mood, they told her that she was so lucky to live in such good situation, since back when they married, life was much harder.

CHAPTER 14

Raffi Makes a Mistake

ANI WAS AWARE that her daughter was unhappy, but what more could she do? She was already giving them a large portion of her salary, as well as gifts and all her spare time to take care of the children so that the young couple could get out of the house and enjoy life. Ani believed that she should never bring up the subject of misfortune and unhappiness with Sara. Ani always believed that, if one spoke of misfortunes, it would make one feel more miserable by just recognizing and remembering one's troubles, so she thought that it was better not to talk about miseries and live life as it came forth. That was exactly how she had lived her life all these years. She neither talked about her past nor complained about the present. She did not care if this attitude was considered to be brave or cowardly but, at least, she knew that it helped her to do what she had to do every day.

The years passed. Raffi's father became sick and died. It was a sad time for everyone. Raffi's mother was lonely, so she moved in with him and Sara. Although she was a nice woman and helped Sara a lot, it meant less privacy and freedom for the couple. But it allowed Sara to spend more time on her knitting. Then one day Raffi's mother fell sick and soon joined her husband in peace. Raffi was sad to lose both his parents in such a short time and became depressed. His friends tried to help him; they took him to little cafes and offered alcohol to ease his pain. At first, Sara was happy to see him spending time with friends and feeling better. But soon it became a habit for Raffi and his friends to go to a café after work every night, drink some arak, and forget their miseries. Raffi often returned home drunk. Sometimes he was more open with Sara and other times he was depressed and said little.

Sara did not know what to do. She felt sorry for him and was sad to see him in such condition. Then she criticized his behavior, but he continued. She knew that everyone in society expected a certain behavior from teachers, and she was afraid that, if he continued drinking heavily, he would lose his position. Raffi loved his wife and children and wanted to give them a better life. But he knew that he was not able to achieve this, and alcohol gave him an umbrella of protection to hide under. Sara was now a beautiful young woman, only twenty-four years old. She looked like a mysterious, beautiful rare flower that had blossomed and become more attractive day by day.

By this time, some of her best friends had finished their higher education. The more ambitious ones were still in school pursuing advanced degrees in Europe, while others married successful men and were living in Beirut. But whether they were in school or not, most of Sara's friends had very comfortable lives. They often visited each other and never paid attention to their social status. They remembered their pure friendship from the old times at school. Sara never spoke about problems to her friends. On the contrary, she always seemed very happy. Even so, when her friends visited her at her home, they could feel the truth. Yet they never said anything but respected her courage and choice.

One night, when the children were already asleep, Sara as usual was knitting a sweater for a customer and was expecting her husband's return, probably drunk. Raffi came home very late and, when he came in, he did not answer Sara's questions and did not even look at Sara, who was worried and in tears. He went directly to the bathroom, washed himself, and went to bed, keeping the sheet rolled tightly against his body. But the next day Raffi began coming home earlier and sober. Sara was happy to find that her husband had become his old self. She tried to direct his attention more to the children, who were growing every day, and to herself as well. But, although Raffi was now much nicer to her, he was distant.

Since the death of Raffi's mother and his depression, they had not been physically intimate with each other. Sara was young and had desires. She was like a fire hidden under the ashes that needed attention. She needed to be physically and emotionally close to her husband, but it was not a subject that she could discuss with him. One afternoon she dropped the children at Ani's house and asked her to keep them overnight since she and Raffi were invited out and would be returning home late. Sara stopped her usual work, prepared a fancy dinner, and spent time in front of her makeup mirror. She made herself desirable and practiced playing the womanly games that she had seen in some movies in order to attract her husband.

Raffi came home early and, since the children were absent, they ate a quiet and pleasant dinner. Then Sara began drawing Raffi's attention to herself. She was finally able to bring her husband to touch her and open up to her as before. While they helped each other undress, she suddenly stopped, shocked as she found the front of his underwear spotted with an ugly discharge. Suddenly he realized his indiscretion and tried to keep his distance and cover himself with the bed sheet. Sara forgot all her passion. With great anguish she wondered what had happened, if he had become sick or had been in an accident.

Raffi was in tears and asked for her forgiveness. At first she did not understand his words clearly. Finally Raffi confessed that the last time he was drunk and walking home with his three friends, on the way they met a prostitute who was standing at a street corner. His friends talked to her and hired her; they insisted that he join them. When he refused, they dragged him to her house and asked him to talk to two of his friends while the third one was in the room with her. Still intoxicated, he sat in the waiting room and then somehow found himself in bed with her. After a short time he had found out that he and his three friends were infected. That was the real reason that he stopped drinking and seeing his friends. He stayed distant from her and the children in order not to infect them. He had consulted a physician and was following his prescribed remedies, but the cure was long.

Sara was already standing at a distance from her beloved husband. She felt hurt, cheated, abandoned and betrayed. She was sorry that she had loved him and had put her and her children's future in the hands of such a weak man. She was heartbroken and sad. She started crying and for just a moment her love for Raffi turned to hate. She always kept her house very clean; her glassware always shined like new. She loved clean, white sheets and tablecloths. She always washed their clothes thoroughly and even ironed Raffi's underwear since she thought they looked nicer and heat killed all kinds of germs.

Now seeing Raffi's blood-spotted underwear disgusted her. She felt dirty and saw her husband as a huge germ. Trembling with anger, she told him that she had accepted her hard life and had struggled in silence and in peace and was happy to share her life with him in the hope of a better future for them and for their children, but she could never accept their life together in betrayal and dirt. Raffi cried and asked for forgiveness. He said that he knew that he had been weak and stupid but he loved her and the children very much.

Sara was unmoved. She told him that, from that moment on, she could no longer lie in the same bed with him as his wife.

She promised to continue her responsibilities as mother and housewife. She expected him to respect their appearance in society, but she would stop being his wife in privacy. She was so serious that Raffi felt she had not left him any chance to defend himself. He knew well that she had the right to be angry with him, but he did not expect such a strong reaction and rupture in their relationship.

Sara took her pillow and blanket and slept on the floor. Both of them slept in tears. Their pillows were wet but neither tried to reach out to the other and reconcile, even though real love was still present strongly in each of their hearts. She was young and had never heard of or seen such a thing. The only man that she had seen naked was her husband, who was pure. But now she had seen an ugly and dirty person who disgusted her. She was afraid of him for herself and for the sake of her children.

Sara knew that prostitutes were the lowest class of Beirut's society. She also knew that many men and young boys visited them, but why Raffi? She had all the passion and love for her husband, but why would he choose a street prostitute over his wife? Deep in her heart she expected Raffi to come down to her, hold her, tell her he loved her, and assure her that he would be cured in the future. But he did not. How could he? After all, he was an honest man and was painfully aware that he had committed a wrong. How could he even hug his wife and ask to be forgiven when he had not been able to forgive himself all this time? So he did not even try to reach out to her. But the next night he asked Sara to sleep in the bed and he chose to sleep alone on the hard floor. He loved his wife dearly and blamed himself for his stupid action.

Sara was disgusted to wash his garments and have any contact with him. She kept all his clothing separate from hers and the children's. And she kept her distance physically and emotionally from Raffi. It was as if a crystal vase had broken in a hundred pieces and no one could put it back together again. Each could hardly believe that their love and life together was finished in one night, especially between two people who loved each other so much. The sole bond between them was their children; they talked to each other only when necessary or for the sake of their children. Each grew alone in solitude; they lived as a couple for the outside world but were strangers to each other. They shared only the common roof above their heads and the dishes on the dining table. They never tried to reach out to each other or solve problems between themselves. Each wore a hard cover like the porcupine or turtle when facing danger. Each learned to play the game perfectly; they remained good parents and kept up pleasant appearances for their friends, family and neighbors. But, in private, they stayed distant and apart.

At one of Sara's school friends' gatherings, she met Maggie, an old friend whom she had not seen for a long time. Maggie's mother was French and her father was a very wealthy Maronite Christian Arab. Maggie had lost her husband to a sudden illness. She was taking care of her family's successful business, for her husband and father had left her with a lot of property and wealth. Maggie was a happy young woman who liked to laugh and enjoy life regardless of the tragedies that she had faced. She gave the news to her friends about the famous two brothers whom everyone heard about and told them that she was dating one of them. Some asked if it was Wahab, since he was known as the more handsome one. She answered that it was his younger brother, Ali, and teased everyone by adding that Wahab was still available if someone was interested.

The two brothers were desirable for any girl. Their only problem was their religion; they came from a Muslim family. Their mother's family was originally from Palestine and their father's family was from Turkey. Their parents lived in Beirut for a very long time and were considered more Lebanese than anything else. The parents were religious and observed all the Islamic laws and traditions. Their father, mother and sister had performed the *haj* – the pilgrimage to Mecca – but the two brothers did not follow any religion and were living a modern life. Both finished their education in Beirut and then graduated from the pharmaceutical faculty in Hamburg, Germany. Upon their return, they had opened a large company and now represented many famous manufacturers, whose medical supplies and drugs they imported. They had become one of the biggest distributors of medical supplies in the Middle East.

Maggie told her friends that, although Ali was very nice to her, he was not ready to propose yet. Plus, there was the problem that his parents were against their union because she was both a non-Muslim and a widow. Maggie talked so much about Ali's charm, his blue eyes and his generosity that all the girls were eager to meet him. So she told them that the next gathering would take place in her house and she would also invite the two brothers so that they could meet and admire their handsomeness.

Sara saw and felt all the excitement and flame in her friend's eyes and remembered the short wonderful time that she had passed with her husband before marriage. The memories made her sad and lonely. Whenever she thought of her past relations with her husband, it always gave her a bittersweet taste of life. She closed her mind and told herself that she could not go there anymore since it could weaken her will to struggle in life.

During the entire gathering, she did not talk much. She was afraid to open her mouth and pour out her secrets to everyone. But, in her heart, she wished she could be as happy as her friend, Maggie. She knew how magical it was to love someone. She knew that, when someone is in love, life with all its difficulties was warmer and worthwhile. She remembered how at the beginning she did not have much but she was happy with Raffi. His eyes, his smile and a few words were worth all the gold and diamonds of the world. But without love, life was cold, ugly and lonely. Finally, she excused herself and told her friends that she had to pick up her children. This wasn't true. But she desperately wanted to leave.

Sara left her friends in sadness and walked on the beach, quite aware she was all alone. She dropped her tears quietly under the hidden shade of her sunglasses. She took off her shoes and walked in the blue water. The cool water woke her up from a deep dream. She did not know why she was thinking of Wahab. She looked far across the sea and imagined that his eyes were as blue as the Mediterranean. She wondered if he was tall or short, fat or thin. She asked herself if he had light skin with blond hair or if he was more like his mother's family, with dark skin and black hair. As she walked under the beautiful warm sun, her skin became warmer as if her blood had started running in her veins for the first time after a long deep freeze. It was more than two years since she had a physical connection with Raffi. They had not made love with each other and he had not even dared to kiss her on New Year's Eve. She felt almost like a single, young virgin girl again.

Sara walked for hours. She was not tired and had plenty of time before the school was over to pick up her children. She did not know why Wahab had captured all her thoughts. She had not even met him and did not know who he was. Probably his ethnic mixture was a reminder of her own past, for she was born in an

Armenian family but spent years with a Muslim Turkish woman. But, from the other angle, being an Armenian woman with two young children and coming from a Genocide family and having a single surviving mother, Wahab was the worst possible nightmare she could imagine.

ଛ

It was Maggie's enthusiasm that had awakened her from her long hibernation. Somehow the idea of meeting Wahab, after all that she had heard from her friend, excited her. After such a long time she felt that, although she was a married woman with two children, she herself, Sara, was alive for the first time. She remembered Fatima, her Turkish-Muslim mother whom she had loved but was separated from. Then she remembered all the nice stories that Ani had told her about the wonderful Bedouins who had loved, protected and cared for her.

Sometimes she imagined herself inside the tents of the Bedouins in the middle of the desert at night and sometimes she looked at the sky and remembered her past life with Fatima. Many times she had asked herself what she really was, why all these separations and sufferings in such a short passage on this earth just for religion or ethnicity? Everyone had two eyes and two hands; everyone was born a baby and died one day. She wondered if all these meant anything to God in Heaven. Did He feel all the sufferings of His creatures? Did He care?

She felt that the warmth of the sun was like two soft hands holding her lonely shoulders, and then she imagined it was Wahab's wide warm hands that were holding her hands. Suddenly, for a moment, she felt a delightful feeling and then immediately the inner guilt woke her from her dreams. She asked herself how she could even bring the name of Wahab to her mouth. Adultery was forbidden and sinful in her religion, and she was still officially Raffi's wife.

Then she defended herself and questioned what kind of a husband he had been to her. Wasn't he just an absentee spirit who was present at the same time? She comforted herself by thinking that she was not doing anything wrong; she was just imagining and playing in a romantic movie in her dreams. At least, for a moment, she felt that she was loved by someone and was well and free of her miserable life and responsibilities.

While walking in the water, she closed her eyes and felt very light. She started flying in the air. She saw herself as a young beautiful girl who had a warm heart and had the right to love life and a man again. She needed to be hugged and kissed and feel loved. What if she were to die in an hour – what had she seen in her life? Nothing, she told herself, except a little happiness and a lot of miseries. But, she wondered, if she were to live a hundred years, would she continue her life like it is now? If she were going to be a hundred, she was just at the beginning of her journey and so she had to change her life.

Then she heard the cry of a child calling her mother. It was as if she received an electric shock or someone poured a bucket of cold water on her head. She opened her eyes, remembered her children, looked at her watch, and ran to school. She was a mother and responsible for two innocent children. For a moment she asked herself why she had kept his unborn son. She could have gone to some old women. Then she would have not been obliged to marry Raffi. At these thoughts, she felt ashamed of herself and blamed herself and asked forgiveness from God. She crossed her face many times and repeated in Armenian "*Meghaim kez der, Meghaim kez der*," a plea that God temper his judgment of her. She comforted herself by repeating, as is the custom in Middle East,

"All that happens is the wish of God and the reason for my destiny." She should be thankful!

She picked up her children and, just by looking at them and hearing their voices, her heart started beating to another melody. The children ran to her and were very happy to see their mother; her heart filled with joy and she forgot all about her freedom. Once home, the children washed and did their homework. Sara prepared the dinner and they ate alone since Raffi was working late like always. Sara left his food on the table, put the children in bed, and went to sleep early. Her walk on the beach had tired her, not only physically but also morally and emotionally. She did not hear when Raffi came in since she was dreaming; her weightless body was flying over the oceans and mountains and was looking all over the universe for the dream man of her life.

When she woke up in the morning, Raffi had already left for work. She gave breakfast to the children and walked them to school. On the way she told them that they should study hard and become the first in their class – only the first, not even the second. Now she knew that the only way to have a better life was to study and learn as much as possible. These were not just words but commitments. She helped them to do their homework, taught them poems by heart, and taught them to sing. She worked hard and saved money, planning to spend it on sending her children to all kinds of private classes. Ani was happy to see that, finally, her grandchildren were fulfilling her dreams. Sako was a little slow but Sarina was very studious and talented.

CHAPTER 15

"I Am Wahab"

ANI COULD FEEL all the changes taking place between Sara and Raffi, but she never mentioned anything to either of them. She felt sorry for her daughter and blamed herself for not having done better in helping Sara to achieve more in school. She blamed her destiny, and was aware that, if her husband had lived, life would have been so much different for her and Sara.

Maggie visited Sara and invited her to her house the following week. Sara had already forgotten her dreams of freedom and was busy with her work and the children. Maggie told her that she was lucky to have her husband and her children since her life was lonely and difficult. She wished that her husband were alive so that she could have life similar to Sara's. Sara asked about Ali, the man who she was so excited about during their last meeting. Maggie sighed. "Being a single woman is always a hard situation in our society," she said. "Some men just want to enjoy life and not take responsibilities. I am planning to travel to France to visit my family and hope to meet the man of my dreams there. Frenchmen are different. Even a bad husband is like a crown on a woman's head." Sara smiled sadly and answered in a mocking tone, "You are absolutely right."

The week passed quickly. Sara took her children to school and asked Ani to pick them up since she was going to Maggie's house and would return late. Sara took a long bath, chose her nicest dress, and combed her long hair. She put on a little make up, then looked in the mirror and admired her beauty. She was not sure why she was paying so much attention to her appearance; after all, it was only a simple girls' reunion as usual.

While she was walking to Maggie's house, she received compliments from strangers in the street but paid no attention. When she arrived, her heart was beating hard and she did not know the reason. She took some deep breaths before ringing the bell. Maggie opened the door. Some of the other girls had already arrived. Everyone told Sara how beautiful she looked and asked what the occasion was for her dressing up. She smiled and shrugged her shoulders like a child.

Everyone laughed and talked. Some told the latest dirty jokes and then the time came to leave. Sara was not in a hurry to depart since her mother was taking care of the children. She was pleased when Maggie asked her to stay longer. Sara helped Maggie and they cleaned and arranged the room together. Then the doorbell rang. Since Maggie was busy, she asked Sara to open the door and said probably it was Ali and his brother, Wahab, because she had invited them over to introduce them to the girls, but they probably had been delayed.

At these words Sara felt short of breath. Her blood rushed to her face, and she walked with weakened legs to the door. She inhaled deeply, wondering what was wrong with her, and opened the door. Suddenly she was frozen in place. A tall handsome man stood in front of her, looking directly in her eyes. His deep blue eyes penetrated her entire body like two sharp flashes and burned her heart like a sudden wound. He smelled of expensive cologne. Raffi never put any cologne on himself, Sara instantly thought. For a moment, she and Wahab did not move and were unable to take off their eyes of each other.

Suddenly, they heard Maggie's voice asking Sara who it was. They both woke up from a deep dream that had lasted only seconds and smiled. He shook her hand and introduced himself. "I am Wahab." At that moment, Maggie walked in from the kitchen and introduced Sara. They did not exchange any words but looked at each other with a smile. Sara felt uncomfortable and decided to leave. With a charming voice, Wahab asked her if he was so unpleasant or scary that he made her leave. Sara laughed and answered, "No one is able to scare me." At that moment, the doorbell rang again. Maggie opened the door and announced that Ali arrived for dinner. She insisted that Sara join them.

During dinner, Wahab was funny but, at the same time, very intelligent and pleasant. Suddenly Sara felt like the old days – a young girl who was laughing, talking and also learning something new. They had such a nice evening that Sara did not feel the passing of the time. Suddenly, she realized that it was getting late and remembered that she had a family to take care of. She felt sad to give up her brief hours of freedom and innocent laughter. When she excused herself, Wahab looked deeply into her eyes and said that he hoped to see her again.

Once at home, while Sara answered her children's questions, she was unable to forget the handsome man she had just met. She was upset by her feelings and tried to turn her mind to different subjects, but nothing helped. It became worse when Raffi came home tired and depressed. "What a difference in personality between the two men," thought Sara. Raffi never had a funny word to say. It seemed that God had given Raffi the saddest face and all the anguish of this world.

Before meeting Wahab, Sara accepted Raffi and all his characteristics since she did not have anyone to compare him to. He was the only man that she had known. But now she had met someone who was attractive, funny, intelligent and successful. What a difference; what a contrast. She finished what she had to do and went to her lonely bed. In her dream, she was again at

Maggie's house looking at the beautiful azure sea and then at Wahab's handsome face.

The next morning at breakfast, looking at her children's innocent faces, she felt guilty. But she defended herself and realized that she had done nothing wrong, even in her dream. She was a very young woman and had a life ahead of her. She had the right to feel happy and comforted. At least now she could think of someone and feel better. She told herself there were people who were in love with actors and actresses. She remembered that she and her friends at school would collect their pictures. Now she was just pleased to have met a very handsome man. What was the harm?

Days passed but she was not able to overcome her thoughts. One afternoon she walked to Maggie's house to visit her. Maggie was happy to see her and invited Sara to join her friends at home. While they were walking toward the terrace, Maggie laughed and teased Sara. "You made a very strong impression on Wahab the other day," she said. "After your departure, he asked a lot of questions about you." Sara blushed. Maggie laughed and said, "Oh, don't get red like a radish. You are an experienced woman now. By the way, you are going to meet Pierre. He is a wonder and delight. I met him some time ago and I am crazy about him."

Sara asked timidly about her relationship with Ali. Maggie laughed and said that they were never serious. He did not mind her leaving him for Pierre. Ali and Wahab remained her good friends. "Actually," Maggie added, "Wahab is going to join us for tea."

Sara trembled at the idea that she was going to see him again. She walked weakly to the living room and saw a handsome, well-dressed man on the terrace. Maggie introduced Sara to Pierre and they shook hands and exchanged some words. While they were having tea, the door opened and Wahab entered. He was surprised and happy to see Sara. She was confused and happy but did not want to show her happiness. They all talked and laughed like young children and watched the sea and enjoyed the fresh air.

When Sara saw the setting sun, she admired the colorful sky and hated the clock that was ticking so fast. She did not want to say goodbye but she had to leave. Everyone insisted that she stay but she knew she could not and left their company with regret. When she was shaking Wahab's hand, he said that he hoped to see her more often and then kissed her hand. Maggie saw the gesture; she laughed loudly and told Sara, "Be careful. Wahab is a very polite but dangerous man."

Sara almost ran to her house. She hated the idea that she was going to see Raffi and continue her responsibilities as a homemaker and mother. Then she asked herself how Ani could live all these years alone and be satisfied with her life. She had lost her husband at such a young age but had never looked for another man and had never complained about her life. Sara wondered what her mother's secret was and wondered what kind of love used to be present between her mother and her father.

Sara felt that she was in love with Wahab, although she had met him only twice. She felt such a strong love and passion for him that she was not even ashamed of her thoughts. After all, she was alone at home taking care of her family, with no pleasure or personal satisfaction.

Sara had become close to her neighbor, Reneé. They helped each other when needed and sometimes took coffee together and talked while working. Sara was always generous; she knitted sweaters for Reneé and her children and, in return, Reneé took care of the children when Sara had to visit a customer.

Ani was still working full-time. As soon as she got home, she cooked something special for her grandchildren and always asked if Sara needed help. Sara started visiting Maggie and her friends more often. Maggie's beautiful house and surroundings comforted Sara since she was still, living in a modest apartment. Sara was not an envious person, even though her mother had often told her about the wealth and life that her father and grandfather had had. In bringing up Sara, Ani had always given her all she could and told Sara that her generosity toward friends was like that of both her grandmothers. For Sara, visiting her friend's house was, in a way, fulfilling her lost dreams of having a better life, even if for only a few hours.

The children were happy to stay with their grandmother or Reneé while Sara was away. Ani knew Maggie from childhood and they were close friends. When Maggie lost her husband, Ani tried to comfort her. Ani was happy that her daughter had a friend to visit. She was aware that Sara and Raffi were working hard and had little joy besides their children.

For a long time, all the gatherings in Maggie's house were innocent. The young people talked and laughed, watched the beautiful Mediterranean, and listened to the songbirds. Little by little, Sara stayed longer to see the complete sunset. Maggie and Pierre hugged and kissed each other in the presence of Sara and Wahab, which seemed natural, since they were in love. But the relationship between Sara and Wahab remained platonic. Yet it seemed that every time they met their love grew deeper, even without the assistance of action or words. Maggie and Pierre were aware of their mutual attraction, but they neither pushed nor pulled them back. Pierre was a Frenchman used to the idea of love.

Maggie was also educated in Paris, and she thought that the true aim of life was to be in love and live a full life.

Day by day, Sara was more miserable to see her nominal husband at home. By this time there was nothing left between them beyond a superficial respect. Raffi could see the changes in his wife; she was becoming more attractive, and taking care of herself more than usual. He had always loved Sara and was attracted only to her. There were nights that he wanted to jump in her bed and hug and kiss her and make love to her until morning. But he never dared to do so. She was so cold and so distant that he never dared to exceed his limits and hurt her. He was aware that he was the real cause of all their miseries. He had betrayed his beautiful wife and had to suffer and pay the rest of his life.

Yet there was still a little door open for them. Had he arrived home one day with a smile on his face and a bouquet of roses in his hand and asked for her forgiveness, Sara would have accepted him and they would have reconciled. But Raffi never took any action. He truly loved Sara but was doomed to watch her from a distance.

One evening, while Ani was watching the children, she started wondering why her daughter was visiting Maggie so much lately. Of course Ani did not harbor suspicions about her daughter's fidelity since she was a simple and pure woman herself. So when Sara returned home late one night, Ani asked her how she could stay away from her children for so many hours. Sara was evasive. Then Ani asked if she had something to share with her mother, if she was going through any difficulty. After all, Ani had always been there for her in time of need.

Sara did not answer immediately, and there was a big silence in the room. Suddenly the door opened and Raffi arrived. For the first time in years, Sara was happy to see her husband return home because she was not obliged to answer her mother's questions anymore. She immediately asked if he wanted to eat dinner. Ani quickly kissed the children goodbye and left.

2❧

Life continued the same. The children were growing but there was not much going on between their parents. Sara was absent most of the time and, when she was home, she was busy cooking, cleaning and knitting. Even at such a young age the children were aware that there was no relationship between their parents. Once Sako asked, "Why my father is sleeping on the floor?" Sara told him, "Your father has a bad back and he cannot sleep on a soft bed." Another time Sarina asked Sara, "Why does Papa never kiss you? My best friend's father always kisses his wife and children when he comes home." Sara always tried to give convincing answers, but the children somehow knew the truth.

Sako was not doing well at school. He resembled his father in that he was charming but not ambitious. Sako played and talked with his friends most of the time. Sarina, on the contrary, was a hardworking pupil. She wrote beautiful compositions and did well in all her lessons. She was a delicate, kind and sweet spirit. She was tall for her age but very thin. She did not eat much, and most of the time she seemed quiet and sad. She was a very sensitive girl who took all the events very seriously.

Ani was worried about Sarina and told Sara that Sarina was always sad and quiet and did not seem truly healthy. Sara thought that by nature some children were born thinner than others. In truth, her mind and emotions had been overtaken by passion. Wahab had stolen all her heart, logic and mind, and she did not want to think about the little problems of her children.

The visits to Maggie's house and their friendship continued. Maggie was happy with Pierre. Wahab and Sara were deeply in love with each other but their relationship remained non-physical. One day Maggie assured Sara that she could trust her and Pierre and that she was aware of her difficulties with Raffi. If she was not happy and satisfied with her husband, she had to give herself and Wahab a chance because he was, according to Maggie, a really precious and great person who was madly in love with her.

"Sara, you are still young. You and Wahab could start a new life together regardless of religious differences."

Sara felt uncomfortable and replied; "I made my vows to my husband in church and adultery is a sin." Maggie did not answer but, at the same time, Sara did not know why she continued visiting Maggie's house regularly.

One afternoon Sara helped Maggie serve tea since it was the maid's day off. It was early and only Sara, Maggie and Pierre were there. After finishing his tea, Pierre said that he had to leave for a short while to complete some unfinished work. Maggie decided to accompany him. Sara wanted to leave also, but Maggie said that it was too early to leave because she had made a great dinner for all of them; besides, she and Pierre would return soon.

Sara enjoyed a lazy moment alone on the terrace, closed her eyes and let the sun warm her entire body. The view was breathtaking and the garden was beautiful with its colorful flowers. The butterflies smelled each flower for a second and then flew to the next one. The sea waves played their soft music and the wind accompanied their rhythm.

While Sara was enjoying the beautiful view, the doorbell rang, and when Sara opened the door, she found Wahab standing there before her. He entered and asked where Maggie and Pierre were. She told him that they would return soon. Both of them tried hard not to look directly at each other since they were afraid of this unfamiliar situation. Sara asked if Europe was as nice as Beirut.

"Every city has its own beauty and charm, but there is something magical about Beirut," he said. "Maybe it is the mixture of its population and diversity, where East and West meet each other on such a small land."

Sara said that sometimes she believed that Beirut was part of the lost paradise. Then she asked him if his house had a similar view.

"My father owns a very large house. The main house is built in the middle of a huge garden and, of course, has a pool in which they wash their hands and feet before the prayers. Various smaller houses are built around the garden in which he and his brother live. His house faces the sea." Suddenly he changed his voice and came closer to her and said, "I dream of you in that house every day and night. I am sure that you are aware how much I love and respect you. I look forward to these gatherings just to see your beautiful face."

He was trembling and she was also completely lost in love and passion. Suddenly he pulled her close and squeezed her in his arms. As Sara tried to say that she was married and had children, Wahab answered that he knew everything about her since he had gone many times near her house just to watch her walk and work from a distance. He closed her mouth with a long warm deep kiss.

Sara had never experienced such a kiss, not even at the beginning with Raffi. His grip was so strong that she was unable to move. But the kisses continued and she felt the fire burning her from head to toe. Wahab picked up Sara in his arms and walked to one of the rooms and closed the door. They continued kissing and touching each other's faces and hair.

Time passed quickly and, when they heard voices outside, they separated immediately from each other. Wahab went to the terrace to breathe the fresh air and Sara went to the bathroom to arrange her hair. When she emerged, Maggie and Pierre did not even look at her. Nor did they ask any questions. Maggie said that she was very hungry and asked everyone to help her serve the food.

They all ate the delicious *mezzes-snaks* – Lebanese specialties presented in small dishes – that she had prepared for them. The table looked beautiful with all the little colorful dishes. Later Sara thanked Maggie and left because it was getting late for her. She did not eat much since she still tasted Wahab's lips. After she left, Maggie and Pierre teased Wahab and said that he looked like a schoolboy in love. He did not answer and left soon.

Sara did not know how she arrived home since she was very shaky and emotional. She still felt Wahab's hands holding hers. Was it he or was it her loneliness and miseries that were pushing her to such emotions and conditions? She did not know the answer. The easiest answer was that she was in love, totally and completely. Moreover, she was proud that she was loved by a man like Wahab. He was educated, handsome, kind, gentle and rich. What more could a man offer her? She asked herself a thousand times why she had married Raffi so quickly. How could she be in love with such a boring man? He had nothing to offer her, nor was he trying in any way to become a better husband. He could have at least given her some compliments and kind words. When he was changing his shirts or even his underwear, he could have at least recognized that they were clean and pressed and nicely folded. Was it so difficult to say "thank you" or ask if she was tired after a day of work?

Wahab, on the contrary, had nice gestures and loving words all the time. He was not pretending. It was his true being. He appreciated every little gesture Sara made toward him. Moreover, he was a happy person by nature.

That evening she did not interact much with her children. Ani had already washed and fed them and they had done their homework. Sara just made sure that they went to bed on time. She did not wait for Raffi. She went to bed, squeezing herself and imagining that Wahab was kissing her. She was all afire, burning in her bed. But soon she heard Raffi enter the room. She froze just from feeling his presence and pretended that she was asleep in order not to say a word. She asked herself why was she playing with fire and if it would eventually burn her. Why was she even going to Maggie's house? What would happen in the future?

If friends and especially her mother learned about her affair, it would become a scandal and she would bring shame to her family and children. Not long ago, her father and everyone in her family were killed at the hands of Muslim Turks. And now, in peace time, she was in love with a Muslim man who was a Turk. What an irony, she thought. She knew well what would happen if she continued going to Maggie's house or if she met Wahab again. What was it that she was looking for? She had to stop and stay home and be the nice wife and mother that she used to be. Then she heard Raffi snoring and remembered who he really was and what he had become. She asked herself, "What about my needs and my own being?"

For more than two weeks she did not go to Maggie's house. Instead she went to the beach by herself, watched the waves, dampened her feet in the cold water, and sometimes added her salty tears to the seawater. She reasoned about her emotions, talked to herself, and went home early to be with her children. After all, she loved them as they were all she had and were her reason for living.

ॐ

One afternoon, while she was walking on the beach, suddenly someone caught her arms from behind and said. "You make me crazy. Where have you been? How could you stay away for so long?" She did not need to turn and find out who he was. She knew his voice, his hands and his cologne well. They forgot everyone around them and hugged each other tightly for a moment. Then Sara came to her senses and pushed him away gently and said, "It is dangerous here. There are people around us." He proposed they enter a movie theater because no one would recognize them in the dark. She accepted and they each went into the theater separately and then sat together.

He immediately held her hands and kissed them lovingly. They talked slowly and softly. "Why have you not been to Maggie's house?" he asked. "I was becoming crazy not to see you. Every day I had walked near your house and watched your every movement from a distance as much as I could. I wanted to be sure that you were not ill."

Sara did not know what to do. The affection that Wahab offered her so sincerely was weakening her resolve. She replied honestly and simply that she loved him but that she had a husband and children and that she and Wahab were from different ethnic origins and religions. She lived in a different world and could not hurt her mother and children.

Wahab replied that he understood her situation well; he also was facing the same issues of tradition at his house. But, for him, love flew above all those boundaries. What he understood was that when two people loved and wanted each other dearly, that should be enough to overcome all obstacles. He added that the difficulties could be solved only by the people who loved each other profoundly that there was always a solution for every situation.

While in the theater, they held and squeezed each other's hands all the time. Sara's body was burning and trembling. Each wished that they were somewhere far from all the boundaries, just the two of them, so that they could hug and kiss each other until eternity. Before leaving she promised to go to Maggie's house and left before the movie ended so that no one would see them together.

The next day she dressed up nicely and asked her neighbor Reneé to watch her children when they got home from school until Ani arrived. As Sara walked to Maggie's house, her mind ordered her to return home. Her logic pulled her back and weakened her feet, but her emotions pushed her forward. When she rang the doorbell, she realized that Eve was picking the apple from the forbidden tree and was somehow aware of the consequences of her action. She insulted herself at being so weak and not having the willpower to leave. Then she asked herself what harm they were afflicting to those around them. It was their life and their love. Their life belonged to them after all.

After all these years that she had suffered in silence, what kind of reward had she received? No one had said a nice word to her. To the contrary, everyone had tried to take advantage of her situation and exploit her. She had knitted so beautifully, yet her wealthiest customers always tried to pay her the least. She asked herself if her husband never complimented or appreciated her, how could she expect others to do so? Finally she concluded her conversation with herself with the thought that her relationship with Wahab was a personal matter and it was not the concern of anyone else how she wanted to spend her time.

Maggie opened the door and was surprised to see her after such a long absence. Then she laughed as usual and welcomed her friend. Once in the house, Sara confessed all her secrets to Maggie, adding that she was confused and needed someone to talk to and Maggie was the only one who could understand her situation. Sara admitted that she loved Wahab very much and suffered in silence. She had thought that by staying away from him she would forget him, but she was wrong. Maggie replied that she was aware of their mutual love since she had never seen Wahab in such a condition. She assured Sara that her secret would stay safe with her and the best advice she could give was to meet Wahab and give their love a chance. Hopefully, they would be able to think clearer and find a solution.

As they walked to the terrace, Sara could hear Wahab and Pierre conversing in French. Sara was amazed by his total command of the language. The maid served lunch and then a warm Turkish coffee and some sweet pastries. After lunch Maggie and Pierre excused themselves and took off for a nap, leaving Sara and Wahab by themselves.

For some time they watched the blue sea in silence. The sun was warm and pleasant; the waves sang a soft melody; and the breeze blew Sara's beautiful hair across her face. Wahab watched Sara with love and gently swept her hair back into place. Each time he touched her hair it was as if an electrical circuit closed, creating a shock within her. She hadn't felt like that for a long time.

Suddenly both couldn't resist anymore. He held her tightly in his arms and they started kissing passionately. Then Wahab picked up Sara like a feather in his strong arms and took her to one of the rooms. He closed the curtains, with just enough light shining past the curtains so they could see one another. They kissed and touched each other while Wahab was trying to take off Sara's beautiful dress. She was unbuttoning his shirt timidly and gently. Sara was ashamed like a virgin bride, but she felt reassured in his arms and understood that he was the man that she had dreamed of all her life. His wide chest covered her and his two hands were wrapped around her as if they were just one being. They made love, kissed and hugged and they stayed together as one.

They did not know how long they were there, until they realized that they were not able to see any light from outside. Sara pulled open the curtain a little and saw that it was completely dark and remembered her life and became worried. She dressed quickly, combed her hair, kissed Wahab goodbye, and left quietly.

When she arrived home, the children were asleep; her mother had left and her husband was already sleeping. She entered her bed quietly and closed her eyes. She was happy for all the good luck that she had. No one in her family saw her come home. Soon she was asleep in sweet dreams with Wahab by her side.

CHAPTER 16

A Surprise

MONTHS AND THEN YEARS PASSED, and still Sara and Wahab's love did not die. They met each other wherever and whenever they could. In the beginning, they chose places that were not frequented by their mutual friends and relatives. Eventually, Sara became so comfortable with Wahab that she started taking her children with her when visiting him for an afternoon. Sara and Wahab even took the children to beaches, parks and places where they could play and enjoy themselves. Sara told Sako and Sarina that Wahab was an old friend but, because he was not an Armenian, if others saw them together they would badmouth them. Therefore, it was important to keep this a secret between Sara and her children, never mentioning his name to anyone, not even to their grandmother, father or friends.

The children always enjoyed their time with Wahab. Sarina cheerfully followed her mother's instructions, but inside she was sad. Sara found more freedom by having her children around. First, she was not obliged to run home to take care of them when a neighbor was unavailable. Second, if anyone saw her with Wahab, the presence of her children made it appear an innocent event. After all, what could she do in the presence of her children?

In summer Maggie invited Sara and the children to her mountain house, which was very large. Sara told Raffi about the invitation and he agreed that it would be nice for children to breathe the mountain air. Since he was teaching summer courses, he was unable to take them for a vacation. He added that a visit to the mountains would also help Sarina feel better because he worried about her health. Sara was surprised to hear this since it was the first time that he gave an opinion about the children.

Raffi said she shouldn't worry about him; he would manage his life in their absence. It was like a dagger in her heart to see how kind and honest Raffi was toward his family and how evil she was to prepare a dishonest trip. But soon the image of Wahab appeared in her mind and she told herself that she deserved to live happily. She thought a mountain trip would be the best opportunity for her and Wahab to be together without worrying about time.

When the day arrived to leave, the children were all excited. Sarina hugged and kissed her father many times and said she would miss him. Somehow Sara knew that she was more attracted to her father than Sako, who was always happy for anything new; the idea of climbing mountains excited him. Both children asked their father to join them but he answered sadly that he could not because he had to work.

Sara and the children joined Maggie and Pierre in their car. They arrived at the mountain house in the early afternoon. The garden was so large that one could not see the end of it. There were many rare green cedar trees, colorful flowers and fruit trees. Maggie turned to the children. "I am sure that you will enjoy your stay here," she told them. "There are many insects, animals and birds both in the garden and the mountains. You can climb the trees and eat their fruit just as long as you are careful not to fall. But, please, don't worry. We even have a doctor present in the house." The children asked if Pierre was a doctor. "No," Maggie said, "but our friend Wahab is going to join us later."

Upon hearing this, Sarina, who had been excited after arriving at the mountain house, suddenly became quiet. Her young face showed sadness again. Sara was too self-absorbed to notice this. Even though she was often a very giving person, at the same time she was self-centered with a strong ego.

Sara and Ani – daughter and mother – were so different from each other. Sara was more selfish whereas Ani was a giver without any ego. Sarina, who was very sensitive to others, was more like her grandmother, Ani, and very different from her mother, Sara.

Maggie showed them their rooms. The view from the top floor was breathtaking. Then the servants served cold drinks and sandwiches. After the snacks, Maggie told the children that there was no danger around there and they were free to explore and enjoy.

Sako and Sarina went out and soon Sako started climbing the trees and was throwing fruit to his sister. Sarina did not eat much but collected fruit for her brother. She was more attracted to the movements of the white clouds in the sky. In her heart, she hated to see Wahab join them. She was enough old to understand what was going on even though her mother tried to hide the truth from her and her brother. Sarina felt bad for her father; after all, he was a very kind and hardworking man. She could not understand why her father did not fight to win over his wife.

The fact remained that Sara was a nice person but, if someone threatened her ego or criticized her, she would go wild to protect herself. She was always right and from her childhood she had learned to cover up all problems. Sarina was not strong enough to talk to her mother about Wahab, so she kept her thoughts to herself. But, little by little, all these thoughts and feelings weakened her health. She had learned religion and morals at school and from her grandmother. She knew what her mother was doing was not right. But she was not able to open her heart to anyone. Raffi and Ani had tried to understand her pain, but how could she reveal her mother's secret to either when Sara had always warned them not to say Wahab's name in front of any person? Sarina had no solution. If she told Ani or her father, she was sure it would result in more pain, so she kept everything to herself.

Late in the evening Wahab arrived with food, pastry, toys and many samples of cosmetics that he had received from different pharmaceutical companies. In addition, he gave a very nice balance scale to Sako and a colorful plastic dishware set and a silver four-color pencil to Sarina. Both children were happy to receive the unusual gifts. While they were playing with their gifts, the adults were enjoying a drink and everyone was looking forward to the fancy dinner.

After dinner, the children were tired. Sara took them to their room and kissed them goodnight. Sako was very tired and fell asleep immediately. But Sarina stayed awake and looked through the large window at the bright stars and the moon. The sky was deep blue and beautiful with all the twinkling stars. She was happy, after all, for the amazing day that she experienced during her first time in the mountains. She was happy at having had the chance to see the countryside's beautiful nature, eat fruits from the trees, smell wildflowers, run after the butterflies and lizards, and look at the beautiful songbirds. She loved the gifts that Wahab brought her. She had never before in her life had such nice presents. And her bedroom in the mountain house was spacious and beautifully decorated.

But still she was thinking of her father, who was alone and sad back home. Why weren't her parents like all other parents? What was her mother doing staying with friends far from her husband? She felt her hot tears rolling down on her face, penetrating her pillow, drop by drop. Soon she fell asleep, dreaming that her father, Raffi, was holding her hand and Sara's.

The three of them walked in a beautiful garden filled with colorful flowers. Sako was running after the butterflies and they were all laughing.

At that very moment Sara and Wahab were walking in the garden, holding hands, kissing, and watching the glistening stars. They were very happy together. When she arrived at the mountain house, Sara felt guilty and ashamed. But as soon as she saw Wahab, she knew why she was there and how happy she was to be near him. She had the right to happiness. Even though Raffi had chosen to live a boring life and was not making any effort to change, she deserved a better life. After all, she had only one life to live and now she had found the man of her dreams. True enough, she always had an inner fight whenever she had to meet Wahab, for her conscience warned her that she was doing wrong.

The garden was quiet; only crickets and night birds were singing serenades to the love-struck couple. The breeze was fresh and pleasant and the sky was crowded with brilliant jewels. The perfume of jasmine and other flowers filled their lungs and took them out of this world. After a while, Sara felt cold, and they returned to the house. Everyone was asleep. Wahab pulled Sara gently into his room and did not even turn on the lights, since the room was romantically lit by the moon. He helped her undress and, for the first time, they were together at night, becoming one and not worrying about time or space. They hugged, kissed and made love all night until neither of them was able to move anymore. The exhaustion pulled them into a sweet sleep while Wahab held Sara, gently and close to himself. Even in their dreams, they were holding each other and smiling.

The week passed amazingly fast. Sarina became friendlier and smiled and ate more. It seemed that the pure air of the mountains had excited her appetite. Wahab was very kind to Sako and Sarina; he played various games with them and conversed with them in a sincere manner. They accepted him as a good friend of their mother's. Of course, they never saw anything untoward between their mother and Wahab. Sometimes Sara even went to their room to sleep with them so the children would not feel that she was out at night.

In the happy presence of Sara and Wahab and the two children, the relationship of Maggie and Pierre blossomed. After a week in the mountains, no one wanted to return to Beirut, especially the children. They had learned to climb cedar trees and in one they had arranged a small corner for themselves as a private house in the tree. They even asked to sleep there at night but Sara did not allow it. Everyone was in a good mood when they arrived home. Sarina had gained some weight and her cheeks looked rosier than before.

That night, when Raffi arrived home, he was happy to see the children and Sara. The children hugged and kissed their father and told him how much they had missed him and asked him to promise that he would travel with them the next time. They showed their gifts to their father but never mentioned the name of Wahab. They talked only of Maggie and Pierre, just as their mother had instructed them.

Raffi was happy to see how healthy his children looked, especially Sarina. And when he saw Sara, he was amazed to see how radiant and beautiful she was. He felt that she was no longer the sad and unhappy young woman he had come to know but was flourishing day by day. Later that day, Ani came to visit them. The children threw themselves in her arms, and Ani was happy to see everyone relaxed. She, too, noted that Sarina was looking healthier.

That night Sara felt that her bed was cold and empty. Her body was calling for Wahab to hold her. She wanted to kiss him, hug him, and make love to him. After passing such an intense week together, she was miserable to be far from him. Finally, she looked out the window and watched the twinkling stars, but they were not as magical as they had been in the mountains when she was with Wahab. Sara closed her eyes and imagined him by her side; she held her lower lip in her mouth and pretended that Wahab was kissing her; she touched her body and fell into a deep sleep. In her dream, she and Wahab kissed and made love to each other till she woke up in the morning.

The rest of the summer passed nicely. As usual, Sara took her children to the beach or other public places and, by accident. Wahab saw them every time, and so naturally he joined them. Sometimes Sara left the house alone and met Wahab at Maggie's house. One day Wahab asked her to visit his house. She was afraid that his parents would see them, but Wahab reassured her that his parents never left their house and no one came to his house, especially during those hours of the day. Besides, if even anyone did, the house was large enough that she could stay in one of its many rooms and no one would detect her presence.

Visiting Wahab in his house for the first time was an exciting but scary idea for Sara. Once they arrived at his house, she realized that it was located far from the other houses. He showed her around and then they found themselves all alone; the magic of their love worked again and they enjoyed the best time of their life. She felt that he was right. Wahab's house was beautiful and quiet, and tastefully decorated with expensive furniture. It was indeed the best place that they could meet. In the past, they worried about Maggie or Pierre. But, in his house, they belonged only to each other and did not need to worry about anyone else. They were tired of lies and pretensions.

Wahab proposed that she leave her husband and marry him. He offered to take care of her children as his own. He told her that he would like to introduce her to his family and friends, travel with her to Europe, and give her the best gifts. Sara had always refused his gifts because she was not able to take them to her home or wear them.

Sara told him that she could not leave her husband. Raffi was all alone; he had no close relatives in Beirut and, since the event with the prostitute, he had stopped seeing his friends. At work he had just an intellectual and formal friendship with the other teachers. As for Sara's mother, Ani, she was also like Raffi. She had no one but her daughter. If Sara divorced and married Wahab, Ani would die of shame and grief.

Besides, by law, her husband would receive custody of the children. And, even if Raffi gave up that right and gave them to Sara, what kind of life would her children face knowing that their Christian mother had left her husband for a Muslim man?

Wahab remained calm. He was a reasonable and patient man, experienced in negotiations involving both business and family matters. He suggested that they wait and see how time and destiny were going to work for them. What Wahab knew but didn't mention was that his parents would object to his marrying Sara. But he was sure that, in a short time, they would love her because of her beauty and personality. Her religion was a problem but, since conversion existed in Islam, it did not seem to be a big obstacle to him. It was always a good deed for a Muslim to convert someone to Islam. Tradition said that when someone converted a non-Muslim to the Islamic faith, he or she would enter Paradise directly. Wahab was not practicing his religion anyway, so he wasn't worried about conversion or its promised rewards. He would ask her to do that only for the sake of his parents.

ع&

 At home, everything was as usual. The children started school. Sara performed all her household responsibilities perfectly. She continued her knitting, and her customers loved her work. Everything was in its place for Raffi. He had no regrets. Except, of course, that he and Sara had not shared a bed for a long time.

 One day Wahab told Sara that he had some good news. His brother, Ali, was moving to Germany to open a branch office for their business. Ali had asked him to act as his agent and rent out his house for at least five years. Wahab asked Sara to rent the house and move in with her children. In this way, he and she could see each other more often, and the children could enjoy the garden and pool. Because his parents rarely left their house, no one profited from their garden except the gardener.

 Sara asked him to give her time to think about this. From that very night, she started preparing her husband by telling him that one of her friends had told her that a nice house was available for rent and that she thought it would be great to move there if they could afford the rent. The children would enjoy the garden and pool, she told Raffi, and everyone would have more room and comfort.

 Sara used all these logical arguments to persuade Raffi to move to the new house, the same way that Eve convinced Adam to eat the forbidden fruit. Although Sara felt guilty, she justified herself by recalling that the sin had started with him, so the consequences were mutual. Raffi was not a difficult person or a fighter; he never insisted imposing his opinions on others and, on many issues, it wasn't even clear if he had an opinion. He always wanted to please everyone. When Raffi agreed to move to the new house, she gave him the address of Wahab's father, and Raffi and Wahab's father signed the papers. The old man was a good shield to protect the identity of the real owner.

Raffi received the keys and came home happily to give the good news to his wife, thinking that may be this would bring them closer together. Sara started packing immediately and, when the children came home, she told them the good news. Everyone was happy. That night, when they told Ani about their move, she became a little sad because it meant she would have to travel a longer distance to visit her daughter and grandchildren. But soon she, too, was happy that her daughter would live in a better neighborhood and in a much nicer house.

Within the week, all the packing was done and they moved to the new house. It was separate from the other buildings on the property and very beautiful. It had a nice view of the pool and beautiful garden. When Sara looked out of the window, she could smell the perfume of the flowers and hear the sound of the sea mixed with the songs of the birds. While she was looking out, she saw Wahab approaching her house with a bouquet of flowers. She ran downstairs and opened the door. They hugged each other and sealed the moment with a kiss. Then he told her that, while she was settling down, he had to make a business trip to France for a month but hoped to return soon to be with her. They kissed goodbye and Sara wished him a safe trip.

That afternoon Sara did not feel well. She thought that all the hard work during the move made her exhausted, so she rested in the afternoon. And she thought that Wahab's departure had added to this depression. But she was not really able to take a nap. The excitement of seeing Wahab at such a close distance, the pure air, the beauty of nature, her feelings of guilt, her memories of the past and present, her relations with her children, her mother and Raffi – all together kept her awake. For some moments, she became a prosecutor – accusing and blaming herself of adultery and living a dishonest life. Then she became a defense attorney and argued that she had the right to live and be happy and continue doing what she had been doing.

Soon she became tired of her game, got off her bed, and started singing from the Armenian opera, *Anoush*. It was an opera that she always liked. It told the story of love between the shepherd, Mossy, and a girl from a wealthy family. One day there was a wrestling competition in the village and two young men were chosen to fight each other. One was Mossy and other was Anoush's brother. Mossy won over Anoush's brother and the entire village praised him for his strength. But Anoush's brother suffered prestige from his loss and turned against Mossy. He forbade his sister from seeing him. Not only would Anoush refuse to respect this demand, but she and Mossy ran away to the mountains. Since life in the wilderness was not easy, Anoush decided to return home.

Upon her return, Anoush asked her parents for permission to marry Mossy. They told her that they were still angry because Anoush, by running away with Mossy, had brought shame to the family. In order to restore their honor, her brother went to the mountains and killed Mossy. When Anoush heard of Mossy's death at the hands of her brother, she lost her mind and passed the rest of her life as a madwoman, wandering in the mountains and singing and talking about her lost love Mossy. In the story of Anoush's love for Mossy, Sara saw her own love for Wahab.

Sara stopped singing and again felt uncomfortable. She made some hot tea. As soon as she finished her tea, she had a wave of nausea and ran to the bathroom. When she calmed down, she looked in the mirror as if she were passing herself through a pregnancy test. Wahab and Sara had taken all kinds of precautions to prevent any accidents. Nonetheless, Sara suddenly was weak and began trembling at the thought of a huge scandal. For anyone looking from outside, it would have been a blessing and a normal aspect of life for a young couple to have a third child. But not for Raffi and Sara. She asked herself what reaction Raffi would have if he knew she was pregnant, especially at the moment when everything seemed to be going so well for them.

Sara looked at her belly and talked to the fetus. "You know very well that you are not welcome in this house. Leave me alone. Go away. I don't want you and I don't love you. If you come into this world, a miserable life will wait for you. You are the result of adultery; you will be called a child of sin. Go find another womb and stay with people who want and desire you."

She was horrified. All her plans were destroyed and she saw only misery for her future. Suddenly she decided to end the pregnancy, if there was one. She remembered that her period was late and she had not paid much attention to it. She ran immediately to the door and started running up and down the stairs like crazy. She jumped ropes and did all the strenuous activities that she could until she was exhausted and fell on the couch. Her heart was beating hard. She was perspiring and was tired, but nothing happened to her. She even felt better and when everyone came home, she had a good appetite for dinner and slept well.

When she woke up early the next morning, her problems started all over again. After Raffi left, she ran to the bathroom and threw up in horror. It was only some water but it tasted bitter, as if her gallbladder was coming out of her mouth. The children were calling her to say goodbye since they were late for school. Sako and Sarina were growing and able to dress themselves, make their own breakfast, and even walk to school together. The school was not far from their new house and it was a safe walk. Almost all the children walked to school and enjoyed talking and playing in the streets.

After she was alone at home, Sara was panic-stricken. She hoped and prayed that Wahab would come to visit her soon. Maybe he had a medication that would help her to get rid of the unwanted baby. But Wahab had already left for Paris, so she had to deal with her problem by herself. As soon as she felt better, she started running up and down the stairs again. She picked up, as best she could, pieces of heavy furniture and moved them around. But nothing happened. It seemed that the fetus had chosen a nice healthy body in which to stay.

Then Sara remembered that there was a woman who helped young girls to get rid of their unwanted pregnancies. But immediately she changed her mind. She remembered a young girl from a famous family who was madly in love with a boy and, after she became pregnant, told the boy, thinking that he would marry her. But the boy was scared and ran away, so she had no choice but to ask for the woman's help. The woman demanded a lot of money and introduced hangers and dirty wires inside her to perform the abortion. She finally lost the fetus but later she developed a severe infection and was sick for a long time. When she finally found the right boy and got married, she learned that she was not able to become pregnant. So he divorced her.

Sara had visited her when she was sick; she remembered her sufferings and changed her mind. She made Turkish coffee and added grinded cardamom and drops of rose water to it. Its perfume filled her lungs and she felt better. Whenever she had a problem, she would make a strong Turkish coffee, which helped her to relax and clear her mind. As she sat down to drink her coffee, she opened the windows. The sweet perfume of jasmine, tuberoses and roses filled the room. The birds were singing to the accompaniment of the sea waves. She looked at the blue sky and felt the warmth of the sun on her delicate skin.

Suddenly her eyes shone. She had a sweet and bitter taste in her mouth just by thinking what she was thinking. She told herself that, since the fetus had decided not to leave her body, she had to play a game. How about giving Raffi a second chance as a husband to thank him for the effort he had made to move into the new house? She could play the nice woman and share her bed with him for a short time. The idea that she could put the baby's existence on his shoulders gave her comfort of mind. This way no one would learn the truth about the baby.

After she made up her mind, she rearranged her bedroom, made his favorite food, and then spent time with her children helping them with their homework. Raffi came home at his usual hour but this time Sara warmly welcomed him and the entire family ate the delicious dinner together. Raffi watched her from the corner of his eye and wondered if there was a change in his wife's attitude toward him. After dinner, Ani visited them. She brought a delicious pastry, and everyone was happy to see her and she was happy to see them settled in such a nice house. Ani noticed the change of attitude in her daughter and was happy to think that the move had brought closeness and happiness to the couple.

After the children went to bed, Sara went to the bedroom and put on a nice nightgown. When Raffi came into the room, he did not find his usual blanket on the floor. He was surprised and then saw his beautiful wife showing him the bed. He was confused. To make it easy for him, Sara turned off the light and asked if he was cured of his disease or if he had visited other prostitutes.

Raffi was excited and happy. He swore that he made that mistake only once in his life. He took off his suit in the dark and was so confused and excited that he struck his foot against the footboard, but he paid no attention to the sharp pain. He rushed to his wife like a thirsty voyager who had been lost in the desert for long time. He did not know where to start or what to touch. He had dreamed of this moment and had fantasized in his dreams every night and now he was not sure if it was real or still a dream.

The beauty of Sara's body was evident even in the darkness. Her skin smelled sweet and it mingled with the strong smell of the jasmine flowers coming from the outside. He kissed her fingers, her toes, and then he lost himself. Soon he went in a deep sleep. Sara was disgusted and angry at herself. The short moment that she passed with Raffi was a real torture for her. But she told herself that even the undesirable act justified its purpose.

Sara had no feeling toward Raffi anymore. She felt that all the bridges between them were broken and there was no way for them to return to earlier days. She imagined Wahab at her side and started touching and moving her hands around Raffi's chest and body. Raffi woke up and asked if he was dreaming or if this was all really happening. She replied that she was grateful for all that he had done to obtain this beautiful house and, for the sake of their children, wanted to give another chance to their life.

Sara did all she could to kiss him in a way that would make him never forget the night that he had spent with her. Raffi again fell asleep. With great effort Sara stood up and went to the bathroom to wash herself clean of Raffi. Then she thought that if she made love to Raffi every night of the week, it might cause her to lose the fetus. This cheered her, for she was so desperate that she was ready to do anything.

When she returned to her bed, she stayed far from Raffi, who was already snoring. She hated herself for betraying Wahab, but she knew it was an important effort and sacrifice that she was making for their future relationship. As planned, they continued their close relationship every night for a week.

Raffi was completely a new person. He was happy. He was coming home earlier. He was still working long hours but, as soon as he arrived home, he played with the children while Sara prepared dinner. The children instantly noticed the change in their parents. They were happy that they did not have to go out with their mother to visit Wahab, that they no longer needed to lie, and that all was going well with their parents at home. Sarina looked much better and had more of an appetite; Sako was doing better at school. Sara had early morning sickness but no one was at home to notice it. Each night she was on her plan, hoping to lose the unwanted child and praying for that all the time.

Raffi was in heaven. He had never imagined that such a change could occur in his wife. When he had seen his wife coming home late in the past, all beautiful and happy, he became suspicious but he had not heard or seen anything untoward. And when he had questioned the children, they always answered that they were either in Maggie's house or at the beach and parks.

One night when the children were asleep he even told Sara that he used to die from jealousy and envy thinking that other men saw her in the street or that she might be attracted to someone else. In the darkness, Sara blushed and did not answer. She was not able to lie to this great degree and afraid that, if she said a word, she would betray herself.

Then Raffi added that he knew that his wife was an angel and that she had the right to be angry and disappointed with him. He deserved all the years of punishment, he told her, unable to see that she had not forgiven him. Whenever she slept with him, she felt like a prostitute. What was the difference, she asked herself. They performed their acts to earn money and she was doing it for her own gain.

CHAPTER 17

A Wish Granted

ONE MORNING, after everyone had left the house, Sara heard a knock on the door. She recognized the tap-tap-tap, and her heart started beating faster. She looked at herself in the mirror, arranged her hair, and opened the door.

As expected, she saw Wahab standing before her. He looked more handsome than ever. Even as she was closing the door, he was kissing her. He said that he had missed her every moment and even the beautiful Parisian girls were not able to keep his mind away from her for a moment. While kissing and smelling her he asked, "What have you done to me? I am not able to function without you. I had a hard time concentrating during important meetings. You have to marry me and become my wife, so that I can see and have you every second of my life."

Sara was happy to see him but had sad eyes and a heavy heart. Wahab looked at her and asked if she had been working too hard since she looked tired. Then he pulled a little box from his pocket and presented it to her. She opened it and found a beautiful dark blue bottle of perfume with a silver script. Wahab said that Soir de Paris perfume was very much *a la mode* in Paris. Then he gave her an album of pictures of all the wonderful places to visit in Paris and a small metal statue of the Eiffel Tower. He said he knew that he could not offer her real gifts, but at least these little ones would not arouse any suspicion. He said they should make plans to see each other since he had missed her very much. Sara was dying to stay in his arms but knew she could not invite him to her bedroom. Wahab respected her house and said that the next day he would stay home waiting for her. Then, after a final kiss, he left.

Once alone, Sara pulled the beautiful bottle of the perfume out of the box. She was grateful for this gesture and reminded herself that Raffi had never given her such a gift. She put a little drop of the perfume on her neck and under her nose and all through the day smelled the sweet perfume and dreamed of Paris. She looked at the images in the album and regretted that she was not able to see all these historic buildings with her own eyes. After the children ate their dinner, Sara went early to bed as she did not want to wait for Raffi. She covered herself with the blanket tightly so that Raffi would not approach her. She dreamed of Wahab. The smell of the perfume took her to the foreign lands and she saw herself in beautiful garments walking with Wahab on the romantic streets of Paris, like the postcards she had collected in the past.

Later that evening Raffi quietly entered the room and left in the early morning before she was up. When Sara awoke, she was relieved because she did not have to face her husband and feel guilty. After the children went to school, she put on a beautiful dress, put a few drops of the French perfume on her dress, and admired herself in the mirror for a while. She was still a beautiful and desirable young woman. She was burning to see Wahab and her pregnancy was not bothering her anymore.

At ten o'clock she left her house and walked quietly to his house, while looking around like a thief. No one was present; the garden was so large and the trees so dense that she felt protected. Wahab was as impatient as she was. Even before she knocked, the door opened and there he was waiting, eagerly awaiting her. He closed the door and they forgot the world immediately. They were kissing, smelling and hugging each other. Wahab told her that Paris was filled with beautiful girls but none of them were as attractive as she was. Whenever he tried to talk with any, as soon as he looked at them, he saw Sara's face and he knew that he was in love.

Then, after kissing and hugging for a while, suddenly he looked at her seriously. "I cannot continue living any longer like this," he said. "I want you at my side all the time. I want to take you on the trips and be with you. Please get a divorce and marry me."

Sara looked at him happily for a moment. She also wanted to be with him all the time, and so she wanted to say a big yes. But suddenly she froze and went into a deep thought. Then tears dropped from her large eyes.

Wahab licked away her tears and asked why she was crying. She sadly said, "I would love to marry you but I am not able to leave my husband. If I did that, I would hurt my children and my mother deeply. I do not have the right to hurt my mother, knowing what she has gone through. My children also would suffer forever, for they would be shunned in the Armenian society if their mother married a Muslim. Besides, your family would never accept my children into their family. They would not even agree to their son marrying a divorced woman with two children."

Wahab responded strongly and passionately. "I have thought through all the problems during my trip and my offer of marriage is very serious. I accept your children as my own. My family will be obliged to accept you; it is my responsibility to work on that. You should not worry for Raffi because he will eventually find and marry another woman. Your mother is probably the most difficult issue. I do not know her, but I promise to give her a comfortable house to live in and I will guarantee her future so that she could stop working." He paused a moment. "You do not need to answer me immediately. I am very serious and my offer is valid for as long as you need to think about it."

Then Wahab offered Sara some tasty chocolates he had brought from Europe and a sweet liqueur in a beautiful cut crystal goblet. They were so happy to find each other that they forgot everyone and everything; their world resumed being only the two of them. Soon they were one and stayed that way until late afternoon.

Suddenly Sara woke up in his arms. It was a warm day. Wahab was still sleeping. To Sara, he looked like a Greek or Roman statue, so handsome and kind. The room was quiet; only the bronze sculpted clock was ticking and killing time. The birds were singing. She looked at the time and realized that it was getting late. She kissed Wahab gently until he woke up, and then she told him that she had to leave. That night they slept in their own houses and in their own beds but, in their dreams, they were united until morning time.

The next day Sara went shopping and bought a lot of food. It was heavy for her to carry but she was a strong woman. When she arrived home and put the packages on the table, she felt a sharp pain and then contractions. She ran to the bathroom and felt very uncomfortable. She was bleeding heavily. Then she felt stronger contractions, like the waves of a stormy ocean hitting her one after the other. She felt herself bleeding more and then a feeling as if something separated from her and dropped down. At once she understood that she had lost the little fetus of her forbidden love that had stayed in her for seven weeks. She became very weak and almost fainted. She cried from the depth of her heart, because, in reality, she wanted to have Wahab's baby. But, at the same time, she knew that it was not right.

Finally she thanked her luck since nature had worked in her favor and her prayers were answered. She rested awhile and, when she felt better, cleaned the bathroom, took a shower, and was happy that the children were with Ani that night. The bleeding stopped and she rested on her bed. She had tears but, at the same time, she felt free. When Raffi came home very late, Sara was already sleeping soundly.

Sara stayed home and rested for two days. Wahab wanted to know why Sara was staying away from him. She hesitated for a moment and then decided to tell him the complete truth; after all, he had medical knowledge and they had to be more careful in the future. Then her tears dropped. Wahab was all concerned for her health and sad at the thought of losing a baby who could have obliged Sara to decide in his favor. He again asked her to marry him, have his babies, and live a comfortable and loving life. He wiped away her tears, touched her face and hair delicately, and proposed to take her to a doctor to be sure she was well. This was what Sara was expecting from Raffi all their married life, and this was the difference between the two men.

Sara refused and said that she knew she was well. After a week, she was a healthy woman again. On the first day that she was able to leave her house, she went to visit Wahab. He was very happy to see her. They hugged and kissed each other gently, talked and dreamed. She asked him to tell her about Paris and his trips to different countries. She looked through his photo albums and foreign books and they passed a peaceful afternoon together.

Life continued as usual. Ani visited them often and spoiled the children with gifts, home-cooked pastry and delicious food. Raffi was still teaching, both during the day and after hours. And Sara worked at home in her knitting business. The love between Sara and Wahab never faded. On the contrary, it grew deeper every day and it seemed normal for them to continue their illicit relationship. Sara had already gently cut Raffi from her life with excuses; she was not able to play the game and be with two men at the same time. But she had become used to her life of being married to one man and having loving relations with another. She was feeling less guilty and no longer scared because now she and Wahab passed most of their time together in his house.

Once in a while, Wahab had a business trip to Transjordan. Sara would then ask Raffi if she could visit school friends in Jerusalem. She and Wahab boarded the same bus, sitting apart at first and then together later on, miles from Beirut,. Whenever they visited Jerusalem, they went to Café al Ahmar. Wahab knew the owner, who always received them with a large smile and gave them their special table, which was secluded. They ordered Turkish coffee and Arabic sweet pastries.

One day Raffi came home happy and told Sara that he had been offered the position of principal of an Armenian school in Iran. The move would mean more pay and a better future for their children. Raffi also knew that it meant leaving a comfortable life in a familiar place and traveling far to a new country. In telling Sara the news, he did not notice the flicker of shock across her face. Sara instantly recovered and congratulated her husband. Inside she was miserable. She did not know how to leave Wahab, but she also realized that the children were getting older and that their future was more important than hers.

She dreaded telling Wahab. But, when she did, he calmly reassured her that, since his firm already had offices in many Middle Eastern countries, it would be easy enough to open one in Iran and spend most of his time there with her. She had to do what was important for her children and, besides, he was not optimistic about the future of Greater Lebanon. Maggie and Pierre had already moved to France and were living in Paris. Wahab met them whenever he visited Paris, and Maggie wrote letters to Sara and invited her to visit them when she could.

Finally, Sara and Raffi made the big decision to go to Iran and they asked Ani to move with them. By then, Sara had begun wondering if living in a new and strange environment would help her end her relations with Wahab.

They arrived in Tehran and moved into the home that the school had rented for them. It was an apartment in a fourplex, and most of the other tenants were Armenian. The apartment occupied the first floor and looked like a private house; it was comfortable but not as nice as their home in the garden of Wahab. Everyone missed the sea, but they had a small garden with rose bushes and colorful petunias that smelled sweet, especially at night. There was also a small pool that they called the "*hoz.*" The garden and the *hoz* were shared by all the neighbors and their children. The Muslim gardener's wife washed her dishes and clothes in the hoz, and she and her husband also washed their faces, hands and feet before their prayers. All the children played and swam in the *hoz*.

Tehran was not as beautiful or as developed as Beirut, even though it was the capital of an ancient and once powerful country. But, little by little, Sara became accustomed to her everyday life. She missed Wahab and, no matter how hard she tried to put thoughts of him aside, she did not succeed.

It did not take long for Wahab to make good on his promise. He moved to Tehran and opened an office in the bazaar, where the country's economy pulse beat most strongly. He then rented an apartment not far from Sara's. His was on the third floor. It had a large balcony overlooking the main boulevard, which was lined with huge plane trees that stood higher than the apartment building itself. His windows also faced a nice park across the street, where there were games for the children, a merry-go-round with beautiful colorful wooden horses, and a little café tucked in a romantic quiet corner. Parents left their children in the play area while they talked and drank and ate in the café.

On warm summer nights Sara took her children to the park, where she and Wahab pretended to meet each other by accident. While Sako and Sarina played in the park, Sara and Wahab sat at the café, drank, talked and dreamed. Once in a while, when they thought no one was watching, they held hands or stole short kisses from each other. Sara felt safer in this new country because she did not know anyone, which meant no one recognized her. And because she never participated in any activity at her husband's school, no one there knew her either.

Ani had found some Armenian friends her age who had suffered similar experiences of massacres by Turkish soldiers in the northwestern cities of Iran. They never talked about the details of the horrors, but they drank coffee and, without words, understood each other's pains.

Both children were doing well at school. But Sara had come to understand all too well that moving to Iran could not end her passion for Wahab. So she continued her forbidden love. She found courage to visit him in his apartment and they continued loving each other.

When the children were not at school, she took them with her but asked them to play quietly so that the neighbors would not hear them. Wahab had a huge closet full of gifts from different companies that he represented – souvenirs from his trips, and all kinds of interesting odds and ends, including beautiful old watches, antiques of all kinds, compasses, scales, and much more. It was almost like a science lab and museum. For the children it was like visiting Ali Baba's cave while their mother was in the company of her lover in the other room. Sako and Sarina liked Wahab since he was a kind man who had become like a relative after all these years. But, in her heart, Sarina never approved of her mother's actions and was sad most of the time. While at Wahab's apartment, she usually did her homework or read books.

Raffi was happy with his new job, which provided him with not only more money but far more prestige than his old job as a teacher. His easy-going, non-confrontational nature was much appreciated by the school's teachers and other employees, who were competent but set in their ways. Meanwhile, Sara had reactivated her knitting business and soon found paying customers.

Wahab traveled often to Lebanon and Europe in his work. Once, after he returned, he told Sara that Europe had forgotten the suffering and loss of the Great War and was heading toward another conflict. The voices of the war's dead soldiers and other victims were silent, but new and loud voices of ambitious people were heard louder and louder each day.

The Great Depression dragged on in America and elsewhere, aggravating age-old animosities. Wahab said the world had become crazy again. He thought that another war, even bigger and worse than before, would soon engulf the world. He felt bad for the youths who would have to fight this war and for everyone, especially the Europeans, who were going to suffer and die because of a handful of ambitious rulers. He talked about an angry man in Germany named Adolf Hitler who had a dangerous torch in his hand and seemed eager to burn down civilization. But, he told Sara, most of the people he met paid no attention to the growing signs of danger and continued their lives paying little attention to Hitler's words and actions. He said that more intellectual Europeans agreed with his analysis of the situation but were powerless to stop the crazy man. The world, he sighed, seemed intent on repeating the mistakes of the recent past.

Within months, Germany attacked Poland and soon the war spread to other countries. Sara felt lucky to live in Iran since the government had declared its neutrality. But store shelves were getting empty and people were losing jobs. Food supplies became scarce. The government started issuing coupons for foods like sugar and flour. People stood in long lines for hours to buy staples like bread. Little by little, stories about all kinds of atrocities started spreading around; they were so horrific that some people did not believe them and thought the Allies had invented them to weaken any support in neutral countries for the Germans, who clearly were winning the war. The real news did not travel fast and the truth was hidden. As the Germans conquered more and more countries, they brought suffering, hunger, homelessness and death to many people.

Ani, who had followed Raffi and Sara to Tehran, had her own little apartment and a job. She visited them daily and the children were always happy to see her. She did not read the newspapers but her face was somber and sad. In her mind, she relived her old history and again heard the voices at night. She was surprised that so many people were enjoying their lives, going to movies and parties, never thinking about what was happening in the world. They did not understand the real meaning of war and suffering. They never heard what she had heard or seen what she had seen.

This time the uniforms had changed colors. Instead of Ottoman khaki, the aggressors wore the colorful black and red uniforms of the Third Reich. But still they acted like Turks – killing, raping and destroying many innocent lives. Ani prayed at night for everyone and asked God to go to their aid and not be absent since He was for the Armenians.

Sara remembered her childhood, her fatherless life and their horrific journey through the desert and wondered how many children were going to suffer as she did. How many would lose their mothers and fathers? How many sisters and brothers and how many wives and husbands and lovers were going to be separated from each other, never to see one another again?

Raffi lost his job when the government closed minority schools and required all children to attend Persian schools. He was unemployed for some time but, finally, because of his education, found a job as an accountant with an engineering company that was building bridges in the country. So he traveled to various cities and returned home for a week or two before leaving again. The children were thrilled to see him when he returned because he brought them little gifts. If he traveled to the country's southwest, where the British Petroleum Company was active, he sometimes was able to buy candy and canned food, which had become hard to find in Tehran.

In both Beirut and Tehran, Sara was more of a liberal thinker than society at large. If she could, she would let women choose their future, where no discrimination or wars were present. People would be free to live their lives as they wished. Life was given to each person for only a short period, so all had the right to live as they wished. If Sara governed society, people could marry and divorce as they wished, regardless of religion. Women would bear children only when they wished and only when it was the right moment for the couple to have new burden in their .lives. Her society would be based on love and respect and be one in which crime did not exist.

The king of Iran, Reza Shah Pahlavi, had close ties with Germany, which had built the train station in Tehran and whose nationals were present in the country. In 1941, the British and Russians protested his rapprochement with Germany and forced him to abdicate in favor of his son, Mohammad Reza Pahlavi. These changes brought instability to the country.

During all this turmoil, Sara again became pregnant. She repeated everything that she had done before in Beirut but this time she did not lose the fetus. It seemed that the little being had decided to be born at any cost. Sara again played the same dirty game with Raffi.

By now Raffi was aware of his wife's affair with Wahab. One day, after a long period when he was suspicious but still uncertain, he followed Sara and discovered her love affair. But he decided to respect his wife's secret and his family's honor. Raffi was all alone in this world. He had lost his parents and did not have any siblings. His wife and children were his only family. He had always loved and respected Ani like an old sister and a mother. He knew how much she had helped his family and was deeply sorry that he did not have the means to give her a comfortable life and many gifts. But he had always treated her the best way that he knew.

He decided to hold his silence in order to keep his family intact. He knew Sara well. If he reproached her, she would not leave quietly but would blame him for everything. This would reopen the old wounds and expose the children to the unwanted truth or shame them. What if he left Sara and Wahab didn't marry her? Where would she end up? In the end, he decided not to confront Sara but take his revenge in his quiet way. Anyway, Raffi was not the kind of man who would fight to get what he wanted. By this time, he was not even eager to have a physical relationship with his wife. Despite past feelings of love, he felt disgusted by her dishonesty. He had failed her only once by stupid accident, but she had continued betraying him during all these years!

He accepted her pregnancy without complaint and, when Sara gave birth to a girl at home, he even seemed happy to have a new member added to his family. Raffi still loved Sara madly and therefore would never hurt her. He especially wanted to keep his mother-in-law away from the truth, because he knew how much Ani had suffered in life. But, since that day of discovery, he had remained sad and heartbroken.

Raffi named the new baby Ruth, after Ruth in the Old Testament. Ruth was not born a Hebrew but was married to one. She was a very respectful young woman who, after her husband's death, stayed with her mother-in-law and accepted the Jewish faith and lived by its laws. This name in its own way brought comfort to Raffi since he hoped Ruth would accept and love him as her own father, although he never shared the profound meaning of Ruth's name with Sara.

Ruth brought much joy to her brother, sister and grandmother. Sara had mixed feelings toward her. She was proud of Ruth since she was an unusually beautiful baby. But, at the same time, she hated her in her heart, because she a constant reminder of her sins. She would feel this dilemma until the end of her life.

Wahab could wait no longer to see his daughter. One morning, when everyone was at school and work, he visited Sara and the baby. He loved Ruth, but it was prohibited for him to have Ruth, his own baby, in his house. Wahab and Sara had each received a different but fair punishment.

Meanwhile, Raffi's poetic talent gained new vigor and he started writing love poems to a woman he called Lara. When Sara read some of his poems in the newspaper, she yelled at him and asked who his new lover was. She wanted to know if it was a new teacher at school or a private adult student. He never answered her and continued writing his poems to Lara. Sara never realized that he was talking to her through his poems. He had made only a name change whose meaning she never understood; he had merely changed the letter "S" to "L."

Despite his weaknesses, Raffi remained a decent person and played his wife's game. He was legally Ruth's father and he gave her his name and officially made her an Armenian girl. He immediately organized a little celebration and baptized Ruth days after she was born. This was his big revenge addressed to the lovers in a hidden message in one of his poems. He accepted a half Muslim-Turk baby of his wife but gave her an Armenian name and the Christian faith. This was the only way that he could inflict revenge on Wahab for stealing his wife from him. But he never let Sara or anyone find out that he knew the truth and kept the secret until the end of his life.

Ani was also in pain and shame, for she had known about her daughter's relationship for a long time but chose to remain silent, for she knew she could not change her daughter's mind. Nor did she want to hurt the honor of her daughter and her family. She never understood why she was being punished by seeing her only daughter, a survivor of the Genocide, fall in love with a Muslim-Turk. So she also joined Raffi's game of denial and cover-up.

๛

Life continued, and so did the atrocities of war and its consequences everywhere in the world. Germans were still present in the country, building train stations and bridges – and who knows what else they were doing? Ruth was a healthy and happy baby. She gave her first smile to Wahab as if she wanted to show that she recognized her biological father.

When Ruth was two years old and Sara walked with her in the street, people stopped Sara and asked if the baby's father was a very handsome man. Ruth had blue-green eyes and blond hair. Another time an American couple asked Sara if she would give her baby for adoption since they were going to move to America and they assured her that the baby would have a much better life and future there than in Iran. The husband even offered her a great deal of money and said that they would send tickets once a year to her and her family in order to visit her daughter. It was evident to Sara that Ruth resembled neither Sako nor Sarina and especially not Raffi. He and Ani each claimed that Ruth looked like their grandparents and, since no one in Tehran had seen them or their pictures, their secret was safe.

Sako and Sarina were happy with their young sister. Because of the big age difference, she was more of a toy to them than a sibling. Most of the time, when the children were at school and Sara did not have rush orders to fill, she took Ruth and visited Wahab. He was happy to see Ruth and called her Fatima, like the prophet's daughter.

Sarina had grown tall for her age but remained very thin. Because of the war, there was still a food shortage in Iran. What little food that was available in the stores was very expensive, and people had a hard time feeding their families properly. Wahab was unable to give gifts to his daughter or make any kind of gesture for fear of making their relationship known. When Sara and her children visited him, he had abundant food in the house, sometimes even exotic treats like rare chocolates. Sara knew he had paid a fortune to buy these for them. But Sarina did not eat even those rare foods. Wahab gave Sara codfish oil, vitamins and calcium tablets for Sarina – items that were hard to find. But, as the representative of Sandoz Pharmaceuticals, he could both find these items and buy them. Ani and Sara prepared all kinds of healthful food and folk remedies for Sarina, but her health continued to fade slowly.

Many knowledgeable people talked about the atrocities that Germans were committing against the Jews and other minorities. But no one took any action, which made Ani angry. "It is exactly like it was with the Armenians," she told Raffi and Sara. "They are again killing, burning and raping the Jews and the rest of the world is turning their face away and trying not to see or hear the truth. If all the governments had criticized and punished the Ottomans for organizing and executing the Armenians when the Genocide happened, no one would dare to kill Jews now. Everyone said that there were many German soldiers in Turkey before and during the Genocide, and that they were training the army. So who knows if they did not practice their methods on the Armenians so that, after some twenty years, they could use more sophisticated methods on the Jews?

"Anyone familiar with Muslim mentality," she continued, "would admit that, when Muslims are against someone, they pull their sword or gun and kill them immediately. They are not patient people and so are less likely to pull people out of their houses and force them to march days and months in deserts and mountains as we had to. For sure, that was not a Muslim pattern. It was probably a German mentality imposed on the Ottomans, and now the Germans are doing the same thing in Europe to the Jews."

Ani slumped back in her chair and covered her eyes, now wet with tears.

CHAPTER 18

Sarina's Mysterious Illness

LIFE CONTINUED mostly unchanged for Sara and her family. Ruth was growing into a beautiful and talented girl. She sat, stood, walked and talked much earlier than most children her age. By the age of two-and-a-half, Ruth spoke Armenian and Persian very well. Sara taught her some children's songs and poems and, by the time Ruth was three years old, Sara would ask her to recite poems in public. She was a very sweet girl but also calm and, in a way, she lived in her own world since Sarina and Sako were at school and then busy with homework. Ruth had an imaginary friend with whom she played when she was alone in the morning. In the late afternoon, when the other children returned from school, Ruth played with them in the garden.

Sara continued seeing Wahab. She always took Ruth with her. She was a small child and no threat to them. Ruth was also a loving girl. She loved Raffi but, at the same time, always told her mother that she adored Wahab. She played with the plane tree leaves that fell onto the balcony and with the tree's fruit, which were like soft balls; when she smashed them, there was something cottony inside. She loved the smell of the leaves and was amazed at the size of the trees. As she grew older, she learned the alphabet and, when she started kindergarten, the teacher was surprised at her knowledge. She could already read and recite long poems.

Iran's political situation changed. The Armenian schools reopened once again and Raffi got his old position back. He was now the principal and taught some classes at the same time.

Since Raffi was earning a good salary, Sara was able to send Ruth to private dance classes in which she excelled, always earning a spot in the school plays and performances. When she began learning how to write, she asked Raffi to teach her Armenian script, since he had beautiful penmanship. She learned how to speak some Arabic and French from her mother and the conversations between her and Wahab. She learned at a young age that her mother had secrets to keep. Ruth never exposed her mother even to the people whom Ruth loved dearly, and neither Ani nor Raffi ever asked her about her mother and Wahab. So she remained honest to herself and to her mother.

When Ruth was five years old, she was admitted to pre-school. After ten days, the principal informed Sara that her daughter was wasting her time in the class since she already knew all the subjects. She suggested that Sara place her in the first grade, where Ruth would be much happier. The first year of school went very well and she was ranked first among her classmates.

Yet something was wrong. Although Sara never hesitated to ask her young daughter to show off her talent in public, in private she never praised Ruth. Instead, she always criticized her. Ruth was the constant reminder of Sara's own mistakes in her life. Her mere presence made Sara think of what she had done to herself and others by her actions. From an early age, Ruth became aware that there was something hidden between her and her mother. She learned that there was always more to the surface appearance of everything that surrounded her in life.

Although Sara was feeling less guilty, she tried to make up with Raffi but it never worked. They were very different and already were far apart physically and emotionally. She never got the courage to divorce him because of family, friends and society. What would everyone say about her children? And, most importantly, how would it affect Ani if she went against her traditions? Sara was not sure what she was. She wondered if she was Muslim or Christian in her heart. Although she could deeply feel the influence of Fatima from her days as a small child, she also felt her Armenian roots strongly. She visited mosques with Muslim neighbors and prayed, but then she went to the Armenian Church and prayed as well. She wished that there were no boundaries and differences between people. There was only one God but so many factions and so much strife!

Wahab still hoped that Sara would marry him one day. They loved each other so much, but both were comfortable with the routine and the *mode de vie* that they had settled into over the years. Sara was even comfortable living a double life while having a single love in her heart. She was a devoted mother and respected her mother and husband the best way that she could. No one reproached her or dared to say anything to her. Some gossiped behind her back but then stopped when they saw how devoted and hardworking and caring a person she was. She helped everyone in the family and neighborhood. It was her way of bribing people to keep their mouths shut.

Raffi continued to love his wife although her bed was closed to him. At least he was happy to be married to Sara and told himself that she was young and immature and that the day would come when she would take him back into her life. Sara played the role of the official wife to Raffi. They went to his office parties and accepted friends' invitations to dinner parties and smiled at everyone. Sara continued working hard at her knitting business to help with her family's finances.

Sarina was always calm and always thin. She did well at school but, little by little, her body gave up on her. She became weak and refused to eat. Once again, she asked her mother why

Sara and Raffi did not kiss each other like all her friends. Sara immediately replied that those were private behaviors and should not be done in public. But she knew that Sarina, now sixteen years old, was not a child anymore and had more questions to ask but did not dare.

Months passed and Sarina lost more weight. Unable to find the reason, the doctors suggested that they take her to the mountains or maybe to the seashore for fresh air. Sara started worrying and begged Wahab for a solution. He gave her more vitamins and fortifying syrups but nothing helped. Sarina was melting like a candle. She started having fevers. Sometimes she vomited and coughed violently. Raffi and Sara took her to the hospital while Ani stayed with Sako and Ruth. Sara cried and prayed all night.

This time a doctor diagnosed her condition correctly. Sarina had tuberculosis. He explained that because she had grown so fast and her body had not absorbed much nutrition, the sickness advanced quickly. There was not much hope for her but they would try all the cures available. Raffi and Sara prayed in the waiting room and cried together for the first time. They finally had a common pain to share. Sara immediately blamed herself for causing the pain and sadness of her daughter, but she also blamed Raffi because of one negligent moment that changed everything. She bargained with God that, if He cured her daughter, she would never see Wahab again.

Sara and Raffi tried to comfort each other. A week passed but no one was able to help. One afternoon, while Sara was finishing an order, Ani went to visit Sarina. Whenever she visited Sarina, she would take some freshly cooked food, feed her, and stay with her until the end of visiting hours. But that afternoon Sara was surprised to see her mother return home early. When she looked at her face, her tears fell without words. Ani then told her that, when she entered Sarina's room, she did not see her on her bed. The young patient who was sharing the room with Sarina told Ani that the night before, when the nurse brought their dinner, Sarina told the nurse that she was very hungry. The nurse happily placed the tray on her bedside stand and arranged her pillows so that she could sit up. Sarina smiled and suddenly closed her eyes and, with a smile still on her face, left this world.

Ani and Sara were in deep pain and grief. They cried and hugged each other. Sara understood that she needed her mother for the first time since Ani had gone through so much grief that she had ways that could lessen her pain. But no one has any remedy for such great losses. One must work alone for long years and, still, this kind of broken heart never heals.

Sara broke like a crystal vase into tiny pieces. She had lost a fresh and beautiful daughter at the age of sixteen. Sarina was such an intelligent and promising girl. Sara remembered her sad face and her questions and her heart ached more. She immediately related her death to her adultery and told herself that she was being punished like King David. Both she and David lost their children as the price of their adultery. Then she remembered the words in the Bible after the flood when God told Noah, "I will no more destroy the Earth but the sin will be paid by seven generations. . . ." Then calmly she answered, "But my father and mother were innocent people. They never harmed anyone in their lives. So why did they lose their son and almost everyone else?" She reasoned that death is random and has no logic and that no one but God knows the real reason for things that happen to people.

Soon their apartment turned into a house of mourning with everyone dressed in black. Ani, Raffi and Sara were in such state of grief that no one, no words and no speech could comfort them.

At the moment of the burial, Ani asked God when He was going to take pity on her. Why did He not take her and leave her granddaughter alive? She had always been ready to go. Was it all her fault? All along, she had cried and complained that she never had a grave to cry over for her husband and parents. And, when she had Vartan's grave, she had left it behind to find her daughter, Sara. Now she finally had a grave to cry over.

All blamed themselves that God had taken Sarina as punishment for their actions. Even Sako thought that the reason his sister died was because he had pulled her hair in their games, or had taken away her candy or ice cream when they used to play together. Everyone was in pain and feeling guilty for being alive. Ruth was the only one who was at peace for she was too young to understand the real meaning of death.

Ruth stayed with one of the teachers at Raffi's school during the week of mourning at home. When she returned, she smiled and continued reading and playing games with the neighbors' children. Soon school started and felt relieved to leave the house because everyone was so sad there. Ani moved in with Sara and her family since she had stopped working and thought that she could be a help to her daughter and grandchildren. She and Sara went together to Sarina's grave, where they cried and tried to comfort each other. Raffi was sad and quiet; he worked and did not talk or share his grief with anyone. On the fortieth day after Sarina's death, he composed a poem titled "For my Sweet Sixteen Daughter," which was published in a major newspaper.

The entire Armenian community mourned while reading this poem, but it was Raffi's only public expression of grief. Sako was sad but continued going to school and walking around the city with his friends. That was what all the boys of his age did in those days. But, as always, he did not do well in school. Sara wore only black. She tried to stay strong like Ani had all her life, but she was unable. She would burst into tears for the slightest reason, which bothered Sako and Ruth very much. It broke their hearts to see their mother cry.

Ruth was the only one who brought joy to everyone. She asked questions, eagerly hugged everyone, and wanted to be loved. She was the only one who hugged and loved and showed affection to Raffi, which brought a smile to his face. Sako did not have much to do with his father and, since he was not studious, Raffi was not happy. He loved Sako very much but neither showed their real feelings to one another.

One morning, while Sara was home alone, Wahab came to see her and give his condolences. He had missed Sara and was very sad for her. But, when she opened the door, she did not invite him inside and showed no emotion. Wahab tried to enter and hug her but Sara told him to forget all their past and leave her forever since her daughter had paid for her sins and she was going to stop seeing him. Wahab had tears in his eyes but did not dare to say a word or touch her hands for the last time. He knew she was very serious and could see that the Sara he had known and loved had died. She did not have her fiery look anymore. Her eyes were still beautiful but were flat and he could see pain pouring out of them. She said goodbye like a ghost and left him standing tearfully before the closed door. He feared that all his hopes and love were forever locked behind that door with Sara. He left her house with a thousand memories and deep pain.

CHAPTER 19

After the War

SARA WAS STILL YOUNG AND BEAUTIFUL. For an entire year after the death of Sarina, she did not leave the house. Her hair turned snow white. She became a devoted mother and daughter and, although she did not resume intimate relations with her husband, she stayed devoted to him as a wife. Raffi now knew that he had Sara all for himself and that was a big gift at last. He did not recognize the irony of the situation. Many times Sarina had hoped she could bring her parents together, but she did not know how to accomplish this. Now, in death, she had achieved her wish!

Raffi was heartbroken but still loved Sara deeply. He pitied her for her suffering but was incapable of helping her since he was not able to cope with the loss of Sarina himself. He continued writing and publishing poems. His after-hours students were his challenge since he loved those who studied and wanted to learn. After all, he was a poet, a romantic and a quiet man.

After a year, a Jewish friend came to visit Sara and Raffi. He brought a nicely bound Old Testament and asked Sara to read it. He said that, by doing so, she would discover that she was not alone in suffering hard times in life with her family. "For thousands of years, all the prophets have had worse and often unimaginable tragedies in their lives, but the important thing is to dry the tears, respect the spirit of the departed, and start living again. And as we say, may her memory be for a blessing," he said.

Sara was moved by his words and began reading the Old Testament that same night. Little by little, she came back to her self – not to the old Sara but to a more composed and wiser person. She knew a French woman who was the seamstress to the royal court and her business was flourishing. Because Ani was watching over Ruth and Sako, Sara decided to ask for work with the seamstress.

Madame Janette was happy to have a hardworking person like Sara, who quickly learned the secrets of high couture and thus earned a steady salary. Sara enjoyed her work since Madame Janette was very kind to her. Sara discovered that being a seamstress was a complete and welcome change. After work she went directly home, where Ani had prepared a delicious dinner and had taken care of the house.

A couple of times Sara saw Wahab in the street. He tried to speak with her but she acted like a complete stranger to him. Wahab continued his work and later started teaching at the University of Tehran, but he never recovered from the loss of Sara.

Sako finished high school and decided to go to work. At first, Sara and Raffi insisted that he should go to college, but he refused and finally they gave up. He worked at various jobs and saved some money and one day announced that he was going to immigrate to America with some friends. They were sure that they could earn more money there and live a comfortable life. Sako could even resume his studies. Sara and Raffi disagreed but finally relented and he obtained his visa. On the day of his departure, everyone was crying and kissing goodbye. Ani hugged and smelled her grandson as much as she could for she was aware that it was likely that this was the last time that she would see him in this world.

Instead of going to college in America, Sako married an American-Armenian girl and settled down among other Armenian immigrants in Southern California. The Armenian community was very tight knit, and Sako had no trouble finding a good job. He sent pictures and letters and, when he had children, he sent pictures of them and everyone was happy for him and his family.

Ruth grew up without Sako's presence. She had lost both her sister and, in effect, her brother as well. Memories of both became faint in her mind. Every once in a while she received a short letter from her brother. Each time it read the same: "We are well and hope you are well too. Love, your brother." But she always remembered Sarina with tenderness. Years earlier, when she was not able to fall asleep, Sarina had told her to close her eyes and try to see all the colorful butterflies. She told her that then she would have nice dreams and sleep soundly until morning. Ruth had tried this many times, and it always worked for her. After Sarina's death, she would also try to see her, but the image was unclear, like a photograph slightly out of focus; however, she could hear Sarina's voice clearly in her heart.

Now that Sara was working for Madame Janette, Ruth missed her mother. Because Madame Janette had rush orders, Sara would stay as long as needed and sometimes Ruth would go to bed before Sara returned home. Raffi often came home with papers to correct for his after-hours students. He also did editing for a weekly newspaper, so he had little free time at home. He would talk for a few minutes with Ruth and then turn to his work, which was an imperfect shield against his pain. As a result, Ani was the only loving and caring person close to Ruth. She had become a real mother to her. She was the one who took care of Ruth and transmitted the family stories and traditions.

Ruth often thought of Wahab. She missed the good times she had spent at Wahab's house. She missed the trips and games; she missed the tall plane trees and the smell of their leaves. She had some little toys and gifts given to her by Wahab and she treasured them more dearly than ever. She continued to be the best student in her class and was considered very talented in every subject. Raffi and especially Ani were proud of her success. Sara loved it when people talked about Ruth's beauty and intelligence, and there were moments that she could recognize Wahab's handsomeness and intelligence in Ruth. Sometimes Ruth would see Wahab in the street and, in private, would excitedly tell her mother that she saw him. Sara would never ask her any questions.

Ruth was a constant reminder of Wahab and, because of that, Sara unconsciously would curse innocent Ruth for the most trivial reasons. She loved Ruth yet, at the same time, hated her deep in her heart. Sometimes she thought that Ruth's birth brought death to Sarina, because Ruth remained a witness and reminder of her adultery and sins. Sometimes she would ask herself why Sarina had died and not Ruth. Sometimes she wondered whether, if Ruth had died, it would have washed away her sins. But, immediately, she would feel guilty and think about something else. Perhaps that was one of the reasons why Ani opened her loving heart to Ruth and poured all her affection on her. As a result, Ruth became a very affectionate girl. She was able to bring together and give comfort and happiness to everyone.

On the day she graduated from Tehran University – with honors, of course – Ruth saw the eyes of her grandmother, father and mother glistening with pride and tears. They were very proud of her achievements; each of them felt that she has fulfilled their dreams fully. Ruth could see the joy in their eyes.

Returning to school, Ruth earned a master's degree. Ani, Sara and especially Raffi were proud that their daughter did so well academically. She was hired by the university as an assistant professor and quickly became popular and well-liked by her colleagues. She had friends from all religions and social classes. During a meeting with her department director, who had studied in

Paris, she was urged to obtain her doctorate in France. The director added that, if an intellectual had never studied in France and been immersed in that country's culture, he never considered him or her completely educated. He told Ruth that he was impressed by her knowledge and talent and was going to propose her for a scholarship.

The opportunity excited Ruth but, at the same time, made her sad. Ani was getting older and Ruth loved her dearly. In reality, Ruth understood that Ani always had been more a mother to her than Sara had. Ani was able to love her unconditionally – a pure and rare love. She was always there when Ruth needed her; after all, Ani had gone through so much that she understood that life was all about love and compassion. She was always courageous and hardworking and had passed all her values to Ruth. Ruth knew that she was a joy to Ani and a kind of glue to Sara and Raffi's relationship. Her departure would break their hearts and make them feel lonely. But she also knew that Iran was going through political and social crises and that, even if she continued living there, she would need to obtain her doctorate so that she could command a better position and salary.

After some days she told her family about the suggestion of her department director. Raffi and Ani immediately encouraged her to accept it. They were sincere and thinking of the impact that this opportunity could have on her future. Sara, too, was happy and encouraged her to accept. But, at the same time, she was happy at the prospect of having her daughter in Paris because she knew that it would give her the reason and opportunity to visit the city that she had discussed so much with Wahab. As much as Ruth resisted the idea of leaving home, Ani pushed her to accept. She knew of Ruth's deep love for her and, therefore, told her granddaughter that she had already lived her life and that Ruth should not worry about her but should continue studying for her future. Ani assured her that it would give her great joy to know that, in the future, there would be a Ph.D. in the family. She had dreamt of this all her life and wanted Ruth to fulfill her dream.

Everyone helped Ruth prepare for the big trip. Friends and relatives gathered in the Hakopian household the night before her departure. Some envied her luck, while others were happy for her. The next morning everyone looked sad. At the airport, Ruth kissed her mother and father goodbye and, when she kissed Ani, she felt that her grandmother was kissing her but, at the same time, smelling her deeply as if she were trying to capture and keep a part of her. Ruth's heart was heavy with sadness, but both she and Ani smiled weakly and exchanged hopeful words with each other.

Ruth touched Ani's long silver hair gently. It was silky soft and the wind blew some of it across her face. Then Ruth ran toward customs since she was unable to stay with them any longer. Once she crossed to the other side of the airport, she felt a continent separating her from her loved ones. Then she cried quietly with the pain of leaving her grandmother, whom she loved so dearly. Ruth felt that she was free but, at the same time, she understood that she was carrying a heavy load of traditions and memories on her shoulders. She felt lucky to sleep for almost the entire duration of the flight from Tehran to Paris. Ruth was very tired, since she had not slept well for days. As soon as she arrived at the airport in Paris, she called home. Everyone was excited to talk to her and, at the end, she and Ani exchanged some words of love and Ruth realized how much she already missed every one of them, especially her grandmother.

CHAPTER 20

Daniel

SHE TOOK A CAB TO HER NEW HOME at Cité Université in the 14th Arrondissement in Paris and found Maison d'Iran, the Iranian boarding house where she was going to live. She approached the information desk and asked the handsome young man behind it how to obtain her keys. He answered her questions in a very warm voice, took her papers, and, after handing her the room key and explaining some regulations, asked if she needed help with her luggage. Her room number was 910 and the young man told her that it was funny because he lived in room number 110.

Ruth was unable to turn her eyes away from him. "Who is he?" she wondered. "Is he married?" She glanced at his fingers but did not see any rings. She looked confused, and Daniel thought that she was already homesick like most of the students who, like himself, came from a foreign country.

He remembered how sad and lonely he felt when he first arrived at the student residence. And, in truth, he still felt sad when he thought of his home country and his family. He introduced himself as Daniel Cohen and assured her that she would enjoy her stay. He said that they would see a lot of each other since he was also studying for his doctorate and lived in the same house.

When Ruth took the elevator to her room, she felt that she was no longer a lonely person in that new world since she felt a warm feeling toward the young man at her side. He opened the door of her new room, set down her suitcases, and wished her a good rest and left. After she closed the door, his voice was still ringing in her ears like romantic music. She was amazed at her romantic attachment for him. How, she asked herself, could she have such feelings for a person with whom she had exchanged only a few sentences? She thought that she had never met such a handsome and kind young man.

Ruth unpacked her luggage and put her empty suitcases under the bed. Then she decorated the empty and cold student room with souvenirs from home. She hung some hand-stamped fabrics and pictures on the walls to remind her of family and country. Although her room was not large, it was clean and modern. Unlike most student housing in Paris, Maison d'Iran was newly built, and Ruth was room 910's first resident.

Darkness had fallen. Ruth knew that the student restaurant was already closed, so she decided to walk to the little café she had seen from the cab window before entering the housing park. When the elevator stopped at the lobby, she walked head down, submerged in her thoughts, without paying attention to the students who were coming in.

Then she suddenly bumped into one of them. Embarrassed, she apologized and unexpectedly saw that it was Daniel standing before her, smiling. He asked her if she needed help. Ruth answered that she was hungry and was on her way to the corner café. Daniel told her that he just finished his part-time job and, if she didn't mind, he would join her since he too had missed the cafeteria hours. She could hardly believe her good luck and happily accepted his offer. She had many friends back home in Iran, including young men. But none had captured her heart. Yet here, far from home, she met a man upon her arrival and her heart started beating faster even though she knew nothing about him or his family. Was this what everyone calls *beshert* – destiny?

Ruth and Daniel walked to the café near the Metro station; it was situated in the corner of a large park called Parc Montsouris.

The café was filled with students from throughout the world. Some spoke French while others talked in their native languages. Their voices were mixed with those of the servers, who loudly called out orders to the counter. The ringing of pinball machines was constant. Some of the young patrons were drinking coffee or tea; others were drinking *panache*, beer or wine. Most of them were arguing politics, philosophy or religion. Others were doing homework, and a few lovers were sitting in quiet corners holding hands or kissing each other from time to time. Many were smoking pungent Gaulois cigarettes. The smoke climbed lazily to the ceiling and blew into intricate patterns each time the door was opened. The entire effect, Ruth thought, was cosmopolitan and exciting – more exciting than any other place she could imagine.

This was the life of most of the Cité Université students in Paris in the late 1960's. Ruth remembered the words of her director that "One should be baptized in French culture to complete the cycle of his or her intellect." Paris was a different world in and of itself. Ruth could feel it immediately just by sitting in the café and looking around, appreciating the *liberté, égalité et fraternité* – freedom, equality and brotherhood – that the French people won in 1789 in the French Revolution and have since tried fiercely to hold onto.

When a busy waiter came to take their orders, Ruth ordered Camembert on a baguette and a cup of *café au lait*. Daniel ordered a *Croque Monsieur* with cheese only, no ham, and *panache*, which was the French name for a mixture of lemonade and beer. They started talking and asking each other questions.

They shared both a home country and a family story. He was born in Beirut, which Ruth knew about from her parents, and this brought them close together, as if they had known each other for many years. Daniel told her that he was Jewish; his mother's family was from Syria. His grandmother escaped Syria during a pogrom just after the turn of the century, when the Syrian government burned the Jewish quarter to the ground, destroying homes and businesses, and mobs killed the Jews. She was the only one in her family who was able to leave the country since her parents were killed in the massacre. She came to Lebanon and met a well-respected man who was also from Syria. His parents had sent him to Lebanon at a very young age because they never felt safe in Syria and told him it was better to settle in a more secure country. They married and had two children, a boy and a girl. They named their daughter Dinah. Like her mother, Dinah married a young man who originally came from Egypt to study in Lebanon, and the couple had two children. Daniel was their firstborn.

Daniel explained that his father's family suffered the same fate as his grandmother. In 1956, Egyptian president General Gamal Abdel Nasser nationalized the Suez Canal, precipitating a crisis that almost led to war with France and England. After America intervened, the canal remained in Egyptian hands. But Nasser then ordered all Jews to leave the country quickly. None of them were allowed to take any of their wealth or belongings – only whatever would fit into one suitcase. Jews, wealthy and poor, left behind their land, houses, automobiles, gold, silver, housewares, furniture and – the most important possession in their ancestral country – the graves of their loved ones.

They carried their memories with tears. They loved their country. They loved its sky, desert, sea and the smell of the air and of the Nile River. They thought that they belonged and were a part of the country where they were born and had grown old, from father to son, for generations.

They spoke the purest Arabic language, listened to Om Kalsoum and Mohammed Abdel Wahab's songs, and felt their heart beating at the words. They thought that the country belonged to them equally like all the Egyptians who lived there. But then they learned that politics rendered them as Jews and not as citizens because they were not born Muslim. They were foreigners in their own country.

The time had come for them to leave Egypt once more but this time they were leaving without Moses. They had worked hard but, again, they left empty-handed, leaving everything behind. They walked toward a new and unknown destination. For Daniel's grandparents the destination was Lebanon, since Daniel's father was already in Beirut. For a while they lived with their son and his family. Then they moved to their own house, worked hard, tried to form a culturally rich family, and gave their two children and their families all they could in an environment that was beautiful but never quite peaceful. Since the establishment of Israel, the politics of the region changed and, as time passed, no one felt safe in Lebanon, especially the Jews.

Lebanon was in conflict. Christians, Muslims, Druze, Kurds, Armenians and Palestinians all had lived there for many years in peace and harmony. It was said that Lebanon was the Switzerland of the Middle East and Beirut was the Paris. Yet all fell to pieces. People turned on each other, kidnapping and killing one another.

Ruth and Daniel agreed on the present and future situation of their beloved sad countries, and Ruth talked about her parents and past. At the end both felt that power-seeking politicians, failing economies and intolerance prevented their countrymen from finding happiness and prosperity. People always accepted each other until others turned them against each other.

They stayed for long time in the café talking, and each second that ticked on the clock brought these two young people closer to each other, as did each passing day. Although Ruth and Daniel were dedicated to their studies, traditions and families, at the same time they were attracted to each other's religion and culture. Life's everyday events drew them closer.

Ani fell sick in her old age and died soon without suffering. Her last words were prayers and blessing addressed to her granddaughter. Ruth was heartbroken that she was not able to be at her side while she was leaving this world, but Sara assured her that she left happy, knowing that Ruth had fulfilled her dreams. Soon after, Daniel lost his father; he traveled home to mourn with his mother and returned with hair growing on his face as required by Jewish tradition. They found consolation in their love for each other.

They respected and loved one another sincerely but did not want to commit to a serious relationship. Each had traditions deeply rooted inside themselves, and both had been taught by their parents that they should marry a person only from within their own people. Neither of them wanted to betray their parents or community by marrying outside of their religion. Ruth knew that this had been one of the main reasons her mother never married Wahab. But she felt times had changed. If one believed in peace and harmony in the world, would not the best way of reaching this goal be to mingle with everyone, love, intermarry and learn to respect each other's values and religions? Then, Ruth thought, peace would descend on the world.

By the time they finished their doctoral theses, they found themselves at City Hall, standing before the mayor and promising to love and care for each other. They did not plan a large wedding since neither had family present in the country. Besides, no religious authority would marry them. The Judaism practiced in France was traditional and conversion was so difficult and time-consuming that it was virtually impossible. And it was evident that Daniel would never convert to Christianity. So they hoped that God would bless them in silence. But, officially, they were blessed in a loud voice by the city's elected mayor. They both asked each other the question: Who converted and married Ruth and Boaz in the Bible? Ceremony was not the key to a happy life, they believed. Honesty and commitment were, and Ruth and Daniel felt strongly that they possessed both.

CHAPTER 21

A World in Change

CITÉ UNIVERSITÉ WAS BUILT IN 1925 in the heart of Paris to bring peace and understanding to its students, who then returned home to help build their nations. The founders thought that, if the students lived for three years in housing where the residents were from more than one hundred countries, they would learn to respect each other's differences and peace would flow from their experiences.

Years earlier when the King of Denmark sent his daughter, the crown princess, to Paris to study, he did so without revealing her origins. Like any other student, the princess lived in a residential hall at the Cité Université, ate at the same cafeteria that other students did, and pretty much participated in the same activities like all her classmates. Later she fell in love with a French student who was unaware that she was a princess; they married and, after the death of her father, she became the queen of her country.

The Queen of Iran, Farah Diba, had attended Cité Université the year before she married the king. She was the one who had pushed the government to build The Iranian House, where Ruth and Daniel lived. There were many stories like this about Cité Université.

But the late Sixties were a different time. The world was changing, and a cultural revolution was being waged by college youths in many countries. Different political parties were in conflict all the time, especially in the Middle East, and Paris had become an intellectual and political battleground. Idealistic youths were drawn from all over. Sometimes Ruth thought that it was like a new game for youth.

Students sang revolutionary songs, burned tires, barricaded the streets, and dug up the old paving stones upon which so many historical events had occurred in Paris and threw them at the national police. The Vietnam War was raging and being denounced by young people throughout Western Europe and the United States. On the streets of Paris, it seemed that the old order was on the verge of being overturned.

Even so, there were some quiet students who went to all their classes and diligently turned in their homework, and there were a few student lovers sitting in quiet corners holding hands or kissing each other in public, seemingly oblivious to the presence of others. They were in their own world, far from revolution and arguments.

Three events especially touched Ruth. One day there was a Vietnam peace rally at the Cité and Ruth was saddened to see that most of the students who attended were dressed in motorcycle jackets and helmets and some even carried baseball bats. (Baseball was not a sport appreciated and practiced in France, yet they had found and carried the bats.) Ruth asked herself why the young boys and girls should attend a meeting for peace when they were ready for a fight. And a fight did occur in the middle of the conference devoted to peace.

Another time she was at a birthday party for her Maronite Lebanese friend, Amira. At the time, Palestinians were widely present in Lebanon and many Christians sympathized and worked with them in their struggle against Israel. Amira's father had a famous restaurant and club facing the beach in Beirut. At her birthday party, a handsome Syrian boy with blond hair and blue eyes lifted his cup to drink to Amira's health and prosperity. He finished by saying that he prayed that Moshe Dayan, the architect of Israel's triumph in the Six-Day War, would be buried soon and that his brothers, the Palestinians, would drive all the Israelis into the sea. Everyone cheered and drank to the toast. Ruth looked at him and asked herself if he was one of the children of the Nazi SS soldiers who went into hiding in the Middle East, married Muslim girls, and infused their hate into the blood of a new innocent Arab generation.

The last experience happened the night she was invited to a friend's room, where they celebrated the birthday of an Iranian student who was working on his thesis about philosophy and Sufism, the mystical branch of Islam. Ruth never drank alcohol because her mother always complained about Raffi's drinking and smoking habits. This had dissuaded her from using alcohol or tobacco. That night she drank only lemonade while all the revolutionary Muslim boys and girls drank straight vodka, without adding water or juice to it.

Less than a week later, the Khomeinist students had suddenly become the most popular among all the revolutionary Muslims at the Cité. After they attained control of the student government, they immediately sought a ban on the nonalcoholic beer served in their little basement café and the demolition of the café itself. Ruth was surprised to see that the first boys and girls who supported these moves were the same ones who just days earlier had swallowed all that pure alcohol in front of her eyes. Now they had turned into puritan Muslims. It brought to mind a famous Iranian author greatly respected by the revolutionary students, – Sadegh Hedayat – who in his book, *Gharb Zadegi* wrote: "Many pretentious intellectuals in Iran drink alcohol and clean their lips with their sleeves and say that drinking alcohol is a sin!"

Like the majority of Armenians in Lebanon, Ruth was an Apostolic Christian-Gregorian. She had gone to church with her mother and especially with Ani. She loved to hear the organ music and the voices singing all the beautiful liturgies. But, after she turned twelve, she became curious and asked many questions about religion. But each time her parents or their priest told her, "It was so, and you should not ask too many questions." But it was not in Ruth's personality to accept indefinite answers. She needed more. She had the fearless free spirit of her mother, Sara, buttressed with a logical mind. When she did not receive what she was asking for, she took *sharia* classes at school to learn the code of law based on the Koran. She learned Arabic and studied the Koran.

Ruth always had the same unknown pull inside her toward Islam as she had for Wahab. She was told that Wahab's parents had made the pilgrimage to Mecca and, thus, were *hajjis*. Sara always took her to mosques and to *emamzadehs* – the birthplaces of prophets but, in some cases, their tombs as well. Ruth loved these holy places. The prophets' graves were protected by *zarih* – the golden fences. People came from all over the county to pray by holding onto the *zarih* or by attaching green color ribbons to it, for green is the prophets' symbolic color.

Many of the visitors, rich and poor alike, showed their devotion by throwing coins or paper money through the fence. The amount depended on their wealth or the bargain that they had made inside their being with their God. The women would pray in their *chadors*, which covered them from head to toe. One could hear their words of prayer or their cries and, as they dried their tears with a corner of their *chadors*, they would take off a golden dangle bracelet or a precious ring from a finger and throw it inside the fence. These were their donations for the poor. Later the *mullahs* – Muslim priests – collected them to help some needy people and they spent some to take care of the property.

Ruth loved the pure lamentations of the people – sad but very spiritual. The sounds of near-silent prayers were heard like the hum of bees mixed with begging and bargaining with God. Then there was the beauty of the tiles and the golden *zarih*, all mixed with the smell of rose water perfume.

But, as she studied more, her brain did not accept some of the laws and logic that were demanded by the Islamic religious authorities. She was not going to betray the religion in which she was brought up and that was older than Islam and had far fewer unreasonable restrictions. But, like Sara, Ruth never gave up loving to visit mosques and *emamzadehs*. She loved to hear all the Ramadan rituals, when the authorities would fire a cannon in the morning so people would say their prayers and eat a meal before sunrise. Another cannon was fired at sunset to remind people of the evening prayers and to break the fast. This would continue for a month. The special smell of delicious food filled the air very early in the morning and late in the evening. Ruth loved all these collective rituals and she loved to hear the prayers – *azans* – that were sung loudly at minarets.

Years before meeting Daniel, Ruth had questioned her religion. At that time, her eyes fixed on a verse in which Jesus said that he had not come to bring a new religion but wanted to make some modifications to the existing one, and he had suggested that everyone should practice the Bible and add his laws to the current practices. Ruth decided to study the Old Testament. At the beginning, it was difficult to understand all the meanings and all the names but slowly she advanced in her search. By the time she had met Daniel, she was quite knowledgeable about Judaism and happy to discover that Daniel, too, was a scholar in Judaism. He knew Hebrew and was able to read the Torah with his beautiful voice and without advance preparation. Like Ruth, he had studied Arabic and knew the language perfectly, and he loved reading the Koran and always said that it was written beautifully. He had gone to a Sunday school operated by missionaries for some time and had studied the New Testament. But his search for spirituality and God had ended with his roots in Judaism.

Ruth was very comfortable in Judaism since she found her answers in the Torah and its commentaries. When she questioned the rabbi of their community, he never told her that she had to accept what was written. Instead, he tried to find an answer and, when he was unable, he said that he would consult all his commentary books and answer her later.

Ruth finally had found her peaceful space in religion; she respected and was more comfortable in Judaism. On Saturdays she went with Daniel to the synagogue and prayed to the only God in Hebrew, Armenian and Farsi, the language of the Iranians. She looked down from the balcony and envied Daniel, who could pray and read the Torah. She was studying Hebrew and promised herself that one day she would be able to read and understand the prayer books in their original language. She kept a kosher house and read many books about the laws, traditions and spirituality of Judaism.

They moved to a small apartment in the heart of Paris. Both worked at research and teaching and established a warm family filled with love and respect for each other. A year after the wedding, Ruth heard from her mother, who wrote that doctors discovered that Raffi had advanced lung cancer and had given him a maximum of six months to live. Ruth was in her early pregnancy and wanted to visit Raffi for the last time. He had always been a kind and very honest man. They both loved and respected each other very much. But Ruth's doctor would not give her permission to travel. Ruth called her father almost every day. He always told her how proud and happy he was that her daughter had the highest educational degree and lived and worked in a city that he always dreamed of.

This was the first time that Raffi talked of his dreams. The last time that they talked, Raffi told her that Sara was treating him very kindly. He was thankful and happy that Sara had kept him at home and in his room surrounded with his books. But he was aware that it had been very hard for her to take care of him. He told Ruth that the precious time gave them the opportunity to talk together and review their life and finally solve many old conflicts and misunderstandings. Ruth made a joke and said that he should not pay attention to Sara's sharp responses. He answered: "One day you will understand all the truth and remember not to break your husband's heart in life."

Ruth was not aware that, on the day she was giving birth to their son Joseph in Paris, he was taking his first breath at the very instant when Raffi was drawing his last.

Ruth was very sad when she heard the news. Daniel tried to comfort her but she received more courage when she saw that their little baby depended entirely on her. She received new energy every moment that she held and fed the baby. Daniel visited them at the hospital room where love and hope of life was present. He was counting the days when he would take them home.

Seven days after giving birth, Ruth returned home from the hospital. Daniel had invited members of the local Jewish community to their apartment. And he had persuaded a courageous rabbi to circumcise their son, even though by Jewish law he was not a Jew.

On the circumcision day of their son, Daniel's mother, Dinah, came from Lebanon to see her grandchild and be present in his *brit mila*. She placed the baby on the lacy pillow and handed it to her son to hold while the prayers were said. Ruth's heart started beating hard and tears dropped from her eyes. She was not sure if the baby was going to suffer or not. It was her first experience. She stayed in her bedroom and listened to the prayers and, when she heard Joseph cry out followed by the *mazel tov* wishes of everyone, she understood that the ceremony had ended. After a short while Daniel appeared and placed the baby in her arms. Ruth looked lovingly at Joseph's angelic face, which seemed peaceful. Daniel smiled and said, "The rabbi gave Joseph a drop of wine so he was drunk and did not feel much pain. Now he would like to drink your milk and sleep for a while." He kissed Ruth and joined the guests, looking very proud and happy.

Daniel's mother returned home to Lebanon. The situation there was not calm and Daniel had urged her to remain with them in Paris. But Dinah answered that she had lived in Lebanon all her life, loved Beirut and that did not want to leave. She was used to her house, to the language and to life there. And she wanted to be buried next to her husband in the Jewish cemetery. Anyway, Dinah said that she was an old woman with many friends from various ethnic communities who visited each other daily, drank Turkish coffee, ate pastries that they cooked and exchanged the recipes. What would she do in Paris to pass time away?

Dinah's daughter and her family and most of Dinah's friends and neighbors had immigrated to Israel with their families after the Six-Day War because, like many other Lebanese Jews, they no longer felt safe in Lebanon, the country where they were born and had grown up. Some left for Europe; others went to America or anywhere that they had relatives and could obtain residency permits or work. But Dinah was determined to remain in Lebanon, her homeland.

ॐ

Ruth and Daniel had decided that their new son would be cared for by a stay-at-home mother. Ruth did not mind that she had studied so hard and earned her doctorate in order to be a full-time mommy. She thought that being a mother was both a very difficult and an honorable job. Besides, she could use her university knowledge to be a consultant or tutor or perform other home-based activities. Yet she would not be able to leave the house for extended times. She knew well what her family history had taught – that children missed their mother even if a loving grandmother like Ani was in her place. During this period, she cooked new dishes and tried to imitate Ani's tasty Armenian dishes and pastries. She also had time to study other subjects that she did not have time to learn about during her prior studies. Ruth called this period of motherhood her "intellectual pregnancy."

While baby Joseph was sleeping, Ruth had a lot of quiet time to think of her past. The most mind-catching for her was her mother's relationship with Wahab. Now that she was a mature, married woman, she could revive long-ago memories, analyzing and reviewing all the episodes correctly and objectively. She was fully aware of the intimate relationship between her mother and Wahab. She had tried to ask Sara some indirect questions but knew that her mother's past experiences of lying in order to protect herself had become a habit and a way of life. She could have asked questions of her grandmother or Raffi, but she never did out of respect for them.

Once, when there had been an argument between Raffi and Sara, Ruth had tried to calm them down and make peace. Raffi had told her, "One day you will find out the truth." She tried to remember and dissect all the past, from the very early age of two-and-one-half, so that she could gather her memories. Ruth remembered all the places that she had gone with her mother and Wahab. Her mother had always asked her not to talk about Wahab to anyone, even her grandmother. As a child, Ruth loved Wahab because he was a very kind person. But she always felt that there was something more to her feelings. She felt that a stream of her blood somehow was joined to Wahab's, but as a child she could not solve its mystery. Later, as an adult, she hoped to discover the truth, but she was never sure and her mother never gave her any clues. Wahab sometimes gave her little toys and her mother explained that he wanted to give her more, but what would grandmother and father say if they saw her with large toys?

As Ruth grew older, she started putting all the facts together. Her curiosity pushed her to find out why she was drawn toward Wahab. All the signs, such as their physical resemblance, pointed to her theory that Wahab was her biological father. Then one day, before leaving for Paris, she was looking for a paper and was surprised to find a nicely folded, old lace fabric in one of her father's desk drawers, which she had opened by accident. The beautiful lace attracted her attention. She removed it from the drawer and discovered a paper folded inside. When she opened it, she was shocked to find six photographs of Wahab and Sara. Ruth was thankful that no one else was at home. She took her time and looked at the pictures very carefully and with love. Although she knew that her mother's adultery was a sin, the pure love between her and Wahab fascinated her.

After she looked at all the pictures many times, she turned them over and saw dates on all the pictures in Wahab's beautiful Arabic handwriting. In one of the photos, the handsome Wahab was alone in a carriage drawn by horses. In the rest, he and Sara were together. Ruth wondered who had taken the pictures. Was it a friend who knew their secret? Or had they asked a passing stranger? She came to the last photograph, which showed Wahab and Sara in a wheat field surrounded by tall wheat and wild flowers. It was a romantic picture, and she could see all the love present in their eyes. She looked at the date and saw that it corresponded to the early months of her creation. So her mother was pregnant with her while the picture had been taken! She looked at Wahab and told him that she always loved him; she wished that Raffi and Sara had divorced for then she would have lived a much different life. She pulled the picture out of the group and told herself that she had the right to have one thing from her biological father in her life. She hid it in her wallet and knew that no one would claim the picture.

She was amazed at Sara's courage and dishonesty; by then Sara had no relations with Wahab. Yet she had hidden her love story memorabilia in her husband's office! Ruth told herself that Raffi, her father, had always been kind and loving toward her. She always had a deep love and respect for him. She had seen how devoted Raffi was to his family and how respectful he was to Ani. Although her mother had not been faithful, sincere and loving toward him, Raffi always loved and respected Sara in public and in private. She never understood his true behavior and character. Was he a weak person with no character, or was he a man who was able to forgive? Or did he love Sara and his children so much that he accepted all in silence?

Ruth remembered that, as a little girl, she was eager to visit Wahab, fall in his arms, ask for his love, and show him her love. But then she told herself that Raffi was the one who took care of her, put her through school, gave her all she needed, loved her, and was there when she was sick or healthy, sad or happy. What had Wahab done for her? He had just given her mother a tiny sperm cell and that was it. He knew the truth but he never showed her any affection after her mother stopped seeing him. She always asked herself the same question: "Which of the facts were more important in her life – the biology or the devotion of a stranger? Was her real father the one who slept with her mother or the one who took care of her?"

This inner struggle and argument were always present in Ruth's mind, but she finally decided to respect the privacy of her family and suffer in silence for the love that she always had for Wahab. Maybe this was her punishment for being the sinful fruit of adultery. But she knew there would be always something emotionally very strong present in her – maybe a curiosity and maybe the magnet of blood and biology.

Finally, Ruth told herself that Raffi was hurt and cheated by his wife once; she was not going to betray him another time, especially now that he was dead. She stayed silent all her life, in a way feeling that she was punished by having to call "Father" the man her mother had married and not to the one who had given her life. She always asked herself why she was punished to be the fruit of sin from the first day when she came to this world. Now that she was more mature and spiritual, she knew that there was always a reason for everything. Maybe this was the reason that made her a loving and compassionate person.

Life continued peacefully for Daniel, Ruth and Joseph. Every day Joseph learned a new gesture and sound and little by little he learned to talk and walk. Ruth was completely fascinated with her baby and recorded his every new movement or word in an elaborate scrapbook. Daniel had devoted himself completely to his son and wife after coming home from work. On weekends they went to different villages or parklands to show Joseph the wonders of this world. They went to Jardin de Luxembourg to watch the boats floating on the big royal pool. They went to see Guignol, the famous puppet show, and ride ponies.

Daniel and Ruth moved to a larger apartment and tried to give the best education possible to their son. After the death of Raffi, Ruth visited her mother in Iran. Sara told Ruth that she would like to move to Paris and live with her and Daniel since she did not want to live alone in Iran anymore. The people closest to her were now dead and she was lonely. Ruth called Daniel, who readily agreed, and she stayed a little longer to help her mother pack and move to France with her.

Before their departure, Ruth went to the Armenian cemetery to pay her respects to her sister, Sarina; her grandmother, Ani; and her father, Raffi, for the last time. She talked, prayed and cried with each of them separately since she knew that it probably was the last time that she would be able to visit her loved ones' graves. She did not expect to return to Iran and resume her old job, which was still available to her. She had seen in Paris the young Iranian students who shouted for the death of the Shah and his family. She knew that a dramatic change had occurred in Iranian society and that the nation was on the edge of revolution.

One day, while still in Tehran, Ruth found herself walking to a street corner where Wahab often used to cross. Suddenly her heart beat faster as she saw Wahab walking in her direction. She really wanted to see him one more time, and he was pleased to see her. He was as handsome as always. His blue eyes were still attractive but his eyelids rested lower on his eyes, making them more mysterious. He first asked her how Sara was doing and then asked about her and her brother. She was excited to give him indirectly the news that he was a grandfather. She thought that he might say something to acknowledge that fact, but he respected Sara's secret and said, in a voice that seemed sad, that he was happy for her.

Then, in a faraway voice, he told Ruth that some years earlier, when he went to visit his family, his mother and father insisted that he should close his business in Iran and leave for Lebanon or anywhere else. His parents had cried and said that they were approaching the end of their lives and wanted to see him married and continuing the family name. They proposed an arranged marriage with an Arab Palestinian girl from a good family. Wahab said that he accepted their offer out of respect for his parents. But he did not care for anyone except the only woman that he loved. In the end, he added, he understood the present explosive situation in Iran and was closing his business and moving back with his family to Beirut and later to Paris. He had a son and a daughter.

Ruth smelled alcohol on Wahab's breath and was sad for him since she knew that alcohol had become his refuge ever since Sara left him. As Ruth said goodbye, Wahab asked her to give his regards to her mother. Ruth was sad to see such an intelligent and charming man broken down. He was almost like a soulless person. He looked like the walking dead. She thought that Wahab's soul died the day Sara had pushed him away forever. She suspected that Wahab was a weak man by nature and that was the reason that, even after so many years of relations, he had not been able to convince Sara to marry him, or to leave her once and for all. Instead, he had wasted his life in a hopeless relationship that did not exist. Ruth looked at Wahab for the last time, as if she were leaving another grave of a beloved one. She was disappointed that he never mentioned or showed her any paternal emotions.

While walking home alone, she wondered if men and women are created differently from birth. As soon as men feel warm and safe in a place, they stay there forever and do not move. In contrast, women are curious and seeking creatures. Even when they feel warm and safe in a place, they always look for adventure in their lives. Then she remembered the story of Adam and Eve in Paradise, which was her joke with Daniel. Ruth always told him that if Adam was going to live in Paradise forever, it would never cross his mind to disobey God and eat the forbidden fruit from the Tree of Knowledge. But, almost immediately after God created a woman to be at Adam's side, she would bite the apple and pass it to her husband.

Once at home, Ruth told Sara that she had met Wahab and relayed all the news. Sara answered her in an indifferent voice that she knew he had married and had children. Even so, the last time that she had met him on the street he had said, "Now that you have lost your husband and mother, and your children have grown and left the country, I still ask you to marry me!" But this time Sara had refused his offer because she had found her true love in Raffi!

CHAPTER 22

The Cohens in Paris

RUTH AND SARA FLEW TO PARIS where they joined Daniel and Joseph in their apartment. Sara tried to help Ruth maintain the home and care for Joseph, but Ruth could not stop comparing her to her grandmother. She was shocked and disappointed to discover that her mother was a very different person than Ani. There was little similarity between Ruth's mother and Ruth's mother's mother. Ruth had to readjust her expectations and feelings toward her mother and was surprised to learn that people can live a lifetime together but still not know each other well.

In the late 1970's, the world was getting crazy again. The war between the Arabs and Israelis in the Middle East had not stopped. It appeared to be like young children's attitudes in games: When one of the political chiefs did something, the opposing politicians retaliated immediately and all the innocent citizens suffered the consequences. In this chaos, a wise man named Anwar al-Sadat, the president of Egypt – after showing his force and bravery in the Yom Kippur War in 1973, which claimed many Arab and Jewish lives – participated in peace talks and finally recognized Israel as a legitimate state. He was courageous enough to sign a peace treaty with Israel, his old enemy, and for the first time a Muslim leader visited Israel. He was a brave man and a true Muslim. But, of course, there were many who were against peace in the Middle East and were doing all to prevent it. These conflicts also played out in Paris. Bombs exploded in Jewish and Egyptian cultural centers and prayer houses.

Once, when Ruth was buying books from the Oriental Bookstore in Rue Petit Prince, she was shaken by a strong explosion. After regaining her composure, she walked down the street to the Jardin de Luxembourg and discovered that the target had been a Jewish kosher restaurant serving the students of the nearby universities who respected the laws of kashrut. Innocent young boys and girls who had been eating lunch were carried on stretchers to the ambulances as a circle of people watched quietly and indifferently. Ruth felt the warmth of her tears in her eyes and she cried loudly, "How come everyone is so indifferent? Is the Holocaust starting all over again and you are just watching in silence? Haven't you learned your lessons yet? The first target always starts with Jews and then it is followed by others." Some looked at her in silent amazement and others felt the guilt and quickly left the scene.

A week later, when she was returning from a concert, again the area was shaken by an explosion. This time the target was the Egyptian Cultural Center. Two cousins – the president of Egypt and prime minister of Israel – had shaken hands peacefully after many wars and much bloodshed, but their decision did not please the policymakers of some countries. In the Egyptian Cultural Center, great lectures were given in French or Arabic about literature, history and Muslim philosophy. One more time a group of extremists showed its anger and vengeance by retaliating, this time bombing a cultural center because of a rare individual – a president who won the Nobel Peace Prize, who saved lives by not sending young men of his country to die on battlefields, and who brought peace and pride to his country.

Everyone was fascinated by Sadat. He became the true symbol of a real Muslim man by respecting his religion and traditions. He was respected by even the Iranians who hated him because some years later he would become the only world and Arab leader to offer his hospitality to his ailing friend, the Shah of Iran and his family. Others had often boasted that they were the friends of the Shah and the queen but quickly deserted them when they lost everything.

Two months before the Iranian revolution, United States President Jimmy Carter and his wife, Rosalynn, wanted to visit their friend, the Shah, and his wife and pass Christmas with their Muslim friends. But later, when the sick Shah was discharged from a New York hospital after treatment for cancer, he could not find a place to stay. He who had golden palaces in Iran and lavish homes in other countries, who was flattered and courted by many governments, found only closed doors. Even the Iranians who shouted "Death to the Shah" in front of the hospital could not understand why President Carter did not invite the Shah and his family to stay at his Georgia peanut farm as his personal guests.

It was only Sadat who would extend an invitation. He was aware that his action was not a popular one but it was a humane one – a gesture that a true friend would offer to an old fallen friend. He was the only one who put his life in danger and invited the Shah of Iran to Egypt. He was a friend when the Shah ruled as the powerful king of Iran and remained a friend when the Shah was abandoned by all others. Later, Sadat was assassinated by members of his own military.

Months after the Egyptian Cultural Center bombing – on the first day of Passover, which was in the spring – Daniel left early to pray at the synagogue. As Ruth and Joseph were getting ready to join Daniel, the phone rang. The caller was a young man who spoke perfect French. He asked Ruth if Daniel was Jewish. Ruth thought that probably the young man was seeking a prayer house or perhaps was a stranger in the city looking for a host family for the holy days.

On Passover night, every family puts out an extra set of tableware for an unexpected guest. And the Passover prayers call on Jews to let anyone who is a stranger or does not have food to eat to join the service of Seder. Some people dedicate the extra seat to the Prophet Elijah, who will appear before the arrival of the Messiah and prepare for His arrival.

Ruth asked the caller if she could help him. The man repeated his question. Again, Ruth asked if she could help. But he only repeated his question, over and over. Ruth calmly told him that, yes, they were Jewish. Then, feeling a threat in his voice, she added, "Yes, we are Jewish, as you are and all the people in the city are. Now how can I help you?"

The voice became serious and harsh. "So wait and see the awful things that are going to happen to your family soon." The line went dead with a sharp click.

Ruth was a brave woman, but this incident shook her. What worried her most were the background sounds during the call, noises that sounded like two-way radio squawks. The two bombings in the city immediately came to mind.

She quickly finished dressing and ran to the synagogue with Joseph. She saw that the building was still standing but there was a police car parked in front of the entrance – something she had never seen before. She hurriedly entered and, when she saw Daniel, she was so happy that she kissed his hands. He asked what had happened. She explained all and asked him to accompany her to the police station. After they filled the complaint, she asked the officer if he knew why a patrol car had been parked in front of the synagogue. He was polite but never gave a direct answer.

The officer told Ruth and Daniel that the police would patrol the street in front of their house for a week and advised them to be careful for a while, watch their surroundings, and report any unusual events. Over the next few days, other members of the Jewish community received similar phone calls. Ruth, who was a very sensitive person because of her family's experiences, always took these events more seriously than Daniel. This incident made her think of the security and well-being of her family. She could see that Muslim immigrants, with their high birth rate, would eventually be able to exert power in France, either by street actions or political involvement. Ruth remembered Joseph's happy face when he left for the synagogue that fateful morning. His beautiful eyes were shining of innocence and joy and leaving France would be the last thing on his mind. Yet she understood that there were parents who have filled the minds and hearts of their children with hate and vowed that she would never become like her grandparents, who waited until it was too late to leave.

There were two lessons that Ruth learned from this event. The first occurred the day after she received the threatening call. She packed all the food that she had prepared for Passover and she, Daniel and Joseph went to the village house where they used to go for vacations. They read from the Haggadah that night, recited the story of the Jews' departure from Egypt, and ate their dinner.

Ruth sat in the garden, and the peaceful atmosphere of that spring night lightened her spirit. She remembered the entire story that they had just read and told herself that life was only in the hands of God. Someone might attempt to kill a person, but if it was not his time to die, the person would remain alive regardless of all. Then she told herself that, if it was their destiny to die just then, they could have had an accident and perished while driving four hours to this village. It might be even right at that moment that the person who had called them had died by another accident. Who knows about the wonders of God!

One evening, some days after they returned to Paris, Monsieur and Madame Levy from their community came to visit them and express their sympathy for what had happened. They told Ruth and Daniel that there were other Jews who had received similar calls. Mr. Levy had asked the telephone company to remove his name from the phone directory and suggested that Daniel do the same.

Daniel replied that, if all the Jews asked the telephone company to remove their names from the directory, then Jews would not be able to find assistance when needed. "Anti-Semites are always able to find you anywhere, even if you change your name or have an unlisted phone number," he said. "So why bother?" Ruth said that she had concluded that life and death were in the hands of God and no one else. "How do we know," she added, "that among us sitting here there is no sickness destroying us right at this moment?"

The Levys were very well liked by everyone and had just started their retirement. They said they were planning to visit their two children and their grandchildren, both of whom were married. One lived in Canada and the other in Israel. A month later a big shock hit all the community members when they received a call from Madame Levy. In tears she told them that while Mr. Levy was eating a carrot, he had great difficulty swallowing it. So the next day they went to the doctor and discovered that Mr. Levy's stomach was completely filled with cancer. The doctors wanted to operate on him, although they said there was just one percent of success. He died exactly six months after the telephone incident. Everyone was shocked by his death, since he looked perfectly healthy. Ruth felt bad and reproached herself. Why had she said what she said that evening? She felt that, in a way, she had predicted Mr. Levy's illness.

By then Ruth was ready to abandon all and move from one country to another to find the best place for her family's safety. After all, she asked herself, don't female cats transport their kittens to seven different locations until they find the safest and the most comfortable location for them? She talked to Daniel and persuaded him to start thinking seriously about emigrating. It would be a major step, especially because they had a nice apartment and Daniel had a secure and well-paying job, generous health insurance, a guaranteed retirement income, and – perhaps most important of all – forty days of vacation per year. Moreover, both were completely absorbed in the French culture and loved the life in France.

But for both of them material things were not all that important. Ruth knew from experience that one could always buy goods again. But it was important to live in a safe environment. The ideal then was the United States. Ruth's brother had been an American citizen for a long time. When Ruth explained the situation, Sako immediately offered to be Ruth and Daniel's sponsor. Soon they, little Joseph and Sara were in Los Angeles. They knew that Los Angeles had earthquake fault lines running through it and like all American big cities suffered from violent crimes. But, by then, Ruth also knew that nowhere in the world was safe anymore. After a while, Ruth and Daniel were able to obtain their Green Cards. At least, Los Angeles offered wonderful weather and the chance for a fresh start.

CHAPTER 23

The Cohens in America

RUTH AND DANIEL decided to raise Joseph in a single religion. Theirs would be an American Jewish family, and Joseph would be brought up as a Jew. His parents agreed that, when he grew older, he would make his choices for his life but, while he was young, it was better for him to stand on the ancient ground of the Jewish religion. Joseph was a talented and intelligent boy and quickly learned English.

Sara was happy in America because she met many of her old friends and neighbors from Iran who had fled the country before and after the revolution. She could spend long hours at the home of one or the other, where over tea and pastry they would lament having had to leave Iran and rejoice that they were in the United States. Sara, too, learned English, although she always spoke it with a notable accent. Ruth and Daniel's English wasn't so much accented as it was inflected. As for Joseph, his English was indistinguishable from any native-born Californian.

Even so, the Cohen household in America was home to many languages, just as it had been in France. Sara and Ruth spoke Armenian together and, when Daniel's family visited, they conversed in Hebrew, Arabic and French. When Ruth's friends visited, they spoke Armenian, Farsi and English. So Joseph, like his father and mother, was growing up in a multicultural environment. It was enriching, but little Joseph was unburdened by this realization.

Sako, who had become a very successful businessman, had rented a comfortable apartment for the Cohens. It was in an attractive and safe neighborhood. Even though a large number of

Iranian immigrants lived there, a synagogue was within walking distance. But the most important thing for a new immigrant was to find the right job and get used to the new environment. Most of all, it was scary for Ruth not to have health insurance, since she was used to the best health care system in the world in France. One of their friends, who had gone through similar difficulties, told Ruth and Daniel, "It is hard to get used to life in America, but people who are determined to work hard make it in the end."

He gave them two pieces of advice. "Life sometimes resembles a cold swimming pool. Just putting legs and hands into the water does not help you get used to how cold it is. Instead, one should plunge immediately into the pool. Then the water does not seem as cold. Also, do not compare life in France with life in America. It's not that one is better than the other. It is that they are different."

Daniel, too, told Ruth, "One should accept things as they are and not compare anything or anyone."

Life is difficult for any immigrant in a new country, but with the years of experience and higher education that Ruth and Daniel had, they expected to find jobs quickly. To their dismay, when they applied for jobs, they were told that they were overqualified. They had never encountered this before. How can one be too good to be hired? Finally, after some months of searching, Daniel was hired for an interesting job but the salary was not high. Friends told them that most of the new immigrants face the same condition with their first jobs. But after some months, they learned the job market and life became better. Ruth found a part-time job so that she could take care of Joseph when he was out of school. They attended Temple Beth Am. The members and the rabbis were very kind to them. They invited them to their homes and became friends. Joseph, too, found new friends, although they were very different from the friends that he once had in France.

"When you live in Paris, it takes a long time to be accepted by your neighbors or co-workers as a friend and invited to their homes," Ruth wrote one of her friends in Paris. "But once you are accepted, they remain your friends forever. Even if you move to another city or country and do not see them for years, as soon as you meet them again, their friendship is present. On the contrary, in America and especially in Los Angeles, people are very friendly; they talk to you in grocery stores while waiting for the cashier. They tell you their entire life story. Also, when you are a new immigrant, many people come to you like angels. They help you, give you whatever you need, and they say, "I understand your situation. I remember that we were just like you when we first came to this country." But once you have come out of your difficulties, they disappear. You think that they were your friends, but then I think the expression is "they dump you.""

Life was getting better for the Cohens in America. They bought a small house with a lemon tree in the backyard. Joseph had become completely Americanized. He was first in his class, doing especially well in math, language and sports. He practiced fencing, and played the violin beautifully, participating in many competitions and often winning First Prize.

Early in November 1984, Daniel's cousin called him from Israel. He said he had heard from a soldier, who was with an army unit stationed in Beirut, that Daniel's mother, Dinah, was very ill. But she was hiding it from everyone since she did not want to bother any of her children. Her daughter, who lived in Israel, would not be able to do much because it was not safe for Israeli

Jews to travel to Beirut. Dinah was sure that life was difficult for Daniel and Ruth in a new country and, therefore, did not want to bother them with her problems.

The Jewish community in Beirut, once very large, had shrunk to only a hundred or so individuals, mostly elderly. They were told to leave the country since it was not safe for Jews to live there anymore. But most of them were emotionally stuck in Lebanon, the country in which they had been born and grown old. Their choice was to stay or immigrate to Israel. If they chose not to go to Israel, it was very difficult to obtain permission to live in the United States or a European country. So most decided to continue living in Lebanon; many, like Dinah, wanted to be buried next to their husbands or dear ones.

There were a few who were like Shlomo Hallak, a fifty-nine-year-old physician. He was born in Lebanon and had a thriving, although not especially profitable, pediatric practice. He loved his profession and was needed in his country. There were so many parents – Christian and Muslim alike – who needed his help for their children. He knew all of them well since he visited the children often in their houses.

He sent his wife and son to Paris, but what could he do in a new country like France? Was he going to start studying all over again and pass board examinations at his age? So he chose to stay since he did not feel any danger for his life and was very satisfied to help others professionally. He had even saved the son of a very famous Palestinian leader from death. All the Arab women loved him because he took care of their children even if they did not have money to pay for his visits. Muslims and Christians, Druze and Kurds – all loved and respected Shlomo, although everyone knew that he was Jewish.

Daniel thought about what his cousin had told him and explained to Ruth that he had decided to visit his mother and ask or force her to leave the country. The political situation was unstable in Beirut. Ruth did not feel it was safe for Daniel to travel, but Dinah was his mother. When they talked to her, Dinal said, *"Inshalah"* – that she would feel better soon – insisting that Daniel did not need to visit her and that he should stay home with his wife and son.

Ruth worried for him but she knew Daniel had to do what he felt was necessary. She told him that she was not comfortable at the thought of his going to such a dangerous part of the world, but she convinced herself that, if something should happen it was meant to be, no matter where Daniel was. They lived on a multitude of faults in Los Angeles and, at any moment, an earthquake could occur. And even when it happened, not everyone died. It always depended on whose name was chosen from the book of life!

Daniel strongly felt his responsibility as a son toward his mother. The education that he had received was to respect parents and help them when needed. He also knew that the Jewish community in Lebanon was so small that it did not have any impact on the country's politics. In essence, no one in Lebanon cared about the Jews. So he bought his ticket and left.

The Iranian revolution was gathering strength and Khomeini's supporters were trying to expand their influence in the Middle East. They had already empowered the Shiites in southern Lebanon. They wanted to buy arms from the United States, but President Ronald Reagan refused to sell them to Iran. Everyone was fighting against everyone else.

ॐ

On the blue Mediterranean, the city of Beirut – now the lost Paradise of the Middle East – had practically turned into hell. Bombs exploded everywhere; each political group kidnapped men from opposing groups, and whoever had guns would use them when needed. The Kurds and Shiites, who were advancing toward the city, occupied any vacant apartments or houses, even if the residents were gone for just an afternoon. The father of one of Daniel's school friends had visited a relative for half a day and, when he returned to his apartment, he found it occupied by a Kurdish couple with six children. He asked them what they were doing inside his apartment. The Kurd replied, "No one was in the house and I needed a roof over the head of my wife and children."

"Didn't you see that I was living in my apartment? After all, when I left in the morning my bathrobe was still damp."

"I also took a bath and used it and now it is wet."

"Didn't you see that there were fruits and food in the refrigerator?"

This time the woman answered. "Yes, we saw the food and the children ate it all."

By then the Kurdish man was annoyed with this questioning. "What is the big deal?" he asked. "Anyway, you are just one person. Why do you need to have all these rooms alone for yourself? Take the small room and leave us alone."

The father of Daniel's friend was obliged to leave his home since there were no legal authorities who could have come to his aid and solve the problem.

No one was safe in the city, not even the head of state or the leaders of the different political factions. But, still, people lived there, celebrated weddings and births, and buried assassinated dear ones. Humans, young and old, became used to all kind of conditions.

As soon as the residents of Beirut heard gunfire or sensed danger, they ran to their houses, closed the doors and windows, and remained inside until they felt it was safe to come out again. Sometimes they were buried in their houses if they were the target, or if their houses were blown up by accident.

Daniel arrived in Beirut without incident and immediately saw that his mother was very ill. Doctor Hallak had taken care of her the entire time. He told Daniel that he had done all he could and that she was not able to travel for the time being. Perhaps Daniel's presence would give her moral support to find the strength to travel at a later time.

Daniel tried his best to take care of his mother. He had a hard time finding food or medication. He could buy what he needed only by bribing people. This was the way of life for everyone. When Dinah felt a little better, she agreed to leave the country with her son. Some of Daniel's old friends – who came from the Christian, Muslim and Palestinian communities and were still living in the country – visited him. They were happy to share childhood memories together and talk about the peaceful times that they had enjoyed before. Most of them looked older than their actual ages. Each of them had lost one or more members of their families to the violence.

Finally, Dinah felt a little better and pretended to be stronger so that they could leave the country. On the Friday morning before their departure, Dinah and Daniel visited the grave of her husband and his father for the last time. A friend drove them to the cemetery and, on the way back, they were able to buy some food for their last Shabbat dinner.

In the afternoon, Daniel prepared the dinner. Their luggage was ready for their departure. It was an emotional event for both of them since they knew that they were having their last Shabbat dinner in their old house where there were so many memories from the old days. Although Dinah did not want Daniel to come to Beirut, now that he was there at the dinner table, she was happy that her son – a man – was blessing her table.

As Daniel recited the prayers of Shabbat and blessed the wine and the bread, the doorbell rang. Dinah said it could be Doctor Hallak, since she had invited him for the dinner. He had asked her not to wait for him because he always had emergencies and so was late for many invitations. Daniel opened the door and, before he could say a word, Dinah watched with horror as two gunmen grabbed her son and dragged him to a new red BMW that was parked in front of their gate. They forced Daniel into the car and drove off immediately.

Dinah tried to call out after them but they had already disappeared. She cried and asked for help. Neighbors came out of their houses to see what had happened. Everyone was in shock. Dinah's Christian and Palestinian neighbors told her that they would never take such an action against a Jewish man, especially a person like Daniel. Dinah knew that they were sincere for, after all these years, even with the existing conflicts with Israel, the Palestinian authorities in Beirut had always tried to show the outside world that they were in conflict with Israel, not the Jews. Now that had changed. It was true that the country was in chaos, but each faction had its own rules of kidnapping and retaliation. Daniel was not a person of interest to them. In tears, Dinah told her neighbors that the men who took her son did not look like Lebanese; they looked more like strangers.

One of the men told Dinah that he would immediately inform the authorities and that she had to tell his family in America. Doctor Hallak arrived and Dinah, who was crying violently, kept repeating that it was all her fault. Why had not she died before her son came to visit her? No one was able to comfort her. She cried, fainted, awoke, talked to herself, prayed and cried. When she came to her senses, Doctor Hallak told her that Daniel would probably be returned tomorrow since he was an innocent person and everyone knew that he was not involved in politics. His abductors had made a mistake; meanwhile, Doctor Hallak would use his influence and contact all his influential patients to see how they could help. She had to have faith and patience. He asked her to swallow the pill that he had in his hand since the best thing for her was to sleep. A Palestinian neighbor promised to stay with her that night.

The fresh bread that had been blessed by Daniel was still on his plate. The chicken soup was still ready, waiting to be served.

There was no news from Daniel or his two kidnappers the following day. The authorities said that they would do their best to find him, but one police officer admitted, "The situation is so dangerous in the city that even we don't know ourselves if we will arrive home safe and see our wives and children every night."

That same Friday night, while Haim Cohen Hallaleh was blessing his wife Sheila and their three young sons at the Shabbat table before starting to serve dinner, the doorbell rang and two gunmen dragged him to a red BMW and disappeared. Sheila and the children remained in the doorway, shocked and frozen with fear like Roman statues, and then they cried for help.

Haim's nickname was Hay. Everyone in the neighborhood knew him and his family. They were well liked by all. He and his wife were born in Beirut and both loved Lebanon very much. When danger became apparent, they realized that they could either stay in Lebanon or immigrate to Israel, because visas elsewhere were not available. They were aware that the Israeli government gave all kinds of aid to new immigrants, such as help in finding jobs, free lodging, free health care and free schooling for the children.

But Hay refused to live in Israel; he loved Beirut and decided to remain there. He and his wife were the only Jewish married couple in their thirties and they had young children. He had many friends in Lebanon from all factions of religion and politics. He loved his wife and his three sons. He was not very religious and followed his religion mostly by tradition. He did not belong to any political party. He was just an accountant in a department store. Everyone loved him at his job; his boss greatly respected him for his hard work and honesty.

When friends asked Hay why he did not immigrate to Israel, he answered, "I have three sons who are born in Beirut. They have Muslim, Palestinian and Christian friends; so do I and my wife. In Israel everyone has to serve in the army, and all the boys are obliged to enter the military after high school. How can I, my wife or sons point their guns if, God forbid, there was another conflict between Israel and Lebanon one day? How can we kill our friends whom we love so much?"

Again, everyone came to support Sheila and her sons. Dinah visited her and they cried together for hours. The anguish of not knowing where their son and husband were tormented them.

Doctor Hallak tried to calm both the women and the children. He assured them that surely a mistake had been made and that the authorities were trying to help and find Hay and Daniel. The next day everyone heard loud shouts of *"Alaho Akbar!"*

coming from the Muslim women who were begging for help in Arabic. Dinah and Sheila went out and were shocked to see that many women and children were running in the street and some were crying hysterically. They asked a neighbor what had happened, and she told them that the two men in a red car had kidnapped Doctor Hallak. All the women had begged the two men to leave him for their community and take them instead. But the two men brutally pushed the women aside, savagely grabbed Doctor Hallak, pushed him into the red BMW, and drove off. It was daytime and so the men were not at home. Some of the women even ran to their houses and grabbed their husbands' guns but, when they came out, the car had disappeared.

During the following days, the gunmen in the red BMW also kidnapped Yehuda Benesti, sixty-eight years old, and his two sons, Ibrahim, age forty, and Joseph, thirty-three. All three worked in their father's gift shop. Then it was the turn for Shimon Tarab, a sixty-year-old retired professor. After that came Solomon Serour, sixty-eight, the only employee of the Jewish funeral house, who stayed late to do his *mitzvah* – good deeds. And others followed: David Sasson, sixty, was a pharmaceutical executive; Shlomo Mizrahi, fifty-four, was an electrical engineer. And there was also Reuben Jammous, fifty-seven. All these men had two things in common: They loved the country that they were born in and they were Jewish by faith. None was involved in politics in any way.

Daniel had called Ruth on the Friday afternoon when he and his mother returned from the cemetery to give her the good news that Dinah had agreed to travel with him to America on the following day. He asked her to kiss Joseph and take good care of herself; in a couple of days they would be together. That he did not call on the following day was normal. Ruth cleaned the house and prepared Daniel's favorite food for his arrival.

On Monday Joseph had his music theory and violin lesson at the Performing Arts School after his regular school classes. On her way to the school, Ruth bought *Le Monde* from a newsstand, picked up Joseph, and drove him to the music school. It had become a luxury for her to buy the French newspaper, which she and Daniel used to receive and enjoy every day in Paris. Once Joseph was in his music theory class, Ruth had two hours of free time. At that time the school was on Thirty-Second Street near the University of Southern California. Ruth walked toward the USC campus. She loved to sit on the benches there, watch the young students, and remember when Daniel would come to pick her up at the Sorbonne. It was a beautiful sunny day, like most days in Los Angeles. She sat on her favorite bench and closed her eyes for a moment, absorbing the warmth of the sun peacefully.

While she was relaxing, she thought of Daniel and about how much she had missed him in that short period of separation. Over all these years, their love had steadily strengthened and the difficulties of their lives had only brought them closer to each other. For a moment she saw Daniel's gentle face approaching hers to kiss her. She smiled at the thought that, by the end of the following day, he would squeeze her in his arms at the airport.

A couple of young students passed by her bench, talking and laughing loudly. It was as if they woke her from her sweet dreams. She took *Le Monde* from under her arm, read the front page headlines, and then turned to the back page, where all the important news was summarized. Suddenly, her eyes caught one story and her heart stopped. The headline said that two Jewish men had been kidnapped in Beirut on Friday night from their houses. When she started reading the article, she thought that she would faint. Daniel was the first person kidnapped that night. At first she did not believe it. She read it again, and then she wanted to cry, to shout, to run and tell everyone. But she did nothing. It was as if her legs were planted in the hot asphalt. She did not have the strength to stand, walk or talk. She sat motionless without a sound, as tears covered her face.

She looked at her watch. She still had half an hour before Joseph would finish his class. Anyway, what could she do at that hour of the day? All the government offices were closed, and she did not know where to start. She knew a few people – some parents at school, Joseph's teachers, some co-workers, members of the synagogue, and the rabbis. But what could these simple people do to fight a terrorist group?! She did not have much knowledge about the American government and institutions. She and Daniel were not even American citizens yet.

As soon as she came to her senses, she read the article again over and over, hoping that perhaps it was not her Daniel or maybe she had made a mistake. The article said that the abductors belonged to a Muslim fundamentalist Shiite militant group that called itself "the Organization of the Oppressed in the World." She asked herself what kind of oppressed people they were if they were oppressing innocent people by kidnapping them.

By now Ruth was thinking more clearly. She got up from the park bench and ran to a telephone booth, dialed 411, and asked for the numbers of the Lebanese and French consulates. First she called the Lebanese Consulate and was able to speak to the general consul of Lebanon in Los Angeles. She introduced herself and asked for his help. She swore that her husband was innocent of any wrongdoing and had no political activities. He was a very kind husband and father. The consul told her that he had been informed of the kidnapping but had no power to help and, in fact, did not even know where to turn for help.

"Even I myself am in danger all the time," he told Ruth. "When I am at home or am leaving for the consulate, even in the U.S., I am not sure that someone will not kidnap or kill me before nightfall. I will try all my best to help your husband to return to his family. But I am not very optimistic for a successful outcome."

Ruth then called the French Consulate. The answering machine message said to call back the next morning after ten o'clock.

She then called some friends. Everyone who knew Daniel was shocked at the news and said that they would visit her after dinner. She did not call her mother, Sara, or brother, Sako. What, she asked herself, could they do?

She finally called the rabbi of her temple. At first, he was unable to say a word. Then he repeated that he was sorry, very sorry. This was followed by a long silence as if he was unable to compose his thoughts. He finally said, "I will be at your house in two hours and, meanwhile, I will talk to some congregants who teach law at USC and UCLA and ask what is the best way to approach the problem and which institutions could be helpful."

Ruth then called Daniel's mother in Beirut. As soon as Ruth heard Dinah's voice, she broke down in tears and asked what had happened exactly. Dinah too was crying. She asked for Ruth's forgiveness since it was her fault that Daniel came to Lebanon. She did not know any more than what was in the newspaper article. Ruth tried to calm down her elderly mother-in-law and told her to pray and not to blame herself. Help is coming, she told Dinah.

CHAPTER 24

Life without Daniel

WHEN RUTH TOLD JOSEPH that his father had been kidnapped, the boy asked, "Why?" But beyond that, he didn't say much and seemed to withdraw into himself. Ruth wished she knew how to console him, but the fact was that she could not console herself. She and Joseph were sad and left all alone in a huge country they hardly knew.

Ruth did not know what to do. She thought about going to Beirut to try to find Daniel. But she did not know anyone in Lebanon except her mother-in-law and, even if she went there, what could she really expect to accomplish? And what about Joseph? He wasn't old enough to stay home all alone. And who would take him to school? Finally, Ruth called the State Department in Washington. A Robert Kingston told her that they knew about the kidnappings. In a practiced but sincere-sounding voice, he advised her to remain in America and have patience. Authorities from several countries were doing their best to free the hostages, he said, especially since the capture of Doctor Hallak. All the Lebanese communities were asking for his freedom.

A friend suggested that she call the Israeli general consul in Los Angeles. He answered the phone and spoke with Ruth in a kind but resigned voice. "The Israeli government is following the abduction of the Jews of Lebanon but, unfortunately, we are not able to help much because, although they are Jews, they are not Israelis. If Israel took any action, then the kidnappers would announce that the hostages are Israeli spies. So we have to be careful but will do our best to help. If we have any new information, I will let you know."

Ruth then called the American Red Cross, hoping that it could help. The woman who answered disappointed her. She was either a very insensitive person or had too much work to do. She told Ruth that their hands were tied and that they mostly "deal with the bodies." Ruth was shocked to hear her words and slammed down the phone.

৵

Several months passed. Ruth now worked full-time in order to support herself and Joseph. Sako and Sara tried to help her as much as they could. When Ruth was alone at night, she was horrified to imagine where Daniel was kept and in what conditions. She needed someone to knock her out so that she could go to sleep and not think. There was no news, not even a single word from anyone about the thirteen innocent hostages who had been abducted by an unknown group. "The oppressed people of the world who drive a brand-new red BMW," Ruth thought bitterly. There was word that the group belonged to the fanatical Shiites of South Lebanon, who were under the influence of the Khomeini government in Iran.

Ruth often called Dinah since she was aware that Dinah's health was deteriorating day by day. Once she even talked to Sheila, the wife of Hay, who was visiting Dinah. They both cried.

"I tried to force Dinah to eat something or drink water," Sheila told Ruth. "But she refuses all, even her medication. She only drinks coffee and repeats that she put her son in danger." Near the end of the conversation, Sheila asked Ruth if she could help her somehow, since she was not able to find a job and their three young children needed food and clothing. Ruth understood that Sheila thought that, because she was in America, she probably was wealthy. What Sheila did not know was that Ruth herself needed help.

Nonetheless, Ruth promised to try to help. She called the people who were helping her and asked them if they could find a way to help Sheila in Beirut. She especially hoped that those who had ties to France could help because France always had a better relationship with the Arabs than most other nations. Lebanon used to be called "the Daughter of France." Ruth also called one of the Jewish organizations on behalf of Sheila and her children.

Nine months passed. On December 24, Christmas Eve, Ruth received a call from Mr. Kingston of the State Department. He informed her in a sad voice that they had found the bodies of Daniel and Hay. Then he added that each was shot three times and their bodies had been thrown into the courtyard of a church in Beirut.

Ruth fainted. It was fortunate that Sara and Sako's family were in her house. Sako picked up the phone and asked the man who he was and then received the bad news. Mr. Kingston told him that Ruth should call him later to see how they could help her with returning the body to Los Angeles. Joseph was in shock and seemed frozen; he was trying to take care of his mother.

In a way, Ruth was now comforted to know that at least Daniel was no longer suffering at the hands of the kidnappers and that his spirit was free to fly where he could find peace and solace. Dinah called Ruth and told her that the Red Cross had Daniel's body and asked Ruth if she could bury him next to his father as everyone had suggested. It was difficult and very expensive to fly his body back to the U.S. Dinah was crying the entire time.

Ruth accepted the suggestion. On the same day, she and Joseph went to the synagogue and the rabbi and the congregants participated in a service that corresponded to his official burial.

Ruth stayed home for a week and respected the ceremony of the *shiva*, Jewish official grieving.

Before the end of *shiva*, she received a call from Sheila, who told her that Dinah had died. Sheila said that at least Daniel was lucky to be buried by his mother but there was not even a *minian*, a minimum of ten men needed to say the *Kaddish*, the prayers at the funeral. But the few members of the Jewish community remaining gave the needed respect to Dinah and buried her between her husband and her son.

Lebanon's ancient Jewish community came to an end with the death of the remaining hostages. Two days later the badly mutilated bodies of Mr. Benesti and his two sons, Ibrahim and Joseph, were found near the same church. All had been tortured to death. A short while later one more dead hostage was recovered, but the rest never were found. Ruth felt that she was lucky to know that her husband had been killed quickly with three gunshots. She also knew that he had lost a lot of weight and that probably he was never fed properly during the nine months of his captivity.

She felt sad for the families who never received any news their loved ones. Years later she met the wife and son of Doctor Hallak in Paris. She was heartbroken since both of them were shaking nervously when they told Ruth, "You are not aware how lucky you are. At least you had a body to bury and were able to put a final dot to your chapter. We never received a body. We do not know if he is alive or dead; if he eats or sleeps. Although we know deep in our hearts that he was killed, still we wait for a confirmation."

Ruth continued her life stoically and with courage. She was young, beautiful and intelligent. She continued working and encouraged Joseph to study hard and pursue all his activities. She told him that was the only way that he could avenge the death of his father – by being a good person and making the best of himself.

After taking the Jewish hostages, the terrorists kidnapped Terry Anderson, a reporter who was married to a Lebanese and living in Lebanon. He was later freed and returned to America. By this time everyone understood that the Jews were being taken by Shiites in a show of force to President Reagan, who had refused to sell arms to Iran. After Anderson was captured, the secret arms deal organized by Oliver North, a Marine Corps lieutenant colonel, took place and that was the reason that he was freed.

Later Anderson wrote a book about his experiences. When Ruth read it, she learned that, while a captive, Anderson had become ill and a man was brought to his tiny dark room to treat him. She understood that this was probably Doctor Hallak. Ruth called Terry Anderson and they talked for a while. He was not able to give her more information than what he had written in his book since he said that he was locked in a small room and had no information from outside. He described the doctor who came to visit him when he was sick. He said they brought him in blindfolded and took him out blindfolded. He and the doctor were not able to exchange any words. He just examined Anderson and prescribed medication that saved his life. After that, he never saw the doctor again.

At the Book Expo of America, Ruth met Colonel North. She introduced herself, and he knew exactly who she was and expressed his sorrow for the loss of Daniel.

Joseph graduated from high school near the top of his class. He won an academic scholarship to USC, finished college, and was accepted to medical school. He loved studying medicine and wanted to become a surgeon. He had turned into a handsome young man, but he was so busy at the hospital that he wasn't doing what most of his friends were doing, such as attending parties and enjoying life.

When Joseph was in the last year of his fellowship program, Ruth tried to introduce him to some nice girls. But he was not ready for any commitment. However, one day he called his mother and told her that he had met a nice Israeli girl who was there on an exchange program. He asked her if he could bring her home for Ruth to meet. Of course, Ruth was delighted and invited them for Shabbat dinner. After hanging up the phone, Ruth started preparing the favorite foods of her son. She prepared the dough to rise so that she could make his favorite *khalah*, or Shabbat bread, for dinner. She felt that there was love in her son's voice. He had never talked that way about any girl to his mother and she was happy that her son was probably in love.

On Friday she set the table beautifully and the delicious smells of the baked bread and the food filled the entire house. She arranged the flowers in the vase and placed the long candles in the shiny silver candle holders. She dressed up and waited for the arrival of her son and his girlfriend. She was happy for him and, at the same time, she was sad because Daniel was not there to see how his son had grown into a handsome man, a knowledgeable surgeon, and God willing, soon a bridegroom. Tears filled her eyes and she immediately told herself that he was always by her side after his assassination and had guided her to accomplish all her responsibilities perfectly.

When she opened the door, she saw Joseph's glowing face. For the first time, he seemed very happy. He kissed Ruth and introduced the beautiful girl by his side. She had long curly blond hair and her clear blue eyes were very attractive. Her name was

Rachel and she captured Ruth's heart immediately. She offered a lovely bouquet of flowers to Ruth. She spoke fluent French with a strong Hebrew accent, which made it more attractive. Joseph showed her around the house. Ruth finished the little touches to the dinner and told them that food was ready to be served.

They washed their hands and, before sitting at the table, Ruth asked Rachel to join her in welcoming the Shabbat, praying over the candles and lighting them. Then Daniel made the prayers of Shabbat. After blessing the wine and bread, Ruth brought all the dishes to the table. Rachel immediately went to the kitchen to help her. She was very friendly and simple. She appeared to be a very nice girl. Rachel loved the food, especially the bread, and said that Joseph had already told her about Ruth's delicious *khalah*. They passed a peaceful and happy Shabbat together.

After dinner they sat in the living room and talked awhile and looked at the family photos. This was the first time that Ruth had a joyous evening at home since Daniel's kidnapping. Although Daniel and his pain were always present, still she was able to enjoy talking with his son and beautiful Rachel. When they left, Ruth talked to herself and, at the same time, to Daniel and said, "Did you see that? Your son is in love. I think we are going to have a wedding soon. I am sure you will be present with all of us under the *khuppa*!"

BOOK TWO

THE JEWISH FAMILY

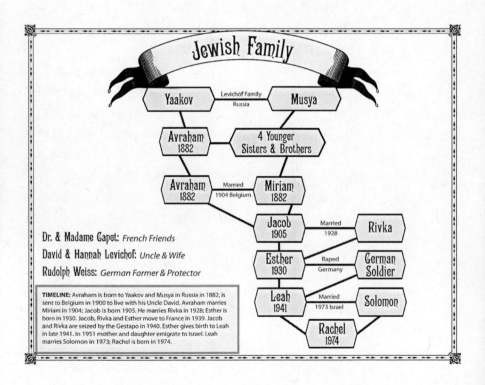

Jewish Family

Yaakov — Levichof Family Russia — Musya

Avraham 1882 — 4 Younger Sisters & Brothers

Avraham 1882 — Married 1904 Belgium — Miriam 1882

Jacob 1905 — Married 1928 — Rivka

Dr. & Madame Capet: *French Friends*

David & Hannah Levichof: *Uncle & Wife*

Rudolph Weiss: *German Farmer & Protector*

Esther 1930 — Raped Germany — German Soldier

Leah 1941 — Married 1973 Israel — Solomon

Rachel 1974

TIMELINE: Avraham is born to Yaakov and Musya in Russia in 1882, is sent to Belgium in 1900 to live with his Uncle David. Avraham marries Miriam in 1904; Jacob is born 1905. He marries Rivka in 1928; Esther is born in 1930. Jacob, Rivka and Esther move to France in 1939. Jacob and Rivka are seized by the Gestapo in 1940. Esther gives birth to Leah in late 1941. In 1951 mother and daughter emigrate to Israel. Leah marries Solomon in 1973; Rachel is born in 1974.

CHAPTER 25

Yaakov and Musya

LEAH'S GREAT-GRANDPARENTS had lived in a small village near Moscow, as had their ancestors for generations. Yaakov Levichof was a tailor who had customers from all of the surrounding cities. Because of his skill and good character, his customers appreciated his work and respected him very much. Like all tailors, he sometimes had difficult customers – people who demanded minor changes after their suits were finished and ready to be picked up. Their demands caused him a lot of additional work, nearly all of which was not even necessary.

Yaakov knew that the real source of their unhappiness was not his work but problems in the customers' business or arguments that they had with their wives or in-laws on that day. They were unloading their frustrations and problems onto his shoulders. The shortening or adding of a half-centimeter was not an important change to the garment but to the customers because it restored their self-importance. They might not be able to control events in their business or their family life, but they could control the length of an inseam.

Yaakov was aware of his customer's moods, but he understood human nature and so would redo a finished piece at no additional charge in order to satisfy his customers' wishes. He was never paid well for his work. Most of his Jewish customers led a modest life like his. They bought suits only for special occasions, such as weddings or for the High Holy Days. Sometimes they offered him vegetables, fruit, chickens or whatever as payment.

Yaakov's wealthy customers were almost all Christians and most of them took pains to make him understand that he should feel proud that such people patronized his business. They would order the best hand-sewn suit that Yaakov could make and, when it was ready, nearly always demanded many unnecessary modifications to justify the price, which was a third less than what they would pay in Moscow. Yaakov understood his customer's little games, but he kept his silence and worked long days to support his family. His wife, Musya, took care of their five children, cooked and cleaned the house, and tended their little garden and henhouse. If she had any spare time, she sewed their children's garments with leftover fabric from her husband's shop.

It was not a prosperous life but it was a happy one. Yaakov and Musya loved each other and their children. The Russian authorities ignored them, unless they needed something from them. Yaakov repaired, free of charge, the uniforms that local policemen brought to him from time to time. When they picked up the work, their payment was no more than a smile and a nod of the head. But Yaakov figured it was a roughly fair transaction because the police left him and his family alone, especially in troubled times.

The Jews never understood why – every once in a while and without warning or provocation – the Cossacks would come riding into their quarter beating people, breaking windows and destroying businesses and houses. On rare occasions they would capture some men and take them away. Their families would live in anguish not knowing if their loved ones were alive or in prison. No one, not even the village rabbi, understood this behavior. He just asked his congregants to keep quiet in order not to irritate the authorities, because everyone knew that they did not have a better choice in life. After all, when the damages were only material, he would ask them to make repairs and live their lives in peace.

The older Jews approved their rabbi's words. But the younger generation – activated by ideas seeping in from Western

Europe – argued with the rabbi and the community elders. They wanted them to unite and fight for their rights or leave Russia and go to Palestine. This caused alarm and fear in the elderly, who repeated their *Shemas* so that the Almighty would give their grandchildren wisdom and reason. Or they would tell the complaining youngsters that it was time for them to get married since they were losing their minds.

As for Yaakov, he told himself in a low voice that the Cossacks looked just like his other customers, that events all depended on the mood of the government and that officials always try to divert attention from real problems in order to placate unsatisfied citizens. After all, everyone in the country was happy that the wrath of the government was turned toward the Jews. The Tsar and his government spread the word that Jews wanted to take over the world and rule over everyone, drink the blood of Christians, and kill their innocent children.

One day Yaakov told his wife that their local policeman asked him to repair some suits and, when he came to claim them, he did not smile as usual but instead had a somber, even grim, face. Yaakov thought that this was a precursor of great trouble. Already he had heard much bad news from his other Christian customers. When he arrived home, he asked his wife to gather together necessary items since he was thinking about their leaving Russia.

Musya looked at him with wide eyes and asked if he had lost his mind. But when she saw that Yaakov was serious, she cried and asked her husband how they could leave their families and friends behind, and where could they go with five children? Finally, they decided to first send Avraham – their oldest son, who was already a young man – to Belgium, where Yaakov's younger brother lived. David was a successful diamond-cutter who lived with his wife, Hannah, in Antwerp. He had left Russia at a very young age many years ago.

Although all Jews were aware that no country was truly safe for them, Belgium's past gave them hope, especially when they thought about the repeated pogroms in Russia. David had sent Yaakov and Musya letters, carried by travelers who visited Russia, explaining about Belgium's history, describing his own situation, and encouraging them to immigrate to Belgium. In one letter he related the history of Jewish diamond-cutters in Antwerp.

In 1585, when the Spanish took over the city, most of Antwerp's Jewish diamond-cutters fled north to Amsterdam. In 1648, the Jews returned to Antwerp but were still subjected to anti-Semitic threats. At the end of the Napoleonic wars in 1815, Antwerp was incorporated into the Netherlands. All religious groups were granted equality, and the Jewish community of Antwerp was officially reestablished in 1816. It was then that the city's diamond trade started expanding.

Yaakov knew that his brother was a highly skilled diamond-cutter and well-established in the trade. David and Hannah had lost their only son years before, so Yaakov was sure that they would accept their son, Avraham, happily into their household. They had their address of many months ago but were sure that David and Hannah had not moved. Besides, Avraham would be able to easily find them due to David's fine reputation.

Yaakov agreed that his wife was right. Seven people were too many to move around easily. He was sure that David and Hannah would take care of their son like their own, but he could not impose his entire family on his brother even though he knew that he would receive them kindly. Avraham was a bright and talented young man, but as a Jew he had no future in Russia. Yaakov and Musya reasoned that, if anything happened to them in the future, at least Avraham would carry on the family name. Once in Belgium, he could learn his uncle's trade of diamond-cutting, and then his future would be secured. So they talked to Avraham and told him their plan. But he didn't want to leave his family, so they promised that, as soon as he was settled, they all would join him in Belgium.

Yaakov decided to confide in one of his customers, a high-ranking official in the local government who traveled abroad regularly. Dmitri Ivanovich was Yaakov's only Christian customer who appreciated his work and was fair to him. When he came into the shop to try on his new suit, Yaakov asked him if he could help his son. "My brother and his wife have lost their son and are very sad and need help," he told Ivanovich. "They have offered to adopt Avraham and teach him his trade of cutting diamonds so, when he returns to Russia later, he would be a skilled worker."

Ivanovich looked at Yaakov sadly. "It is a good idea to send Avraham away to learn a trade," he said. "I don't see much of a bright future for our youth here." Without saying so, he had told Yaakov that Avraham should not return to his homeland. He then brightened up and promised to help him get a job on the trains that carried travelers to border towns. Once there, Avraham would have to find his way across the border and then to Belgium.

Ivanovich then advised Yaakov that, if Avraham wanted to be safe, he had to look like a Russian, which meant cutting his hair and hiding or cutting the side curls. Yaakov was a religious man but was more liberal than his fellow men in the village. He thought that the safety and freedom of his son were worth the loss of his hair. The hair could grow later, but the gift of life was given to individuals only once.

Yaakov thought that it was a good sign that four of his children had reddish hair and light brown eyes. Even better,

Avraham was born with golden hair and blue eyes. If he wore Russian clothes and cut his hair, no one – not even the most anti-Semite Cossack – would recognize his origins. Yaakov did not have enough words to thank his customer, so he offered the new suit free of charge to Ivanovich and added that he would be always thankful to him and that all his suits in the future would be sewn free of charge for him.

Once at home, Yaakov gave the good news to his wife and son. Everyone was happy and sad at the same time. They did not reveal their plan to the other children or relatives. A day before his departure, they told the other children and their grandparents that Avraham was leaving for a neighboring yeshiva to study for some time. Avraham kissed his siblings and, when it came to his mother, he broke down like a child. They hugged and cried for a moment since Musya did not think she would ever see him again. But she was happy that, with God's help, he would have a better life and no Cossacks would be able to hurt him or his family in the future.

As Yaakov and Avraham walked to the house of Yaakov's father for the last time, Yaakov gave him all the advice that he could think of for his son's future at that last moment. The grandfather was surprised to see his son and grandson at such a late hour. They told him their secret and Yaakov added that his son really needed his blessings before his departure. With tears in his eyes, the old man said, "This is a wise decision because I don't think there is any future left for us in Russia. But people of my age don't have a choice. We must remain." He went to the back room and brought out two small gold coins. "I have kept these pieces for your wedding day, Avraham, but you will need them more now. Keep one for your future and spend the other one on the needs of your trip."

Avraham knew that the two coins were the only wealth that his grandfather had saved for his future. He tried to refuse them, saying he had all he needed for his trip. But the old man insisted. He also gave much advice and, at the end, he put his two hands on his head and recited the blessing of the Cohanims, while Avraham bent to kiss his wrinkled and trembling hands for the last time. His grandfather pulled him with all his strength against his chest and kissed him farewell, his tears a mute testimony to his belief that this was the last time that he would see his firstborn grandson. Avraham had also tears in his eyes. As he and his father were leaving, the old man gently tapped Avraham on his back with his frail hands. "Remember that you are a Jew and honor your traditions," he said. "And when the right time comes, marry a fine Jewish girl and have many children."

Yakov took his son to his tailor's shop. They entered quietly by the rear door. He asked him to sit on the stool and made a prayer and, with a guilty and shaking hand, cut Avraham's hair, giving him a Russian boy's haircut. Then he gave him simple black pants and a gray shirt with large sleeves and told him to change clothes. While Avraham was changing, Yaakov collected his son's curly hair from the floor and put it gently in a small fabric bag that he had sewn the day before. He pulled the cord tightly, tied a knot, and placed it like a sacred piece in a drawer. When Yaakov looked at his son, he was surprised to see a young Russian man standing in front of him. He took Avraham's old garments and cut the *Tzizit* from the four corners of the shirt and put them in another little bag that he had prepared. He handed it to Yaakov.

"Keep the *Tzizit* in your hidden pocket with the two gold pieces that your grandfather gave you. They would provide protection and good luck. When you arrive in Belgium, knot them back onto your shirt."

Then Yaakov put Avraham's old garments in the same drawer with his hair and closed it gently, as if they were going to be the most precious objects for him for the rest of his life.

Avraham looked around the shop for the last time as if he were trying to remember every inch of his father's workplace. Then they walked quietly toward their final destination through the dark forest as Ivanovich had directed. The moon shed enough light for them to find their way on the narrow road. Their march was without incident, and early in the morning they arrived at the railroad station where they said their final farewell.

Avraham left for his new destiny while Yaakov returned home with a heavy heart. At least he had a long walk during which he could clear his head. Since he was alone in the forest, he cried his heart out without shame and, when his tears dried up, he prayed for the well-being of his son. He remembered the day Avraham was born, then remembered every moment as he grew up to become the handsome young man he was. He remembered how the three generations – Avraham, himself and his father – walked together to their small synagogue and then listened with pride when Avraham read from the Torah for the first time. He watched his life like a movie in his mind and repeated the favorite scenes in the darkness of the forest. Sometimes he had a smile on his face and then a warm tear dropped from his tired eyes. Despite all his sadness, he was happy and sure that Avraham was going to have a much better life for himself and for his future grandchildren in a country where there were no Tsars or Cossacks.

When he arrived home, he found that Musya had prepared his breakfast. The water was boiling in the samovar and she looked at him with red eyes. He knew well enough that she had not slept all night and had cried and prayed for her firstborn son. He arranged his hair with his hands and wiped off the remaining tears in his eyes and put an artificial smile on his face and approached his wife, letting her know that all went as planned, that their son was going to be well, and that she should be happy as they were going to join him soon.

Musya smiled bitterly and replied that she had started planning what they needed to take with them. She knew her husband's pain and did not want to add to it. Both of them drank a cup of hot tea together in order to reassure one another that everything was fine. But even the hot water did not pass easily through throats tightened by the immense sadness of separation. Yaakov entered the small dark bedroom where his remaining innocent children were asleep in their beds. He lay down sad and exhausted in his bed. In his dream, he was still walking with Avraham through the dark forest and, once in a while, he gently touched his short cut hair.

CHAPTER 26

Avraham Makes His Way

AVRAHAM ARRIVED AT THE RAILROAD STATION with the letter of recommendation from Dmitri Ivanovich. But Avraham Levichof was now Alexi Chernoff. The stationmaster hired him, gave him a train employee's uniform, and explained his responsibilities. His train would leave in three hours and, until then, he was free to do as he wanted. He changed into his uniform, put his street clothes into his small suitcase, and walked around the station grounds. Once he found a quiet place, he repeated the *Shema* quietly to himself. Although he was an inexperienced young man, he looked and behaved like a much older person. But inside he was just a boy who was scared of an unknown future and very sad to be away from his parents and siblings.

Avraham loved Russia and the village where he was born and had grown up. But now he was sleeping on a narrow bed in a shaky train. He knew that from this day forth he would be at the mercy of his destiny. The train conductor seemed to be a kind man but some other railroad workers made him uneasy and even fearful. Avraham was not used to close contact with gentiles, especially those with foul mouths. He mustered up his courage by thinking of the Biblical Avraham, who left his city of Ur with faith and hope, also for unknown places, and became the patriarch of his religion. He also remembered the kind face and soft hands of his father. As the train lurched slowly along the uneven tracks, Avraham's eyes closed and he fell into a deep dream.

Avraham worked aboard the train – sweeping floors, moving luggage, closing and opening windows as the train passed through tunnels – and when it reached its border town destination, he quickly changed into his street clothes and disembarked. When the conductor found his abandoned uniform, he thought little of it. Some men just weren't cut out for train work, and poor Alexi Chernoff had worked two days without pay.

Gold, luck and cunning got Avraham out of Russia and across Europe. He overcame many difficulties and, after months of struggle, finally arrived in Antwerp. He found his uncle at the address that his father had given him. Uncle David was surprised and happy to see his nephew. His wife, Hannah, was a kind woman who spoke only a few words of Russian. She fed Avraham and prepared his bed in their son's former room, which had remained empty since his death. Avraham could not believe that his uncle lived in such a beautiful house with all the modern conveniences. For him everything was new and amazing and he thanked God for his good luck, especially after such a long and tiring trip.

David and Hannah were very happy to receive Avraham in their house and, from the first moment, they accepted him as their own son. David asked many questions about Russia and the family and the two spoke through the night in Russian. Avraham gave him the good and the bad news about everyone. David told his nephew that Yaakov was very smart even as a young boy and he could see that he had remained a wise man to accept the separation and send Avraham out of the country, since Russia was going to blow up soon. People were not happy with their Tsar, and he had just heard that more pogroms against Jews had taken place in different villages in the last few months. A stricken look flashed across Avraham's face and he asked if they were anywhere near his parents' village. David said no, but Avraham wasn't entirely reassured. As Avraham prepared to go to bed, David told him to sleep for as long as he needed. Then Hannah would take him around and show him the city. Later he would introduce him to his work and to their community.

The next morning Avraham was ashamed to wake up so late. He was surprised to find himself lying on clean white sheets in a comfortable bed. When he had gone to bed he was so tired that he didn't even notice. In fact, he was not sure where he was or what day it was. He quickly dressed and, as soon as he walked out of the bedroom, he smelled the delicious food that Hannah was preparing for him. They communicated in sign language and broken Russian, because Hannah spoke French and Flemish like most people in Antwerp.

After lunch Hannah showed him some pants and shirts and suggested that he try them on since she thought they would fit him. Later Avraham and Hannah went to the post office and sent a coded telegram to Yaakov, letting him know that Avraham had reached his destination and was healthy and happy. At the end Avraham asked his father to hug his mother, grandfather, brothers and sisters for him since he missed everyone very much. Then Hannah showed him around the city and took him to her husband's atelier, where David worked. Avraham was surprised to see how his uncle turned ugly stones into shiny beautiful diamonds. The next day Hannah took him to a school where she registered him for lessons in the French language. After a week, Avraham started a regular life that embraced work and study.

In the mornings he walked with his uncle to work and in the evenings he went to school to learn the language. Afterward, late into the night, he did his homework. David taught his nephew all the tools of the trade and was very proud because Avraham made rapid progress in learning both diamond-cutting and the French language. While Avraham would need years of experience before he became a master diamond-cutter, he clearly had the aptitude for such an exacting trade. David was proud to introduce him to his community and happy that finally God has given him another son who could take his job after him and would say *Kaddish* when he and Hannah left this world.

Everyone liked Avraham, who was happy to live among such nice people, especially his uncle and aunt, who treated him like their own son. He knotted back his fringes to his shirt. When he prayed, he remembered his parents and asked God to protect them, give them good health, and to someday reunite the family.

CHAPTER 27

A Story Ends in Russia

AVRAHAM'S PARENTS AND HIS FOUR SIBLINGS never made it out of Russia, but Yaakov and Musya were proud that their son had become a skilled diamond-cutter at such a young age and that he was living well with his uncle and aunt. As the years passed, Russia became a more dangerous place for Jews to live.

It was not widely known that the Tsar's son, Tsarevich Alexei, had hemophilia. When the doctors were unable to cure Alexei, his mother, the Tsaritsa, looked everywhere for help. Finally, in 1905, she turned to Grigori Yefimovich Rasputin, a semiliterate peasant who had achieved the reputation of a healer through prayers. Every time that Alexei began bleeding, the Tsaritsa called on Rasputin, who subsequently calmed the boy and stanched the bleeding. It appeared that Rasputin was effectively healing him. Rasputin seemed to enjoy the power he had found in the court, and many people believed he was a visionary mystic and prophet. But others feared his growing power.

By 1915, with Russia doing poorly in the Great War, everyone – from peasants to nobles – wondered who was running the country and gossiped about the relationship of their Tsaritsa and Rasputin. The peasants were unhappy, as were the educated youth in the cities, so it seemed to the government that accusing the Jews for all the country's problems was the best way of calming unrest.

Once in a while, Avraham received news from his father. He always wrote asking them to leave Russia and join him in Belgium, but he knew that it was a very difficult move for them.

Later the letters became rare and then stopped altogether. Avraham received news about his village only when a visitor arrived from Russia, which was in turmoil. The Tsar was aware that the end was near, yet he tried to remain in power. His Cossacks continued taking out their revenge on the Jews, as if by killing Jews and destroying their villages they could stop the revolution.

One morning the police officer at Yaakov's village brought him a pair of pants to repair. He was smiling and in good spirits. But when he picked up his pants the next day, he was somber and thanked Yaakov for his work for the first time. He told him that it was a pity he did not leave with his son to wherever he went. Now, he said, it was too late and he left the shop almost in tears. Yaakov was frightened and immediately locked the door and ran home. He asked Musya to pack some necessary objects and food and told the children to stay alert since they were going to leave immediately after dark.

He did not know where they would go or how they would get there, but his instincts told him not to remain in the village. He pulled the hidden savings box from the closet, divided its contents into six parts, and sewed them inside the fold of the sleeves and under the coats of each family member. That, he said, was for emergency use. They should keep their jackets on at all times and not lose them.

They had an early dinner and waited nervously for nightfall. But late in the afternoon they heard the voice of a police officer commanding everyone to leave their houses by the order of the Tsar. As soon as Yaakov opened the door to see what was happening, he felt a sharp pain and tasted his hot blood in his mouth. Before staggering to the floor, he told his wife and children to hide, but it was too late. While he was trying to regain his footing, he heard the cries of his wife and children. Suddenly all was quiet and peaceful for him. Some Cossacks were swinging their bright swords in all directions, killing the innocent men, women and children of the village. Others, who had torches in their hands, threw them at the synagogue. As the flames began consuming the modest building, the rabbi rushed inside to save the Torah. As he attempted to leave with the heavy scrolls in his hands, he was cut down and left to burn in the flames.

There were all kinds of smells in the air – the smell of burning wood and straw mixed with the odor of charred human flesh. These shameful smells filled the air of the small, peaceful and pious Russian village where so many people prayed to God for His blessings and waited in hope for the arrival of the promised Messiah. The Cossacks laughed as they took the farm animals and whatever they could find as reward for their sinful acts.

One day Hannah asked Avraham to come home earlier that evening since she had some guests for dinner. When Avraham arrived, he heard the voices of some men and women and understood that he was not as early as his aunt had requested. He immediately changed out of his work clothes and, when he entered the living room, his eyes were immediately attracted to the face of a beautiful young girl. Her name was Miriam. Hannah introduced Avraham to Miriam and her other guests; she wasn't quite able to disguise the fact that she had arranged the dinner in order to introduce Miriam to Avraham. Later Avraham had to admit he did not remember much about that evening except meeting her.

It wasn't long before David and Hannah's dreams were realized. Before their deaths they were able to take part in the wedding of their beloved nephew and the beautiful Miriam. Nine months later, David held the little baby, Jacob – named after his brother – in his arms for his circumcision ceremony. Avraham wrote to his parents about the good news that they had become grandparents but received no answer from them.

Avraham was sometimes surprised at the power of life. After all that he had witnessed in life and after all the horror and unfairness and injustice he had seen, he often asked himself how he could marry and bring a son into this world. He was unable to answer his own question, but nonetheless he was happy to have a devoted and loving wife and a precious son who sometimes even pulled him out of unpleasant memories and pushed him toward happiness. Miriam and baby Jacob imbued Avraham with the energy and purpose to live his life – to wake up every morning and work for their well-being.

The news in Europe was not encouraging either. The Germans had already started their aggression and Avraham thought that it was going to inflame the entire continent. This would be a very ugly and cruel period in history. His entire heart and mind were occupied by his immediate family and by his kind parents and innocent siblings. He was aware of the pogroms and revolution raging across Russia and guessed that his family was among the innocent victims. But, without definite word, he still clung to a slender reed of hope, which warmed his heart.

Belgium chose neutrality in the Great War, but the Germans invaded the country anyway. Despite overwhelming odds, King Albert I stayed in Belgium to lead his troops.

Like nearly all men of his age, Avraham joined the army to serve his adopted country. Although he did not believe in wars, it was the only way that he could fight against the injustices that his family in Russia had suffered. Soon his unit was sent to Flanders, a prime killing ground of the Great War, where casualties would mount into hundreds of thousands. It would be immortalized in the poem "In Flanders Fields," where poppies sprang up from the battlefield. The Great War was not only the most destructive war up until that time but a totally unnecessary one. Decades later historians would still puzzle over the events that led to it.

Avraham received many wounds and lost a leg on the battlefield. That he survived made him luckier than many. When he finally returned home, he found two frail, worried and sick people waiting for him with love and hope. He was happy to be home – he now realized that Belgium was his home – and reunited with Miriam, Jacob, David and Hannah after a long separation. Everyone thanked God; they were happy to be able to hold each other in their arms.

Miriam, David and Hannah were sad to see Avraham with only one leg. Even little Jacob asked many questions, but everyone was thankful that at least he was alive and had returned home. The news of the atrocities of the war was coming out little by little. Although the Allies ended up as the winners, in reality only America could be considered a winner. All the European countries suffered greatly and ended the war with huge losses in men and treasure. A generation of young men had been nearly destroyed; the Ottoman and Hapsburg empires and the Romanov dynasty were brought down; and the British Empire was mortally wounded.

Even before the United States entered the war, many young Americans volunteered to join the French army. Most ended up as ambulance drivers. Meanwhile, few newspapers in Europe or America wrote about Armenians being massacred in Turkey by the Ottoman Empire, which was an ally of the Germans. Before the war, German military personnel and diplomats were heavily present in the country, advising and shaping its military and later witnessing the atrocities of the Armenian Genocide. But the European countries were absorbed with their own miseries of the war and, after the armistice, only a handful of people helped the Armenian survivors. As for the rest, Turkey was too far away and the Armenians were too few and poor to worry about.

As time passed without word from Yaakov, Avraham and David became increasingly worried. They sent telegrams and letters but received no answer. They were unable to do anything but wait. Then one day a diamond buyer told them of all the cruelty against the Jews and intellectuals inflicted by the Tsar and his Cossacks in a futile attempt to remain in power. So the Red revolution occurred and Tsar Nicholas II, his wife and their innocent children paid with their lives for all the injustices of their country that did not start but hopefully ended with him.

The news of the end of the Romanov dynasty was of no consolation to Avraham and David. They feared the worst about Yaakov, Musya and their children. Although they did not know it at the time, Avraham was – as predicted – the sole survivor of his large family, and it now was upon his shoulders to carry on the family name and traditions.

After the war, the leading nations held many meetings and signed many treaties and agreements. Everyone hoped that human tragedies like the Great War would never happen again. Some even thought it was the war to end all wars. However, the goodwill and hopeful deeds did not extend to the Jews. The anti-Semitic ideas of the Tsar found nourishing environments elsewhere. In the countries of Central and Western Europe, where anti-Semitism had often flourished, hatred of Jews found new strength. Likewise, a virile patriotism was still taught at schools, encouraging the children to love their countries and die gloriously when needed. The lessons of the killing fields went unnoticed.

ॐ

Despite the romantic image of American expatriates living the good life on the Left Bank of the Seine during the 1920's, life was still difficult for almost everyone in Europe after the war. Belgium, which was devastated by the German invasion and the bitter fighting in Flanders, did not receive reparations from Germany. After a period of alliance with France, Belgium returned to neutrality in the 1930's – a decision that would not save it from events in the future.

More than a year after the fall of the Tsar, a Jewish refugee from Russia arrived at David's home. He was a diamond merchant who once counted the Romanovs among his customers. Avraham asked him questions about his parents' village and then learned the fate of his family. For a long time he felt guilty to be alive and living a peaceful and prosperous life. He cried quietly when he was alone, and every morning and evening at the synagogue he recited *Kaddish* for his parents, siblings, grandfather, and for all the souls of the village.

Avraham, by then a master diamond-cutter, took over his uncle's business. David had become too weak to do the painstaking work of diamond-cutting. But he visited Avraham often and admired his skill and was proud that he was highly respected by his customers.

Some months later, first David and then Hannah died. This was a sad time for Avraham and Miriam since they loved both of them dearly. Even Jacob seemed to sense a great loss. David and Hannah were such kind and caring human beings. They loved and helped Avraham to learn and have a secure life. Avraham again went to the synagogue every morning and evening and said

Kaddish for his uncle and Hannah and prayed that God would bless Jacob with their memories.

Jacob continued his school. He was a talented student who became a handsome young man. Later he went to medical school in Louvain and became a pediatrician. He returned to Antwerp and practiced at the main hospital. He was respected by all his colleagues and patients. At an international pediatrics conference in France, he met Doctor Phillipe Capet, who was chief of the pediatrics department at the hospital in Poitiers and was doing research on the effects of the BCG vaccine, which was prepared from a living attenuated strain of tubercle bacilli and used to protect children from tuberculosis. Doctor Capet and Jacob soon became good friends. Although Doctor Capet was much older than Jacob, they had a common bond. Like Avraham, Doctor Capet, too, had been injured seriously while serving at an army field hospital during the war and he had to deal with the consequences until the end of his long life.

Doctor Capet's wife, Madeleine, was a schoolteacher and they had five children. Jacob and the Capet family maintained their friendship and continued meeting each other at different conferences. On one occasion Jacob and his parents were invited to visit the Capet house at 42 Rue de Blossac, next to the beautiful Blossac Park. While Doctor Phillipe Capet and Jacob walked through the park discussing medical matters, Madeleine, Avraham and Miriam sat on a bench, talking and feeding the sparrows.

One day while Jacob was at the hospital, he met a new young nurse by the name of Rivka. It struck him immediately that she was very appealing and probably Jewish. By the end of the day, he felt strongly attracted to the young nurse and, in the days that followed, destiny brought them closer to each other. Soon Jacob was in love with her and asked for her hand in marriage. A year after the wedding, Rivka gave birth to a little girl, whom they named Esther, after the happy memories that they had from Purim Festival when Rivka used to dress up like Queen Esther every year.

In the Bible, Esther was chosen by Persia's King Ahasuerus to become his wife. The king loved her very much but his prime minister, who was a power-seeking man, was irritated by the behavior of Queen Esther's uncle, Mordecai, who never bowed in his presence (because Jews bow down only to their God). So the prime minister plotted an evil plan to annihilate all the Jewish people. Queen Esther was Jewish herself, although no one knew this. When she was informed by her uncle about the plot, she arranged a big festivity, invited the king and his minister, and unveiled the plot to the king. She finally was able to save her people from the massacre. Since then – every year on the holiday of Purim – Jews read the *megilat Esther*, the story of Esther. It is a festive day, one of joy and gratitude. Children and adults dress like kings and queens and share pastries with friends and neighbors.

By 1938 Jacob and Rivka's Esther had become a talented girl of eleven years. She was among the best students at school and played the piano beautifully. She was the love and joy of her grandparents and parents, all of whom spoiled her with abundant love and affection.

CHAPTER 28

A New World War

ONCE AGAIN THE WORLD WAS BECOMING TOO SMALL for ambitious people. The news from Germany was not good. In the 1920's a small young man, filled with hate and named Adolf Hitler, expounded his ideas of racial purity and national destiny. But hardly anyone took him seriously. However, Avraham knew exactly what was happening. As time passed, he warned his son of a new threat from Germany. He told Jacob that he had heard Hitler on the radio and thought he sounded like the anti-Semites of Tsarist Russia. Avraham said that Hitler, was a dangerous man and that the Jews should prepare themselves for terrible problems.

Jacob listened politely but was busy at the hospital and did not have much spare time. He was neither involved in politics nor interested in religion. Instead, he and Rivka were always busy with their very demanding work. Their patients needed their attention and, at home, they wanted to spend their time with Esther and their parents. By 1939 they finally felt the danger and realized that it might be too late to flee. Jacob told Rivka and Esther to pack up their essential belongings since they were going to France soon. Jacob believed that France was the country of exile for all religious or political refugees, because French governments have always given asylum to refugees of all kinds. He was sure that Hitler would not attack France, which had perhaps the strongest army in all of Europe – one that could protect the country of freedom, equality and fraternity.

Although Avraham and Miriam encouraged their son and his family to leave Belgium, they refused to join them. Avraham was tired of running away. He decided to face evil once for all at his home. He had already fled the Tsar and his Cossacks as a young boy, had faced the Germans in the humid bunkers of the Great War as a soldier, and now it was time for him to stay at his home where he had worked and was retired. What could he lose? In a way he was proud to invite evil to attack and show that he was not afraid of it, whether it be in the form of a Cossack, a German soldier of the Great War, or a German in a Nazi uniform.

By the end of the week, Jacob and Rivka had left their positions at the hospital. Their colleagues were in tears, and so were Jacob and Rivka, who dearly loved their profession and everyone who worked with them. Once at home, they felt that they were ready for their new destiny. Again, they asked and even urged Avraham and Miriam to join them. But they refused and told Jacob and Rivka that they should look for a better life elsewhere because they were young. They hugged one another, kissed and cried. For a moment Jacob, Rivka and Esther were not able to depart. Finally, it was Avraham who pushed them gently out of the house, where a taxicab was waiting to take them on the first step toward their new destination. Miriam showed them the little place inside their coats where she had hidden three beautiful diamonds that Avraham had cut and showed Esther a corner of her coat, explaining that it contained a gift from her grandparents for when she married.

The train station was crowded as were the roads, so much so that they were no longer safe. Jacob had decided that the train was the best way to travel to France. Although they knew many people in France, only Doctor Phillipe Capet had given them an open invitation to his house. So Jacob decided that was where they would stay until they could find permanent quarters.

On May 10, 1940, soon after they left Belgium, the Germans invaded the country and the Nazis began evacuating Jews from their houses. Among them was an old man who smiled and held his head up proudly, limping on one leg and holding the arm of his wife as they were taken to a train station with thousands of other men, women and children of all ages. There they were tossed aboard freight cars without benches or windows and taken away.

It was a miracle, thought Avraham and Miriam as they sat on the floor squeezed next to each other, that they had not been separated. They were lucky to be in the first group, which was sent almost directly to the gas chamber. They stood proudly, holding each other in their arms, as naked as they were on their wedding night. As Avraham patted the snowy hair of his wife, he asked her gently to breathe deeper the air sent to them by Nazis so they could join each other more quickly on the other side of this cruel world, in a place where peace, love and light were waiting for them.

It was late at night when Jacob, Rivka and their beautiful Esther arrived in a small northern village in France. They didn't know of Avraham and Miriam's fate but, instead, thought that the war would be over soon and they could return home. For months they lived in a small but clean *auberge*, where Jacob and Rivka taught Esther math, science and literature. There was a small piano in the breakfast room where she was able to practice. But, as the months passed by, the news steadily got worse and they felt in danger. They contacted Doctor Capet and were invited to go to his house in Poitiers.

When they arrived late at night at the old wooden gate in front of Doctor Capet's house, Jacob took the clapper and struck the iron bell at one side of the gate. While awaiting a response, he realized that a big Nazi flag was waving in front of a nearby house. The Germans had already begun occupying France. Marie, a cousin of Madame Capet, opened the gate and welcomed them warmly but, at the same time, escorted them quickly inside. They entered the large kitchen, which was dark except for a bit of light coming from the stove. A long table in the middle of the room was made out of solid brown wood and many chairs were set around it. This was the Capet's everyday family dining room. Marie guided them to the next room, which was the formal dining room. There Phillipe and Madeleine Capet awaited them.

After the greetings and some small talk, Marie served dinner. The table was set nicely with large white dishes and polished silver. Around the room there was beautiful antique furniture from Poitou, a region of central France rich in history. Madame Capet was especially proud of a beautiful buffet. She had explained that it dated from the French Revolution, when an anti-monarchist had used a sword to carve away a fleur-de-lis, which was the symbol of the hated monarchy. When her father acquired the buffet, he repaired it and the missing parts were restored. Everyone had admired his masterpiece until the day that a friend, who was an official antique appraiser, said that it was a nice piece to decorate a dining room but, if were in its original damaged condition, it would be unbelievably valuable.

For Jacob, knowing the Capet family had been a wonderful experience. He loved the stability of French life. One time he and Doctor Capet visited a house in Saint Soline, a village some miles outside of Poitiers. Doctor Capet had shown him a well-thumbed Larousse dictionary, which had been given to his mother when she had graduated from high school. All the furniture, books, clothes, and pictures in both their main house and the village house came from previous generations and brought forth memories of ancestors and the past. Furniture or even pieces of clothing were often kept in the same place where parents had placed them.

Jacob found this amazing, for he had nothing from his grandfathers or grandmothers. There were no family keepsakes to remind him of the long ago, nothing to trigger old memories. Now what he had received from his father and mother he had left back home in Belgium, and he was not even sure that he would see either parent again. This contrast between multi-generational continuity and near constant upheaval, he told himself, was exactly the difference between a Frenchman and a Jew!

Marie brought the first course to the table and Jacob came out of his musings, drawn by the smell of the hot vegetable soup. After the long trip, the soup was a pleasure to have. Madame Capet offered them cold milk, which she always had with her soup. The main dish was served and then the salad and cheese. The goat cheese was homemade and, with red wine, it was very delicious. By the time they were having coffee with a cube of dark chocolate, the women had gathered together to talk. Phillipe Capet told Jacob that he was welcome to stay in his house for as long as necessary. But, he added ominously, Germans had recently arrived in Poitiers, occupying the house of a neighbor, which was now their headquarters. He proposed that Jacob, his wife and their daughter occupy the third floor of their house and try to stay invisible in the daytime so that the Nazis would not learn of their presence. He told Jacob that he hoped the Nazis would leave their city soon, especially after hearing stories of their brutality.

After dinner, the Capets showed their guests to their bedrooms on the third floor. There were many books and an upright piano for Esther. The Levicof family was very tired and emotionally exhausted, so they went directly to bed. But it was some while before they fell asleep, for they worried about their parents, each other and about their unknown future. They had lived a decent and respectful life, but now they were not sure how long they could enjoy the comfort of a safe bed.

In the morning Jacob missed dressing up and running to the hospital. He could hear his patients asking for him. He knew he could help many of them, but now he had nothing to do with his time. He listened to the beautiful bird songs from outside the window. It was a sunny and mild day, and the old trees covered the wall and its windows. No one, Jacob thought, could see inside from the street.

కు

The Capets were like their parents – hospitable and kind hosts. Life continued calmly. The Levicofs ate their breakfast and lunch on the third floor because the Capets wanted to maintain their daytime lives without change. But, at night, Jacob, Rivka and Esther quietly climbed down the stairs to the dining room where they joined the Capets and Marie in a delicious dinner served with the nice silverware and beautiful china.

One day Madame Capet showed Esther a lot of slates piled in a corner of their garden. "These slates come from our roof," she told her, "when we repaired and changed them some months ago. I have kept them so that, when you will marry one day and have children, I hope you will come to visit us. I will ask your children to jump on the slates until they break in tiny pieces. I have heard that if I mix the slates with the garden soil and plant red tulips, after five years I will obtain black-colored tulips. This is a secret that a dear friend has shared with me recently. I would like very much to see the black tulips growing in my garden."

Esther politely nodded her head. Deep in her heart, she admired Madame Capet's hope for life and a future in her advanced age. But she thought, "What is she saying? I'm not even sure if I will be able to see the next sunrise. Is she trying to give me courage and hope, or is she trying to buy time in showing future plans to the Angel of Death?"

Twenty days passed and the Nazi flag was still hanging from the house down the street, the one taken away from its original owners. The Germans did not leave as the native French of the city had hoped. One morning there was a knock at the gate. Madame Capet, who was ready to leave the house to go shopping, opened the gate and was confronted by two German soldiers, who asked for Doctor Capet. Madame Capet was a petite woman who, as a child, was heavily influenced by her schoolmaster father; later she also became a schoolteacher. So she had a very strong personality and, being the mother of five children and coming from a traditional French family, she had kept her authority. Although the two soldiers were very tall, she maintained an air of superiority, told them that she was ready to leave, and asked why they disturbed her. The soldiers apologized for bothering her and said that they were sent by their commanding officer to deliver a message. He wanted to see her and Doctor Capet at his office immediately. She coolly told them that her husband was seeing a patient. As soon as the office visit was over, they would comply with the request.

The soldiers left and Madame Capet returned to the house. She told her husband of the soldiers' request and they were sure that it had to do with their guests. No one from their household had denounced them. Probably a neighbor or passerby had seen Jacob's family from a distance. Or who knows!

The Capets walked down the avenue to the German headquarters. When they entered their neighbor's house, they were amazed to see that the Germans had comfortably settled in and were using everything in the home as if it belonged to them. They were escorted to the office of the commanding officer, a major.

After a formal introduction he said, "We have learned that you are hosting Jews in your house."

Madame Capet understood that she could not protect the Levicofs by lying, but she thought might be able to save them by telling the truth. "Actually, my husband's colleague is visiting us," she answered firmly. "They have attended many international medical conferences together and exchange their knowledge by visiting each other once in a while. It is also a good occasion for me to visit his wife because we have become good friends. We are not aware of their religious beliefs. In our family we have been taught that it is rude to ask about religion or other personal matters. Our guests are very educated and interesting people, and we discuss subjects that are much more interesting than you can imagine."

Doctor Capet, a much more reserved person, was quietly proud of his wife's sharp tongued-reply. He knew well that she always spoke her mind eloquently and pointedly, but he did not expect that she would be so brave to behave the same way before a Nazi chief.

The German officer was taken by surprise and, for a short moment, was unsure of what to say. But he quickly regained his composure. "I have been informed that you are serving the food with silverware," he said. Doctor Capet was momentarily speechless at this accusation, but Madame Capet answered instantly.

"Sir, that is what we possess. Even if you should come and have dinner with us, I will be obliged to serve you with my silverware."

The major was again silent for a moment, digesting the words that were thrown to him strongly by a woman half his size. Then he collected his authority and said, "My soldiers will arrest your guests as the law requires." The Capets left saddened, but they knew that they had done and said all that they could.

Within minutes German soldiers arrested Jacob, Rivka and Esther and took them to the headquarters. The Capets never heard or saw their friends from that moment on. Even years after the war had ended and their neighbor returned to his house, they were unable to find any trace of their beloved friends.

"I am sick to my stomach whenever I remember seeing Jacob and his family leaving our house with the soldiers," Madame Capet always repeated later. "And I am sick to think about what happened to them, especially after the war when we learned about all the atrocities that the Nazis did against Jews. I wonder if they died in prison camps or in gas chambers, or from hunger or cold, or did they end up in Doctor Mengele's hands. What a pity to destroy all that education, talent, youth and beauty. When my mind wonders about them, I block it immediately and try to think of something else! But this torture is a gift from the Nazis to us until the end of our lives."

Whenever Madeleine Capet went to meet a guest at the train station, she always pointed to the tall trees across the road from the train. "You see these beautiful strong trees on the hill facing the train station?" she would ask. "When the Germans started bombarding Poitiers, this hill lost all its trees and vegetation. There were only huge holes with their big mouths open to the sky. When I passed this hill I had an ache in my stomach because I told myself that Poitiers had become like Swiss cheese in a dark color and that we would never have our nature back to us. But, after the war, the spring rains started falling and, by the end of summer, everyone was surprised to see the green grass growing and the roots of the old trees coming back to life. That's when I learned about the power of nature. So whenever I see a plant growing in a stone, in the cracks of a road or any unimaginable place, I tell myself, *Regardez, la force de la nature.*"

Doctor Capet never talked about his dear friend, Jacob. He always had a sad face whenever his name or the war was mentioned. "I couldn't believe my ears how strongly Madeleine talked to the German officer," he would tell friends. "I was sure that we were going to be arrested. I think because she was so sharp and spoke with such authority that he was intimidated and unable to take action against us."

CHAPTER 29

Death and Life

JACOB, RIVKA AND ESTHER were taken to a small dark room in the basement of the commandeered house. They were calm and resigned. Jacob and Rivka did not worry for themselves as they had lived full lives. They had read the Torah and knew of the history of the Jewish people. Nothing had stopped evil in all these centuries. Now, evil had taken the face of the German Nazis. But they worried about their beloved, beautiful and young daughter. She had seen nothing of this world; she had not tasted and experienced much of the good part of this life. It was too soon for such a talented girl to end up like this in the hands of cruel individuals. They prayed to God to help their daughter.

Soon they were transferred to a new location with other Jews and then were put aboard one of several large trucks, squeezed in with Jews from different places and carried off to an unknown destination in a convoy. They were not fed properly. No regard was made for their comfort or hygiene. No one took them to a court of law, nor were they asked any questions or told what their crimes were. Their only sin was clear: All were descended from Abraham and Sarah of thousands of years ago who believed in one God.

Esther kept close to her parents, who were not afraid of death. They had seen the many faces of death at hospitals. But this was not a usual situation. Jacob and Rivka knew that death was the end for everyone and was the only way to eternal peace. They were afraid of what atrocities might be committed on them and their daughter but, when they remembered the calm and peaceful faces of Jacob's parents during the last moments of their farewell, the memory gave them strength and hope. After all, what good would come from complaining and crying? They should never give the enemy the pleasure of seeing them in fear and pain. And so they accepted all the sufferings in silence. They did not even have much to tell each other. Instead, they just put their cold hands around each other whenever they could.

They rode for hours without stopping. Jacob was sure that they had left France, but they were so tightly packed in the truck that he was unable to read road signs. It was dark outside when the trucks stopped. Everyone was ordered off and told to line up on the road. Jacob saw that they were in a forest and near railroad tracks.

At first it was chaos. There were children and elderly who had natural needs and some walked a short distance away to attend to these needs behind some trees. The soldiers were also tired and distracted and, for a moment, they did not give harsh orders. Jacob pulled Esther toward himself and Rivka and told her, "There is no future here. Join the other children behind those trees and then run as fast and as far away as you can. You can save yourself. God will help you. Just run."

He pushed her away. Esther did not have time to think, to ask questions, or even to say goodbye. She walked quickly into the forest and then began running, without aim or destination, just as her father had told her. She was not seen by the German soldiers.

The train arrived after an hour. It was dark by then and the captives were cold and dispirited, not knowing anything about their destination or fate. Jacob, Rivka and the others were pushed like cattle aboard the freight cars. Esther's absence went unnoticed. Everyone was in shock and clutched by the fear of the unknown. They were trying to understand what was happening to them and why and trying to survive and keep their families together. Just a day or two earlier, they had been doctors, teachers, merchants, musicians, parents and grandparents – successful and respected members of their communities. Now they were treated like farm animals.

Jacob and Rivka were taken with the rest to a camp. They were registered, with a long number tattooed on their arms, and then they were separated by sex and age and taken to different barracks. Healthy adults like Jacob were put to work. They toiled for long hours, subsisting on meager rations and counting a day without being struck by a guard as a good day. Jacob was assigned to the camp hospital, which was really just a large clinic. The operating room, if one could call it that, did not correspond to the normal requirements and the expected medicines were scarce. Regardless, he often found puzzling experiences. Some patients were in such bad shape that Jacob expected them to die in just a few hours. He would operate and administer all the drugs that he could even though he had no hope of a cure. Yet some would recover and return to work, which always pleased the camp officials. The reverse was also true. Some patients were admitted with minor problems and then their condition would deteriorate rapidly and they would die unexpectedly.

Every day Jacob was amazed to see how everyone, especially some elderly or weak and sick men, were fiercely holding onto life, even without proper food, hygiene or medicine. Occasionally, he and Rivka saw each other for a short while. Rivka's beautiful long hair was shaved to her scalp and, from the short shoots, Jacob could see that it had turned from a shiny black to a dull gray. On each occasion that they met, she gave her brave, sweet smile and he saw how her grief had marked her beautiful face with long and short deep wrinkles.

One night they called him for help in the women's barrack. When Jacob arrived, he saw Rivka, reduced to a child's size and suffering from fever. The other women begged him to help her because she had cured many of the women's ailments. But this time Jacob was sure that he was correct in believing his patient was passing her final minutes. Perhaps she was just holding onto this cruel life in hopes of seeing her beloved husband one more time. Jacob gently called out her name several times. Finally, Rivka opened her eyes and looked at Jacob with a forced smile. She suddenly looked very peaceful and, without saying a word, she closed her eyes forever. Jacob kissed her face for the last time and, before the burial detail could come to take her away, he recited the *Kaddish* in tears and then returned to his barrack.

Now Jacob was all alone in this world. He had blocked his brain from thinking about the fate of his parents and his daughter, Esther. After experiencing life in the camp, he was quite aware of his parents' fate. But Esther was in the hands of her destiny. Every time a new group arrived, he anxiously looked to see if she was among them. But tonight he liberated his soul and cried without voice. He prayed that God would have pity on their innocent daughter and would spare her from all dangers. Now he was ready for the final solution in their camp, where musicians were playing in the courtyard the same beautiful music that he used to listen to while sitting in the balcony of a concert hall with his beautiful wife and daughter.

On the day he was called to take the final shower, he held fast to the corner of his coat, now torn in many places, and felt where his mother had hidden the beautiful shiny diamond that he had kept all this time in the hope of presenting it to Esther on her wedding day. He blessed his father and smiled, since he knew no one was going to touch his dirty coat and that it would be burned with the rest of the prisoners' garments, which were covered with filth and insects.

He entered the chamber with a peaceful and smiling face, listening to the beautiful classical music played by Jewish violinists who used to play in the Berlin Philharmonic before the Evil came to power. He saw Rivka and Esther in their beautiful long gowns in the balcony waving at him and showing him his seat. He used the last of his strength to force open his lungs for a deep breath. Jacob Levicof, who used to walk the halls of a major hospital and greet everyone from the doorman to the nurses and patients, calmly walked to his fate, paying no attention to the two SS soldiers who were telling each other in German, "I cannot understand the Jews. They know that they are going to be gassed in seconds, yet they are praying to their God who is not helping them when they need Him. Look at that tall man who is walking so straight and has such a big smile on his face as if he is going to a party! Amazing, isn't it? Maybe this is the reason that we are killing them. I think no one is able to understand them, not even the Fuhrer!"

CHAPTER 30

A Life Saved

ESTHER RAN IN THE DARK as fast as she could. Sometimes she fell down but always got up immediately and continued running just as her father had commanded. After a while, when she had lost all her strength, she stopped and looked around. She saw only trees and bushes. There was no sign of a human being in that dark forest. Once in a while, she heard a night bird or an insect's voice. She was cold, thirsty and hungry but that was not important. Since being taken from Doctor Phillipe Capet's house, she had not had a decent meal and had already learned to live with the bare minimum. After traveling through the night, she witnessed the victory of light over darkness. Although it was not the season of sunshine, still the sky was announcing the coming of the day. Now, Esther was able to clearly see her surroundings and, since she was exhausted, her instincts ordered her to rest in a safe place for the day and continue toward her unknown destination at nightfall.

She looked around as fast as she could as the early morning fog was getting thicker. Finally, Esther found an inviting corner formed by some tall bushes, trees and large stones. She added some more branches over the space, giving it a room-like look. She took a large leaf and used it to collect the morning dew and drank it instead of the hot chocolate she once had each morning. She found some berries and ate them with appetite. Then she lay down on the humid floor and shaped her body like a snail, inserted her head inside her coat and fell asleep immediately.

When she woke up, a thick fog had covered the forest. She was not able to see even a foot in front of her. Despite having had almost nothing to eat for the past twenty-four hours, she was feeling much better since she had slept nearly a full day. But concepts like the name of the day or the time of the clock had no meaning to her. She did not even know if she was real or not. Her surroundings reminded her of the fairy tales that she had read. She was all alone in this world with only two cut diamonds from her grandparents. And even though she had them in her possession, she was not able to feed herself or obtain comfort. The air was humid and she knew that it was going to rain. Like the day before, she walked around and picked some berries, hoping to find other sources of food as well. After she ate her sparse meal, she gathered some more branches to protect her space from rain.

Whenever her mind wondered about the fate of her parents and grandparents, she blocked out those thoughts and reminded herself that she should keep safe and run as her father had told her to. The rain started falling, but it was not too hard or for too long. There was no fog now, so she looked around to see if there were signs of any people nearby. She saw and heard nothing. Since she was exhausted mentally, she assumed her snail position once again and slept for a very long time.

When Esther woke up, she felt better. Peace and silence were the rulers of the forest. It was dark but, since her time in the forest, she had learned to see in the darkness like owls. She decided to run again, thinking that she would finally reach a safe place. She ran, she walked, and she ran again through the night and, by the arrival of daylight, she felt tired and hungry. She remembered the Shabbat dinner in her grandparents' house and smelled the delicious food that her grandmother would serve them on Fridays. She did not let her tears appear on her face but, instead, looked for berries and plants and decided to find a place to rest.

In this part of the forest, the trees and plants were not as dense as before. Esther found a flat place where she could stretch her body for a while and told herself that, after a little rest, she would continue her march. But since she was very tired, she immediately fell into a deep sleep.

Suddenly she felt that vultures were ripping her hungry body to pieces. She felt the taste of her blood in her mouth and, when she opened her eyes, she was amazed to see that she was not dreaming and that an SS soldier was raping her while she was asleep. He was still in his uniform. Esther knew German well and begged him to leave her alone, but he became more savage and bit her lips again and held her completely down. She tried to move but was not able to protect herself. He was more excited to discover that she was a virgin and continued his savagery without pause.

Esther cried and begged but nothing helped. He was a very tall and strong man. She looked only once at his face and saw that he had blond curly hair and blue eyes. Esther closed her eyes, tried to push her spirit out of her body, and asked God to take her immediately. She felt no more shame and pain. He continued his actions, not caring if she were alive or dead, until he himself was not able to move anymore. He rolled off her and lay still for a while. Esther was unconscious.

After a while, the soldier looked at his watch and became worried because he might be late for duty. He was not concerned about concealing his crime. After all, it would be her word against his, and he knew his commanding officer would find in his favor and then wink at him with a knowing smile. He stood up, arranged his uniform, and cleaned his boots with her jacket. He then looked at Esther and said to himself, *"Schöne frauleine, Zehr Schöne frauleine aufwiedersehen!"* He jumped on his bicycle and continued down the road as usual, whistling some marching song.

෨෧

Esther was left on the ground for who knows how long. An elderly farmer, collecting pine cones and branches for his fireplace, saw something in the distance resembling a human body. He told himself that nowadays even the peaceful forest was not spared of the effects of war. As the old man approached Esther, he recognized what had happened and his body shook with disgust toward his fellow Germans. He was sure that one of the young SS soldiers from the nearby village had committed the crime. He covered Esther's body with the pieces of her torn garment and her coat and pulled off his large woolen scarf and wrapped it around her neck. He tried to wipe away the dried blood around her lips and started shaking her gently to bring her out of the unconsciousness.

Esther opened her eyes with pain; she was surprised to see a gentle old face watching her with care. She felt all kinds of pain inside her being. She was shattered and broken and felt dirty. The man introduced himself as Rudolf Weiss and asked if she spoke German. Esther just nodded her head and closed her eyes with shame and desperation. He asked her to make an effort and see if she could stand up. He told her not to be scared since he was going to take her to his house and would take care of her. She begged him to leave her alone because she wanted only to die and was hopeful that God would grant her wish. Rudolf told her that he understood her wishes but that she was too young to give up on life. Right now all looked so dark for her but the time would come when she would be able to see a brighter day.

With Rudolf's help, Esther stood up. She wrapped the pieces of her coat around herself. Rudolf told her that his farmhouse was not very far from where they were. They walked slowly and Rudolf told Esther that recently he lost his wife of many years and that their only son, Max, had been called into the army and was killed in Poland. When they arrived at the farmhouse, he asked her to sit on a comfortable chair while he heated some water. Then he brought some clean and nicely folded garments and told her that, although they may not fit her perfectly, they had been washed and ironed by his wife and she could wear them for the time being. He directed her to the bedroom, where she cleaned herself and changed into the new garments.

Because of Rudolf's kindness, little by little, the shattered body and spirit of Esther started healing. But before long, each morning she started throwing up the little food that she was eating. In the beginning, she did not show her pain, but then Rudolf realized that Esther was not eating or drinking. When he asked her the reason, she told him about her condition. Rudolf did not want to disturb her since she was slowly coming back to her normal existence. In just a few short weeks he had come to love her as if she were his daughter and so he was very protective of her. From his experience with his wife, he understood that Esther had to be pregnant, but he did not want to tell her right away. She was just a child who had become a woman and would soon be a mother at such a young age.

Rudolf Weiss was just a simple farmer but he was not a simple man. He understood that, as a stranger and rape victim, Esther was not safe. He quickly devised a plan and told her he was going to change her name to Else and introduce her as the wife of his deceased son to his neighbors, friends and family. Since Esther was a tall girl and looked much older than her age, no one would suspect anything. That way she would have a reason for living at his farm. They created a history for Else, and Rudolf told her many details about Max's life.

As the weeks passed, he and Esther adopted each other as father and daughter. They did not have many visitors and they lived peacefully with the minimum of supplies and comfort, while outside, not far from them, innocent people were dying and cities were burning.

Soon Esther felt a little bump inside of her flat tummy. She had no answer as to why she was gaining weight, especially since she was not eating much. Soon Rudolf started talking to her about her future responsibilities as a mother. She cried and begged that he leave her alone so she and her baby could die. But Rudolf tried to reason with her and show her a brighter future. She asked him how she could love the baby fathered by a rapist, an SS soldier. But Rudolf told her that babies were the miracles created by God and, as soon as she saw her baby, her heart would open to love it and she would forget all about the father. He urged her to put him and his short existence out of her life for good and not let his presence steal even a second more of her life. This was the only way that she could have her revenge over those short brutal moments.

CHAPTER 31

Leah

A BABY GIRL was born at the farm with the help of an experienced midwife. Esther herself was a child but now she was also a mother. She looked at the newborn infant with hesitation. But, as soon as the midwife placed her in her arms, she forgot all about the donor of the sperm and her heart opened to an enormous source of love. Esther decided to name her Leah.

Germany, now defeated and occupied by four foreign armies, was going through one of its most difficult times. The Fuhrer had started a glorious war but all had ended in loss and shame. Life was hard for the nation's citizens. Food was scarce and, with each passing day, the war's toll on German lives became more apparent. People were trying to understand how and why the war started and how an educated and cultured people like the Germans ended up committing all those atrocities. The land of Beethoven and Goethe was disgraced.

Esther spent her days taking care of Leah; she was a beautiful little girl with blond curly hair and blue eyes. Esther thought that Leah looked exactly like her grandfather, Jacob, and had the sweet smile of her grandmother, Rivka. Esther maintained her adopted identity and, when Leah was five, she enrolled her in kindergarten as the daughter of Max and Esle Weiss.

All three lived a simple but happy life filled with love and kindness. Esther worried about Rudolf. He was in his late seventies and clearly an old man who was growing weaker day by day. Esther loved this kind man and he loved Esther and Leah. They were the hope of his life. Esther had learned to do many tasks on the farm, such as caring for its few animals and tending to the vegetable garden. When Rudolf felt his end approaching, he took Esther to his bank and added her name to his account. He made some changes to his will and made sure to have his signature notarized. And, in his own hand, he wrote a letter describing how he found Esther Levicof and how, for her own safety, she became Else Weiss, widow of Max Weiss and daughter-in-law of Rudolf Weiss. He had his signature on this also notarized but he would not allow the notary to read the letter.

Leah was ten years old when Rudolf kissed them farewell and closed his eyes peacefully. His gentle smile was still on his kind face. On the day of his burial, Esther cried and grieved for the first time, because she realized that she had once again lost a father. But, at least this time, she knew how he died and where he was buried. She never learned the fate of her parents and grandparents. She had nothing but her own being left as a gift from them and two beautifully cut diamonds in order to remind her of her grandparents.

Esther felt sad and lonely. She was grieving everyone she had lost. She began to feel that her hidden depression was not healthy for her daughter. She then remembered Rudolf's words that she was still very young and beautiful. And she was an accomplished pianist, practicing almost every day on the farmhouse's old upright piano. Leah attended the public school in the nearby village and was at the head of her class. Esther realized that her daughter was surrounded by only Germans and no one was around to teach her their Jewish heritage. In addition, as news of the atrocities continued to be revealed, she wondered how she could live in a country where her family had been killed as a matter of public policy.

To see or hear a train tortured Esther's spirit. Often she thought that the very air that she was breathing was mixed with the ashes of God-knows-how-many Jews. In contrast, Israel was a young and independent Jewish country. Jews from all over the world were moving there and were welcomed. No one would dare to discriminate or persecute them just because they were Jews. Finally, one day she decided to take Leah and immigrate to Israel. There her daughter would grow up in her faith, and Leah's secret would be kept in her heart forever. Her revenge would be that Leah would grow up as a one-hundred-percent Jewish girl.

Esther collected their belongings and sold the farm that she had inherited from Rudolf. Before leaving for Israel, she and Leah cut some beautiful flowers that Esther had grown in a special section of the farm. They went to the cemetery where Rudolf was buried. Esther and Leah arranged the flowers nicely on his grave. They thanked and prayed for his kind spirit and said farewell.

CHAPTER 32

A New Life in Israel

SOON THEY WERE ON THEIR WAY to a new life. Esther had worried that she and Leah might have trouble being admitted to the country, even with Rudolf's letter. But the immigration official treated it as routine. They settled in Tel Aviv and Leah immediately started school. She and her mother had to learn Hebrew, starting with its alphabet, so unlike that of European languages. They also had to learn the customs of their new country, but many new immigrants were likewise struggling to establish themselves in Israel.

Esther and Leah were not alone. They were always able to find a store clerk or even someone on the street who could answer their questions in German or French. When Esther and Leah spoke German to each other in public places, sometimes there were sharp eyes that followed them. Esther understood their feelings well, and she was grateful to Rudolf for bringing her close to Germans and to the German language and giving her a peace of mind. She had seen the good and the evil that exist in all humans and societies.

The Promised Land was neither paradise nor the land of milk and honey. It was still a very young country, built mostly by traumatized people who had experienced discrimination, pogroms and the Holocaust. There were many challenges for the government and its citizens. But Esther felt at peace for the first time in her life. Outside her little apartment, in the markets and on the streets, it looked like the halls of the United Nations building. Adults and children spoke in all different languages. Esther felt alive again. The government cared for its citizens; there was free education and counseling, and health care was available for everyone. People were working hard in the Kibbutzim, Moshavim and everywhere. Although most had deep psychological injuries, they worked hard and proudly to build their country as they built gardens and orchards in the deserts and on the seashore.

స్త్రీ

Esther bought a piano for their small apartment and started giving piano lessons. She saw many people, young and old alike, with numbers tattooed on their arms. They never talked of their experiences but tried to maintain a proud bearing, with heads held high and backs straight. When she became close to some, she asked them if they had seen her parents or grandparents, but she never received an affirmative answer. It was as if they were drops of dew on the face of a beautiful flower that had evaporated without leaving a trace.

At a concert she met a new immigrant, Paul Levi, a soft-spoken lawyer from Belgium. Paul also had been taken by the Nazis. He had passed difficult times in the camps and lost his entire family. Nonetheless, he retained his wry sense of humor and gracious manners. He reminded Esther of her parents and grandparents and they became closer and married within the year. Leah loved her stepfather, who became like a real father to her. Life continued for them in a loving atmosphere regardless of the small and big wars that continued to occur with their Arab neighbors. In those early days of Israel, many of its new citizens had hopes that one day soon these conflicts would end and the Messianic Era of Peace would dominate the region.

స్త్రీ

The Promised Land had kept many of its promises, but the Messianic Era was more of a mystical idea than a reality. It seemed that Jews were always called on to struggle against anti-Semitism, and this time it was in their own country and with their half-brothers who were also Semites – the Arabs. Every year Paul – an infantry officer – had to serve in the army for a month like nearly all Jewish adults in Israel. When Leah became eighteen years old, she too was obliged to join the army and later to serve her month each year. Esther finally understood that, as long as she lived, there would never be true peace anywhere in this world. In this little corner of the world lived two peoples, both descended from Abraham and both believing in the God of Abraham. Yet they were in constant conflict, and from time to time it would break into outright war.

During one of these wars – the Six Day War in 1967 – Paul was killed in battle. Esther faced a new grief that she added to her collection. Once more she found herself alone. At least she was lucky to have a beautiful and loving daughter like Leah. Sometimes she would look at her daughter's face and, for a moment, see German features and coloration. But Rudolf had taught her to forget the past bitterness and enjoy her gifted daughter, who had turned into a dedicated Jewish Israeli girl. Each time she saw Leah in her army uniform, she told herself what a wonderful revenge it was that a half-German girl, the daughter of an SS brute, had become a pure Jewish girl serving in the Israeli army!

Leah had become a beautiful young woman. After finishing college, she found work in Jerusalem. Leah loved Jerusalem, where east and west met and where all the religions and conflicts are present in such a small space. She often visited her mother in Tel Aviv and their time together was very special. But Esther never shared memories of her past with her daughter, and Leah never asked any questions about the past. Esther still played the piano, which remained her sole permanent companion.

Leah married Solomon Ohayon, a young pharmacist whose parents were from Morocco, and a year later a beautiful *Sabra* girl was born to them. The children who are born in Israel are called *Sabra* – the name for the cactus fruit, otherwise known as the prickly pear. This fruit has many spines on its outer skin so it hurts when held in hand. But as soon as it is opened, the real fruit inside is very sweet. So the Israeli-born are compared to this fruit since they are rough when attacked but, in reality, they have a kind heart. They named her Rachel. She had inherited the curly golden hair and clear blue eyes of her mother and the darker skin of her father. Neither Leah nor Rachel ever learned the origins of the coloration of their hair and eyes. Somehow Rachel's face had that special charm that brought east and west together. Esther enjoyed her only grandchild and, when her time on Earth came to a close, she finally found the real peace that she had sought all her life. Leah buried her mother in Jerusalem, where she is waiting for Resurrection Day.

The conflicts continued. True peace was never established between the Arabs and Israelis, regardless of all the efforts and mediation of powerful foreign states. There was, at least, a cold peace between Israel and two neighbors, Egypt and Jordan, after the bitter Yom Kippur War of 1973. Everyone had hoped that this peace would affect other neighboring countries and the Palestinians. But there was no resolution of the conflict, and so Israel remains as it began – a small country on a constant war footing.

The positive side of the story is that there is now one country that will accept Jews from throughout the world with open arms. Whenever there is a problem for Jews anywhere, at least they have peace of mind knowing that they can move to a country in which they will not be persecuted. They will be accepted in Israel, where they can speak their language and practice their religion freely, and where the Shabbat is the official day of rest.

In the midst of all the turmoil, Rachel grew up to be a wonderful girl. She got used to what happened around her every day. She attended a school where Israelis and some Palestinians studied together. She and her mother often went to shop at Palestinian stores in East Jerusalem. Rachel loved to mingle with people there, a result of the influence of her father and his parents, who continued to live in Morocco, a progressive Arab country that treated its citizens without much discrimination. Her father spoke Arabic at home, even in Israel, and understood the Arab world view well.

Rachel graduated from medical school. While working at the hospital, she often treated wounded Palestinians and Israelis without discrimination, and she was happy to speak Arabic with her patients. Sometimes, when wounded men and women were brought into the emergency room, she was not sure which one was the bomber and which ones were the victims. Her job was to take care of all of them.

After her residency, she won a two-year fellowship from the Weizmann Institute of Science to do research with other doctors at Cedars Sinai Hospital in Los Angeles. Although her parents and grandparents were sorry to see her travel so far, they were proud of her being accepted in such a prestigious program. Both her mother and her grandmother secretly were praying and hoping that Rachel would finally meet her *beshert* in Los Angeles and marry and fill their arms with grandchildren.

BOOK THREE

THE PALESTINIAN FAMILY

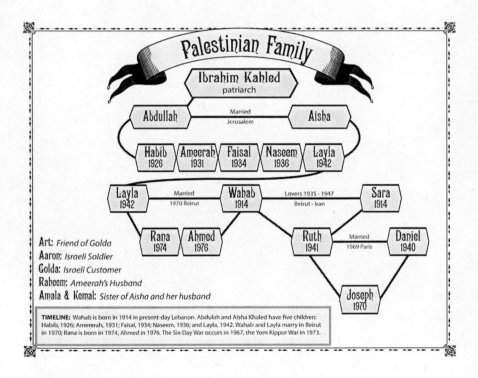

Palestinian Family

Ibrahim Kahled
patriarch

Abdullah — Married Jerusalem — Aisha

Habib 1926 | Ameerah 1931 | Faisal 1934 | Naseem 1936 | Layla 1942

Layla 1942 — Married 1970 Beirut — Wahab 1914 — Lovers 1935 - 1947 Beirut - Iran — Sara 1914

Rana 1974 | Ahmed 1976 | Ruth 1941 — Married 1969 Paris — Daniel 1940

Joseph 1970

Art: *Friend of Golda*
Aaron: *Israeli Soldier*
Golda: *Israeli Customer*
Raheem: *Ameerah's Husband*
Amala & Kemal: *Sister of Aisha and her husband*

TIMELINE: Wahab is born in 1914 in present-day Lebanon. Abdullah and Aisha Khaled have five children: Habib, 1926; Amererah, 1931; Faisal, 1934; Naseem, 1936; and Layla, 1942. Wahab and Layla marry in Beirut in 1970; Rana is born in 1974, Ahmed in 1976. The Six-Day War occurs in 1967, the Yom Kippur War in 1973.

CHAPTER 33

The Khaleds

IBRAHIM KHALED lived with his wife and grown children in East Jerusalem. Their ancestral house was made from the beautiful stone that was unique to Jerusalem and it sat on the top of a hill. From there, Ibrahim and his family had an inspiring view of the entire city of Jerusalem. He had loved this view from childhood even though, since the creation of the State of Israel, the view had changed considerably, since Jerusalem became a city where modern and ancient life and architecture blended together.

As far as he could go back in his family's history, this house had belonged to the Khaleds. His father and grandfather had lived there, and Ibrahim hoped that his children and grandchildren would continue the family tradition and keep the house in the family for generations to come. Unfortunately, three sons had died in childhood from disease. Allah finally took pity on him and his wife, and their youngest child, Abdullah, was robustly healthy and had grown to become the stick in Ibrahim's hand in his old age. The couple loved him more than the pupils of their eyes.

They had a large garden with many old olive trees that protected them from the summer heat. The family usually drank tea and coffee under the shadow of the oldest tree. It seemed to them that olive trees were like humans – no two looked alike. Each had its own characteristics, leaned in different directions, and grew its branches in unique ways.

Ibrahim was a well-known importer of arts and crafts. He knew the best craftsmen – some were women – in the neighboring countries. He bought their amazing work and resold it to the gift and souvenir stores throughout Jerusalem and kept some of it to sell at his own store. The merchandise was made from a variety of materials, including textiles and various metals. Wooden pieces inlayed with mother-of-pearl were a specialty of Damascus and Jordan. He also bought baked clay items, hand-woven rugs and fabrics and, especially, jewelry from the Bedouins.

When Abdullah was young, he used to accompany his father on buying trips and thus learned the ways of the business world. But, after Abdullah married, he took over his father's retail store. The sign above the door read "Khaled & Son Gift Store of Jerusalem." He worked hard and prospered. Many tourists, having visited the holy places, stopped at the store to buy gifts and souvenirs for their friends and families.

Abdullah and his wife, Aiesha, had five children. They had given them beautiful Arabic names and later the meaning of each name surprisingly corresponded to their evolving personalities and character. Their oldest son was called Habib, which means *loved*; their oldest daughter was Ameerah – *princess*; their third child was a son they named Faisal – *strength*; their fourth child was another son, whom they named Naseem – *soft wind*; and their youngest child was a daughter they named Layla, which meant *born at night, rapture* and *elation*.

Layla was really all that. Her dark shiny hair reminded her parents of the deep nights of Jerusalem, and her sparkling black eyes reminded them of the brightest stars in the sky. Her parents were proud and happy. She was a delight. It seemed that her joy carried everyone to another sphere of existence. From a very young age, Layla was a highly intelligent girl. She was different from her siblings in that, even as a small child, she discussed matters with her grandparents and parents and asked a lot of questions. Like her grandfather, she loved to sit in the highest point of their garden and watch the beautiful city of Jerusalem. She was always amazed and curious to see the two armed camps, replete with concrete walls and bunkers, barbed wire fences, and minefields. She heard about these from her grandfather but did not understand really what he meant. Why would people bury metal to hurt others who walked on the ground?

ॐ

The two groups of soldiers remained face-to-face, and each side's national flag waved large in the air. The Jordanian flag was red, green, white and black whereas the Israeli flag was only white and blue. One day, as Layla learned how to mix and paint colors on paper, she began experimenting. She went to her father, who was resting under a tree in the garden, and asked, "Why are there all those soldiers and flags?"

He smiled at her and began to explain that the flags represented two different countries and two different... but before he could continue, Layla spoke up. "I think I have found the solution. I learned at school today how to mix colors. If we eliminate the black and add yellow, all the problems will be solved."

Abdullah looked at his daughter with wide eyes and asked how was the problem solved. She answered, "The Jordanians will have red, green and yellow and, anyway, the fabric is white for both flags and the Israelis have only one color, blue. So, if we put all the colors together, they can have a palette of all colors like the rainbow in the sky, and there will be no problems anymore because Allah made the rainbow to bring us the promise of peace and no more floods and destruction."

Abdullah was amazed at her reasoning and intelligence. He said nothing for a moment and then told her that she should not worry about these matters and should not repeat her solution at school or at the store. "We have a lot of envious merchants who are jealous of our success," he explained. "If they hear such an argument, we may have problems in the future. Be a child and enjoy life. Leave these complicated matters to adults to solve." Then he sighed and his face showed his sadness. Layla saw this and climbed into his arms, kissed his cheeks, and promised not to tell her solution to anyone else.

The Khaleds were Palestinian Arabs but they had Jordanian nationality. They lived a quiet life far from politics and conflicts. They wanted only to run their business honestly, treat their vendors and customers with respect, and live happily with their immediate and extended families. They said their five daily prayers and, when there were problems, they talked to their Allah. East Jerusalem belonged to Jordan and, although the Khaleds were Jordanians, they always felt that they were treated differently and more like minorities because they were originally Palestinians. They were used to such discrimination and tried to live in peace with everyone.

Abdullah and Aiesha sent their children to the best schools they could afford and told them to study well and, especially, to learn languages. Knowing several languages would help the children be successful should they decide to take over the business of their father and grandfather. All the children knew Arabic and later learned French and then English. When they were young, they would go to their father's store and talk to tourists in order to practice their language skills.

When Ibrahim grew old, traveling became hard for him. He gave up going on buying trips and stayed at the store with some of his grandchildren while Abdullah traveled throughout Jordan and Syria to buy goods. As soon as Abdullah returned from a trip, Ibrahim would stay home and sit under the big olive tree, and his wife and daughter-in-law would serve him tea or coffee. When his friends came to visit him, they would prepare the *nargilleh*, the water pipe, and they would smoke and talk.

The children grew older and life continued. Habib did very well at school and, when he graduated, he helped his father at the shop and on trips for a year. But one day he told his parents that he expected more from himself and wanted to go abroad to continue his education. His parents and grandparents were happy to hear that he was ambitious but asked him to consider studying near home or at least in Amman, which was only about fifty miles from Jerusalem. Habib promised to seek out the best possibilities. After some time he informed them that he had received a substantial scholarship from an international organization and had decided to study medicine in Paris. His parents were happy that their son was going to be a doctor – the first one in the family – but they were sad that he would be so far from them. That night Abdullah discussed the matter with his father, who encouraged Abdullah to respect his son's decision since he thought the future was not very clear and reassuring for them in East Jerusalem. A medical degree from a prestigious French school would give Habib far more choices than his parents and grandparents had.

Once in Paris, Habib often wrote letters to his parents. He was happy with his life. A year later both Ibrahim and his wife died of old age. Two years after this, Abdullah and Aiesha's oldest daughter, Ameerah, told them she wanted to study in Beirut. Ameerah was a very attractive girl who, after finishing high school, had gone to work for her father at the store. But, like her brother, she was ambitious and wanted to do more than sell handcrafted merchandise. Her parents were not happy about this until Abdullah remembered the advice of his late father. He then told his wife, "It seems we do not have much choice. She is not happy here. She has refused all the Palestinian and Jordanian young men who asked her to marry them and now she is a little too old to get married easily in our society. At least in Beirut she would have a much better chance to meet a nice person, like your sister, Amala, did. Beirut is only one hundred and forty-five miles from Jerusalem, so we can visit her when we miss her or if she gets married there. It would take us only two and a half or three hours to drive there. Call Amala and ask her opinion."

Aiesha dropped some tears of sorrow and answered, "I was preparing her dowry for some years, hoping to see her wed in Jerusalem. But now times have changed and girls want to study and travel like boys."

The next day Aiesha called her sister, Amala, and told her about her daughter's wishes. Again the tears flowed. Years ago, Amala had married a wealthy businessman whose parents were a Lebanese Arab man and a Turkish woman. Kemal Haddad was born, educated and had grown up in Lebanon. He was skillful in banking and real estate, and so he and Amala had a beautiful house in the city and another one for summer vacations in the mountains. She traveled to Europe and enjoyed life. She laughed at her sister's tears and told her that she should be happy and proud that her daughter was such a smart and ambitious girl. Then she told her sister not to worry, since she would talk to her husband to get his opinion and would call her back.

The following day Amala again called her sister and told her that her husband thought Ameerah was a very intelligent girl for deciding to study in Beirut since it was the best time for anyone to live in the most beautiful city in the Middle East. He thought that she would have much better opportunities in Beirut than in

Jerusalem. He told Aiesha that he and Amala wanted Ameerah to live in their house. Their children were studying in France, so they had enough space for her to live comfortably. In addition, they could supervise her like their own daughter while she was studying and, therefore, her parents would feel peaceful and happy.

The Khaled family prepared for the departure of their daughter and decided to take a week of vacation. Hassan, who had worked for Abdullah for many years, would run the store. Whenever Abdullah traveled, he left the store in the hands of Hassan, who did his job like a son. They also gave him the keys to their house so he could see if anything needed to be done while they were absent. And they informed Habib, hoping that he could join them in Beirut. Aiesha often worried about Habib, living alone in Paris. Was he eating well, did he keep his apartment clean, and was he studying hard? She told herself that perhaps she and her sister could find a nice girl and push him to marry so he would no longer have to live alone.

The day arrived for the trip to Beirut. The Khaled family rented a large van and driver whose job was driving people from Jordan to Lebanon and Damascus and back. Some of the trips were for sightseeing and some for business or family reasons. Everyone was excited, especially Layla, who had read all about the countries of the Middle East and their histories. If the Khaleds drove nonstop, they could reach Beirut in less than three hours. But they decided to stop and visit various villages and towns along the way. They visited the ruins of Baalbek, which had stood through the reigns of eight Roman emperors over three centuries. Much later Baalbek gained additional fame as the site of a well-known musical festival, the Festival of Baalbek. Many regional singers performed there, such as the late Egyptian Om Kalsum, the most famous Arab woman singer of modern times, who was well-loved and popular even in non-Arab countries like Iran.

Much later America's Ella Fitzgerald and Lebanon's beloved singer Fayrouz performed in Baalbek. In the early 1970's, with the Israeli-Palestinian conflict growing, Fayrouz became much more popular with the song "Ghods" – *Jerusalem* in Arabic. Every pro-Palestinian and even Jews from Arab countries sang it in the universities of Paris.

The Khaleds' trip took place in the early 1950's. From the mid-1950's through the mid-1970's, Lebanon experienced its Golden Age, when it was known as the Switzerland of the Middle East and Beirut was the Paris of the Middle East. The city then was a paradise, with green hills, snow-capped mountain peaks and a sea of saltwater washing up upon a beach of soft sand. This small country held incomparable richness in terms of geography, delicious climate, history and architecture. In coastal towns like Juniyah the beautiful houses were made of small stones with red tile roofs. And in ski resorts there were elegant villas with pools and all the modern comforts.

For more than twenty years, Beirut was a center of higher education – a refuge for Arab intellectuals who had turned against the policies of their governments and, in doing so, had formed a special and unique multicultural society. Beirut was a hub of international trade, regional finance, transportation, shipping and communication. It was also a center for entertainment, art and fashion. The best apples grew up high in the nearby mountains and, in spring the perfume of orange blossoms filled the lungs. At a time when people in surrounding countries still were unaware of the look and taste of bananas and avocados, nearly everyone in Lebanon was using them as everyday foods.

In the early 1950's, big developments started flourishing in Beirut. Among the two million inhabitants of Lebanon, there were well over a dozen religious and ethnic groups. Today, Lebanon remains a nation of immigrants, many of them exiles who fled from wars and massacres in their native countries. In the old days there were rarely any physical barriers between the Muslim and Christian areas. Many companies established their headquarters in Beirut and their managers even brought their wives and children to live in the paradise of the time. Beirut's tall buildings often housed people of many different religions and nationalities, and they became good friends and enjoyed their lives.

When the Khaleds arrived at the house of Amala, they thought that they were entering a king's palace. Amala and Kemal received the family with kisses and tears and, when Habib appeared at the door, Aiesha thought she would faint from excitement and happiness. They all went to sit on the terrace of the house, which faced the Mediterranean Sea. The sun was still warm but the sea breeze was cool. The servants brought tea, coffee and pastry, and the children had sherbet with a touch of rose water. The siblings were all over their brother, Habib. They had missed him greatly. Aiesha's happy eyes hardly left his handsome face. Soon Layla started asking him about Paris, its people, buildings and even the colors of the French flag.

Later Amala took her sister and Ameerah to the room that they had prepared for Ameerah. Aiesha immediately told her daughter, "You should thank Allah that your aunt and uncle can offer you such a beautiful room. You have to listen and respect their rules. You have to take care of yourself, study hard and get good grades and, by the wish of Allah, get married soon." Amala laughed. "Don't worry if she doesn't obey," she told her sister. "We will bring her back to you immediately. We are sure she will have a great life and future here and will make our families proud of her."

The Khaleds stayed awhile with Amala's family. Habib helped his sister register at the university, and they all were invited to fancy restaurants on the beach side of the seashore drive. They walked on the beach and the children ran and swam in the water and, when it grew dark and was time to leave, all were sad. Aiesha and Amala introduced some nice girls to Habib but were not able to make a match. Habib left for Paris to continue his studies, which were going well, and the rest of the family returned to Jerusalem minus Ameerah. The trip home was much faster. Although they saw a large Palestinian refugee camp, it was too late in the day for them to stop.

Prior to the 1950's, the government built camps or low-income housing for international refugees. In the 1920's it was for Armenians who came from Turkey and Syria, and in 1948 for the Palestinians fleeing Israel's war of independence. Historically, these camps disappeared as their inhabitants integrated into society or traveled to other countries to join relatives. But the Palestinian camps had changed little over the years and were thickly populated with poor people. This was also one of the reasons that Abdullah did not want to stop on the way back from Beirut. He did not want his children to see how their fellow Palestinians lived in these camps, for he feared that they would no longer take pride in their heritage. He always paid a portion of his income to the mosque and another portion for the Palestinian refugees. He knew that many of his relatives and friends donated to the cause and that many Arab countries, especially oil-rich Saudi Arabia, gave a great deal of money to the cause. But whenever he traveled, he wondered in quiet despair what the authorities were doing with all those donations to keep people living in such poor conditions?

Abdullah never wanted to be an activist or militant. He cared for his family and friends, dealt honestly with all in his business, donated generously to righteous causes, and had a peaceful conscience before his creator. He believed that politics was not his responsibility. He just wanted to live a normal peaceful life with his family and be able to pray and work in his ancestral land.

CHAPTER 34

Raheem Enters the Picture

EVERYONE WENT BACK TO SCHOOL AND WORK, and Aiesha cleaned her house and prepared dinner for her husband and children. She was sad that Habib and Ameerah lived so far from them but, at the same time, she hoped that they would have a better life than their parents, which is every mother's wish. She always had news from Ameerah and Amala. Her sister's family was doing well, and Ameerah was successful in her studies. She was happy with her move to Beirut, and her aunt and uncle had opened her eyes to a completely new and fascinating life. They took her to parties where everyone was attracted by Ameerah's beauty.

One day Amala told her niece that one of her husband's cousins had returned from Paris. His parents invited all the available girls from good families to an extravagant party in the hope that their son would get married and settle down. He was both bright and handsome, and his family was wealthy. But everyone said that he was always in love with different European girls yet never married any. Ameerah's aunt thought that he was a little old for her but added that her husband as well as the husbands of most of her friends who had great lives were also much older than their wives. An older husband, she said, could be very good. Then she said, "My father always used to say, 'What benefit could a hungry Romeo offer his Juliette? After marriage, when Juliette and her children were hungry, the love of Romeo would fly out the window.' "

Ameerah did not answer, and her aunt continued. "His mother asked me to invite you because she likes you. Anyway, it is an occasion to meet other single available young men at the party. Tomorrow, after school, we will go to my favorite boutique and I will treat you to a nice evening gown." This cheered Ameerah, who agreed immediately.

On the morning of the party, Amala asked her hairdresser to come to her house and do their hair. Both she and her niece looked beautiful. After Ameerah put on her gown and looked at herself in the mirror, she was surprised to see that she had become a beautiful woman. Her aunt Amala whistled and said, "You look like a real princess from *The Thousand and One Nights.*" When Kemal arrived, they all went to the party.

The house was beautiful and romantic since it had been decorated with hundreds of lights. Inside there were many people dressed in the latest fashions from Paris. The smell of expensive perfumes and delicious food was mixed with the sweet scent of jasmine and other flowers from the garden. Soon Amala and her niece were welcomed by the host couple and then they met many friends. Everyone was talking and laughing happily. There were some foreigners present, too – people from Egypt and Jordan, from Syria and Turkey, and from France and Greece.

Ameerah was confused. She felt like an art critic attending a new gallery show. She had been to this house before, but each time she visited she discovered paintings, sculptures or antique furniture that she had overlooked on previous visits.

Her aunt and uncle were talking to their friends. There were many young boys and girls standing in a circle, talking and laughing. Some voices were so fake that Ameerah wanted to be alone in the beautiful terrace facing the sea. She smelled the scent of night flowers mixed with the sea breeze that brought the smell of the water and salt to her lungs.

Ameerah loved being alone and daydreaming. This was one reason that she had not married yet. None of the boys of her age were mature – at least not as mature as Ameerah. Conversations with both boys and girls of her age bored her. Standing there, she was engrossed in her dreams when suddenly she heard a warm voice behind her.

"Who is the beautiful princess in the dark, and what is she doing alone on the terrace when everyone else is inside enjoying the party?"

She abruptly came out of her reverie and turned toward the deep and well-modulated voice. In the dark, she saw only a man of a certain age but could not see the details of his face. She timidly dropped her eyes down and did not answer. He introduced himself as Raheem Malik and extended his hand to Ameerah. She shook his hand and repeated her name automatically. "Ameerah. Ameerah Khaled."

Raheem kept her hand in his warm large hands and asked, "Are you from Beirut, and what are you doing with your life?"

Ameerah tried discreetly to pull her hand out of his while she smelled his expensive cologne and searched for an answer to his questions. Finally, she said, "I love to look at the Mediterranean and smell the brisk sea air and dream of nothing special." Then she asked if he was a friend or relative of the family and what was he doing in Beirut.

Raheem replied, "Unfortunately, I am forced to stay home out of respect for my parents and participate in the party that they have thrown for me. Otherwise, at this time of night, I would have been at a nice restaurant eating dinner quietly with friends."

Ameerah understood that he had just arrived from Paris and was the man in question for all the girls who were present at the party. She was curious to, at least, see his face, so she pretended that she was getting cold and wanted to go indoors.

As soon as they entered the room, people pulled Raheem aside to talk to him. He obviously was very popular with everyone at the party. Ameerah followed him with her eyes. She saw a handsome man standing under a large crystal chandelier with several beautiful girls around him. He had dark hair and deep blue eyes. She looked away and calmly pulled herself to a corner where she could hear his warm voice answering questions from his guests. While listening, she became fascinated with the beautiful silk Persian rug that covered nearly the entire floor of the large living room. Ameerah had learned in her father's store to appreciate woven textiles and rugs, and she realized that the Persian rug that was spread in front of her was more exquisite than any she had ever seen before. She was curious to know how many knots were in each square inch. The flowers in the rug looked so real that she became totally engrossed in the rug and forgot where she was.

Suddenly she smelled the familiar cologne and felt a warm hand on her shoulder. The man with the big smile looked at her. "Ameerah, what are you dreaming about this time?"

In simple honesty she answered, "I am asking myself how people could weave such a beautiful and complicated design."

At that moment Amala and Kemal approached them. "Well," Amala said, "we see that we do not need to introduce you to each other. I was wondering where you were, Ameerah." As the party wound down, Ameerah and her aunt and uncle thanked Raheem and his parents for the beautiful evening, and Amala invited them to their house and laughingly added, "You should come as soon as possible before Raheem has time to disappear as usual from Lebanon."

Once Ameerah was alone in her bed, she heard the beautiful voice of Raheem and felt his warm hand on her shoulder. It took a while for her to fall asleep, and then she dreamed that she and Raheem were sitting on the beautiful Persian rug and flying in the sky. He was showing her the green countryside and describing the trees and other objects in his rich, warm baritone voice.

It did not take long for Raheem and his parents to accept the invitation and visit Amala for an informal family dinner. Everyone could see that there was chemistry between Raheem and Ameerah. His parents also found the young girl very attractive and, after some more visits, they officially asked Amala's permission for their son to marry her niece. Amala spoke with Ameerah and understood that she was willing to accept Raheem's proposal. She called her sister and asked for permission, adding that it was a young man that every family in Beirut was hoping to have as a son-in-law.

At night, while everyone else slept, Aiesha and Abdullah sat under the old olive tree where all the family problems were solved. Aiesha told her husband everything that her sister, Amala, had said about their daughter's suitor. Despite Amala's enthusiasm, Aiesha was sad for she understood that, if Ameerah went through with this marriage, she would no longer live in Jerusalem. But soon she added that Beirut was not too far away – an observation bathed in tears. She and her husband continued to discuss the matter, an effort made difficult by their never having met their prospective son-in-law.

Finally, Abdullah said, "If they like each other, the distance is not a problem for us. Ameerah has refused everyone here. If she returns, she might then marry a man from Saudi Arabia. Do you think she would be then happy to live in a harem with many women? How about the distance from here to Riyadh or Jidda?

And the climate? We have to trust Amala and our daughter's judgment. He can't be a bad husband. Look at your sister. She is happily married and her husband is his cousin. The same blood runs in both their veins. If he chose our daughter among so many girls, then it is the will of Allah."

Soon they all started getting ready for the wedding day. The Khaleds again traveled to Beirut. Habib flew in from Paris. Everyone was eager to meet Raheem. In her wedding gown, Ameerah looked and behaved like a princess. Raheem was a handsome man, probably fifteen years older than Ameerah, but this was not so different from other couples. Abdullah was eighteen years older than Aiesha, and Kemal was a dozen years older than Amala. This age gap was a normal thing among Muslims in the Middle East. After the wedding, the couple left on their honeymoon for Cote d'Azur, on France's Mediterranean coast. Later they would meet Habib in Paris. He was engaged to a beautiful French girl, and they were planning to marry as soon as she graduated from the university.

Raheem had a beautiful apartment in Avenue Foch, and he had told Ameerah that, because of his business, they would live some months of each year in Paris. The Khaleds returned to Jerusalem and a year later they again traveled to Beirut to be present for the birth of their first grandchild. While they were waiting for the arrival of the baby, Amala tried to introduce some nice girls to Faisal, but he had his mind in another direction and was not ready to settle down. Aiesha loved two of these girls, who were attractive and from nice families, but Faisal was no more than polite whenever he met them. In order not to hurt his aunt and mother's feelings, he told them that he would decide which one he favored by the time his sister had a second child. "*Inshallah*, God willing, that will be next year," he said, which provided sufficient hope to the matchmakers.

Meanwhile, Ameerah gave birth to a healthy boy. The Khaleds stayed for the naming ceremony and the circumcision. Aiesha remained behind while her husband and children returned to Jerusalem. The boys had to return to work, and Layla had to continue her schooling. After a week, Aiesha saw that she was not a big help to her daughter because her in-laws loved and helped her. Besides, there was also a nanny for the baby. Aiesha realized that she was needed more in her house than here.

Two years passed and Ameerah had a second child, a daughter. She was very happy with her family. She, Raheem and their two children traveled all over Europe and the Middle East. And, thanks to her husband's generosity, she was able to spoil her parents and siblings with gifts.

After Faisal and Naseem finished their schooling, they worked full-time in the family store, which had grown considerably, as had the family's import business. Abdullah was happy that his sons were following him in the family business and he proudly changed the store's name to "Khaled & Sons Gift Store of Jerusalem."

CHAPTER 35

Faisal Makes His Decision

IN THE 1960's, EGYPTIAN PRESIDENT NASSER became the voice of the Arab nations and also became very powerful in the region. Yasser Arafat formed the Palestinian Fatah movement and began calling for war to eliminate Israel. Later the Palestinian Liberation Organization, known everywhere by its initials PLO, was founded by Nasser with Ahmed Shukhairy at its head.

In late December 1964, Fatah began attacking Israel. In less than two years, more than a hundred terrorist attacks resulted in many fatalities and injuries. Each attack, big or small, received wide publicity in the Arab world. Nasser often referred to them in his impassioned radio addresses, and many Arab youths – especially those in Palestine – were attracted by his fiery words. Young Palestinian men were encouraged to join Arafat's Fatah in order to liberate their country.

Among those drawn to this message was Faisal Khaled. More and more he stayed out late, often missing dinner. Aiesha tried to understand what was happening to her son but he answered that he was out with friends. It was accepted that, at his age, he should be allowed to set his own hours. Aiesha agreed but was not comforted. She was aware that the behavior and the attitudes of her third child had changed markedly, but attributed this to the normal growth process and told herself that he would change as he matured.

One day Faisal told his father that he had to do some official work and was going to be absent from the store. He left home early and returned at noon. Aiesha was surprised to see her son home so soon. She offered to fix him lunch but he declined and thanked her with a lost voice and said that he was not hungry. While Aiesha was in the kitchen he came in, hugged his mother and kissed her hand and said that he was going for a short trip and that she should give his love to everyone. Aiesha's heart sank. Tears fell from her dark eyes, and she asked Faisal if his father had given him permission. He answered that he was an adult and knew well what he was doing. Yes, he was sure that his father would insist that he stay in the store all day. But he needed to do what he had to do, and it was for the betterment of everyone whom he loved. He abruptly turned and left immediately.

Aiesha fainted. When she came to, the kitchen was cold and dark and she started crying. Soon, Layla, Naseem and Abdullah all arrived home. When they saw her crying, they were alarmed. All Aiesha would say is, "Faisal has left us." Finally, Abdullah asked Layla to bring her a glass of cold water and he calmed her down and asked the children to leave the room. He asked his wife to tell him the entire story.

Abdullah's face grew paler with each word since he knew exactly what his son meant. There were many excited, desperate or patriotic young men who had joined the Palestinian resistance. The recruiters knew how to attract them, but Abdullah thought that his sons were different and soon would follow the example of their brother, Habib, and continue their education. That evening, no one was hungry for dinner and each of them slept sadly in their beds, laying their heads on wet pillows.

Days passed. Aiesha expected news from her son but heard nothing. She was amazed that the gentle, loving boy who had grown up in her arms had left her without sending back news. He had loved and respected his parents, she reminded herself, so what could have happened to him? Each time she wondered, she blamed herself for covering up her son's late homecomings at night. She never thought it would lead to any harm. After all, he was a young man and needed to see friends. Aiesha did not want to discuss this with Abdullah, sine she knew her husband was tired and did not want to disturb his sleep.

One morning, about a month later, Aiesha heard a knock at the door. She ran happily to open it because she thought it was Faisal. Instead, she was surprised to see a stranger standing there.

"Is this the house of Khaled?"

Aiesha uneasily said yes, and showed the visitor into the house.

"I am here to congratulate the family for giving such a brave and unselfish son to the cause of justice. Everyone in Fatah is proud of him, and Mr. Arafat himself asked me to visit you." Aiesha was shocked and confused. Finally, she asked, "How is my son Faisal doing? Why doesn't he come home, or at least write or call us? Everyone in the family is worried and sad because we haven't heard from him."

The man pulled a picture out of his pocket. "This is the last picture of your brave son. He cannot contact you since he sacrificed his life for all of us some days ago very bravely. Now he is with Allah and soon, when we have our country back, he will be remembered as one of our heroes." The man put the picture on the table, walked briskly to the door, and closed it behind him before Aiesha could ask any more questions.

She was shocked to her core. Her shaky hands grabbed the last picture of her son. The photograph showed Faisal holding a rifle with one hand and a grenade with the other. He was in uniform like a soldier! Suddenly she burst out crying. She kissed the picture of her son, who had a cold look and a much different face from that she knew all these years. Aiesha slumped down to the floor. Her sobs were eventually quieted by a deep sleep. After months of mental torture, at least she knew where her son was and that he would never return home.

Aiesha remained on the cold floor for hours. In her dream, she could hear people calling her and feel them shaking her. But she ignored everyone because she was walking with Faisal on the soft sands of Beirut, not far from Ameerah's house, asking him if he had made up his mind about which of the two girls he was going to marry. Faisal did not answer but smiled at his mother. Suddenly, Faisal pushed her in the sea and she became all wet. She opened her eyes and saw the worried eyes of her husband, son and daughter around her. Layla was crying and was calling to her. Naseem had a glass of water in his hand, and Abdullah was trying to give him an empty glass in exchange for the full one. In a weak voice, Aiesha asked, "Why did you wake me up? He was trying to choose one of the girls to marry. Why did you push me into the sea?" Then she closed her eyes again, desperately hoping to return to sleep. She was holding tightly the picture of her son against her heart.

Abdullah tried to revive her with kind words and asked what had happened. As soon as she came to full consciousness, she told them that she wanted to die and could not live anymore. Finally, she told them about the visit from the stranger. She pulled her hand away from her heart and showed them the picture of Faisal. "He told me that this was Faisal's last picture and that we should all be proud of him. And that he is with Allah now. I want him here. Why did he go to Allah? We have such a beautiful mosque in Jerusalem. If he wanted to pray, that was a holy place. Why had he gone so far away?"

Then she pulled her hair and cried. Abdullah asked her to think about Layla and Naseem, who were present in the room.

With a gentle voice, he told Layla and Naseem that he was tired and needed to sleep, but they had to eat their dinner and force their mother to eat also. He went to his room, closed the door, and fell into a fitful sleep. The children took only little bites of the meal that Aiesha put on the table. She refused to eat despite their pleadings. Finally, the children went to bed, leaving their mother lying on the rug, holding the picture of Faisal against her chest and hoping to see him again in her dreams.

The children were awakened early in the morning by their mother's screams. "I've killed him, I've killed him!" Layla and Naseem rushed to their parents' bedroom where they saw their mother holding the hand of her husband, who lay lifelessly in the bed. Naseem immediately called their family doctor but, when he examined him, he informed them that Abdullah had died many hours earlier, probably of a heart attack. He offered some sympathetic words and a sedative to Aiesha, who was sobbing uncontrollably.

Suddenly, Naseem became the man of the house. He contacted the *imam* of their mosque, who was a friend of his father's and knew him to be an honest and kind man who was loved and respected by everyone. By late afternoon, everything was ready for the burial of Abdullah Khaled, since their religion required that a dead body must be buried before sunset on the day of death. Aiesha dressed from head to toe in black and, during the funeral service, asked the *imam* to also pray for their son, Faisal. That was when everyone learned of Faisal's death. She told them that he had died while on a business trip, and gave a white shirt of his to the *imam* and asked him to formally bury it at the side of his father. Once the grave was covered, there were four generations of Khaleds in the ground. Naseem and Layla tried to comfort their mother but, in truth, they also needed to be comforted. Everyone was shocked by the double funeral. Friends and neighbors advised Aiesha and her children to go to sleep early and told them that Allah would give them the strength and force to continue their lives.

Some friends of Faisal and Naseem, who knew nothing of Faisal's actual fate, were almost hysterically shouting that his and his father's blood were on Israeli hands, for it was because of the Zionist existence that the Palestinian people suffered.

That night, when Aiesha was alone in her cold bed and her tears were washing her pillow, she remembered the comforting words of the *imam* at the funeral. Then she remembered the words of the unknown visitor, who told her that her son had joined the martyrs some days ago. As she kept thinking, she remembered the news she had heard on Arab radio glorifying a young Palestinian hero who had attacked a supermarket, which resulted in the death of a housewife and her infant daughter. There were also many people who were wounded and transported to the hospital. The Palestinian gunman was shot dead by the police, although the radio announcer described it as a glorious and selfless sacrifice by the young man, who had given his life for the cause of his people.

Aiesha remembered that she had asked herself what the benefit was to the Palestinians of killing a woman who was shopping for her family and her innocent baby. She had also been sad for the young man's family and had told herself that he could have helped the cause of his people by more positive actions. Now she knew that the young hero was her own blood and flesh, her dear Faisal. He was such a gentle young man who, like his father, was kind and considerate of everyone. Then she wondered, "Who was the person capable of influencing and changing the heart and mind of my loving son?!" She had no answers. Instead, she could only offer abundant tears and sorrow.

CHAPTER 36

A War Casualty

BY THE TIME Layla finished her schooling, she had turned into a beautiful young girl. She had a lot of responsibilities, for she was taking care of the house and her mother, who had become like the walking dead. Aiesha wished and prayed that Allah would take her so she could join Abdullah and Faisal. She spent most of her time at the cemetery, crying and talking to her departed husband and son.

Naseem had grown into a responsible man who was supporting his family by running the gift shop and distribution business. He was a kind man who worked all day and late into the night trying to figure out what was going on around him. Habib was a doctor who practiced in Paris, married and with two children. Ameerah continued to live *la dolce vita* with her husband and children in Beirut and Paris. Both Habib and Ameerah were deeply saddened by the deaths of Abdullah and Faisal. But they lived far away, could not see their mother's situation, and did not learn of their father's death until after his funeral, so they were not as affected as Layla and Naseem.

Habib and Ameerah wanted their mother to visit Paris or Beirut, but she refused and said that she was in her land with her husband and son. They also asked Layla to continue her studies abroad, but she told them she could not leave her mother and brother alone. She was working at the store and doing much of the housework and cooking as well. Serving customers and taking care of the diverse activities of their business served as a welcome distraction for her sad spirit. She had loved her father very much and was sad that no one was aware that he had not been in good health. She also missed Faisal, Habib and Ameerah. But the one she missed the most was her mother. Although she was present physically, there were no long conversations or animated interactions like before. To keep her mind sane, when she finished all her responsibilities, Layla boosted her spirit after dinner by reading books in various languages on many different subjects.

At the beginning of 1967, the political situation in the Middle East was very tense. Tourists no longer visited Jerusalem in large groups, so business at the local stores dropped sharply. At Khaled & Sons, the main customers were businessmen who were in town for a few days and wanted to buy some souvenirs for their families. Naseem was gloomy and pessimistic. He did not say much or share his thoughts with Layla. He did not even realize that it was a very difficult time for her as well. She remembered the happy days of the past and, although she was living with her mother and brother, she was really all alone. She had kept current with a few friends, but they were either married with responsibilities of their own or had very different interests from hers. So she preferred to stay alone by herself instead of wasting time with them.

By the end of April, Naseem had withdrawn most of the business' money from the bank. Every night he brought cash home, and he and Layla would hide it in safe places. Then one night he told her that, because the store was doing almost no business, he had decided to close it for a while and travel. He told her that, if she saw that business conditions were improving, she could open the store and run it with their longtime employee, Hassan. Or, since Hassan was a very honest man, she could ask him to run the store alone since she had her hands full with their mother.

Naseem promised to write or call often, but he said Layla had to understand that he needed time for himself to find out what he really was looking for in life. He also told Layla with passion that, on his return he would take her to the Mediterranean beach in Tel Aviv and they would swim and enjoy the sun together.

Although young, Layla was not a child. She had seen the changes in her brother and noticed his new friends who would stop at the store and invite him for tea in a café when business was slow. She was not a politician but listened carefully to the radio stations and read the newspapers every day. And, of course, she had read many history books and knew that, where there is a fire hidden under the ashes, one day it will blaze up to unthinkable proportions. She always told herself that people wanted to put out such a fire in either of two ways. Some people would look at the ashes and admit that, while there used to be a fire there,   it was now out because of the ashes and there was no danger of it reigniting. So they would ignore it and continue to live their lives. But realistic people would look at the ashes and, to be sure and safe, put their fingers inside to see if the fire was really out completely. And, when their fingers got burned, they knew that the fire was likely waiting for the right moment to roar back to life.

When Naseem kissed his mother and told her that he was going to travel, she kissed him back. "Allah be with you!" Naseem hugged Layla and told her again, "Soon, I will return and we will go together and swim in the beaches of a free Tel Aviv." Layla hugged her brother and begged him to take care of himself and told him that she always loved him very much and hoped that he was not putting all of himself, instead of just his finger, into the ashes. She said that she would wait for his safe return. She took the Koran in her hands and, as was the custom, stood at the doorway and asked him to kiss the book and pass three times under it.

On his last passage, Naseem ran out of the house and Layla followed him with her tears in her eyes until she could see only tears. She kissed the Koran and placed it respectfully on the mantel, with tears still washing her face. She looked at her mother, who was lost in thought and looking far away. She went outside, sat under the olive tree, looked at beautiful Jerusalem, and asked, "Why?"

The Arab radio stations continued to broadcast the bombastic and incendiary speeches of Nasser. More terrorist attacks occurred in Israel and the number of heroes on Fatah's and PLO's list grew. All the governments of the region blamed each other for the conflict and said that they were getting ready for a bloody war. Major countries played political games in the region for their own benefit and sold arms to one country or another. The United Nations took no meaningful actions.

On May 14, 1967, Egypt demanded that U.N. peacekeeping forces be withdrawn from the Sinai Peninsula. U.N. Secretary General U Thant agreed to remove the troops on May 18. Five days later Nasser closed the Strait of Tiran – Israel's shipping link to the Red Sea. He justified his actions by saying Egypt was prepared to fight Israel for the rights of the Palestinian people. He declared that his soldiers would not only walk on the bare sands of Palestine but on sands soaked in the blood of Israelis.

On May 29, Nasser addressed the Egyptian National Assembly. "God," he said, "will surely help and urge us to restore the situation to what it was in 1948." Syria had already sided with Egypt. On May 30, King Hussein of Jordan signed a pact with Nasser and, on June 4, he was joined by Iraqi President Rahman

Aref, who proudly announced, "This is the moment to wipe Israel off the map."

On June 1, the Israeli government, with Moshe Dayan as Israeli Defense Minister, was feverishly preparing for war. In the early morning of June 5, the Israeli radio announced that Egyptians had opened fire and that Israeli forces were returning it. The Israeli radio later reported that, in the prior few hours, the Israeli Air Force had attacked and destroyed enemy aircraft, which were mostly on the ground. But, at the same time, the Egyptian radio announced that its forces were winning the first day of the war. A fierce ground war took place between Egypt and Israel, in which Israel prevailed. After the Israelis won all of the Sinai, Nasser accepted a ceasefire.

Then, Israel turned its forces to the Golan Heights, where Syrian artillery was shelling civilian targets in the north of Israel. On June 9, Israeli troops attacked Syria and, after a fierce battle between the two armies, Israel conquered the Golan Heights on June 10. The way was open to Damascus, but the Israeli army did not advance.

Uncharacteristically, King Hussein made a bad judgment call. He ignored Israeli pleas to stay out of the upcoming war and attacked West Jerusalem. Jordanian artillery and air forces also attacked the suburbs of Tel Aviv, Netanya and other cities in Israel on the first day of the war. Israel counterattacked, and the Jordanian Legion, after a fierce tank and artillery battle, was driven out of East Jerusalem, allowing the city's unity to be restored. Now Temple Mount and the Wailing Wall – *Kotel*, the Western Wall – were returned to Israel after a very long time.

Israeli Defense Minister Moshe Dayan, Chief of Staff Yitzhak Rabin and the chief chaplain of the Israel Defense Force, General Rabbi Shlomo Goren, soon visited Eastern Jerusalem.

Rabbi Goren blew the *shofar* (ram's horn) at the Western Wall, signifying its liberation.

"The divided and split capital of Israel has been reunited," he proclaimed. Israeli paratroopers raised the Israeli flag above the Western Wall and everyone sang "Hatikvah," the Israeli hymn. Soldiers prayed and cried with high emotions and said *Kaddish*, the Jewish prayer in memory of the dead, for their friends who did not survive to see the glorious day.

By June 10, the war had ended and, on the next day, a truce was signed between Israel and its Arab neighbors.

After the end of the Six-Day War, the pan-Arab ideology of Nasser collapsed in the Arab world and, following his death later that year, the outlawed Islamist movement – the Muslim Brotherhood – began to gain favor among the masses. Hafez al-Assad became prime minister and then president of Syria. Meanwhile, Arafat worked furiously to take over Fatah and make his Palestine Liberation Organization the only voice of all the Palestinians.

Layla woke up very early on the fifth of June. Most of the time she would wake up early or even in the middle of the night because of the loud noises or cries of her mother. She would run to Aiesha's room only to find her deeply asleep. Layla knew that her mother had nightmares but still, at the slightest sound, she would run to her room to see if she could help her. She prepared a cup of tea for herself and sat under the olive tree. The weather was beautiful; the sun was already up; and the birds were singing. She looked around the garden and up at the beautiful sky and asked herself why the world was moving toward destruction. Life was so short and beautiful and yet, in such a short time, she had lost almost everyone.

She watched the ants working hard during those early hours and remembered her father and brothers and prayed that the spirit of her father would watch over Naseem so that he could keep his promise and they could be together again. When she walked into the house later, her mother was up and looking for her. She asked her mother to sit under the olive tree while she prepared her breakfast. Aiesha drank tea and coffee but seemed almost indifferent to food and had lost so much weight that her daughter could hardly recognize her. Layla hoped to force some food into her body.

Aiesha was in a good mood that morning and, for the first time in a long while, ate a full meal. She told Layla about her sweet dreams. "Faisal, Naseem and your father were sitting under a beautiful tree covered with flowers. There was a river separating me from my husband and sons. They did not see me but, as soon as Abdullah heard my voice, he ran like a gazelle in his young years, jumped across the river, and picked me up in his arms. Then Faisal and Naseem welcomed me. I am sure they are going to come and take me."

Then she looked at Layla with love and said, "I thank you for all your hard work and sacrifice, but you should leave this city and go to Paris and live near Habib and Ameerah far from here. Promise you will do so."

Layla had tears in her eyes since she could understand the deep meaning of her words. Her mother's eyes were shining with joy and peace; Layla had not seen her like this for a long time.

Suddenly she saw movement down in the city and recognized soldiers and tanks. She immediately told her mother that she was cold and they needed to get in the house. Aiesha went to her regular chair, and then she sat on the floor and then lay in her bed. As Layla was washing the teacups and plates, she turned on the radio and heard that, since early morning, Israel and Egypt were at war. She was shocked. Although everyone had felt the tension for more than two years, people were hoping that the major powers or the United Nations would bring peace to the region.

She switched back and forth from Arab to Israeli stations. Each was claiming victory over the enemy. Then she heard gunshots and explosions in the distance just as a radio announcer said that Jordanian artillery and infantry were advancing into West Jerusalem. Much later she heard that the Jordanian Air Force had fired on many suburbs of Tel Aviv.

Meanwhile, Aiesha was in her own world and almost asleep again. Layla looked from the garden to Jerusalem. The beautiful blue sky of hours ago had changed color to dark gray and, in places, almost black. She understood that the situation was dangerous. She returned to the kitchen, filled all the buckets and pots that she could find with water, and stacked furniture against the doors and in front of windows. She was alone and knew that she had to rely on her own strength and intelligence. As the day advanced, so did the sound of guns. She could only listen to the different radio stations and try to figure out which of the broadcasts was more accurate. As night approached, Layla did not turn on the lights. Instead, she and her mother ate under the dim light of a candle and then went to bed early.

The following day the sound of artillery and small arms fire were grim evidence that a fierce battle was taking place. Layla listened to the radio and stayed indoors with her mother. Late that evening Layla heard a deafening explosion and then felt a deep peace. When she came to her senses, she was cold and did not remember where she was or what had happened to her. She looked up and, through a tiny hole in the roof, she could see the beautiful sky of Jerusalem filled with twinkling stars. She smiled at one of the brightest and asked how her father was doing, and then she again fell into a deep sleep.

In the morning, Layla woke up very early. It was still dark but she could feel that night was hardly fighting to keep its kingdom since it was time for the sun to rise. She looked around and was surprised to see that everything in her room had moved and there was a little hole in the ceiling. She tried to stand up but saw that she was covered with books and other items. She had some bruises and small cuts but otherwise was not injured. Then she remembered the loud explosion and understood the house had received a shell from one of the armies. What was the difference which one? The important thing was that their home had been hit.

As soon as she could stand she called out for her mother, but there was no answer. She ran to Aiesha's room but she wasn't there. When Layla went to the living room, she saw her mother lying on the rug, in a pool of blood. Her hands were holding the last picture of Faisal against her heart. Her face was pale but she had a peaceful smile. Layla touched her cheek and realized that she had died many hours ago. She understood that probably she had her dream again and that was the reason she had such a peaceful smile.

From her father's funeral she had learned that she had to bury her before nightfall. The artillery sounds were growing louder and she was aware that she would not be able to transport her mother to the cemetery. Besides, the *imam* was probably not available to conduct a service. Suddenly, she felt a force inside her being. Layla went outside and took a shovel and started digging under one of the trees that faced Mecca. After she was satisfied with its depth and size, she ran back into the house, took the cold body of her mother to the bathroom, and washed her using water from one of the buckets that she had saved. Then she wrapped her in a clean white sheet and took her to the grave that she had prepared.

She was so intent on her task that she did not even hear all the horrible noises of war around her or worry about her own safety. She placed Aiesha in the grave and then ran back inside to fetch the bloody picture of Faisal that her mother had held to her chest. Layla covered the picture of Faisal with a clean white handkerchief of her father's and placed it on her mother's chest. She then brought the Koran outside and read some prayers, imitating what the *imam* had done. After she put the book back on the half-broken mantel, she returned to the grave and started throwing earth on her mother. She was crying, talking to her mother and to Allah. Her hands and arms were sore. It took her a long time to cover the body entirely; she knew she had a lot of time before sunset.

By then she became aware that the sound of the guns had diminished considerably, but she was not concerned with the outside war. She had her own war inside her house, inside her being, with everyone against her. Everyone who loved her was gone. Somehow all her loved ones had deserted and betrayed her. They had left her all alone in this world.

Exactly at the moment that she was throwing the last shovel of earth on her mother, she heard a loud and long sound of the blowing of a ram's horn. Jerusalem was peaceful now. The sky was returning to its vibrant blue color again. She heard voices from the distance like the mumbling of bees, then a very loud group sound. And, before she walked in the house, she saw a large Israeli flag flying in the sky.

Layla threw herself in her mother's habitual chair. She was exhausted; a fly sat comfortably on her wet cheek and she was not even able to move her hand and chase it away. She either had fainted or was asleep since the fly took all its time to wash its face with his two narrow arms and then lick Layla's cheek. It was as if it were showing this person the insect's superiority over the powerful humans!

When Layla woke up after a deep sleep, she was rested and had forgotten what had happened. She looked around. Everything seemed calm but there were some holes, large and small, on the walls and roof of their house, some blood on the rug, and some furnishings were broken and out of place. Only then did she remember that she had buried her mother just hours ago. Tears washed her face, but she realized that it was only a cold body that she had buried. In reality, her mother had died when Faisal and her father died. At least Aiesha was now at peace, for every moment of her life after that day was a torture for her.

Layla then remembered her last words and cried bitterly since she was sure that her brother, Naseem, had joined the PLO and was also dead by now. But she had no proof – only her mother's prediction and her inner gut. She remembered that her mother had asked her to leave the country and join her sister and brother in France. She smiled bitterly and in tears said, "Mother, Naseem promised to take me to Tel Aviv to swim. I have to wait for him. Whenever he made a promise to me, he kept it!"

She told herself that she had to keep herself strong and not become like her mother. She had to clean and restore the house because Naseem would be tired when he returned. She went to the kitchen, ate a few bites of food, and made a pot of strong coffee. She returned to the living room to start planning how she would repair the house. Layla remembered her grandparent's stories and attachment to their land and house, and she told herself that she would never give up their house or the name on the front of the store and would make them proud of her.

ॐ

Many Palestinians who lived in the West Bank fled because of the war. They feared for the safety of their families. Some came back after the end of the war but many did not. During and after the war, Israeli forces also ordered some Palestinians to move for strategic and security reasons. Some were allowed to return after a few days and others received offers from the Israelis to resettle elsewhere. Fortunately, the Khaled house was not in a strategic or security zone and Layla was able to clean up the damage and later hired workers to repair the house. The East Jerusalem Arabs were given the option of retaining Jordanian citizenship or acquiring Israeli citizenship. They were recognized as residents of united Jerusalem who could vote and run for the city council. Most chose to retain their Jordanian citizenship. Many people were still confused and believed that soon Israel was going to leave the lands and cities that it had conquered during the war.

As soon as security returned to Jerusalem after the Six-Day War, many tourists visited the city. Layla contacted Hassan and informed him that she was opening the store and needed his help. Hassan, who had fled to Jordan during the war, returned to Jerusalem one night with a lot of difficulty by crossing the Jordan River. Beginning the following day, it took them a week to repair, clean and rearrange the store. Then they opened for business. Layla worked all day and, in the evenings, she sat under the old olive tree, eating a simple dinner. There she could visit her mother's grave and cry for her sad fate.

After a month, she realized that, if she continued her routine, she was going to end up like her mother. So she met the *imam* who had buried her father and explained all. The *imam* praised her brave spirit and promised to arrange a formal burial for her mother. After a week, everything was organized; the plot next to her father was prepared to receive Aiesha. Finally, she received a proper burial and prayers that she deserved. Her soul was at rest.

Layla donated some money to the *imam* so that he would invite all the members of his mosque to a memorial dinner in the memory of her brother and parents. Every month she paid a percentage of her income to the mosque as called for by her religion and gave money also to the Palestinian refugee fund. She planted some new olive trees in the place where she had first buried her mother and, after some time, she felt her spirit was elevated. She could feel the presence of her parents and Faisal in the bright stars. Ameerah and Habib insisted that she should join them, but Layla told them that she would when the time came. For the moment, she was doing fine in Jerusalem and needed some time to clear up her mind.

CHAPTER 37

Layla Meets Golda and Aaron

BUSINESS IN THE GIFT STORE WAS BOOMING. Layla and Hassan added more shelves with new merchandise. Besides foreign tourists, many Israelis also visited Jerusalem. Layla happily practiced the various languages she spoke with visitors from many different countries. One afternoon a group of older women entered the store and, as soon as Layla and one of the ladies made eye contact, it seemed that they had known each other for years. A connection was created between them.

After the women bought some souvenirs, Layla saw that the one with whom she had made eye contact looked frail and tired. So Layla offered her a chair and told her kindly that she could rest in the store as long as she needed. The woman accepted immediately, thanked her with a rough accent, and introduced herself as Golda. Her friends asked her to join them because they had other places to visit. But Golda told them that she was tired and, since the nice young woman had offered her hospitality, she would sit there and wait for them to return.

After Golda's friends left, the store became calmer. Layla asked if she could bring her a cup of tea or coffee. Golda was pleased with the offer but asked for only a glass of cold water. They started talking and, despite, being complete strangers, felt an odd feeling of friendship. Although two women could hardly be more different than Golda and Layla's mother, Aiesha, Golda reminded Layla of her mother. In a sudden burst of emotion, Golda said, "I am a Holocaust survivor. My parents and I, as far as we could remember, lived in Germany and were Germans, just like everyone else. But one day our entire life was changed. The Nazis took us to the camps and we were reduced to poor and hungry people overnight. Later we were separated from each other, and I learned that my entire family was killed. I was the only one to survive and I do not understand the reason. My daughter was much younger and stronger, but she did not make it."

Golda's voice broke and it took a moment for her to continue. "After the liberation, I had no one to turn to and did not know where to go. Then I learned about the possibility of going to Israel. Although it was far away and very different from what I was used to, once in the country I found many people in my situation. Much later, during a ceremony of the survivors, I was surprised to find my younger brother. He lives in Haifa, is married and has two sons. Later I had a position teaching at the University of Tel Aviv until I retired some years ago. I do have some friends in the building where I am living and, at my age, I cannot ask more of life."

She paused to finish the glass of water.

"I often come to Yad Vashem, the Holocaust Memorial Museum. When I enter it, I feel I am visiting the graves of my loved ones. After crying and talking to them, I return home somehow comforted. But today we came to Jerusalem for the first time to pray at the Western Wall. This was the wish of my parents and husband. Somehow I felt their presence and saw my daughter's beautiful face."

Then Golda apologized for talking so much about her life. She said that, as soon as she saw Layla, it was as if they had a connection. Although Layla did not resemble her daughter, still she saw her daughter in Layla. Then she added, "Who am I to tell you all this? I can see in your eyes that you have gone through hard times yourself! I am sorry, and I hope we will have peace between our two sister nations from now on. It was a waste of life for both sides – what a tragedy for everyone!"

Golda was so sincere and kind that Layla opened up and, for the first time, she told her story to a complete stranger. Neither felt the passage of time.

Suddenly they both jumped, startled by the loud noise of Golda's friends returning to pick her up. Golda and Layla hugged each other and Golda told her that she planned to come often to pray at the Wall. Layla closed the store and went home happy. She felt that their encounter and discussion had given her new energy. She decided to take the opportunities that were available to her and learn Hebrew, which would make her life easier and enable her to understand better both the new government and her new neighbors.

On the way home on a bus one of the women teased Golda unkindly. "Well, it seems you have added an Arab terrorist to your circle. How do you know that her father and brother were not the ones who killed your nephew? How could you hug her just months after the Six-Day War?"

Golda was hurt by her friend's remarks. She knew her friend well and that she always had a big mouth and was against everyone. Golda sharply told her, "Actually, you are right; her brother was the one who killed my nephew. But I am not sure if my nephew did not shoot him back before dying! I believe that, as long as we have people with such big mouths like you on both sides of the camp with their *Lashon Hara* (bad-mouthing), they will continue to keep the fire of conflicts and wars burning." Then she turned her head toward the window and did not talk to anyone for the rest of the trip. Instead, she thought about Layla all the way back to Tel Aviv.

ॐ

Life was busy for Layla, and many changes were happening in Jerusalem. Golda came almost every week and they ended up becoming good friends. Since Layla loved to read, they exchanged books and ideas. Another time Layla invited Golda for dinner and, when the hour became late, she stayed overnight. The two discussed all kinds of things under the ancient olive tree, and Golda appreciated the view over Jerusalem. For the first time, Layla did not feel lonely at home.

After some time, Golda invited Layla to her home, noting that it was close to the beach and had a nice view, which she was sure that Layla would enjoy. Layla thanked her but refused. Golda was upset. "I came to your house and slept there; why wouldn't you come to my house?"

Layla replied, "It is not your house that I am refusing. It is a horror for me to travel on a bus. I always try to walk and not take buses. Whenever there is a terrorist attack or something happens, the police stop the bus and order us out onto the street. They ask all kinds of questions and sometimes they search our bags and purses. I feel so deprived of my rights – so frustrated and hurt. But everyone thinks it is normal."

Layla continued to share her story. "One time I was so frustrated that I responded bitterly to the young soldier who was searching my bags and asking me questions. He took me to the station. His superior asked me questions and I told him that I was tired of being treated differently in my own land. And we talked a lot. At the end he apologized and said that, when a bomb explodes, everyone is hurt. Bombs do not spare Arabs or distinguish age and religion. He told me the police were trying to protect everyone, Jew and Muslim alike. Then he handed me a card and said that I could take a cab paid by his office. I thanked him, returned the card, and told him that I was not a beggar; I just want to be left alone and live like a normal citizen!"

Golda was touched by her story. "One of my best friends has a car," she told Layla. "He also had experiences like ours in the past, and he still drives. I am sure that he would be happy to drive with me next week. If you stay a week, we can drive you back. If not, I hope on the day of your return there will be no incident and you will return home without humiliation, which I know well."

The following week Golda and her friend entered the store and she introduced him to Layla as Art. He shook Layla's hand and said, "I am so happy to meet you. I was so anxious to meet this beautiful and intelligent girl whom Golda was talking about all these past months. Well, I have not yet discussed any subject with you to judge your intelligence, but I can approve the part about the beauty." They all laughed.

Layla picked up her little suitcase and accompanied Golda and Art to his car. He asked her to sit in front so she could have a better view while traveling. Art said that while the distance between Jerusalem and Tel Aviv was only thirty-nine miles and that it usually took no more than forty minutes of driving time, he was going to drive slower so that Layla could see the sights and enjoy her first trip.

There was not much traffic on the road; occasionally, they passed some trucks, buses and military cars. No one stopped their car, so Layla felt more at ease and observed the passing scenery. This was the first time that she was traveling in Israel. She had much information but mixed feelings about the country, yet it was only a short distance from her house. She could probably even walk to the border. As they rode along, Golda and Art talked about how Israel was addressing irrigation, housing and many other civic matters. Then they arrived in Tel Aviv with its small and tall buildings. Art stopped the car in front of a building and asked the women to get out so he could park the car a short distance away.

Layla was able to smell the sea even before she saw it. Golda opened the main gate and they took the elevator to the fourth floor. Golda opened the door of her apartment, kissed the *mezuzah* – a small piece of parchment inscribed with two Biblical passages hidden inside the decorated little piece of metal – and invited Layla to enter first.

She showed her the apartment and then took her to a bedroom that was decorated with a young person's taste. There was a picture of a handsome young boy on the desk. Golda saw the question on Layla's face. Her eyes filled with tears and she said, "I did not tell you since it is still very fresh for me. He is my nephew – my brother's oldest son. He was a very talented and handsome young man. He was studying at the University of Tel Aviv and was brilliant. When the war broke out, he volunteered for the army because he believed he had a duty to protect and save his county. He died in the Golan Heights, and they told us that he had shown a lot of bravery. He died so that I could live peacefully. It is not fair!"

Golda took a moment to regain her composure, and then continued. "He would be very happy to know that you have stayed in his room. I am sure you would have become good friends if you both had met before."

Art came in and the subject changed. Golda prepared tea and coffee with cookies. They sat on the balcony and looked at the beautiful scenery before them. The water was so calm, blue and nice that no one would imagine the country had just ended a horrible war. After they all rested, Golda told Layla that she was going to start preparing dinner, so Layla was free to walk on the beach and enjoy the remaining two hours before sunset. Because

Layla did not know the streets, she did not want to be out after dark. However, the next day she would learn her way around the neighborhood.

Golda handed Layla a set of keys and wrote the address on a piece of paper. "You know enough Hebrew to ask your way if you are lost. You will be surprised to learn that many newer immigrants' first language is Arabic."

While Layla was in the elevator, she looked at the key chain and saw the name "Yaron" under the plastic tag.

She walked on the soft sands. At first, she expected that someone would make a remark to her and stop her, but everyone was enjoying the God-given beauty of the sea, which was spread in front of all equally. No one paid special attention to her except some young boys, who whistled when they saw her. Layla ignored them. Mothers were relaxing under the sun while their children played in the water. Some adults were talking and arguing, and there were young couples holding hands, walking and kissing once in a while. There were some large, newly built hotels with famous names. She walked and walked. She could feel only the warm sand under her feet and warm tears on her face.

Layla looked at the distant horizon and told Naseem that she was in Tel Aviv, still waiting for him. "You promised to give me news but you did not send even a single word. This was not like you. What happened to you, and where are you?" She cried so much that she felt her tear ducts were empty. Although the sea breeze was cool, her heart was burning. The sun was shining and she felt that somehow its rays were lightening her darkened heart. She looked at her watch and understood that it was time to return. When she rang the doorbell and unlocked it, the smell of delicious food came to her.

"Good," said Golda. "Just in time. Dinner is ready."

Layla asked if she could help set the table but Art answered that was his responsibility. The candles were lit, and the plates were set nicely. They had a delicious dinner and sat on the balcony afterward and watched the sun set and later the stars appear. It was quite late when Art said goodnight. Golda told Layla that she usually got up late in the morning but, if Layla awoke early, she could go to the beach and watch the beautiful sunrise.

Layla slept very well and thought of Joseph and all the things that had happened to Golda during her lifetime. She fell into a deep sleep and, in her dream, she saw that they were all at the beach – she, her mother, father and Golda were talking while watching Naseem and Yaron, who were running like little children on the sand, laughing loudly and throwing water on each other.

Layla woke up late. It was already warm. The two women had their breakfast; Golda showed Layla books and some pictures of her students. Art came to the house and proposed taking them to Dizengoff Street. At first Layla refused, but they insisted. The three shared a late lunch in one of the restaurants and looked at store windows.

In the evening, Layla went for a walk on the beach and told Golda that she was going to watch the sunset since it was her last day. Layla had already learned her way around. She walked along the street for a while and then headed toward the beach, where she took off her shoes and walked a long way on the sand, appreciating the view and talking to herself and to her brothers. She wondered if there was not enough room for everyone to live peacefully and enjoy life. There was plenty of space everywhere from Jerusalem to Tel Aviv with a lot of open land. Even on the beach of Tel Aviv there was sufficient space for everyone to enjoy God's sea and sand!

Sunset was approaching. Layla found a large stone and sat on it. It was pleasantly warm, as if the stone had collected all the heat from the sun during the day and was offering it to Layla. With no one around, she felt calm and serene. She thought about her own life and just enjoyed the most glorious view of nature. The vast blue sea and the sand were painted with the colors of the setting sun. Layla was fascinated and completely absorbed by the magical view.

Suddenly she heard a warm voice asking her in Arabic, "Have you ever seen anything more beautiful than this glorious sunset?" For a moment Layla was shocked, since she thought it was Naseem talking to her. She turned toward the voice and saw a handsome young man whose face and eyes also reflected the changing colors of the sunset. He had dark hair and skin almost like hers and a very kind face.

"You are right," she answered. "It is beautiful."

The young man continued the conversation. "This is the most precious gift that God has offered us humans to look at and enjoy and, yet, as you see, there are not so many people around to appreciate it."

He introduced himself as Aaron and asked permission to sit down beside her. They talked more about the beauty of nature. Later Aaron told her a bit about his background.

"My parents are from Tunisia and I was born there too. By the time I was ten years old, they decided to leave the country because they did not feel it was safe to stay there anymore. Our choice was between France and here. First we went to France but life was hard there. We missed the warm sun, the sea, our past habits and way of life. One day I heard my father telling my mother that sooner or later they were going to end up in Israel and it was better to emigrate while the children were young, since it would be better for their future not to move later. Everyone still loves France and thinks about the life that we had there. Now we live a small city in the suburbs of Tel Aviv where many Tunisians live. They try to keep their old habits. They even have built a synagogue like the one they had in Tunisia."

Sunset, Aaron explained, was a special time of day for him. "My father died some years ago. Whenever I have time, I come to this same spot and watch the sunset. I remember seeing the same sea from a different angle all my childhood. This was a moment for my father and me to be together. We would talk and enjoy nature. When I am here, I can feel his presence by my side."

Layla felt amicable toward the unknown young man. She also told him who she was and what she was doing there and that she was remembering a missing family member.

Aaron smiled bitterly. "I am in the military service and I just came back from the war. It is so sad that we have to kill each other in order to continue living. Why can't we be friends and respect each other?"

It was getting late but both of them were happy to find another soul who reflected goodness and thought the same way. Layla looked at the horizon and saw the bright stars twinkling at them. She told Aaron that Golda was expecting her for dinner and would become worried. Aaron accompanied her to the building and they said goodbye. Aaron added that he hoped to see her soon or, if he traveled to Jerusalem, that he would like to visit her at the store if that was agreeable.

Layla laughed. "How do you think I earn my living? No one asks my permission. They just enter the store and, if I already know them, we wish each other a good day." They laughed and said goodnight.

Golda immediately noticed the sparkle in her eyes. She teased Layla that she had become like all Israeli girls, kissing boys at the beach. Layla blushed and told her all about Aaron. "He was a very kind, respectful and deep young man. I was happy that we could both ignore our religious differences and accept each other as friends."

The next day Layla thanked Golda and Art for their hospitality. They drove her to the Central Bus Station (Hatakhana Hamerkait Hahadasha), where she would catch a bus to Jerusalem. Golda prayed that Layla would have a nice trip, free of any unpleasant events or bad feelings. She hugged her and wished her a safe trip and told her that she would see her in two weeks.

When Layla boarded the bus, she sat in the first available seat and did not even look at the person sitting next to her. As soon as she sat down, the man stood up and took another seat in the back of the bus. Layla thought that he probably did not want to sit next to an Arab but, at that moment, a modern young girl with short hair and a V-neck, sleeveless blouse laughed. "It was great what you did," she told Layla in Hebrew. "I do it all the time. I cannot understand why they won't sit next to a woman. We are not going to eat them."

Layla smiled and responded, "I did not do it intentionally." Since her head was down, she did not see that her seatmate was an ultra-Orthodox Jewish man.

☙

The following weekend Aaron entered the store when Layla was alone. She was surprised and happy to see him. After some time, Golda again invited her for dinner and invited Aaron as well. He was almost the same age as Yaron. She was happy that at least he was back from the battlefield safe but sensed that he was surely sad of heart and spirit. The friendship between Layla and Aaron continued. Nothing happened physically between them, since they knew neither of their families would approve of, agree to, or even understand such a union. But, when they were together, they completed each other. They took special care to see each other far from the city, because many people knew her in East Jerusalem.

One day, when she was visiting Golda, they met each other at the beach to innocently watch the sunset as usual. Aaron kept to himself and said little. Layla looked at him and asked what was going on with him. He told her that he had received orders to go to Israel's border with Lebanon because of rising tension between Israel and the PLO. Some extremist Shiites based in Southern Lebanon were firing Katyusha rockets into northern Israel.

(Hezbollah was officially formed in 1985 and backed financially by Iran. It became the main politico-military force among the Shia community in Lebanon. Hezbollah follows a Shiite Islamist ideology shared by the leader of the 1979 Islamic Revolution in Iran, Ayatollah Khomeini.)

Aaron did not know when or if he would be back and was thinking that he would miss her very much. He suddenly turned to her. "I hope you know by now how much I love you," he said. "There are so many countries and places in this world. My service is over in less than six months. Promise me that, when I am back, we will leave this country and travel to a place where we can live together happily forever."

Layla was moved and saddened by his impassioned words, for she also loved him but knew that a future together was impossible. The divide was easily bridged between friends but was too wide for marriage. Still, he asked if she would give some thought to his suggestion.

"What will happen to our children?" she asked timidly.

"Well, we will decide what to do when we have them," Aaron replied. "They would become real Israeli-Arab children. We will teach them both languages and both religions and traditions and perhaps they will find a better way than we have to deal with problems. Maybe they can prove to everyone that there can be love, peace and respect between both cultures and religions. We have the responsibility to teach them this idea correctly. By the time I return, you have to tell me which continent and country would you like to live in, since I will be happy to be anywhere with you."

Suddenly Aaron took Layla's hands in his own trembling hands and sealed his proposal with a warm kiss. And from his pocket he pulled out a simple little ring with a greenish blue stone from Elat, an Israeli seaport.

'This blue stone will protect you from the evil eye, and I feel a part of me will be always by your side," he said.

Both had tears in their eyes and he pulled her into his arms, squeezed her against his chest and kissed her lips tenderly.

Layla was burning because she was ashamed of Aaron and of herself. She gently pushed him away but both kissed each other again with a lot of love for a short time. Holding hands, he accompanied her to the gate of Golda's apartment building and repeated that he loved her. His final word was "*Lehitraot*" – "see you soon." He did not hear Layla's answer: "*Inshallah*" – "God willing."

The next morning, as Layla was boarding a bus to Jerusalem, Aaron rode in an Israeli army truck, heading north to protect the population of the border area villages.

Layla continued her life, but her mind and heart were with Aaron in the south of Lebanon and north of Israel. She listened to the news on the radio. Every day there was something happening to one or the other side. Now both sides belonged to Layla. If a Palestinian died, she was sad for his family and, if an Israeli was dying, she had the same feeling for his family. Every time that she received news from Aaron she was happy that he was safe. As the weeks went by, she looked forward to seeing him again. When she was alone, she would look at her ring and smile. But she had not yet decided where or even if they could be together. Paris was a great city, as her sister Ameerah often wrote her. But how could she present an Israeli husband to her sister and brother? Although they prided themselves on being modern Muslims, they would never approve of her decision.

One day, while Layla was walking to the shop, her eyes caught the large headline in the *Jerusalem Post*. "Two Soldiers Kidnapped by PLO." She felt her knees weaken and thought she was going to fall down in the street. She paid the boy and grabbed the paper. She could hardly believe her eyes. There was a picture of Aaron and another young soldier. The story reported that the PLO had kidnapped the two young men and that the army had no more information about them. There was a plea from both families for the safe return of their sons.

Layla had tears in her eyes. It was too much for her to take this last blow. She continued walking to the store, her tears washing the sidewalks of Jerusalem. When Hassan arrived for work, she left the store and walked directly to the cemetery and talked to her parents. "Is this how you punish me for loving a boy from another people? He is a very kind man. If you had known him, you would have approved and loved him – I am sure of that. Did you forget that he is also a descendant of our great prophet

Ibrahim, our common ancestor – right? Please help me; help us to bring him back home safely. I am lonely and miserable."

Days turned into months. There were more newspaper articles about the two missing soldiers, and prayers for their safe return were said often in the synagogues. Layla prayed in Arabic and asked that Golda and Art pray at the *Kotel* – the Western Wall – in all the languages they spoke. But nothing happened. There were no news, no letters and no word of any kind. They had disappeared as if they had never existed.

Exactly one month before Aaron would have finished his military service, the PLO printed a picture of the two soldiers in a Lebanese newspaper. The article said that they had been executed. Their remains were never returned to their families. Layla told herself that, if the PLO had given a chance to Aaron and to themselves, they could have found many common grounds to respect and love each other.

This was all that Layla could take. She talked to Ameerah, who was visiting Beirut, and told her that she was going to leave Jerusalem. Hassan would manage the store and visit and take care of the house as necessary. Ameerah was very happy with her sister's decision.

CHAPTER 38

Layla Meets Wahab

IT WAS A SUMMER DAY IN 1971 when Layla sadly boarded the car that would take her from her beloved Jerusalem. She sat near the window, pushing her face against the cold glass, looking out at the precious city that she loved so much. This was the only place that she knew, having lived here all her life. She always believed that it was the oldest and the most beautiful but also the most tragic city in the world. She did not want to leave but had finally concluded that she could no longer live in a city where she had suffered so much and looked forward to so little. After much anguish, she accepted the invitation from her sister, Ameerah, to move to Beirut.

Layla had lost nearly all that she loved in her life and now was leaving behind her ancestral land, her house and even the graves of her loved ones. This trauma had transformed Layla into a completely different person. She had suffered much: the loss of her parents, brothers, home, business and the man she loved but would never marry. Her dreams had changed and so had her beloved city of Jerusalem. It was no longer the city that she knew before – an ancient but classic Middle Eastern city comprised of small earthen houses huddled on narrow streets of earthy colors.

Jerusalem was changing rapidly. It seemed like new buildings and streets were being added every day. Layla's neighborhood had been transformed, and many of her family's old friends had either died or abandoned their houses out of fear or force and moved God-knows-where. While part of the city looked modern with new tall buildings, other parts started resembling matchboxes lined up side-by-side. Even the air she used to breathe was different now. There was an invisible but overwhelming sense of insecurity, suspicion, hatred and hostility felt by Arabs and Israelis alike. She had no one to love or to look after; the Khaled's famous store no longer warmed her heart. Even its sign, which used to make her grandfather and father so proud, brought tears to her eyes. She had no hope for the future of her people in Jerusalem or the city itself. She was sure more violence and wars would ravage this holy city.

Layla was tired and disappointed, even though she had the chance to know and love Golda and Aaron and receive their love and respect and understanding in return. But other Jews viewed her with hostility – first as a Palestinian, second as a probable enemy, then a possible terrorist and finally a *goy*. She again looked at Jerusalem and thought that there was a similarity between her and her beloved city.

She told herself, "Oh Jerusalem, you are the envy and the love of all people near or far. Everyone in the world is in love with you; they are like persistent suitors ready to marry you. O Jerusalem, I know that you are in love only with God for all these centuries. O Jerusalem, I know that you have tried hard to keep the memories of your love deep in your heart and belly, but it seems that God has forgotten and abandoned you and us."

She then thought that, perhaps, Jews have a good reason to go to that simple stone wall to pray and cry. Jerusalem has tried to keep God's memories and gifts for a long time, but humans have tried to take away everything from her. Those stones have been the only sign of resistance to all the human and natural violence. They have seen so much cruelty and human history and tragedies during centuries, yet they have been able to resist and remain standing high, one on top of the other – maybe because they have been built with love and fate, with the energy of the deep and true love still sparkling inside each stone. They are standing in order to keep the faith in people and remind everyone of the real meaning of life. Yes, they have witnessed all the changes of the city and have received all the supplications and tears of the people in silence for centuries. Layla's tears washed her face as the car took her slowly away from the city that she loved so much.

Since the car was traveling in the south of Lebanon, it stopped near a Palestinian refugee camp. Layla was shocked to see the poor condition of the people. She remembered seeing Beirut in all its beauty and prosperity. The contrast between the two places was enormous. Then she remembered reading in a newspaper that camps were established on a temporary basis to help refugees survive in the past. Then, when arrangements were made, the refugees were resettled permanently elsewhere. Layla was saddened to see the living condition of her fellow people. With the exception of the refugee camps in some areas of the south, Lebanon was – at least in regional terms – a prosperous country with a large and relatively mobile middle class. Later, as the bus approached Beirut, its beauty and wealth appeared. No one could imagine that such a jewel of a city was so near the grim squalor of the refugee camps.

Ameerah was waiting for Layla; they had not seen each other a long time. They kissed and cried and then Layla's niece and nephew hugged and kissed her and they all went into Ameerah's house. Ameerah was as beautiful as ever; she really did look like a princess. Ameerah said that they had much catching up to do. She was aware that her sister had gone through a lot but she also knew that Layla had to put away her sadness and enjoy life. She suggested that they go shopping the next day and buy some fashionable new dresses for her. Layla thanked her sister but said that she was content with her life and appearance and that the joy of her being with her sister and her children was the best gift for her.

Everyone was nice to Layla, especially Ameerah, who knew that her sister had endured so much all alone and had taken care of everyone and carried all the burdens of the family by herself. Ameerah was also acutely aware that, in contrast, she had enjoyed living her life. Layla was younger than her sister but looked older. Her troubled past had marked her face and personality.

After a week Ameerah announced that she would hold a big party. "My husband's cousin, Wahab, has finally decided to stay awhile in Beirut because of the insistence of his parents," she informed Layla. "They told him that they are getting old and would like to see their son married and settled before they die. Although he is of a certain age, everyone admits that he is still a handsome man."

Ameerah had more to tell Layla about Wahab. "It is known that he was in love with an Armenian woman very long ago. She was married and everyone was against this love. He even followed her to Iran in the hope that she would divorce and they would get married, but it never happened. He was heartbroken and, for some time, his refuge was alcohol. But he came to his senses and now he teaches at Tehran University and is an important and prestigious businessman. My husband thinks that, even at his age, he would be able to marry any girl from the best families, including girls who are still in their twenties. After all, he is very attractive, extremely wealthy, well-educated and kind. His past belongs to him. Anyway, all people have secret stories in their heart and this should not stop them from living their lives."

Ameerah laughed and continued. "You bury the past and continue living in the future with joy. Once you are named Mrs. Whoever, you have his children for your own security, spend his money, share his glory, and live a great life – right?"

Layla looked at her sister with puzzlement. She was amazed at her shallow thinking but admired her practicality.

Layla had completely blocked her past. She was happy to spend time with her sister and her children. Ameerah's husband, Raheem, worked all day, and so they were able to do whatever pleased them, such as shopping and eating in fancy restaurants. They visited friends who were very nice and complimented Ameerah and Layla, although Layla was sure that they would talk differently when they left.

"I never care what they say in my absence," Ameerah told her sister. "The important thing is that they never dare to say an unkind word in my presence, because they know I would never talk to them anymore. They would not be invited to our sumptuous parties, nor would they receive generous gifts from me. So they flatter me when I am present and I leave the rest for their personal consciences."

Wahab and his elderly parents arrived at Ameerah's house for dinner and Layla was presented to them. "I do not think that you remember her from our wedding day," Ameerah told Wahab. "Layla was a very young lady at the time. She arrived last week from Jerusalem and I have not had time to inform all our friends and family."

Wahab's mother replied, "Well, we know that you have good taste and want to keep all the treasures to yourself." Everyone laughed and suddenly Wahab asked if she knew of the Al Ahmar coffee shop in Jerusalem and if it was still standing after the Six-Day War. Layla answered positively and added that it was located not far from their store and was even more successful than in the past.

"Omar, the owner, is now old but opens the store himself every morning and welcomes people with his kind smile." Then she told Wahab that she was surprised that he knew of such an ordinary and small place in Jerusalem. Wahab's blue eyes took on a faraway look and, with a sad smile, he answered that he used to do business in Jordan and often visited the coffee shop.

"Omar is a friend of mine and a very kind man," Wahab said.

The servants cleared the dinner table and arranged the dessert table with pastries, colorful fruits, coffee and tea. The women exchanged recent family news on one side of the living room while the men talked politics and business on the terrace. Wahab and Raheem discussed with grave seriousness the local political situation.

"It is true that Lebanon is very prosperous for the moment," Raheem said. "But I see a big storm approaching. I am especially worried for Beirut. Just as we always pick the nicest flower in the garden, so does trouble. Wealth is very apparent in the city. All the major foreign countries are present with large companies and their political intrigues and interests. Beirut is the only democratic free city in the region. Like Iran, Lebanon has three major difficulties: the presence of fanatics and Islamists, obvious and concentrated wealth, and a large population of poor people. This is a dangerous mix."

Wahab and Raheem went on to discuss Lebanon's history after World War I. Many camps were established in the 1920's to absorb Armenians fleeing Syria and then again in 1948 to accept the displaced Palestinians. The Armenians and others from the 1920's either were integrated into Lebanese society or went abroad. Their refugee camps disappeared but the Palestinian camps developed into quasi-cities. Successive waves of rural migration, notably from southern Lebanon and in the wake of the military conflicts in some other sections of the country, created permanent slums densely populated by poor people.

"This is also true in the case of Iran," Wahab said. "The population is increasing considerably. Young men are leaving the villages and their families for the large cities, but they have no skills or plans – just hope of having a better life. Well, disappointment hits them hard. If they are lucky to find a job as a servant cleaning a house of rich people, they see the extreme wealth and compare it to their own family's poverty and grow to hate the government, their employers and even their parents and themselves. They are easy targets for diverse political groups and religious leaders who use them to advance their own ambitions. Both Iran and Lebanon, as well as many other countries in the region, are going to blow up one of these days."

Raheem replied, "You have just arrived here after a long absence and, perhaps, you have not had time to see and feel the difference. Do you remember in old times we used to have friends from every religious and ethnic group? Muslims, Christians, Druze and Jews lived together and we were all very friendly. Christian Maronites and members of Phalange were best friends with neighboring Muslims. We did not have barriers between Muslims and Christians. That has changed. Unofficially, we know that Muslims live mainly in West Beirut while Christians reside in the East. The majority of Jews and Armenians have left the country, and soon it will be time for many other groups will follow in their footsteps."

Raheem continued talking. "Cracks are showing up in the foundation of our beloved country and our unique society because of inflation, overcrowding and fears of violence by extremist groups. Soon we are going to lose our peace and prosperity. Barriers and separation are going to be built among us. I am sure that many envious people already have plans for our houses in their hands in order to use at the right moment."

With a heavy heart Raheem paused, for he truly loved Lebanon. "I have not told Ameerah, but I am transferring most of my capital to Paris and planning for us to leave the country before the storm."

"I can't agree more with you," Wahab said. "This is one of the reasons that I am planning to leave Iran. All my friends think that I am crazy because so many of us are prospering now more than ever before. After my last trip to Paris, I visited a friend who is the assistant to the prime minister of Iran and told him that I smell the storm and that they had to get ready for it. He put his finger on his lips and pointed under the table and at some corners of the room, meaning that we were being listened to by SAVAK, the secret police. Later he asked me seriously if I had lost my mind to talk that way. He said I should know better than most how much the country is progressing. I then realized that he was too lost in his glory to accept reality."

Wahab went on to share his vision for the future. "I am planning to arrange something for my parents, but I know they would not leave Lebanon. I hope to persuade them, at least, to move to the mountains. In a few years, my contract will end with the university, and I will move – probably to Paris. May God protect these two beautiful countries that I always loved! We have traveled so much to so many parts of the world, but nowhere can you find the beauty and the good life of Beirut or Tehran. They are really the brides of the world. It is true that not all members of the population in these cities are prosperous, but there is a simple happiness that most people share, even the poor ones (less fortunate ones). But this is also changing since the new generation is comparing and asking more and more. Young people are no longer satisfied to thank God every moment like their parents. We have it all in both places: the sea and the mountains, the sun and snow at the same time. Especially in Beirut. It is the city in which East and West blend well."

For a moment both Raheem and Wahab were silent, saddened by the catastrophic future they foresaw for Lebanon and Iran and distressed that they were powerless to prevent it.

It did not take long before Layla and Wahab were married in a quiet ceremony. His parents and Ameerah were very happy, but Wahab and Layla had no special expectations from each other. They looked more like father and daughter. They both had a deep love in their hearts for their beloved lost ones that filled their being. They never shared their past since they did not need to do so. They understood each other and respected the mutual silence. Probably this was their most common ground: mutual understanding that each had a past love who was very special and would always remain secret.

Layla remembered Ameerah's cynical words. She was Wahab's wife; she carried his name, lived in comfort, received his respect, and one day would bear his children. Wahab was very kind and generous. For their honeymoon, they traveled to Hamburg and then to Paris. She could not call it a honeymoon since she was still in love with Aaron and spent most of her thoughts with him. When she yielded her body to her husband, she felt guilty that she was betraying Aaron.

In Paris they met Layla's brother, Habib, and his family. He was a successful and well-established physician with beautiful children and a very kind wife. Wahab told Layla that he was planning to move to Paris when his teaching contract expired, and he took her to visit some houses that were for sale. He said that Raheem and his family were also planning to move to Paris. Layla was happy to know that she would finally live in a city where she would be reunited with her sister and brother.

After a week they found a beautiful house in the 16th Arrondissement. It was a vast apartment with windows overlooking the old large green trees of the Bois-de-Boulogne. Wahab told Layla that it was now her responsibility to furnish their apartment little by little whenever they were back in Paris. For the time being, they had to live in Iran until his contract ended and he closed his business office there.

Wahab was happy with Layla at his side after all these years of living alone with no special purpose but a lost dream. It was almost as if she was his daughter. No one ever knew if he missed, loved, had thoughts of or experienced any feelings about his daughter, Ruth. Now, at least, he had the opportunity to take care of his young wife, Layla, who was probably the same age as Ruth.

In Layla's presence, he found the warmth and hope of life again. He also appreciated that, unlike most women, she did not ask personal questions. She was an intelligent and curious woman who loved learning but also had the great quality of never inquiring about his past life. Of course, this enabled her to protect her past too. He was sure that she had her own secret story but it was natural for him not to pry. He was happy with the unwritten contract of never telling, never asking.

During their stay in Paris, Wahab took her to some stage shows and places that he had promised Sara a long time ago. Layla was happy to see and learn more about Paris. She had read so many stories about this amazing city and once it even had crossed her mind that she could live there with Aaron. But the presence of Habib and Ameerah in the city changed her mind.

After two weeks, Layla and Wahab returned to Tehran. Wahab had a modest apartment; she discovered it had a bachelor-style furniture and decor. Layla realized that the spirit of the man who lived there had died years ago. The next day Wahab resumed his regular responsibilities and Layla began rearranging their home. Some of his friends came to visit them and everyone loved Layla and complimented her on the amazing changes to the apartment.

Four years later Wahab and Layla were happy and surprised when she gave birth to their first child, a daughter named Rana. Wahab's parents, although old and fragile, came for the birth of the baby. They were very happy and thanked God that He had given their son a child, especially at his age. Two years later Layla bore their second child, a boy they named Ahmed. With his birth, Wahab's parents thanked God for the real miracle and decided to go to Mecca to offer their gratitude. Wahab and Layla moved to a large, comfortable house and lived a quiet and good life.

The long-expected turmoil started in both countries slowly. Wahab and Layla followed first the Yom Kippur War and later the crises in Beirut and elsewhere in the region. Lebanon was going through a bitter civil war, just as Wahab and Raheem had predicted that night on the terrace. By then Raheem, Ameerah and their children were living permanently in Paris. They looked forward to the day when they could return to their beloved country, which was being looted and destroyed right at that moment.

After some time and within the space of a single year, both of Wahab's parents died of old age but in extreme happiness, since their wishes were finally fulfilled and their beloved son became a husband and father. Soon Wahab, Layla and the children moved to Paris to live there permanently. They enrolled the children in French schools and, as the children grew older, Layla was happy that they were growing up in a relatively peaceful atmosphere. The Khaled & Sons store in Jerusalem was doing well and their house was still standing. Layla was happy because Rana and Ahmed were doing well and were attractive and intelligent children. They both finished their studies and went to the university. Rana decided to go on to graduate school, but Ahmed decided to work in his father's prosperous business. Everything was going smoothly. Later Wahab and Raheem visited Lebanon many times but only for a short time and for specific business reasons. Each time they returned gloomier than before and did not talk much about it to their wives.

Layla tried to push her children toward marriage since it was the right time for them. By then Ahmed had already learned many secrets of his father's distribution company but no longer saw this as his future profession. He was always in conflict with his father. Although Wahab provided his children and wife with all the necessities and luxuries of life in modern-day Paris, his age and personality caused conflicts with his children – especially with his son and particularly when he would revert back to his old drinking habits. Ahmed was looking for a father figure, not a benevolent gift-giver and tired grandfather.   Suddenly his behavior and character changed. He became religious and started praying five times a day. Then he did not come home when expected and was even absent for family events. Layla remembered her brothers and worried.

"What do you expect from a young man of his age?" Wahab asked Layla. "He has fire in his belly. He has to discover the world and then he will be the same as he used to be. You worry for nothing."

But Layla could see the presence of Faisal in Ahmed. She started asking him questions but, instead of answering her, he began asking questions about her past life in Jerusalem, her experiences during the Six-Day War and the treatment of the Arab population by Israeli soldiers. Then he would talk to her about the Yom Kippur War, the rights of the Palestinian people and many other subjects. Layla tried to talk to him about Golda and asked him to understand the other side's problems.

Finally, one day Ahmed coldly confronted Layla. "You are not my mother. You are not a Palestinian. You are a traitor. They have brainwashed you, and I am ashamed of you."

With tears in her eyes, Layla told him, "Ahmed, my dear son, you are just a young man. You have grown up in wealth and comfort, but life is very short. You cannot even understand what war and conflicts mean. I have seen death and destruction on both sides. We are all humans living a short life in this world. There are people who will promote human conflicts for their own gain. Ordinary people suffer, just as my family and I did, while the ambitious ones are happy to take the glory and money.

"I saw the suffering of Golda and, after almost fifty years, we now see that the antiques and gold looted by Nazis are being discovered in Switzerland, Argentina and Brazil. And now even our own people have spent the money that was given to them for the betterment of refugees. Instead, they use it for their own needs. They had the glory during international conferences and were fed well with the best food whereas my brothers received the titles of heroes and martyrs and died probably in hunger and cold! I know what I am talking about. You know only what they want you to know. I have suffered so much in silence and it may be my fault for never sharing this with you or anyone else. I wanted you to grow as a free spirit – in peace, harmony and far from hate and suffering!"

Ahmed laughed bitterly and left the room. He never shared his thoughts or opinions again with his mother or anyone else in the family.

೪ಀ

One day in 2002 Ahmed asked his father if they could visit Jerusalem together. He said that he wanted to see his grandparents' house and gift store. Layla was not in good health to travel with them. Ahmed's sister, Rana, was taking important exams. Wahab was happy to travel with his son, who had distanced himself from them recently, and he was also happy to visit Jerusalem after such a long time. He felt as if he was returning to his youth. So he readily agreed and added that they would travel to Jordan and other places together. And, while in Jerusalem, he would take him to his old friend, Omar, and they would drink real tea and coffee, and Ahmed could finally taste the best baklavas in the world.

Then, looking lost in the far past, he told his son he used to go there very often as a young man.

CODA

CHAPTER 39

God Answers Ruth's Questions

RUTH WAS STILL SITTING on top of David's gate in Jerusalem as she had been since that tragic day on August 30, 2002. A long time had passed and many people had forgotten her, but she had not forgotten anyone. Her tears were still washing the paving stones while new green plants were growing in the cracks of the Wall.

She asked many questions. She asked about the fate of the people who have such a short stay in this world and suffer so many tragedies in their lives. She knew the secrets of everyone who was passing through the gate – heartbroken Arab and Israeli mothers; Christians who were stricken by death, sickness and tragedy; and tourists who were visiting Jerusalem and praying for miracles from above in order to improve their everyday lives. Meanwhile, more bombs were exploding and, off in the distance, more blood was soaking into the red soil.

Four wars in the span of a quarter century had not solved any problems in the region; neither had two world wars that preceded these conflicts. For the major powers of the world, the Middle East was like a set of children's building blocks that could be arranged and rearranged endlessly. Ruth thought if she had a voice she could preach to the people of the world from her place and explain all. But she had only a huge pocket of tears.

As she watched the horrific events below her and cried for the victims, Ruth thought of all the political and military leaders who played important roles in the region. While some of them tried their best to work toward peace, others continued adhering to rigid positions that guaranteed no progress could be made.

She remembered their acts and their deaths, one by one.

In 1994, when Yitzhak Rabin, Yasser Arafat and Simon Perez shared the Nobel Peace Prize, the world found new hope for the region and, for a while, Ruth did not shed tears. But it did not take long before her tears fell again ever harder, when the dreams of a real and permanent peace were shattered by another bullet. Rabin was shot by an Israeli law student in 1995 who claimed, "Rabin intended to give our country to Arabs."

King Hussein of Jordan, after so many courageous fights and negotiations, lost his life's battle to Hodgkin's lymphoma in 1999. Hafez al-Assad – the president of Syria, who played such a complex intriguing game in Lebanon among Palestinians and with Israel – died of a heart attack in 2000. Chairman Arafat, the leader of guerilla underground military operations, was elected the president of Palestinian National Authority. Many people had pinned their hopes of peace on him but, after further violent struggles in the region, he was put under virtual house arrest at the end of his life. He died from a blood disorder in 2004 in Paris. The political career of Ariel Sharon, the prime minister of Israel, ended with a massive stroke that made him permanently comatose.

Saddam Hussein, the former president and absolute dictator of Iraq who lived in amazing palaces and patterned his rule after that of Hitler, was tried and convicted of multiple crimes by the American-backed Iraqi government and executed in 2006.

Ruth thought that all these important personalities could have played a positive role in educating children, creating jobs for the youth and giving comfort to the families who had suffered so much and desired to live their short lives in peace. But many of these men misused their powers, failed to take advantage of opportunities, and finally lost their lives to clogged arteries, unseen viruses or fanatical doctrines. Most of these leaders wore bloody gloves, by choice or by force of the events. In the end, they added more to the suffering of the families by deceiving their youth and dragging them into acts of destruction. Many followers believed in them and in their ability to give them a better life and future. Yet the work stayed unfinished. They all died like ordinary people. As it is written: "We all come from the same place and go back to the same destination." Some left behind their good names, while others added more horror stories into the already existing sad pages of the world's history books.

Early one morning, as Ruth heard the voice of the spiritual *azan*, the call to prayer, she looked at the beautiful Temple Mount Mosque, the golden dome of Al- Aksa. She knew that the Prophet Mohammad was miraculously transported from Mecca to Jerusalem and, from the Dome of the Rock, he ascended to heaven.

Then she heard the beautiful liturgies – organ music, songs and prayers from inside the various Greek, Armenian, Catholic and other Christian churches crowded into such a small area. Jerusalem was also the place where Jesus lived and preached, suffered and died and was resurrected.

Ruth turned to God and said, "Tell me, You are the only one who is able to answer my questions. You started with Your Prophet Moses. When You gave him the Ten Commandments, didn't You say that You had worked all six days of creation and rested on the seventh day, the Shabbat, to enjoy Your creation? You commanded that we do likewise. It is the Number Four in the Tablets. Well, the Jews understood the meaning of Shabbat and kept Saturdays holy. Why, then, did You change Your mind after some centuries and allow Christians to honor Sundays as Shabbat? Later, why did You allow so much latitude that others could declare an alternative day? Muslims believe that the Shabbat is actually Friday.

"Did Your computers mix up these dates or did someone do it to create chaos among nations? Do You know how many times I felt real conflict to respect Your orders and live my life? Most of the student-parent meetings were held on Saturday mornings. Most of the important gatherings and parties were held on Friday nights. And so on. The list is long. Couldn't You keep all the religious leaders on the same page? Can You imagine how nice and peaceful the world would look if everyone had the same day to pray and rest? Neighbors could enjoy each other. Even You could have had a peaceful Shabbat.

"Now we come to the temple that was built and destroyed twice. You have said that it would be built again. For thousands of years, people have looked to Jerusalem. They have cried on *Tisha B'Av*, all day and night, and prayed for its reconstruction. But what have You done? Again You have created another major conflict. Why did You bring the Prophet Mohammed to the Dome of the Rock? Couldn't he ascend to Heaven from the same Mecca in which millions of people pray to You? Are the gates of Your paradise so narrow that there is only one entrance to such a huge garden?

"I know all this is Your business. Who am I to ask You questions? But I am curious to know how You are going to build Your new temple. Everyone knows its required design and location. But how can one build it where there is already such a beautiful mosque standing on its grounds? Couldn't You at least push the Rock a bit to the left or right?

"Oh, dear God, I have too many questions and no answers, but my mind goes toward Your favorite prophet, Abraham. You tested him, loved him and promised him children. Why did You wait ninety years to finally give him and Sarah a son? I think that all conflict in the regions come from You and then from Sarah. Had she believed in You, she would have waited longer. She would not have forced Hagar into her husband's arms and then expelled her and their son, Ishmael, into the wilderness. Why did You open Hagar's eyes after so much suffering in the desert and promise that Ishmael would live long and create a big nation? Couldn't You open the eyes of Sarah before she offered Hagar? Couldn't You have revealed to her that she could have a son? Then we wouldn't have all these problems.

"Since You promised Abraham that his descendants would become as numerous as the stars in the sky, You should have given him peace of heart and mind. From his tomb in Hebron, Abraham, too, is crying for his children. He calls his sons and asks them to teach wisdom to their children so that finally they can live together in peace."

ॐ

Ruth waited for answers to her questions. God was silent. Looking around, she saw that the Jerusalem sky was blue and beautiful; the sun shone in all its glory. Below her, some people were walking and pointing to the amazing places in Jerusalem. Others were dressed in black, mourning the deaths of their loved ones. A young boy was praying loudly at his *bar mitzvah* at the *Kotel* (the Western Wall from the original holy Temple). His proud grandfather and father were praying with him. His mother, some distance away, was proud of her son's spiritual achievement but worried in her heart for his future, for in five years he would be called for his military service in the Israeli army. She prayed that, by then, a solution would be found to the conflict with the Arabs and that everyone will live harmoniously in peace.

Ruth talks to herself and to God. She continues crying for her son and his beautiful bride. She sees the wedding gown lying, waiting somewhere in this world, for the beautiful Rachel to wear it. Then she cries harder. Finally, Ruth opens up her heart for the first time over the delicate subject that she had never talked about to anyone. She asked God the question that was bothering her for sometime.

Since her presence on the top of the gate, she heard various discussions from rabbis and students scholars who were exchanging their opinions with each other. One of the arguments was about an old law concerning a *mamzer* – a child born to a married woman outside of wedlock. By Jewish law, the child is not accepted in society and this person is relegated to stay outside the gates of Jerusalem. A *mamzer* can only marry another *mamzer*, thus paying for the mother's sin. Now, Ruth had found an answer for her misfortunate life.

She was never told by either parent that she was a *mamzer* for sure, but she had always suspected from her own inner feelings that Wahab was her biological father. Now, after listening to the conversations between the rabbis, she learned the term of *mamzer*, its laws and how it reflected her life.

She asked God, "What was my sin that caused me to suffer and pay for my mother's actions all my life? I always tried to live an honorable life and respect Your laws. What did my innocent son, Joseph, and his beloved Rachel do to suffer in this life? How many generations must pay for my mother Sara's sin? I thought that You had compassion for orphans! You understood the reason for Sara's actions. Is the science of psychology absent in Your domain? Do You judge humans only by respect of Your laws and their choices of Free Will? You know that most of the time people's actions reflect the experiences of their childhood. I know we have free will to choose our actions. Don't You think that man should come to a special level of understanding in order to choose his actions or even to have the intellectual luxury to understand the real meaning of free will? My mother, Sara, paid for her actions dearly and repented the rest of her life. Why did she have all those sufferings, at such a young age to begin with? At least You know that she was not a mamzer but an innocent victim who lost so much in her childhood!

"Well, God, I see that Your laws are complicated to understand. I thought my mother was considered innocent after leaving Wahab, her greatest love, because she worked hard day and night in order to sustain her family needs, and she repented and changed herself and returned to Your laws. Now I see that even I, who had nothing to do with my mother's actions but was born as a fruit of her love, is considered a *mamzer* and punished regardless!

"What about Ani, and my Armenian grandparents? Why did they suffer? What about the Palestinian Layla? Why did she lose every person that she loved in her life? What about the Genocide that killed more than a million Armenians, and what about the six million Jews who were killed in the Holocaust? Were they all *mamzers*?

"No, I am sure that more secrets exist in Your Kingdom.

"It is written that death is a punishment. As I saw my dear ones flying toward the blue sky, regardless of the horrific situation, they were all happy. No one was sad. So death cannot be a punishment. Besides, everyone who is born will die regardless. On the contrary, living on Earth is a punishment.

"We work hard all our lives to create families and foster friendships. We accumulate objects but, in the end, we leave everything behind and ultimately turn to dust. The purest, the most powerful, the most knowledgeable and even the weakest creatures on Earth are all aware of Your ultimate power. Although we pretend to be brave and ignore this truth, everyone who is born knows that he or she will die one day. When? No one knows, but this fear of not knowing is a constant torture. In the end, all that we have owned belongs to You, as we leave our possessions behind, willingly or unwillingly. Isn't this extreme power of Yours satisfying enough for You?

"Perhaps You take into consideration the laws of reincarnation. Do we remember who we were before being born? Do we know what is expected from us? I do not remember anything. So why do I have to pay for an unknown knowledge? Where is my free will?"

"I beg of You – be generous to us. Why do we all have to suffer so much in order to become a handful of dust again? Give us enough knowledge and intelligence to live this one short given life happily and in peace."

Ruth was crying harder now and continuously asking more questions. All her life Ruth had accepted her fate in silence and without complaints. This time it was a much bigger pain and punishment that she had faced. She had nothing to lose anymore; at least she had the right to ask her questions.

૨♥

Saddened by her pain, the angels are unable to function. They come together to ask their Creator for a solution. Shortly afterwards, they have smiles on their faces, and one of them volunteers for the task of going to tell Ruth the result of their discussion.

Ruth is unaware of the angels' presence because her eyes are drenched in blinding tears. Nearby a bloody explosion deafens her ears. She has no more questions to ask God. "Who am I to ask God questions? I am no one – a handful of dust, another broken toy of His." She had no more words to form sentences.

Suddenly, all the chaos around her disappears. She sees an Israeli woman in labor at a hospital in Jerusalem, giving birth to a beautiful baby girl. As the nurse cleans the baby, she tells the young couple, "*Mazel tov*, you have a beautiful daughter with golden hair." The nurse asks the mother if she and her husband have a name for her. The weakened voice of the mother and the excited voice of the father proudly pronounce the name: "Rachel."

Ruth then turns toward a crowded hospital in Gaza. Many women are in labor, but Ruth is drawn into a room where a young Palestinian woman is giving birth to a little boy. As the nurse cleans the baby, she says, "*Mabrouk*, you have a handsome boy, with a lot of black hair. Do you have a name for him?"

In a weakened voice, the woman answers, "Youssef." Another nurse opens the door and announces the birth of Youssef (Joseph, in Hebrew) to the father, waiting anxiously for the good news.

Both babies cry impatiently. Ruth feels their presence. She asks if she could see them one more time. Suddenly, Ruth sees into the future a beautiful, young, blond girl and a strong, young, man with dark curly hair walking happily together in Jerusalem's main square. Ruth can see that they are very much in love with each other. They hold hands and talk animatedly.

Ruth is now looking at the two babies who are not crying anymore. They are in the loving care of their parents. It seems that the angel has shown them their future as a young couple in Jerusalem. The babies are aware that they must wait patiently for their first encounter.

The angel tells Ruth that her questions have been answered. She does not have to stay and cry on top of the gate anymore. Her loved ones are waiting for her. The angel adds that God has created everyone with free will. Good and evil are choices spread before all, and she should have faith not only in God but in people as well. No one said making choices was easy. One day two wise people will be able to open the hearts and minds of the others. By their actions, they will implant and spread permanent love and peace in the region. No one said this world was an easy place to live in. Success requires wisdom, hard work and loving hearts.

Suddenly Ruth sees the same bright path that spread over the dark sky of Jerusalem on that tragic Friday afternoon of August 30, 2002. The light and its warmth envelop Ruth and pull her up toward the beautiful blue sky. She does not resist anymore. For the final time, she looks back with a smile to the main square in Jerusalem. She prays to God to implement the blessings conferred upon the babies.

THE END

About the Author

Dr. Rosemary Hartounian Cohen is a sociologist with a doctorate degree from the Sorbonne, Paris. She is an author, a journalist, a motivational speaker, devoted wife and mother.She is an accomplished artist who uses various mediums, including oil and charcoal, while her specialty is silk painting.

Dr. Cohen has taught University classes around the world and currently teaches at city colleges in Los Angeles. Her book design silk scarves and neckties was chosen by Publisher's Weekly as one of the best products presented at the Book Expo of America in 1999.

In 1985 Dr. Cohen founded Atelier de Paris in Los Angeles and has served as its president ever since. She is fluent in several languages. She is the founder and director of the Liana Cohen Foundation, a charitable non-profit organization which organizes music competitions and festivals, encourages youth to study music and arts and provides the healing touch of music and arts to grieving families and survivors as well as well as victims of drunken driving, alcohol and drug abuse.

Among her books are:

Korban – The Sacrifice of Liana

Terrorists or Martyrs

The Survivor, Translated and Published in:
Armenian, Farsi (Iranian) and French

Anoush – The Daughter of King Shen